# Abyrinth's Fire

## The Abyrinth Embermark Chronicles: Book 1

Written by

## M.R. Goodrum

ISBN: 978-1-966274-24-7



Line editing by

Linnea Schroeder of

Twinflower Manuscript Services


Cover by Miblart

Map of Europa
Estland
Livonia
Rus
Swedan
Lituania
Biała Ruś
Netherlands
Polska
Warszawa
Germania
Belgium
Galacia
Bohemia
Praha
Slovakia
Moldova
Francia
Austria
Hungary
Switzerland
Moldavia
Slovenia
Croatia
Sarajevo
Serbia
Italia
Ottoman Empire

# Chapter 1

We were out in the city, just the two of us with our bodyguards in close proximity. I had two security men, one older, a former soldier named Kazuch, but I forgot the younger one's name. Kazuch was my father's age, early forties. He had a beard and mustache that had gone mostly white, like his short, cropped hair, and a face that resembled abused leather. Like most of my father's soldiers, he wore dark green with gold trim, which was cut in the style of a military uniform, and was spotlessly clean. He carried a pulse pistol on one hip and a short sword on the other. When I wasn't otherwise occupied, I could hear him mumbling something to himself, and he was constantly checking and rechecking his gear.

The younger guard was dressed the same, though his lean frame made the uniform stand out. He couldn't have been more than a few years my senior, yet he carried himself with professional pride and seriousness. He was too young for facial hair, and his head was crowned with a mop of tightly curled, dark brown hair. They both wore my family's crest on their breast, a crowned red griffin breathing flame, wings outstretched above a golden sun.

Cousin Milka had her one guard, an older, broken-down soldier who was closer to retirement than the front lines. He moped around in her family's colors, brown, like rich milk chocolate. Fine if you are eating it, but it looked terrible on a uniform. I had known Milka since birth; she was two years older than me. When we were younger, the age difference mattered, but now that I was seventeen and she was nineteen, we were much closer. Closer than my brothers or my younger sister, Dominika.

It was a perfect day in downtown Warszawa, not too warm and delightfully sunny. This was the common man, working-class part of the city, where most of the blanks lived. As boring as they were, the blanks grew food and made the things that kept our society going. Among the things they made were some of the finest dresses and ball gowns in all of Polska. With their access to ports on the Baltic Sea, they brought rare silks and cloth from all over Europa. My trials were coming soon, and of course, after I passed them, Father would be hosting a gala in my honor. Naturally, as the guest of honor, I would need a new gown. Maybe two. Just in case.

"Jafra, how much are you allowed to spend?" Milka asked.

"Mother said no more than a hundred and fifty złoty, but if I stay under two hundred, I'm sure Poppa will be ok with it."

"Whoo, such extravagance!" she cooed. Milka was a pretty girl who had been married for less than a year. Her husband was generous, but their wealth couldn't approach ours. Father was the Lord of Central Polska, and we lived quite comfortably. Milka looked at me with laughter in her wide, brown eyes, her honey-colored hair braided and pinned up. Her hawk-like nose and high cheekbones complemented her figure. She wasn't as busty as I, but her long legs and wide hips were all in fashion these days with the male of the species. We looked so different. My hair was black as a raven's wing, also pulled up with short, silver pins. She liked off-white dresses, whereas I could usually be found in brightly-colored day dresses with abundant frills and lace.

"You only turn eighteen once." I smiled at her. "There will, of course, be a grand ball for my coming of age. I'm sure that no expense will be spared. You might want to choose a new gown for yourself."

"Are you excited? Wondering what brand you will receive?"

"Of course. Mother is already shopping me around, trying to arrange a good match. The better the brand, the better my options."

We walked the streets of the garment district, surrounded by dull brick two- and three-story tailor shops. Off in the distance were the uptown skyscrapers. Buildings up to a hundred stories high, with spines of steel and skins of the finest marble, granite, and glass. Each edifice was adorned with columns, arches, and carvings that showcased the genius of our stonemasons. House Sobieski has ruled over this region for hundreds of years, since before the Night of the Comet. We took a city that was once dirty and plagued by crime, and with sweat, gold, and the blood of my ancestors, we built it into one of Europa's shining gems. I was admiring the city, not really paying attention; that's why the sound of bombs going off took me entirely by surprise.

"Oh my God!" Milka screamed as a titanic explosion erupted to the north of us, towards the downtown districts. We were shaken, and I actually fell to my knees. I got dirt on my favorite lavender skirt, but that was unimportant. Sirens started blaring at us from every direction. Dark smoke was coming from the direction of the disturbance. Everyone on the street was rushing around like chickens with their heads cut off. I assumed they were looking for a place to hide. Our guards were on us in a flash, putting themselves between us and whatever danger might be out there. I saw the look of fear on Milka's face, but that didn't deter me.

"Kazuch, get us over there at once!" I commanded.

"Lady Sobieski, it's my job to protect you, to take you away from danger, not towards it." He was speaking to me, but had his pistol out, and was frantically looking for threats.

"This is our fief, and we are responsible for the safety and security of our subjects. Take us there at once!" I said, heading towards the ground car.

The younger bodyguard had anticipated my choice and pulled up in our executive hover car. I'm not sure exactly how they work, but I'm told they utilize the same technology as the airships. With it being such a lovely day, we had the top down to enjoy the sunshine. The car was a dull pewter color, with copper tubes and armor plates running from end to end. There were stubby steel legs that dropped down when the motivator was not being powered. Inside were two rows of two seats facing each other in the back cabin, and four seats in the front, reserved for the driver and guards. We climbed in, and the younger guard activated the drive.

Guards for the nobility were always channelers. Wielders, like the members of my family, could manipulate the power to do amazing things, channelers had power and could use it to motivate machines, and most people were blanks, who had no abilities at all. The younger guard directed his power into the motivator, and we darted off at top speed.

We skimmed along the surface, careening through the city streets, barely missing terrified citizens who were running around, fearing for their lives. Another explosion rocked the city, and I could see a tower of flames rising from the direction where we were heading.

"Faster!" I demanded.

We might have increased speed a little bit, but my driver kept his eye on the road and got us to the bombing site without hitting any pedestrians. He pulled up and helped me out, then assisted Milka in disembarking. The square was in complete chaos, filled with smoke, and bodies littered the ground. People were lying around everywhere. Some were dying. Some were already dead.

I stopped an older woman who was fleeing the scene with two small children in tow. "Pani, what happened here?"

She looked at me, not sure if she recognized me. "I was downtown to file some papers for my grandchildren when cars started blowing up." She pointed at a building a few blocks down the main thoroughfare. "Groups of men piled out of steam cars and started shooting people!"

"I'm glad you are safe, grandmother. As a member of your ruling family, I will personally see to this outrage!" I told her, meaning every word.

The woman gave a wan smile and continued to drag the children away. I arrived at the scene of the crime and saw that the battle was still ongoing. Shots rang out, echoing around the cavern made by the surrounding buildings. Screams filled my ears, and it took everything within me not to turn and run with my subjects.

"Milka, let's go!" I said, pulling the hem of my skirt up high enough so I could break into a run. The shoes I wore were not appropriate for running. Truthfully, they were not really meant for walking, so much as they were to show off my excellent taste in footwear.

"Jafra, no! We can't fight. My brand is not for fighting, and you don't have one yet!"

She was right. I'm not sure what I was thinking at the time. I was athletic for a rich girl. I had taken dance, tumbling, grappling, and I like to swim, but I had never thrown a fist in anger, except for hitting my younger brother Jurek. What a terrible child he was. It was stupid and childish of me, but I wanted to get closer. I needed to see what was going on. Even though she was the elder of the two of us, I had been getting my way for years now. Reluctantly, she followed me, our guards close behind. The younger guard pushed ahead, pulling his sword as he stepped to the vanguard.

"I'm terribly sorry, but I've forgotten your name," I said to my surprisingly competent guard.

"Urban, milady," he said, not turning around. He held his gleaming blade up, his eyes fixed on the path ahead of us. We rushed through the carnage, stepping over the injured and the dead.

We were getting close when Urban stopped and turned to me. "Miss, I can see that your brothers, Stefek and Krystian, are just ahead. It looks like they are fighting masked men in the government quarter. For your own safety, I cannot allow you to get any closer." His tone was respectful, but firm as iron.

"You have excellent eyes, Corporal," Kazuch said. I turned to see him peering through goggles that had a magnifying extension on the right lens. He fiddled with the wheel, moving it back and forth, trying to focus. "My lady, I think we are already close enough to the action. I would recommend we wait here for your brothers and their soldiers to deal with these criminals."

"I want to get a bit closer," I pleaded. "Not all the way. Just closer."

In the end, they had to obey me. If there was imminent danger, I was sure they would override my authority and save me against my will. With Urban leading the way, we moved towards the fighting at a much-reduced pace, keeping to the side near the local ministry buildings.

The boy's eyes were indeed true. When we were several blocks away, I saw my older brothers engaged in battle with two dozen men. They had about the same number of our soldiers at their backs, but as wielders of Abyrinth and sons of the local lord, they felt duty-bound to lead their men.

We were coming from the open plaza, but the fighting was taking place on a wide boulevard, framed by walkways and, beyond them, stone-faced government buildings, solid and stoic in their brutalist architecture. I wasn't upset to see that these architectural monstrosities were damaged, just that a horde of cowardly blanks was perpetrating it. Their bodies littered the ground by the hundreds. I could see several casualties wearing the colors of House Sobieski, and it pulled at my heart and brought tears to my eyes to see them harmed, or worse.

"Milka! You and your man go back to the rover and call for medical units! As many as they can send!" She nodded, and they rushed back to where we had left the car.

My oldest brother, Stefek, was out front. I know that he loves me, but I wouldn't say we're friends. He's twenty-two, a good four and a half years older than me. I'm tall for a girl at five feet eight, but he towers over me. Last I knew, he was about six feet three inches and a lean two hundred and twenty pounds. I'm not sure if he's still growing, but he is taller and stronger than Father by quite a bit. On his thick head, he had short, dark brown hair, almost black. He had a square jaw, and his beard and mustache were thick for a boy his age. I guess he's a man now, no longer a boy. The brand he received on his eighteenth birthday was called Chronoburst. Stefek can pause time locally, just for himself and only for a few seconds at a time. It may not sound that awesome, but he has mastered its usage in combat.

To anyone watching, including me, he was disappearing and reappearing a dozen feet away in another location. I watched him almost take a spear to the midsection, then he blinked out. A second later, he was behind the terrorist, hacking at his neck with his long, one-handed sword. Before the man's head could hit the pavement, he was off to the next opponent. I have seen him do similar things in his endless practice sessions, but to see him actually take a man's life… it shocked me to my core. He was a good-natured boy, but now, my brother scowled and had hard eyes. The way he swept through a horde of enemies, hacking and slashing at them without quarter, he had become an efficient killing machine.

A weird thought struck me: would he return home to his young wife, his dark green, military-style uniform coated in the blood of strangers? How would she react to that?

I'm closer to my second-oldest brother, Krystian. At twenty, he is still three years older than me, but he doesn't treat me like a child. He was just under six feet and thinner than Stefek. They are both physical specimens, but Krystian doesn't take himself nearly as seriously as our older brother does. He has shoulder-length, straight black hair, and his lack of facial hair only highlights his beautiful, noble features.

His brand was Steel Thorns, and he was a virtuoso at using his abilities. He wore the dark green of our house and was utterly confident as he worked his way around the battlefield. With a thought and a wave of his hand, he could cause metal to flow into other shapes. When an opponent approached him with a sword, he caused the man's steel to reform into razor wire that enveloped the man's arm. He didn't directly harm anyone, but he turned their steam cars into giant spiraling tubes of razor wire that trapped the terrorist and made it easy for Stefek and their troops to finish them off.

My brothers were in front, fighting fiercely to provide protection and security for our people. Soon after I arrived, the incident began winding down. A few of the terrorists were still on the edge of the conflict, either taking cover to get off a few shots or looking for a way to flee the scene. I felt safe enough to approach; my bodyguards followed, weapons at the ready. We skirted the periphery of the scene until we were at most twenty feet from older brother.

"Stefek!" I called out to him. "Leave some of them alive. Take prisoners for Father to interrogate!"

Krystian continued to weave his steel traps, but Stefek stopped in his tracks. He was panting, covered in sweat and blood. The look on his face was a terrible thing. He wasn't my brother, but instead, a vengeful demon. Behind his thick beard, I could see his jaw tighten and his eyes squint in concentration. At the sound of my voice, he paused, then his manner softened visibly. "Jafra, you should not be here," he said, anger and annoyance in his low growling voice.

"It is my duty as well as yours! We're all House Sobieski."

"We are, but you won't always be a Sobieski. Not for much longer," he said, breathing hard, his uniform torn and covered in gore.

I'll be honest. His words hurt me. I knew that Lady Roksana Sobieski was deep in negotiations with several prominent families. Possibly even with a couple of royal families. I had known from childhood that I would get married and live in another city, or perhaps even another country. I would adopt a new surname, but I would always be a Sobieski until the day I died. His bluntness, the callous way he had, in his mind, already tossed me aside... it hurt.

"I may not always have the same name as you, brother, but I will be loyal to Polska forever, and Sobieski blood runs through my veins!" I'm slow to anger, but I was livid at the insult.

"Are you ready to pick up a sword and join us, little sister?"

"Hardly," I replied. "Fighting is men's work."

Brother harumphed in derision.

"She's right, Stefek. I'll have the men collect a half dozen of these scum. Once we get them in the dungeons, I will personally 'interview' them," Krystian said calmly. He had always been ice to Stefek's fire.

My oldest brother grunted in agreement; his full head of steam had dissipated, and the crazy look in his eyes had departed. Sheathing his sword, he got his men to begin the cleanup.


After prayers, we all picked up our utensils to attack the evening meal. It had been three days since the attack at the Kievan Rus embassy, and the men in our family had spent hours behind closed doors. Acts of violence like the attack downtown had only happened once or twice in my lifetime. This was the first incident I was aware of since I was old enough to be mindful of the broader world around me. I had the equivalent of a university-level education, and for the record, had academically excelled far beyond either of my older siblings. Why they thought it was ok to shield us women from the harsh realities of the world was a source of irritation and frustration for me. I sat there, with the whole family around me, eating in near silence, and I just stared at my plate. I had had enough.

"Father!" I called from my seat, halfway down the table. He looked up, roast beef hanging expectantly from his silver fork. Mother continued eating, but my older brothers and younger siblings abruptly stopped. "What was the cause of the attack on the embassy three days ago? The people are concerned… and so am I."

Oskar Sobieski was in his early forties, but seemed much older, due in part to the way he carried himself and the silver threads in his black hair. His mustache and short beard hadn't turned grey yet, but he was always in the dark green of our house, his uniform spotless, with gold braid and buttons.

He furrowed his already wrinkled brow and lowered his food-laden utensil. "Why bother yourself with such things, Jafra? You should be preparing for the trials. I know your brothers passed easily, but succeeding, in fact, just surviving, is not guaranteed."

"I know they told you I was there with Milka. We saw what looked like an army of foreigners attacking the seat of government. Civilians died, as did more than a few soldiers wearing our livery. Do we know why they bombed our city, and do we know if they will return to kill more of our citizens?" I could hear my voice rising in pitch; I used every bit of my control to try to calm myself.

Father looked at me appraisingly, maybe for the first time seeing me as an adult and not his baby girl. He took a deep breath, then let it out slowly. He was a severe man, not given to frivolity or even pleasantries. For him to maintain his temper must have been a true test of his willpower.

"Ok, if you want the ugly side, I will tell you. All of you." He looked each of his children in the face, one by one. "Here are the facts, as we currently know them. There were over a hundred invaders. They had no papers, but they all carried Biała Ruś rubles. They were hired thugs, and they had no idea who paid them, except that he was a tall German with a thin mustache and thinning brown hair. What they were able to share, before expiring, was that their mission was to bomb the embassy and to kill as many Biała Ruś men, women, and children as they could."

"They were all blanks," Stefek said. "They hated Krystian and me with unbridled passion. I know some blanks are envious of the channelers, and even more so of wielders like us, but I was surprised at the level of their hatred. They cursed us every moment that they still had tongues with which to spit their venom."

"My darling. You wanted the truth, so this is what we fear, based on what we know. They were paid and organized, but by whom, we don't know. There's a subversive faction out there that wants war with Rus and the West. They don't value human life, not even their own. I fear that this may be the first in many more attempts to overturn the monarchy and force a war that would spread across all of Europa."

I was stunned by the horrible possibility. I had never known war, and had no desire to see my brothers go to foreign lands and risk their lives. Then it struck me. If there was war, they intended it to be here, in my homeland. I trembled with fear.

"Thank you, Father. I needed to know."

# Chapter 2

"Show me your brand," I said to Milka. She had barely gotten through her trials, and she still had a bit of trauma about the whole thing.

"No! Is that why you invited me over?" As I suspected, she was still touchy about it.

"Not entirely, but I'll be getting mine soon, and I want to see yours."

"You've seen your brothers' brands, and I assume your parents' as well. You don't need to see mine." Her mood was sour; it would take a bit of wheedling to get her to give in.

We sat on green, velvet-covered divan chairs in my private quarters. Bright light filtered in through the golden linen drapes, casting long shadows at this late hour of the afternoon. She rubbed her feet on the thick carpet and sulked. I walked over and poured fresh, hot tea into her cup, adding an extra pastry to her saucer. Nothing.

"I've never asked this of you before, but I want you to read me," I said. She looked at me, not sure what to make of it. "I know what your brand does. I've known for almost a year now."

"I don't like my gift. I only ever bring people pain when I tell them their future."

"How does it work exactly?"

"As you know, all wielders and channelers can tap into Abyrinth. Channelers direct it through machines to make them work. Wielders are exclusively from the noble class, and after they receive their brand, they can access the special power associated with that design. The hard part is that we don't get to choose what conduit is burned into our skin."

"Milka! I know all that! How does your power work? I want to know if war is coming."

"I can't read the future of the world, or the country, or even this city. I can see the destiny of a single person, what major events will happen in their lives in the near future."

"Near future only? You can't see when I will die?" I asked, only half light-hearted.

"If you are dying soon, I guess I would." She still looked sullen.

"You're right. That's not a great ability." Anger. "Take off your shirt."

"No."

"Why not? I've seen boobs before. I have two of my own."

With a groan, she turned her back to me. "Get the buttons."

I undid the three uppermost buttons on her tea gown, the white lace bright against the pale blue cloth, and pulled it down to expose the brand. After surviving the trials, the mark appears on the back, positioned along the spine, and several inches below the neck. I looked at hers, amazed that I had never asked to see it before. The mark resembled copper foil, set into the skin and raised slightly above the surface. I had only seen the ones in my family, but from my limited experience, they were all round, with dark coloring in the voids of the design.

"It looks like a small Delphic Oracle," I mused aloud. "From the Hellic period." I traced the lines with my finger. "It's beautiful. You should be happy with it."

"Sure. Let's see what you get." She grabbed my hand firmly, looking deeply into my eyes. I could feel a warm sensation pulse through me, making my arm tingle, and then it spread throughout my body. As this was happening, the seal on her back began to glow. The metal began to glow with a brilliant light. Her eyes took on the look of someone reading intently.

"Your life is in flux. Everything will change during the coming year." Her voice took on an odd quality, sounding as if she were speaking to me from another world. I wanted to pelt her with questions, but it felt like the wrong thing to do while she was in this state. "I see two men. Two men who will vie for your attention. There will be more attacks on Polska, targeting its citizens and targeting House Sobieski. We will be on the brink of war with Rus and their allies. Your trials will test you to your very limit. I see…" She paused, seeing but not able to verbalize the visions she was receiving. "This… this never happens when I…" She sounded confused and troubled. "I see two possible futures related to your trials. I see you barely surviving, and going on to be one of the strongest wielders in generations."

I couldn't help myself. "And the other?"

She gripped my hand so hard it hurt. Tears began to form in the corners of her eyes, and she went pale, like she'd seen a spirit. "I only see darkness down the other path. The other possibility is that you don't survive the trials."

It was not unheard of. The trials were different for everyone. I suppose because the payoff is so great, the challenge is correspondingly difficult. Less than one in a hundred died, but it did happen.

She shrugged her shirt back on, and I couldn't help getting lost in my own thoughts as I robotically did the buttons at the back of her neck. She prophesied my death, and she was more shaken than I was at the prospect. I wasn't afraid of death; I had never given it a moment's thought in my nearly eighteen years. She wept and tried to comfort me, but I think she cried more for herself than she did for me.

Shortly after Milka left for the day, I went down to the casual dining room. We had a larger space that could comfortably seat a hundred, but we also had a smaller room for just our family. The small dining room was attached to the kitchen. I always preferred to eat there, with the smell of bread baking and bacon frying. I would listen to the chef and her cooks gossiping while I ate. Karina brought me tea and biscuits, and I sat for a few minutes to enjoy the gardens through the spacious glass double doors. The light shining in made the sage green walls glow softly. I mulled over Milka's reading of me. Two men? That certainly sounded exciting. I'm not being conceited when I say that I am considered an attractive person. I was an adorable child, and since the change, I have been blessed with a generous bust, flat stomach, shapely hips, and long legs. I know many girls find fault in their reflection, but mirrors have never been my enemy. I'm not the fairest in the land, but I have gotten many stares from both boys and men when I am out in public. I was going to be matched soon, and I assumed that whoever he was, he would be one of the two men Milka saw. But who was the other?

My mind went to the most titillating part of the prediction, but then the rest fell on me like heavy rain from water-fat storm clouds. Both my brothers passed their trials when they were eighteen, and to the best of my knowledge, did so with relative ease. My cousin had predicted that I would struggle, that I might not even survive. Or worse yet, not pass but still live. A noble without a brand was unheard of. My mind wandered, imagining all manner of catastrophe, and I sat there not eating, just staring outside.

"Jafra! Are you ok?" Krystian said, breaking me from my trance.

I turned with a start. "Yes, I'm fine." I pushed my dish away and turned to speak with my brother. He must not have been on duty today; he was wearing a simple white shirt and tight blue britches. He had his hair pulled back and tied with a leather thong.

"You looked like you were a million miles away," he said, sitting across from me.

"Perhaps I was. You know, my trials are coming soon."

"Really? Eighteen already?" He smiled wryly. He was my favorite brother, and a big reason why was his sense of humor. He has always been easy to speak with. He took my hands in his and looked me straight in the eyes. "You're going to be fine. We Sobieskis don't just survive, we thrive."

"Did you make that up yourself?"

Krystian probably had the best sense of humor of all of us. He generously laughed at my lame joke. A plate full of leftover pot roast and potatoes magically appeared in front of him. He gave Karina a thankful nod, then dug heartily into his snack. I swear, the boy could eat more than any two grown men and still couldn't put on weight. Disgusting as it was, watching him scarf down his food took my mind off my future.

"Ok, let's talk," he said, wiping his mouth with a linen napkin. At night, he went out with his friends and drank alcohol, often to excess. I didn't think Mother knew, and if Father knew, he would have gotten his ears boxed by now. This early, he asked for an orange juice and set it on the table within reach. "Your birthday is in about a week. You haven't asked Stef or me about it, though I'm guessing you are dying to." He looked at me with his ice-blue eyes, the same depthless eyes that Father and I had. There were times that I needed to talk with someone, not my girlfriends, and not our parents. Kris had been there for me in the past, and he was offering his help now.

"I'm scared. I know that you and Stef passed your trials with childlike ease, but I fear that I will have a much harder time." It was hard to admit my weakness, but there it was.

"I'm not sure where you're getting your information from, sister. Who told you that we had an easy time of it?"

I've had that impression for years now, and I wasn't sure exactly where the idea started. "Not sure. It may have been from Stef himself. You know how he likes to boast." That was true. Our older brother was nearly perfect. Strong and dependable, good-looking, loved by women, respected by men. He was above the rest of us, and he knew it.

"That might be possible; he is one of his own biggest fans. But I know you didn't hear it from me, because I lie when it suits me, to Father, to my instructors at the military academy, and definitely to women, but I have never lied to you, little sister. The trials were hell. For me, for Stefek, and I presume, for everyone who has ever gone through them."

"Sorry. I didn't mean to downplay your accomplishment." I lowered my gaze, not wanting him to think I didn't recognize that he was a powerful wielder.

"Don't worry, I don't take offense easily. I just want you to know the truth before next week. The trials are no joke, and I had a tough time getting through them. Stef almost died."

This was shocking news to me. People often prefer not to discuss their experiences in trials. Milka absolutely refused to tell me about her testing. My brothers had always seemed invincible, unflappable. The idea that Stefek had barely survived... actually made me feel a little better somehow. Selfish, perhaps, but that's how I felt.

"Is it true that the harder the trial, the more powerful the brand?"

"I've heard that too. I'm not sure if it's a fact, but there may be some truth to it. Stefek's Chronoburst makes him nearly unbeatable in one-on-one combat, or even four-on-one. It's an incredibly valuable gift, and he had to fight like hell to earn it."

"So, tell me about your trial." I looked at him expectantly, expecting him to spill his guts.

"I won't do that, dear Jafra." He could tell by my reaction that I was about to explode on him. "As you probably know, everyone has a different experience. It is somehow... tailored to the person, created to test them to the very limits of their capability. What is difficult and traumatic for me could be no more troubling than a walk in the park for my older brother, or for you, even." He could tell that his vague platitude was not satisfying me. "If I tell you what I experienced, you'll be expecting the same. The best thing that you can do is to enter with a blank slate. No preconceived notions, no expectations."

I looked at him dubiously.

"I'm not saying that you should go in completely unprepared, but if you are expecting one kind of challenge and you get something completely different, you'll be in a worse condition than if you had stumbled in off the street." With his long, thin fingers, he lifted my chin to make sure that I was meeting his eyes with mine. "Eat that morning. You'll have butterflies, and you'll think that you can't get anything down. You'll need the energy. Sleep well the night before, even if Karina has to bring you a tonic. Be alert from the second you enter the chamber and be prepared to react swiftly and decisively."

A lot of that was just common sense, but I did appreciate his taking the time to tell me.

"There is something I thought I should mention, while we are on this subject."

He looked at me quizzically. A faint smile touched his lips before he gave me the satisfaction. "What is that, dear sister?"

"You are aware of Milka's ability?" I asked him

"No, not really. I've always found her a little dry and skittish. We've not really kept in touch, even though I know you have her over all the time."

"Her brand gives her limited—very limited—foresight. She can see one person's immediate future. I asked her for a reading."

His tight brow furrowed in concentration as he weighed the value of my information. "How accurate is she supposed to be? I've never given any credence to these types of things."

That was a good question. I never bothered to ask her how often her predictions came true. Half the time? Most of the time? Rarely? I just assumed it was every time. He could tell by my hesitation and the stupid look I gave him that I didn't know.

"I already said that I don't believe these things, but let's get past that. What did she predict for you? What does the future hold for Lady Jafra Sobieski?" Damn his smirk.

"Well, two predictions."

"Tell the one pertaining to your challenge."

"That's the one that she was not completely clear on."

"Oh my God," he said, literally slapping his own forehead.

"She was a little freaked out by it. She said that for the first time, she saw two possible outcomes, and that either way, I would struggle to survive. In one of the possibilities, I would just barely pass, and I would receive a strong brand, stronger than has been seen in generations. The other possibility is that I die."

"That's not saying much. Every trial is potentially life-or-death, and I hope you receive a strong brand. The truth is, I'm not sure that you have a choice. I have never heard of anyone choosing not to go through the trials." He sat back in his chair, seemingly relieved.

Of course, he was right. As scared as I was, I would enter the chamber, and if it was God's will that I die, then so be it.

"What was the other prediction that our clairvoyant cousin had for you?"

"She said that I would have two men in my near future, both trying to win me."

He leaned forward, now truly interested. "Now that's better. Two men, eh?" He looked me over like a piece of meat. "I would think that there might be quite a few who would be interested in you. Being purely subjective, you're not bad looking."

"'Not bad looking?' I might faint from the excessive compliment."

"Ok, I'm your brother, I've known you all of your life, and to tell the truth, I've never really looked at you." He looked again, like a butcher summing up a side of beef. "Somewhere along the line, you became a woman. I can see two men competing for you."

"I think that was supposed to be a compliment?" I asked.

"Of course, dear. You were always a beautiful child, but you now possess the curves that would drive men wild. Once they find out how smart and loving you are, they will be drawn to you like a moth to flame."

"You don't think I need to worry about it?" He almost had me convinced.

"Why should you? I'm not sold on Cousin Milka's fortune-telling tricks. More than likely, you'll be promised to some lord in the middle of nowhere, get married, and raise a pack of wild dogs like Stef and me. No drama."

As much as I loved my brother, I really hated him at that moment.

# Chapter 3

The week before had been torture. I was obsessed with Milka's predictions to the point where I couldn't sleep. The day had finally arrived. Today was my birthday, and to celebrate, I would go through a trying ritual that could either grant me a mysterious, random power or possibly kill me.

Taking my older brother's advice, I took a sleeping draught the night before so I would have at least some sleep. Following his other recommendation, I tried to eat, but it was impossible to get down more than a few bites.

"Jafra, I have faith in you. I know you will do our family proud," my father said. I looked up at him; he was a few inches taller than I, though I often forgot and felt like a child when he was a few feet taller than I. He was a busy man, and we didn't speak one-on-one all that often. It's not that I didn't know him; it was more a situation where there were five children, and I was lost in the middle of the pack. The boys would carry on the family name, and regardless of how well or poorly I performed today, I would not.

His salt-and-pepper beard and hair were neatly trimmed; his emerald-colored suit was pressed and perfect, his many medals and awards gleaming on his broad chest. It seemed that his reassuring smile was almost a struggle for him to maintain. Mother, of course, was nowhere to be seen. She had already experienced a lot with the boys, and though I was her favorite, she couldn't bear to see me in distress.

Krystian had finally coughed up a few minor details. As a result, I was not too surprised to be presented with a bright white, rubbery body suit to put on. I wasn't used to tight clothing, so it took more than a little effort to wedge my newfound curves into the suit. There was a significant gap in the suit on the back, just below the damned, choking collar. A blank, circular copper disk with slightly raised edges was placed on my back with a bit of adhesive. Krystian had also told me that part. Other than white rubber sneakers on my feet and a white length of silk to tie back my hair, I had nothing else on. The suit was too tight and form-fitting; I felt like I was standing naked before Father and the Trial Warden. There were a few other officials around the periphery of the cave mouth, but I couldn't focus on them, and for the life of me, couldn't tell you how many there were, or any details about them.

Warden Birk, originally from Germania, was the official administrator of the Brand Binding ceremonies throughout Polska. His wild, white hair served to accentuate his severe, wrinkled-beyond-recognition face. He wore large spectacles with wires that extended from the temples to the dull metal backpack he wore. The top half of his uniform looked tight and similar to what Father wore, though it was bright white, and the bottom flared out into what resembled a lab coat. Beneath, he had on dark pants and scuffed leather shoes. Worn leather straps held his backpack in place, and whatever the contraption was, it was connected by a series of wires and rubber tubes to a wide metal belt around his middle, which was eight inches tall and two inches thick. The thing looked ridiculous, but he was a member in good standing of the Steam Guild, so I was warned not to giggle.

We had descended down a ravine over a hundred feet to reach the entrance of a cave that may have been there for millions of years, ripped from the limestone buried beneath our soil. The river that had carved the ravine was long gone, and from above, you could only see the mass of trees that grew from a hole in the ground.

"Let's get the formalities out of the way!" His scratchy voice echoed in the deep ravine. "State your name for the record!" he bellowed.

"Jafra Nicola Sobieski," I replied. I tried not to sound nervous, but his gruff manner was unsettling.

"Lineage?" Again, the barking almost made me jump.

"Eldest daughter of Lord Stefek Sobieski and Lady Roksana Sobieski. First of my name," I replied loudly, so all could witness my noble origins.

"Do you enter the Star Chamber of your own free will, and accept the fate you are destined for? Be it glory, mediocrity, or death?" The last word rolled off his lips and came out as a tortured hiss. I felt a chill pass through me, but I did my best not to let it show.

"With a sound mind and no reservations, I agree to face the Fires of Abyrinth. For the honor of my house, for the love of Polska, and the well-being of the Polish people."

"Very good," he said, looking at me for the first time. "Follow the path behind me, through that crack and into the chamber beyond. There, you will find a pedestal that holds the gem we call Abyrinth's Fire. Place your hand on the gem, and this will begin your trial." He lowered his head so he could look at me over the frame of his glasses. His watery, bloodshot eyes locked with mine. "At that point, there is no turning back. If you do not return in one hour, we will assume that you have perished, and we will send in a team to collect your corpse." He spread his lips in what could generously have been called a smile. "I wish you the best of luck, my lady."

He turned to the side, making a path for me. I didn't want to turn my head to see those behind me. I knew I was not my father's favorite, but I was his favorite of the girls, and even though he said a dozen times how much faith he had in me, I was sure he had almost as much anxiety as I did.

There was the faintest rustle of a breeze and the soft crunch of pebbles beneath my feet, but otherwise, it was eerily quiet. The rock wall was two dozen paces, and in seconds, I was standing in front of a massive crack. The opening was about three feet wide and at least ten feet high. I placed my hand on the dull stone, hoping to feel something that would either reassure me or send me running in terror.

Just stone, nothing special.

I peered into the gap and was met by inky blackness. Light from the ravine penetrated only a few feet before being swallowed by the impenetrable darkness. I stuck my arm in and couldn't see past my elbow. I was given no lamp or torch, so I entered, feeling my way along.

With a hand on each wall, I took careful steps for what seemed to be miles, but in reality was most likely only a hundred yards. Halfway to the end, I saw a light filtering in from the opposite end of the crevice. It got brighter and brighter until I broke out into an open chamber in the solid stone. The walls and ceiling appeared to have been carved into a dome; the floor was unnaturally flat and smooth.

When they said I would be entering a cave, I expected it to be craggy and rough, but the room was anything but. Only fifteen feet in diameter, the walls were smooth, with no other exits or features of any kind. There was a metal plaque set into the back wall, but it was too dark to make out the inscription. The only illumination was the light of Abyrinth's Fire, a gem the size of a grapefruit that emitted blinding white light. The gem sat on a metal fixture atop a machine, the likes of which I'd never seen before. The machines in my country were all based on steam for propulsion. They would have gears, wires, springs, and pipes. They often made one think of them as mechanical insects, with their intricate details and shiny surfaces. This device was unlike anything I had seen or even heard of. It was pale yellow and orange, with dim lights flashing beneath its shiny surface. There seemed to be no controls, no levers or buttons, nothing to manipulate. It grew from the ground, or at least that's how it appeared. Rock encroached on the bottom, cementing it to the chamber's center.

I reached out my hand, ready to begin the program. I stared at my hand, with its long fingers that usually ended in colorful nails; the several rings and bracelets I wore daily were left at home. Hovering less than an inch above the stone, I searched with all of my senses to see if any sound or energy was coming from the gem. Aside from the pure white light it gave off, there was no indication that it was special or powerful. I was almost tempted to take this lightly as I placed my hand firmly on the gem. I was wrong.

# Chapter 4

I was no longer in the cave; I was outside, and it was a brilliant, sunny day. When my eyes adjusted, I saw that I was standing in a field of knee-high waving grass, the blades tickling my bare leg. That caught my attention. I looked down to see that, instead of the rubber suit, I was wearing a simple white cotton nightgown with no design. To be honest, it was nothing more than a bag with holes.  It was the only barrier between my pale, pasty skin and the blistering sun above.

Which way to go? I thought to myself. There seemed to be nothing of interest in any direction. There was a soft whooshing sound as a passing breeze bent billions of blades of grass. A pair of hawks circled above, moving in great lazy circles, coasting on the wind. The earthy scent of grass mixed with wildflowers, wild herbs, and clover was enough to make me long for a simple country life. I stood there, unable to make a decision, when I saw a butterfly drift by me. It had bright orange wings, framed by thin, black and brown bands. I hadn't been in the country recently, and it was larger than I remembered. My mind was starting to wander when I saw another, perhaps its twin. Then, a third, a fourth…

Turning, I saw hundreds of the stunning winged insects heading towards me. I ducked, though I knew that butterflies were not known to be that dangerous. They swarmed past me and kept on the path set by the first. A cloud of the most beautiful butterflies was travelling in a specific direction, and I took it as a sign. I tramped along behind them. The sun was directly overhead, so I had no idea which way was east or north and so on.

Alone with my thoughts, I followed the insects as they flew with conviction in a singular direction. No deviation in course, no stopping to smell the flowers. The monotonously level ground eventually gave way to a slight incline. At the crest of the gentle hill, I saw a figure. As I drew closer, I could see that it was a child, a young girl about six years old. She waved to me as I got closer, but she did not attempt to come to me.

"Bonjour!" she said as I finally reached her perch. She had long blonde hair that needed a good combing and a face that was radiant, despite needing scrubbing.

My French was passable, much better than my German or Russian, so I spoke her language. "Bonjour, petite princesse," I replied. "What is this place?" I asked, waving my hands around.

"We are in what you call the Heart of Abyrinth. In this place, time, distance, and even reality are foreign constructs. Do not believe what you see or hear, smell or touch while you are here. You desire to be connected to Abyrinth, and before that can happen, you must be tried and judged. If you prove worthy, the power will flow through you and help you to do wondrous things."

"If I am not found to be worthy?" I asked.

She just smiled and took my hand in hers. Apart from the different hair color, we looked like sisters. Neither of us had shoes, and she wore the same plain, sack-like dress that I wore. Her face was soft and rounded like that of a child, but there was an ancient wisdom in her eyes. I met her gaze and felt humbled.

She started walking down the other side of the hill, pulling me along. "They call these trials for a reason. You will face three challenges. Fail any one of them, and you'll not receive a connection to Abyrinth." She halted, jerking me out of my comfort zone. "Fail, and there is the chance you will never see your world or family again. Take these challenges lightly at your peril."

I didn't respond, but chewed on her words, internalizing them. I thought I was being serious, but did she see some hesitation in me? Some lack of commitment?

We continued our stroll down the hill towards some trees, not too far down a path that was worn into the field. I noticed that, despite it being midday only a few moments ago, it was now sunset, growing darker by the minute. The stand of trees turned out to be a forest, trees the diameter of lampposts, and others were as big around as two men abreast. They stood so tightly together, you couldn't see more than a dozen feet into the woods. The bark on the trees was shades of black and dark grey, and they looked wet as if they were bleeding clear sap from high up on their trunks. Low branches reached for us, leafless fingers that poked cruelly at our simple clothes as we tried to navigate the rough trail.

"I'm scared!" the girl said, her high-pitched voice even higher since the sun went down.

I looked down at her, and she returned my stare. The worldly, adult eyes were gone, and now there was only a child with a child's innocence. Her declaration of fear was mirrored in her expression, and by the way she gripped my hand as firmly as she could manage with her tiny, soft hand. She had led me to the dark, scary forest, yet now it was she who was afraid to enter.

"Why did you bring me here?" I asked.

"What? I was lost, and you said you would help me get home!" I looked into her watery eyes and saw absolute conviction. Perhaps this was a real little girl who had been taken over, possessed by the spirit that controlled the trials. A cold wind blew across us, raising my skirt, freezing my skin, and covering me with goose bumps. The girl was also freezing and began to weep openly.

I could have gone back, taken her back to the hilltop where we met, but when I turned, I saw more forest behind us. We were in a clearing, ten feet on a side, and the only discernible path was the one we had been traveling. Part of me knew that this was planned, and it was clear what direction we were meant to travel. The cold was sinking into my bones, and I used my other hand to keep my dress from flying up in the breeze. She started a low, moaning cry, so I squeezed her hand more tightly, and we resumed walking.

"What's your name, little one?" I asked, hoping to take her mind from the general discomfort of our situation. She sniffed loudly, clear mucus running down her tiny face.

"Chloé, mademoiselle."

"Je m'appelle Jafra," I replied. "Where do you want me to take you? Are your parents nearby? Do you live near here?"

She shrugged, and again, tears flowed down her rosy cheeks.

I stopped short when I heard a howl. There is no mistaking the sound of a wolf calling to its pack. I was uneasy before, but now genuine fear filled me, making me catch my breath, causing every muscle in my body to tighten all at once.

Heedless of her ability to keep up, I pulled at her arm and picked up our pace to a near run. The dim light of the moon and stars was the only illumination; night had fallen, and it was dark as pitch in the forest, and there was another howl from somewhere far behind us. Then another, originating from the direction we were travelling. I could barely keep us from crashing headfirst into trees, as dark as it was. I wanted to break into a sprint. A big part of me, a part that lived in my conscious brain, wanted to release her hand and save myself. Howls were coming from the sides now, and there would be no safe direction to flee. We passed into a slight clearing, and I decided to make my stand.

"I have to fight them. They have us surrounded." She looked at me as if I had lost my mind. "Feel around on the ground. Find the biggest stick that you can!" As I gave her the instruction, I set the example by squatting and feeling around with my hands. All of the branches began at least a dozen feet over our heads. The only hope of obtaining a tool for defense was to find something on the ground to use as a makeshift weapon.

It was dark at eye level. It was darker still near the forest floor. I scrabbled around, only finding dirt and piles of dead leaves. At home, there was always a broken-off branch in the garden that wasn't wanted; now I wanted one more than anything.

"I found one!" she said excitedly. She helped me to my feet and handed me what she had found. It was almost three feet long and about as round as my wrist. I couldn't have hoped for a more perfect club.

"Merci," I said. I leaned down and hugged her small frame to my chest. I squeezed her, not only to calm her fear, but to find my own center. And perhaps as a last goodbye. "I don't know from which direction they'll come, but stay behind me!"

Another howl, much closer. Two more. They could smell us and were closing in.

I gripped the club in both hands and held it out like my brothers held their swords. I was as prepared as I possibly could be. When they finally melted out of the tree line, I almost felt a sensation of relief. I could see two wolves in my peripheral vision, but the only one that I could concentrate on was the one directly in front of me. I had never seen a wolf in person, and it was much larger than any breed of dog that I had ever seen. On its head and back, it was dark grey with black streaks; its coat looked rough and bristling around its shoulders.

It began with a rumbling growl that vibrated in my bones and made me catch my breath. For several seconds, I couldn't breathe. The wolf opened its muzzle slowly, revealing a deadly jaw lined with fangs. The front teeth were not long, but looked to be sharp as daggers. The canines—aptly named, with two on top and two on the bottom—were at least an inch long and gave the beast a demonic countenance. Drool dripped from the mouth; the jaw clenched, and the growling sound grew louder by the second. I could see in the sickly yellow eyes that an attack was imminent.

The wolf leaped at us, like a spring releasing its tension. Its front paws were outstretched, mouth wide enough to deliver a fatal bite.

I surprised myself by swinging my log at the exact right moment. I mentioned before that I have a bit of an athletic background, and I swung my club with all the force my arms could produce. It cracked the animal on the side of the head, changing its trajectory and sending it to the leaf-strewn ground in a whimpering heap.

My instinct was to hit it again and again until it stopped moving, but its pack had other thoughts. They leapt at us, and it took all the control that I could muster to rotate myself between the wolves and sweet Chloé.

I swung again, trying to connect with the wolf on my right, while the one to the left crashed into me. I was able to score a glancing blow at my target, but I wasn't able to enjoy my success after being raked by razor-sharp claws. The wolf on my right tore through my flimsy dress and my skin at the same time. Blood gushed from my wounds, soaking into the pristine white material.

I kicked to the left while attempting to land a more solid blow against the wolf to my right. I connected solidly with the shoulder, my wooden club making a meaty thud as it struck the furry bastard. As I was having some success, the one to my left clawed at my left calf before sinking its fangs deep in my flesh. The pain was excruciating, but blacking out was not an option.

Chloé was screaming at the top of her lungs, and I wasn't sure if she was more terrified by the wolves or traumatized by how much blood I was losing.

"Get back!" I screamed at the wolves. The first one that I had struck was recovered, so now I again had three of them snapping at me with their vicious fangs; one of them had my blood on its muzzle. While two tried to rip me apart, the third went after the girl.

I tried to move between us, but one of the wolves that had been threatening me moved around for easy access to the tender meat on the little girl. I didn't think about my welfare; I could only imagine what these wild animals would do to little Chloé. I threw myself over her, covering her with my body. Claws ripped my skin, vice-like jaws clamped down on my arms, back, and side. The pain was much worse than I could have ever imagined. At some point, I blacked out.

# Chapter 5

"Let me help you up," said a smooth male voice that was unfamiliar to me.

Where am I? I opened my eyes to see how bad my injuries were. I realized that I was not in pain, even as the memories of foul claws ripped my skin, and fangs dug in and ripped my muscle, spilling my organs on the forest floor.

I was lying on a smooth, glassy surface that was cool to the touch and glowed faintly. Above me was the source of the voice. It looked like a man, but I could tell immediately that it was a machine. It stood over six feet tall; the head would have been oddly small if it were a man of the same height. There was no mouth, per se, but rather a slit in the metallic skull, either brass or copper, covered by a translucent layer that gave it a high-gloss finish. There were no eyes or ears. Instead, it had what looked like two-inch-diameter camera lenses, arranged vertically in the center of the expressionless face. The neck was constructed from metal shafts, connecting the head to a body and pelvis that resembled metal boxes stacked atop one another. The legs were again shiny, copper-colored metal shafts that, to a degree, mimicked human bone structure. The automaton's whole body was covered in a thick layer of the same glossy material.

"Miss Jafra, allow me to help you."

Perhaps I should have been scared or at least a little more cautious, but I took the proffered hand, and I was effortlessly pulled to my feet. There was no heat from the hand, only the sensation of touching rubber that looked like glass. I didn't know if I should look in the top lens or the bottom, so I stared vaguely at the space between them. It stood there, waiting for me to speak or do something. I made it wait.

The room looked like the interior of a clock. The ten-by-ten-by-ten-foot space was walled with metal panels with a smooth, uniform surface. Two of the walls on opposite sides had axles protruding from them with gears and cogs that were interlocking and ready to be set in motion. The whole room seemed to vibrate, so lightly that it was almost imperceptible. On one wall, behind the mechanical man, a panel had been polished to a mirror-like surface. I caught a glimpse of myself and was taken aback once again. The simple cotton dress that had been torn and soaked with my blood was gone. My hair was neatly tied into a single ponytail that trailed down my back. I was again wearing the rubber suit that I had entered the cave in… how long ago was that?

"Where am I?" I asked.

"You are in the Clockwork Conundrum. This is the second part of your trials. Survive, and you will be allowed to move on to the third and final challenge."

"Survive?" I asked. "What is the goal? How can I pass this level? And most importantly, what dangers should I be wary of?"

"So many questions. Unfortunately, that is part of the challenge. Good luck, Lady Jafra." The robot bowed, then sank through a glowing panel on the floor. I almost thought it was my imagination when I saw what looked like strings or spiderwebs woven around the square. When the robot was gone, the light ceased, and the fibers stopped jumping, sinking into the floor as well.

Pure Abyrinth, I thought to myself. I had no basis for my conclusion, but deep in my spirit, I knew it to be correct.

Machinery ran on either steam power or Abyrinth, and whatever this clockwork puzzle was, it seemed like it might run on one or both of the power sources.

I had never been able to see the mystical energy before, and I had never heard that anyone else could either. It's like oxygen, something we know exists and is essential for survival, yet is odorless and invisible. They say that this energy we all rely on started after the Night of the Comet. I find it hard to believe that there was a time when we didn't have Abyrinth, given its essential role in the growth and prosperity of Europa and the New World. According to legend, five hundred years ago, society was hardly advanced at all, and though steam was in its infancy, machines had just started to become part of modern life. Since then, we've flourished, creating wonders that our ancestors could never have dreamed of.

What did I learn just now? In this place, at least, the power is expressed as fibers or webs. I touched the square where the robot had been standing, and it was solid. My fingers traced the edges and found nothing.

There had to be something that I was missing. Putting me in an empty room with no doors is not much of a challenge. I was trapped in a perfect cube. Each wall had panels of equal size, five across, five wide, and five high. To my left, the wall had a large gear with dull steel teeth. It wasn't attached to anything, and I couldn't determine its purpose. I grasped two of the spokes in the two-foot-diameter gear and pulled with all my strength. Nothing.

I pulled as hard as I could. Still nothing.

When I took my hand off the device, I saw something in the shadow I cast. As my hand moved farther from the metal, I could see hair-fine filaments spanning the gap. Under direct light, they were very hard to see, but now that I knew what I was looking for, I could see them all around me. They were clear, but they seemed to glow with a faint trace of light, taking on a silvery quality. The silky fibers between my hand and the gear were straight, pulled tight like guitar strings. My eyes had been opened, and now I could see them everywhere. Little bits of starlight were attached to the boundaries of the wall and floor plates, and some floated in the air like ash after a fire.

With a bit of concentration, I applied a pulling force on the Abyrinth that clung to the wheel. I found that I was not pulling with the strength of my arm, but with the will that I exerted.

I should have been shocked, amazed, but I expected the strings to move the gear, and so they did. Slowly at first, as if it resented being asked to perform its intended function. I heard the tiniest squeak, and the gear turned, and an opening perpendicular to it opened. I continued turning until a two-by-six-foot door opened, or more specifically, three of the two-by-two-foot panels. I couldn't see into the next room, but it was clear what I was meant to do. I mentally tied off the strings of force and continued to the next room.

On entering, the door closed behind me as the floor, walls, and ceiling in the new chamber were dimly illuminated. The primary source of light was the floor, each square panel lit and shining brightly, until the one before me winked out. I stood just outside it and peered down, down, down. The floor panel was gone, and a bottomless chasm lay beneath.

"Hello!" I called out, but it was so deep that there was no echo. I stuck my hand in the void to make sure it was real. There was definitely a hole in the floor. There was no frame around the hole, and I couldn't quite figure out how they were held in place.

To my right, and a few paces ahead, I saw another panel darken, and I had to assume that it too was gone. Before it could register with me, a third panel straight ahead blinked out, then a fourth to my left. On instinct, I turned around to see that three panels had disappeared along the wall I had passed through to enter this room. There were only twenty-five panels on each facet of this cube, and every few seconds, another would cease to exist. My mind went blank, and I couldn't decide what to do when I started falling.

The glowing panel I was standing on evaporated, and I fell. I didn't usually panic, even when surprised. Instinct took over, and I flailed, grabbing the tiles on either side. I felt fibers of power around the edge of the hole, and hanging from the edge, I could see them. They stretched from the floor to my fingertips. Or did they issue from my fingers and reach out to the floor? My upper body strength was nowhere near Stefek's or even Krystian's, but I was sure that I could do at least one pull-up.

I was nearly out of the hole when the floor tile on the left disappeared. I screamed and gripped with my left hand for dear life. As I was hanging there, I was under the level of the floor, and I saw another tile go, then another. Time was running out. It was pretty clear. I fall? I lose.

I concentrated, and I could see the fibrous whisps of Abyrinth hovering around my hand, drifting through the air, settling on every surface. I felt like a spider sitting in a web, the silky strands all connected, giving me feedback on anything in my realm. At my command, the power gathered together to form a rope that I knew was visible only to me. The rope grasped the tiles of the walls and ceiling, on the far end, and wrapped around my arm. I could control it with the power of thought and persistence of will.

The last tile gave way, and for half a second, I was falling. Then my steel-strong fibers wrapped around me, and at my command, carried me out of the pit and into the room. The floor was gone entirely, but the walls remained. I sat buoyed by a handful of the thick cords of pure Abyrinth. They held me gently, and with a silent, mental command, I could turn in any direction, move anywhere in the room. It was like being in the hand of a benevolent giant, safe and cared for.

Looking around, I could see that the ceiling and four walls were intact. Some of the panels glowed, while others did not. One of the panels went dark, and the one to its right lit up. I lay in my web, watching as the seemingly random patterns continued to change. I looked for a pattern, but the flashing on and off was completely random.

This was not just torture; it was meant to be a test. Trying to develop a skill in me or testing my worthiness. I had to think, to concentrate. The first test was to see what I would do in a no-win situation, where not just my life, but the life of an innocent child was at stake. Whoever engineered this test must have felt that my self-sacrifice demonstrated I was worthy of advancement.

This test has shown me that Abyrinth has a physical form, which can be seen. And manipulated? This test was designed to introduce me to the concept of harnessing power in its raw form. Stefek uses the power to pause time, but he'd told me in the past that he no longer had to think about the mechanics of it. He wills time to stop, and it does. The same with Krys. He looks at something metal, and in his mind, he sees barbed wire, razor wire, and rose thorns as long as his fingers; the metal obeys his command.

Both of them, and everyone else I knew, accessed the energy to wield their abilities, and it became more of a reflex than anything else. The channelers harnessed the power similarly to blank engineers who channeled steam into the engines that ran much of the country's machines. They tapped into it and directed it toward any device that had been modified to run on Abyrinth. To the best of my knowledge, what I was learning was something entirely new. I could see Abyrinth, and if I was correct, it was flowing out of me and becoming… if not tangible, maybe ethereal?

I was connecting with the power physically, but I knew, as everyone knows, that the power is also a manifestation of will, guided by the mind and harnessed by the spirit. I had escaped falling to my death, but there was more to learn, and that's why I was stuck here.

I thought the lights were slowing down, but I saw that there were fewer of them instead. It had started as a nauseating light display that caused my stomach to nearly disgorge the large breakfast that Krys had insisted I eat. Now, there were not half as many as when the light show started. I had to work it out. Four walls and a ceiling, each with twenty-five panels, that was… one hundred and twenty-five squares, and half of them were illuminated when it began. Now, there was half that.

I had the sinking feeling that I didn't have all the time in the world. I would have to solve this puzzle before I was in total darkness. I racked my brain, trying to think how to relight the panels, or… I couldn't really think of anything else. Then I had an idea.

I reached out with the power. It existed to a degree in everyone, but until today, I was considered a child, and children were strictly forbidden from tampering with

Abyrinth. I didn't know how to do it, so I visualized the energy within me, rolling around like I'd eaten something bad, then flowing from my hands in silvery-white strands. I could see it clearly now. Like a snake, the power I was wielding curved and rolled, wanting to break free from my control. No, damn it! I was in charge here!

I saw a lit panel near the center of one of the walls. I touched it through my energy tentacle. It did nothing. That's good! The other panels were flashing rapidly, and I could have sworn they were flashing even faster. The one I held was stationary.

This was good. The space right next to my square lit up, and I grabbed it. I had two side by side; they were lit and not changing. Progress. Towards what? I wasn't sure.

I was able to snare one directly above the first square, then a minute later, one just below. It was getting harder; fewer than twenty lights were going around, not counting the four that I had trapped.

A feeling of desperation set in. Every time I checked the walls and ceiling, there were fewer lights. I grabbed at one that was going very fast, and though I wanted to pause it above my stack, it settled in a third row. Damn.

I created six more tentacles, one over each square that I would need to complete a three-by-two square rectangle. As soon as one of my preferred spots was lit, I would pounce on it. I got one on top of my stack, then another on the right side. The lights were dim, and the room was starting to grow dark. My heart grew heavy as I saw that only three lights were still circling the room. I had five of the squares I needed to complete what I hoped would be a doorway, but I felt like I would need six of the squares, in proper order, to make a six-foot by four-foot door. I saw a square on the ceiling blink out and vanish. I needed one of two specific squares to light up, and there were only two... no, there was now only one unclaimed light, working through its random pattern.

I could see the light zipping around the walls, staying for less than a second before moving to the next location. I tried not to follow it with my eyes. I focused on the two power tendrils that I had, each hovering, waiting... It landed on the bottom right, where it would complete a door near where the floor had been.

My adrenaline was raging so hard that it affected my reaction time. The square was precisely where I needed it to be, and... I missed!

It seemed darker. I kept focusing on my captured light squares and waited patiently for the loose one to return. Was it on the ceiling? On the wall behind me, opposite where I was creating a door? I wasn't even sure that it hadn't been extinguished. I was still alive, so I hadn't lost yet.

I waited precious seconds, praying for the firefly to land in my field of vision. Out of the corner of my eye, I saw a light! I couldn't freeze time like Stefek, but when the light appeared again, it seemed to pause for a while—enough time to collect it and complete a doorway that was in the middle of the wall.

All along, I wasn't sure if this was what I was meant to do, but when the rectangle was complete, the squares became so bright that I couldn't see them anymore; I only saw the doorway. Not with my arms, but using Abyrinth, I pulled, and the door opened. I could see a lit hallway through the opening, and using the fibers in the air, the cords that made

up my spider's web, I carried myself up to the door. I stepped
through, and everything went black.

# Chapter 6

I woke up in a bed that was more than twice the size of the one I slept in every night. The room was dark, the wan light outside telling me that it was morning, and the sun was on its daily trek through the heavens. I rubbed sleep out of my eyes and noticed that the sheets on the bed next to me were rumpled, as if someone else had been sleeping there. I was terrified, not knowing if I had been drugged and taken to some lord's manor and defiled.

I touched the spot between my legs. There was no blood on my hand as I brought it up to inspect it. My maidenhead must still be intact, but sleeping next to a stranger would ruin my reputation and throw a wrench into my mother's negotiations for a husband.

Maybe a woman had been sleeping there. I had a few friends who might have invited me over for a ball, and I had spent the night after sneaking a brandy or two. I had stayed over at the homes of my classmates on several occasions. Could this be Daria's or Milena's house? I very much doubted it. They slept in twin beds, just like I did. This king-sized bed seemed fit for a man. I wanted to believe that my innocence was intact, but a feeling of dread ate at my soul, that my situation was far worse than I had hoped for.

I climbed out of bed and saw what I was wearing: a sheer negligee of light shell-pink satin, with darker rose-colored lace. The chemise fell to mid-thigh and barely contained my breasts; my dark pink areolas were visible through the diaphanous material. I wore nothing on my lower body; every contour and every curve was on display. I didn't own any pajamas or nightgowns like this. It was definitely not my style, and the thought of sleeping with my groin uncovered was abhorrent.

Walking around the massive bed, I saw a man's clothes tossed carelessly on the ground. Muddy leather dress boots lay a few feet away near the armoire. Near the bed, there was a pair of dark brownish-red wool britches, tailored and cut for a nobleman. Over the arm of the nearby divan was a light, white cotton shirt, slit halfway down the front with laces that hung loosely from the sides of the opening. Draped carefully over the back of the chair was a dark blue military uniform jacket. The stiff, high collar featured intricate, hand-stitched gold embroidery over a ruddy field, matching the trousers. It had a long row of polished brass buttons down the front, with the same red material as trim where the lapel folded over. The wide cuffs had the same embroidery and colors as the high collar. There were no epaulets or rank insignia. This must not have been his formal uniform jacket, but more of a working uniform. I had no idea of his position, whether he was a lowly infantryman or a general, but from the colors, I knew what country he called home.

"How on earth did I wind up in a Rus soldier's bed?" I asked aloud. From the furnishings in the room, I knew he was no enlisted man. No, he was an officer for sure, and most likely of noble birth.

Everything in the room was stained and polished wood. The thick headboard on the Dresden bed was a deep shade of cherry. It had a gently sloping top, with highly detailed carvings of floral designs that filled the open area. The footboard was the same, and the pattern was mirrored on the wardrobe, the armoire, the divan, and four chairs set around a small table by a large window. Without even kneeling to take a good look, I could tell that the rug beneath the bed was of high quality. There was a brass bowl on a stand with an uncorked bottle of champagne sitting in tepid water.

At the sound of my exclamation, a thirty-something maid barged into the room unannounced. Her dirty-blonde hair was pinned back tightly, and her uniform consisted of a white apron over a light blue, knee-length dress.

The maid didn't seem at all put off by my near nudity. She spoke quickly in Russian, and though my command of the language was shit, I understood her perfectly. "Madam, if you are awake, I can prepare your clothes and then make up the room."

I had so many questions, but I wondered how to get information without sounding like a mental patient. She recognized me, so apparently, this is where I was supposed to be. I nodded, and she went to the wardrobe, selecting a couple of dresses. She held them out for me to choose. I was freaked out, and at this point, I didn't care. I chose the yellow-and-white floor-length day dress with a wide drape of light-green lace that surrounded the deep, wide cleavage. It took us twenty minutes to wedge me into it, and when we were done, my corset was so tight that I could hardly breathe, and my tits were pushed up and half falling out. Another twenty minutes were spent on my hair and applying a little color to my cheeks.

"You'll be taking breakfast on the patio?"

"Yes, thank you."

"The colonel is already there, meeting with the Minister of War and the ambassador. I will bring your plate at once, madam," she said, before curtseying and walking briskly off to the kitchen.

I lifted the bottom of my skirt so it wouldn't drag on the ground, and I began walking towards the large outdoor patio just outside of the guest dining room. The house was enormous, and every hallway had long, tightly-woven floor runners, which tended toward darker colors. The wooden floors beneath were stained dark and oiled to a light sheen. Every few feet, there was a photograph or a painting in a heavy wooden frame, gilded in gold. They held images of people in formal attire; the women wore the latest fashions, silk and satin dresses that displayed not only their taste but also their great wealth. The men wore military-style uniforms, all in the same color scheme as the one left on the bedroom floor.

What confounded me was the faces. They seemed blurry to the point that if I met them on the street, I wouldn't be able to recognize them. Try as I might, squinting, getting within an inch of the canvas, I couldn't make the faces come into focus.

Almost as much as waking up nearly nude in a strange bed frightened me, this intentional concealing of their faces had me even more on edge. Part of me felt like I was in terrible danger. I would bide my time and, as soon as possible, try to get outside the estate and find my way back home. If this were Rus, then I was a long way from my native Polska. I knew no details, had not even a vague idea of my situation, but I was already fretting over having the money to take a train, much less an airship. I can't remember ever being out in the world on my own, and just the thought had me squirming with anxiety. My family merited armed security, and even when I could fool myself into thinking that my friends and I were alone having private conversations, in truth, one of Father's men was always within twenty feet of me.

I wandered aimlessly and got lost a few times before finally finding the dining room. One entire wall was lined with three pairs of double doors that opened onto the patio. Towering, cottony clouds floated like icebergs across a bright blue sky. The grounds were extensive, featuring finely-maintained lawns, a rose garden in the distance, tennis courts near the house, and stables behind a ten-car garage.

That wasn't what caught and held my attention. Like the pictures on the walls, the men at the table had blurred faces. Everything else was in focus. Their uniforms, the food in front of them… only their faces were obscured. I felt a chill run through me, and a scream built in my chest and was about to tear from my mouth, when he spoke to me.

"Darling, I didn't expect you so early." He turned to the other men. "She had a long night, if you know what I mean." He laughed with them. I could make out features, eyes, nose, mouth, that sort of thing, but I couldn't see much more. It was like they hid their faces behind thick panes of filthy glass.

"Good morning, madam," one of the men said, bowing deeply at the waist.

"Jafra, you really shouldn't be here. We're making plans, battle plans, and they really wouldn't interest you." He waved, and a man came over and gently took me by the elbow. I was led back inside, where my meal was served. Before my escort had ushered me back inside, I saw maps on the table where they sat. Maps of Polska, complete with details written in ink in the margins. I wasn't sure, but I felt that these Rus had intentions for my beloved country. I need to learn more.

I sat in the smaller dining room, gazing out at the trio of men who were engaged in an animated conversation. The one sitting down, the colonel, was my husband? They were looking at my homeland, and if one of them was the Minister of War, their intentions could only be bad. How had I gotten married into a family, to a man who wanted to harm my people?

I've heard that Russian cuisine is not very good, and my breakfast did nothing to refute the stereotype. I waved at the maid as she swept through the room for the hundredth time.

"Excuse me." For some reason, I could speak Russian much better than I should be able to. "I forget, how long have the colonel and I been married?"

She stopped and looked at me quizzically. "Almost a year now, madam?"

I thought long and hard about the next question. "Are we at war now? With any country?"

She thought for a moment, stroking her sharp jaw with her long, thin fingers. "There were the Slav uprisings about two years ago, but they are again part of the empire."

"Thank you," I replied, and returned to my plate.

After a meal that I had a difficult time ingesting, I was bustled off to tea with some ladies of the court. Again, I could only see blurs where their faces should have been. I could see the maid just fine, but everyone else's identity was hidden. It was still before noon, and the ladies were wearing clothes that I would have saved for a night on the town—bright red, full-length gowns, dark greens and blues. One lady, introduced as a duchess, wore a long, concealing black dress, along with a white lace parasol.

We sat in the corner of an outdoor café, enjoying a warm Moskva afternoon, and we were brought mimosas; there was no tea to be found. I only had a little wine with dinner sometimes, so I was not much of a drinker. I sipped my drink and tried to gather information.

They chatted every minute when a waiter was not around, and they started with the usual fare. What lord has taken a new mistress, who would and would not be invited to the next formal ball, that sort of thing. They were all much older than I, and even though I spoke very little, they seemed not to notice and probably preferred it that way.

The conversation eventually turned to current events; the ladies discussed how their husbands were frequently away, always in high-level meetings that they were not privy to. There was a lot of speculation back and forth; one would make a wild theory, and the rest would shoot it down. When everyone had contributed, they turned almost as one to look at me.

"What can you tell us, Jafra, dear?" the woman in black asked. "Your husband is superior to all of ours. I'm sure that he probably knows everything these men are up to." They all leaned forward expectantly, their featureless faces staring at me.

I was caught by surprise. I listened so intently that I didn't take the time to fill in my backstory. I could make up something, but these were not unintelligent women, and they were every bit as cunning and resourceful as their high-powered spouses. I finally settled on a longshot, tell the truth. "Whatever I say here must, of course, stay with us." They all nodded in agreement. "He was meeting with the Minister of War this morning and an ambassador. I went outside to take my breakfast with him, but he sent me away, presumably so they could speak in private." I paused, trying to read anything from their body language. "I did notice a map of Eastern Europa on the table. Polska was in the center with lots of writing around the edges."

There was a buzzing that went on, some of them whispering excitedly to each other.

"I'm not sure what it means, but I fear that the winds of war are blowing," I said.

The woman in black leaned in, as did the others. We formed a tight circle, trying to keep out the prying ears of the wait staff. "I think you might be right!" she said excitedly. "If there is to be war in Polska, all of our husbands will be sent. The tsar always claims that we will roll over them like wheat in the field, but we all know it could take months, maybe longer!"

The woman in dark green added in a conspiratorial tone, "That's usually how it works, but we have a truce with them right now. If we break the truce and make a surprise invasion, our army can take them by surprise and strike a devastating blow!"

"I've heard that too," a woman in red added. "If we take out their leadership, the war would be almost over before it even began."

There was a lot more chittering like that, the women discussing the politics of declaring war on my homeland. They all seemed very excited, knowing that they wouldn't be asked to fight. They were all the wives of princes and dukes; their husbands would fight, but most likely, they would direct the action from the safety of a bunker in the rear.

The lady in black turned to me. "You're Polish, are you not, dear?"


I thought that the ground cars in Moskva were ugly monstrosities. They lacked the sleek lines of our ground cars.

As a woman of means, I always traveled in hover cars with a dedicated driver. He offered his hand as I carefully pulled the hem of my dress up to place my foot on the polished steel footboard. I climbed into the back and relaxed into the plush, blue velvet-covered cushions. The car itself was too angular, unadorned, flat slabs of metal welded together into a mostly featureless box. Like most limousines, it had room up front for my driver and two security men. They put up the glass shell to protect my hair, and seconds later, we were coasting down the bustling city streets of the capital. It truly was a spectacular city, one that I had never been to before. The architecture was primarily composed of stone and brick. The buildings were easily as high as the tallest skyscrapers in Warszawa, and from what I learned in university, their population was nearly double ours.

The people were divided into two groups, as far as I could see. The young were beautiful, with women boasting long blonde hair, slender figures, and modest curves. Their blurry features are typical of many Poles and Slavs, including sky-blue eyes, high cheekbones, and long, straight noses. The men were much the same: tall and strong, with mostly short hair, the same ice-blue eyes, and handsome faces.

The other group consisted of older people. I wasn't sure at what age it happened, but at a certain age, their access to youth and beauty was cut off. Older women dressed in full-length, drab-colored, woolen dresses, with sarafans, shugays, and multiple shawls. They padded around in felt boots, carrying goods in enormous backpacks or pushing oversized carts laden with their wares. The men were equally unappealing, with their hunched backs and worn pants, shirts, and vests. I wondered if that would happen to me someday.

It took almost an hour to navigate the traffic and arrive at my home. The colonel's estate was massive, set on hundreds of acres of land with orchards and a small forest teeming with game. We passed through the main gate, guarded by a pair of ever-vigilant, armed men. They recognized the driver, my security detail, and looked in, recognizing me. As they let me through, I was still flustered by the blurred faces. Why did every person except the maid have their faces concealed?

Back in my room, I rested and thought about what the ladies had predicted at lunch. Would Rus invade my beloved Polska? I felt like a prisoner here, alone and without friends. I was so frustrated and scared that I wanted to burst into tears. I wanted to sleep and then wake up in my own bed in my father's house. I must have drifted off, and I was startled by a light hand on my shoulder. Looking up, I saw the maid looking down at me. She gave me a thin smile as she helped me to a sitting position.

"The colonel is waiting. It's time for supper, madam."

She tightened up my hairdo, put a little powder on my cheeks and forehead, and even dusted the gap between my breasts. Now that I was presentable, she walked with me to the formal dining room. The table could seat a dozen, but it was only the two of us. The blurred face of my husband didn't even look up when I entered the room. He had already started eating, a sharp knife in his right hand, and a silver fork in the other. His gold-trimmed crystal wine glass was half full, and it sloshed as he attacked his steak. I was seated at the far end, and a plate full of food magically appeared. He didn't greet me, and never looked in my direction until he had completed his meal.

"I'll be going to bed in an hour," he declared. "Be bathed and properly dressed when I get there." Without further ado, he pushed away from the table and retired to his office.

I had lost my appetite and stood. I had a dark feeling that I was a witness to the beginning of the end of my world. My husband had no desire to look up at me, so I wiped off my steak knife and slid it up my sleeve. The same maid, the one whose face wasn't obscured, walked with me to the bedroom. She helped me out of my clothes, and when I was completely naked, she helped me into a bath that she'd previously prepared. I should have been able to luxuriate in the steamy, hot water, but my mind was racing a mile a minute. If what they were saying was true, my family was in grave danger.

"I'm sorry. I've forgotten your name," I said. I had never seen her before this morning, but I wasn't sure that I believed it myself. It had been the longest, most confusing day of my life.

"Elena, milady," she replied with a knowing smile. She helped me dry off, then brought in a nightdress for me to wear. Like what I woke up in, the gown was, at best, insubstantial. Sheer chiffon panels fluttered in the slight breeze from the open window. Darker, lilac lace held the whisps of cloth together.

I stepped before a full-length mirror, held in a heavy wooden frame, to examine myself. My breasts were on full display, large and yet defying gravity with utter contempt. My stomach was still flat and firm, and my legs were long and toned. The matching thong was ridiculous. The triangle of sheer fabric did nothing to hide my bushy pubic area. In fact, it seemed to accentuate the area. Turning, the cord that ran between the cheeks of my ass served no purpose other than to help hold on the bit of cloth in the front. From behind, it looked like I was nude from the waist down. My raven hair was allowed to fall loosely to the middle of my back. I had to admit, I looked very sexy.

A clomping sound came from the hallway just outside the room. Elena jumped to attention, hands at her sides, chin slightly raised, eyes facing straight ahead. He entered the room like a tidal wave, sudden and with undeniable force. He kicked off his boots, tossing them in the corner. Without even looking at the maid, he gave his instructions.

"Champagne!" He pulled his white shirt over his head, exposing a muscular chest, far hairier than any of the men in my family. Dark, curly hair was thick across his chest, down between his ribs, and disappearing below the top of his trousers, which he was now pulling off.

"I'm drained, Jafra. Get in position; I need to make this quick and get a good sleep tonight. Lots to do tomorrow," he said as he finished removing the last of his clothes. His thing hung there, swaying between his legs like an obscene pendulum. Protruding from a patch of hair that was twice mine, it was half a foot long, and I could see the tip of it trying to poke through the loose skin it was sheathed in. I had seen my little brother's when he was being potty trained, but I had not seen one since, and definitely not a strange man's penis. "Take me in your mouth until I harden, then get on the bed as I told you." His tone gave little room for disagreement. But I had to know something.

"Before I do, I wanted to ask you something."

He grunted and sat on the edge of the bed, his soft penis hanging over the edge. He lay back, waiting. I could smell the sweat on him; the odor from his groin was especially strong. "I saw the maps of Polska this morning when I came out for breakfast."

"I told you not to bother yourself with things that are above your station. The only thing you need to concern yourself with is performing your wifely duties."

"The ladies in my circle thought that we were on a war footing and that Rus would launch a surprise invasion of Polska. Part of an invasion and eventual annexation."

"We will take over all of Europa, eventually. Polska is the closest nation that opposes us, so naturally, they need to be subjugated." He spoke like a teacher to a child, and I could hear the annoyance and impatience in his voice. "Get started."

"I imagine that taking me as a wife was part of some agreement. Forging alliances through marriage? If you invade Warszawa, you'll be trying to kill my father and brothers. That would be breaking a treaty."

He sat up, and even through the mask of the blur over his face, I could tell that he was suddenly furious. He stood and grasped me roughly by the arm. His grip was like a vice, crushing my tender skin and putting pressure on my bones. "How dare you question me! You are no longer a filthy Pole, you're a Princess of Rus, and you'll live longer if you try and remember that!" He ripped the sheer negligee off me and threw me to my knees. "You're my property, and I'll use you any way that I choose."

He grabbed a fistful of my hair and shook me violently. The pain was intense, and I felt a sharp twinge in my neck. I didn't know what level of violence he was capable of, but I assumed it ranged from leaving me with bruises to broken bones and possibly death.

What he didn't know was that I was armed. I had the steak knife from dinner behind my back. I gripped it and plunged it into his thigh, just below his privates. I aimed for his femoral artery, and I must have gotten lucky. The five-inch blade came out when he threw me across the floor; he stalked towards me with murder in his eyes, but his leg was fountaining blood. When he realized how serious the wound was, he tried to cover it with his right hand and struck me with his left. His left was not his dominant hand, but it still sent me reeling. My head swam, and I saw light flashing in my vision. He kicked me in the side, and I felt a rib or two break. The pain in my side made the punch seem insignificant by comparison. He kicked me again, then a third time, and I rolled into a ball to protect my face.

When he was sure that I was conquered, he leaned down to whisper in my ear. "I was going to fuck you and go to sleep. Now I have to go to the surgeon and get stitches. You will die tonight, and I'll keep your head to present it to your mother after I kill her husband and sons." He said those threats in a low, ominous voice, and I was certain that he meant every word.

I can't die here, I thought. Not like this!

He was a fool for not noticing that I still held the knife. He was only inches from me, and I rolled over and plunged my knife under his sternum. His eyes went wide, no longer mocking me. He let out a groan and started to wobble on his one good leg. I pulled out the knife and, rising to my battered knees, I got a handful of his hair and looked in his glassy eyes.

"This is for Polska!" I said as I jammed the blade up to the handle into the side of his neck. "And for House Sobieski!"

He died, and I had still never seen his face. I was shaking, and my adrenaline was pumping nervous energy through my veins.

I barely heard when she entered. Elena looked at the body on the floor, then looked at my disheveled hair and the blood flowing from my busted lip. Her face held a look of horror. "What happened here, Mistress Jafra?" She pulled a sheet from the bed to wrap around me.

"He attacked me, pulled my hair, and punched me in the face. I stabbed him." I felt numb, not ashamed to admit my crime. "I'm happy that he's dead."

"Why, my lady?" She shook me and lifted my gaze to meet her eyes.

"Your country is planning to invade my country. This pig was ready to break an oath, breach the treaty with Polska, and kill my family. Call the Okhrana. I am prepared to die."

"You know that the price is death, and you still fight to protect your loved ones?"

Her eyes were hard as steel, her expression eerily neutral. I could feel her stare boring into me, searching my soul for some answer.

"Yes. I don't want to die. If I could get outside the walls of this estate, I would walk every mile back to Warszawa. If you felt the need to turn me in, I would understand." I lowered my head in resignation. I meant what I said. I had been terrified, but now, after the decision was made, the deed was done… I felt a lot better.

She took my face in her hands, and her touch was gentle but firm. I looked into her eyes and found a kind and sympathetic smile. I was confused and tired.

"You have shown great courage, Jafra Sobieski. You are worthy of a brand; you demonstrated intelligence, resourcefulness, judgment, kindness, and now courage. Touch Abyrinth's Fire to receive your blessing." She kissed me on the forehead, and all went black.

I opened my eyes, and I was back in the cave. I was in a tight bodysuit, my hair tied back, no blood seeping from a busted lip, no broken ribs. I was in a state of shock, and it took several minutes to realize that I was back in the testing chamber and that I was unharmed. They'd said that I had an hour before they sent people in to recover my dead body, but I was sure that I had been gone for several days. I was confused, disoriented, and a little hungry.

Right in front of me was the gem. It still glowed brightly, but instead of the intense white light, it radiated a blue hue, like the sky on a perfect summer day. Elena was the only face I could see in the last challenge, and I realized after the fact that she was the spirit that resided in the gem. She was the robot man who left me trapped in a puzzle, and she was a young girl for whom I sacrificed myself. It would take me a long time to absorb and analyze everything that had happened in that other reality, but it was time to go. With more than a bit of trepidation, I placed my hand on the glowing stone.

Energy coursed through my hand, up my arm, and then arced through the metal circle affixed to my upper back. The pain was intense, and I was sure that it was real pain this time. It went on for several seconds, and I wanted to pull back my hand, break the connection, but I couldn't. I had been brave in the test, I had suffered in the test, and I could be strong for as long as it took to uphold the honor of my family.

When the electrical shock had become too strong and I feared that I would pass out, it was suddenly over. I could smell my flesh burning, but then again, it might have been my imagination. I took the long, lonely walk through the crevice in the rock to return to the outside world.

"Jafra!" my father said, with more enthusiasm than he typically showed for matters concerning his oldest daughter. Rushing forward, he swept me up in his strong arms and held me for several long seconds. I could almost feel the relief flowing from his tense arms and chest.

"We were nearly ready to send the recovery team," Warden Birk said dryly. "You were in the chamber for a bit over an hour. You're alive, and I can see that you've received your brand. I declare you to be an adult and a certified member of the ruling class. Use your power wisely, and only for the benefit of almighty God, your country, and family."

"Can I see it, Księżniczka?" Father asked. Of course I would show him, but it was respectful for him to ask. I felt like our relationship had changed, evolved. What had been days of both physical and mental torture for me had been only an hour of indecision and anticipation for him.

I turned so he could see what I had been given. "Please describe it for me, Panie Ojcze."

He didn't reply for a bit and instead stood behind me, studying the seal. "I've never seen the like, and I've seen many. At the top of the design, there is a single, open eye. It has what appears to be rays of power, radiating in every direction. Directly below, towards the bottom, there is what looks like Abyrinth's Fire, and to either side are waves of mystical energy, curving and yet reaching upward like the twisting vines of a plant." He looked for several more seconds, and I began to feel uncomfortable. "Do you know its name?'

I wasn't sure where I had heard it. I was fairly certain that the spirit had never spoken the words, but still, I knew the name of the gift I had been given. It would be a part of me until my dying day.

"Abyrinth Embermark," I said.

# Chapter 7

It was less than a day after successfully completing my trials that I received an invitation to visit a friend's estate. Katarzyna Czartoryski was the adult daughter of Lord Bartek Czartoryski. I had met her at a few formal functions, but it had probably been two years since the last time we crossed paths. Her family lived west of Warszawa, in Pruszków, near the lake. I'm not sure why I accepted the invitation. I hardly knew them, and I was still recovering from my trials.

The trip would take an hour each way, and I let my mind wander as we drove. I watched the downtown area fly by, then we entered a more middle-class section of town, with small shops and factories. There was more dirt on the roads, and some trash in the gutters. The downtown was very strictly patrolled and kept in pristine condition. The further we went from downtown, the fewer rules and standards there were.

"Are you sure you want to continue, miss?" my guard Kazuch asked. "This part of town is not safe, especially for a person of means."

"Then I'm glad that I have two armed guards to protect me," I said. I was surprised at the old bodyguard's caution.

"It also doesn't hurt that you have one of the most powerful brands in ages," Urban said over his shoulder as he propelled the limousine.

Kazuch's instincts had always been very reliable. I thought for a moment that it might be safer and make sense to call and cancel the visit. I couldn't finish that thought because I passed out in the back of the car. As I did, I saw the glow of Abyrinth coming from a woman standing on the side of the road. I didn't get a good look at her before my eyelids grew heavy and I fell into a sleep.

I woke up to find that I was lying on a couch in the middle of a dark room. Only a single lantern lit the room, and the corners were lost in shadow. I took inventory of myself, and to my relief, I was unharmed, and my clothes were still on. I heard shuffling and the murmurs of two people from somewhere behind me. When I moved my head to try to see more, it caught their attention, and the talking ceased. Footfalls approached me, and an older woman came around to stand in front of me. A man about forty came from the same direction, carrying a chair. He put it in front of me, a few feet away.

The woman sat and looked at me. She was probably in her mid-thirties, but she carried an aura that made her seem much older than she was. Her hair was dirty blonde, bordering on brown, and cut short in the French style. Her features were sharp, from her hawk-like nose to her sculpted cheekbones and down to a chin that came to a rounded point. She wore a white button-down shirt and grey trousers like a man. She wasn't necessarily unfashionable; her clothes were odd, but quite becoming. Her light blue beret was the only spot of color on her otherwise drab appearance. The man returned with a small wooden box, which he set on a one-foot-diameter glass coffee table. Both of them had a halo of energy around them. Abyrinth.

"Why have you attacked me? Where are my men? If you've harmed them in any way, I'll have you skinned alive!"

"Dear child, I rescued you. There was a woman on the side of the road, and she used some sleeping power against you and your bodyguards. She was going to have her thugs drag you off to God knows what terrible fate, but I arrived and paralyzed them. We took them into custody and are deciding what to do with them." She looked at the man who'd brought the box. "Put the light on, please."

I saw that we were in a quaint little home. A woman and two other men were tied up and lying on the ground across the room. She opened the box and withdrew a cigarette. I could see that the box held dozens of perfectly rolled cigarettes, stacked neatly, like cordwood. A thought came to her, and she turned to me.

"Would you care for one, Jafra?" She held out the cigarette.

"I would not care for a cigarette. Only answers," I said, trying to maintain my composure and stop my head from swimming. I should have been terrified, but I was too angry.

She lit her cigarette, taking a long drag. As she inhaled, the light from the coal lit her face. Her face seemed as gray as her trousers, and she looked tired. "Your security men are unharmed. They're sleeping in the next room over. They are channelers like you and me. I am happy to report that they are unharmed by these terrorists." She exhaled a puff of smoke.

"I'm not a channeler," I replied. The nerve of this woman. "I am a wielder." I could see the cloud of energy hovering around her, clinging to her as if she had a static charge. "As are you."

"All wielders are channelers. Not all channelers are wielders. We control the same power, but the nobles can do so much more than pour this mana from heaven into dirty metal machines." She took a heavy drag, then held her breath as she regarded me. She was sizing me up, trying to decide my worth.

"Everyone knows that," I replied. I could hear the petulant child in my voice. "It's by right of birth that we can receive a brand and can control our miraculous abilities." The answer came to me without thinking. It flowed out by reflex.

"Straight from the teachings. You must be an excellent student," she said after letting the smoke out of her lungs. "You are on your way to becoming an excellent little robot."

"What house are you from? Who are your parents?" I asked. "Surely, you must come from superior breeding."

"You mean inbreeding. I know that you're just a product of your upbringing, but that excuse will only carry you so far. You are blessed with wealth and privilege, but do you really think that the blood flowing through your veins is any better than, more noble than anyone else's?"

Honestly, I did think that the line I came from made me better than most. Certainly better than channelers and infinitely better than blanks. I could guess the answer she wanted from me, but I couldn't spit out what to me sounded preposterous.

"Spoiled rich girl. You may be a good student who has learned the teachings, yet it seems you're not much of a student of history. Before the comet, before Abyrinth was discovered, we were all the same. Of course, there were rich and poor, the powerful and the powerless. Because you owned a mansion and people followed your commands, it didn't mean that you were superior." She crushed the last vestige of her cigarette in her bare palm, then left the butt on the table. She looked disgusted by our conversation. "Over the centuries, noble blood has mixed with the blood of the commoners in every land, at every level. There are bastards everywhere; some have risen to power. Men and women who, if they cared to trace their ancestry, would find farmers and tradesmen in their family trees." She pointed a bony finger at me. "Don't think that having a title or a metal plate fused to your spine makes you invulnerable. Since the dawn of time, when the noble class gets out of line, the proletariat rises up and removes a few heads. It was shortly before the comet came that the French had a revolution, and a lot of well-bred necks were cut."

She had points, and maybe some of them were true, but I have a defiant streak in me, and sometimes, against my own interests, I'd provoke a confrontation. "This is all very interesting, and maybe I am a bit conceited, but what does that have to do with those people trying to kidnap me?"

"Your father, the king, and all the rest of them are focused on the Rus, and well they should be, but there are other dangers closer to home. The elites around the world have been hoarding power, not just their stranglehold on the levers of government, but actual power. Let me tell you a secret." She was passionate about this. I was starting to worry if I would get out of there alive. She lit another cigarette.

"I changed my mind. Could I get one of those?" Why did I say that?

She was a little surprised, but offered me a cigarette. Crossing the room, she held it so that I could take it with my lips, then she lit it. With difficulty, I drew in air until the end formed a coal.

I had seen my father smoke when I was younger, but he'd given it up several years ago. I saw Krystian smoking with his friends out by the stables, but I don't think it was tobacco they were smoking. I sucked air through the stick and felt the hot smoke burn the back of my throat, and I felt it burning all the way down. I desperately wanted to cough, but that would be a sign of weakness, and I didn't want that. I immediately felt a little lightheaded, and I kind of liked it.

"There's nothing in your blood that makes you different or special. Us royals, the nobility, are wielders because we jealously guard access to Abyrinth's Fire, not because we are genetically superior." Her face was hard, with bags under her eyes and wrinkles forming around her mouth and forehead. I could see the energy filaments floating around her, clinging to her. She was definitely a wielder.

"Are you saying that common people can become channelers or even wielders?" This woman was clearly insane.

"Anyone, even the blanks that we look down on, could have powers if they were allowed access to the stones. Only a select few know this dirty little secret, but if it gets out, our world will come crashing down."

I took another puff from my cigarette. I wasn't really enjoying it, but I did feel very grown-up and sophisticated while smoking. "I don't believe you, but even if it were true, what are your goals? And how am I involved?"

"Those are better questions." She released another cloud of smoke. "My goals are my own. Maybe I'll share them with you someday. I'll answer your second question. There are hundreds of brands that are gifted by the stones, and thousands of those who can use their power. So naturally, there are multiples of each one, except for the three prime brands that form the Abyrinth Triumvirate. You carry one of the prime brands. They are incredibly powerful and are unique in the world. Your signet will not be given to anyone else until after your death."

"Are you saying that there are people out there who will try to kill me so one of their nobles can receive my brand?"

"No. If you die, there is no guarantee that the brand will go to one of their people. It could be given to anyone anywhere in the world. If they know where it is, it's more likely that they will try to control the wielder."

"Brands are not made public, not published anywhere. Hopefully, I can stay anonymous."

"I found out," she said plainly. Her penetrating stare was unnerving.

She was correct. I thought that my semi-private ritual would be held confidential, but there must have been a spy among those present—someone who was on the lookout for one of these special brands.

She continued, "If they can control you, that will give them enormous power. If they find the other two and dominate all three? Their power will be unchecked. They will be able to commit political assassinations, defeat armies, and rewrite the structure of our society."

"So, what exactly do you expect from me?"

"Revolution is coming. People are weary of the power inequity in the world today. If everyone could become a wielder, then we wouldn't need to follow the orders of the inbred nobility class. I'm part of a secret society devoted to capturing the stones and making them accessible to everyone. The Brotherhood of Virtue has been working under the surface to bring equity to our civilization. We are prepared to take bold actions to free the stones, remove them from government control."

I could understand how the channelers and even the blanks would like to improve their lot in life. I didn't believe what she was saying, but I felt a kernel of truth in it. She looked earnest, like every word she said was gospel. I just wanted to leave, but I knew I had to hear it all before heading home.

"You are a third of the Triumvirate. With your power, you can learn to be sensitive to all brands, to know what a person's ability is without pulling their shirt off. I can teach you to read the flows." She got close to me. So close I could smell what she had for lunch. "We need you to seek out the other two brands that will complete the Triumvirate. With all three, we can bring justice to the people."

"What are these other brands? How will I know when I find one?"

"We don't know yet. They are not in Polska, but we believe that they are somewhere in greater Europa." She could see the doubt, the outright disbelief in my face. "Go home. Think about what I've told you. I will contact you after your Ascension Ball. I can see that you have doubts, but I assure you that I am on your side, the side of the people. In time, you will feel comfortable trusting me, and you can benefit from my group's intelligence."

"I don't even know your name."

"Call me… Hedwig."

"Like the saint?" I asked.

"I aspire to her greatness. Through you, I will bring peace and prosperity to the Polish people."

# Chapter 8

I think Mother was afraid to speak with me just prior to the trials. I saw what she went through with Krystian, but I was oblivious to her suffering when it came to be my time in the chamber. Most royal and noble children passed, but it was not guaranteed.

"I can finally breathe again," Mother said.

Lady Roksana Sobieski was a refined and elegant woman. She turned forty-one a month ago, and she was a couple of inches shorter than I was at about five feet six inches. She wore her long, lustrous black hair up, resembling a beehive and held in place by gold combs and jeweled pins. Mother loved gold and wore it everywhere on her person. She always wore four to six rings, both simple bracelets and diamond-studded bands. She had a locket with pictures of her parents inside, and her earrings were gaudy, with wide gold rings holding more diamonds, dangling like icicles hanging from the edge of a roof in winter. She almost always wore long, white dresses made from yards and yards of the finest white silk satin. She often wore a bodice of the same material, and her brocade looked like spun threads of gold. She held a white fan and cooled herself as we talked on the veranda.

"I survived, just like the boys did. I learned a lot, and I'm prepared to learn more about my brand."

"What is it, dear?" she asked me. I was always my mother's favorite, and even after surviving the trials, she was still worried about me. "The scholars say that they've never seen that design before." Most, if not all, brands were repeats, given to other nobles. Mine was unique and appeared nowhere in the archives.

"I don't know all of the details. I'm still learning." That elicited a perturbed stare. "I can see and manipulate Abyrinth." She stared at me, and I could tell that she was confused. "When I concentrate, I can see the energy flowing around, attaching itself to things, people, floating through the air. When my driver channels to make the car go, I can see the energy leave his hand and enter the machine."

She sat quietly, thinking for a few moments. "That's very interesting, dear." When she said it that way, she didn't mean that it was interesting. She essentially meant the opposite. "I just worry that with a brand that is… of limited utility, it might make it difficult to find you a proper match."

Always with the matchmaking. She had the invitations to my Ascension Ball printed months ago. Aside from making me happy, which was truly an afterthought in arranged marriages, it would have to be a match that benefited Father and the family. Before the comet, marriages were often based on the wealth of the two families involved, as well as the social standing of the respective fathers. If you were of noble birth, you could only be wed to someone of equal or greater status. That all changed after the gems were discovered.

Many people believe that the Night of the Comet and the gems are related; in fact, most do. Generally, I don't think people like coincidences. A massive comet lit the summer sky over two hundred years ago, slowly burning its way from north to south. It's believed to have crashed near the South Pole, but expeditions there have yielded no results. What we do know is that over the next fifty years, caves like the one in which I faced my trials showed up all over Europa, the Orient, and even in the New World. No one understood the science behind this new source of energy and why channelers could harness it to make various machines work, much less what it made possible for the wielders to do the incredible things that we can do. In the archives were recorded several hundred different brands and the abilities each one made possible. One of my brothers could make metal reform at will. The other could stop time! All of the scholars, the scientists, the theologians, none of them could explain why we nobles were able to do the things we could now do.

In this new society, raw power, physical power, and mental power were valued over gold and silver. Many blanks had attained great wealth, but they were powerless against a penniless wielder who could tear down their mansions or boil their blood. Before the comet, a person was judged by the value of their family's holdings and the rents they would produce. That was still important, but it paled in comparison to the feats their brands allowed them to do. The better the brand, the more influential a husband could be found for me.

Mother lifted her teacup to her mouth, unsure how to proceed. I could see the lines of energy all around us, and I willed loose strands to wrap around her teacup. I had found out that I didn't need the wispy, ghost-like strands to be connected to me. I could control the weave remotely, and it operated as if there were muscles applying force to the braided cords of energy. She was shocked when her cup was pulled firmly from her grasp. At my command, it floated in the air and hovered over the table where we sat. I didn't want to make a spectacle in front of the help or anyone else until I had a better handle on my newfound capabilities. She watched as I caused the cup to bob in the air, some of the hot tea spilling onto the glass tabletop.

"Now, that's certainly more interesting than what I thought you were describing," she said, that loving smile returning. She looked at me with renewed pride, all the while thinking of how to capitalize on my powers. I caused the tendrils of Abyrinth to constrict, easily smashing the cup into wet shards that spilled out between us.

"I can move objects, and I can do so much more, Mother."

As she checked herself for stains on her pristine, white dress, she reprimanded, "But did you have to destroy the cup? It's part of a set!"

"I apologize, Mother. Let me show you a few more things that I can do."


The ball was set for the coming Saturday night. I had successfully purchased a new ball gown without encountering another terrorist attack, and I met the girls in the town's arts district. That area features the Warszawa Royal Theater, the Polska Cultural Institute, several art galleries, an opera house, the Warszawa Zoo, and numerous excellent restaurants. I didn't often eat haute cuisine, but Milena suggested it, and I readily agreed. Milka was there along with Daria, Elżbieta, and her sister Anna.

We were shown to a small private room where we wouldn't have to mix with the common people. The dining room boasted the most exquisite furnishings, with no expense spared. The waitstaff held wooden chairs for us, with the softest red velvet cushions. The silk table linens were of a very high thread count and were a brilliant white. The place settings had a charger and plate, both of the finest porcelain. Light-blue napkins were folded into swans and set on the plates. On the left side of the plates were a dinner fork and a smaller salad fork. On the right, there was a serrated knife, a soup spoon, and a dessert spoon. We each had two glasses, one for water and another for wine. In the center of the table was a bouquet of regional flowers, poppies, tulips, and carnations.

A waiter came by pushing a cart, and an older man approached, dressed in a white jacket held together by a small chain, a bow tie, black pants, and shoes that shone like glass. His short hair was slicked back and plastered to his thin head; his pencil-thin mustache was waxed and stood out like the wings of a small bird. Though he was a server, he seemed to hold himself in very high regard.

I generally tried not to publicly correct an inferior's behavior. I found his airs amusing. I was concerned that Daria was going to give him a correction that he'd never forget. She was hot-tempered at times.

His cart had a pitcher of steaming hot tea, another with hot coffee, and water, which he poured for each of us as a reflex. We each got a hot drink and waited for him to leave before we started chatting.

Melina Nowak leaned in. "So Jafra, I was talking with Zofia, who spoke to your older brother."

"Which one?"

"Krystian. She told me that he told her your brand was unique. That it has never been seen before, at least not anywhere in Europa."

"It's not good form to ask people about their trials, or what brand they were given," Milka said on my behalf.

Melina had light-brown, shoulder-length hair, trending toward the heavy side. Her rounded facial features scrunched up in mild irritation. She was technically noble, being the third daughter of my father's uncle. She was nineteen, and her prospects of finding a good match were dubious at best. Despite her loud, maroon-colored chiffon dress, I quite liked her.

"Normally, that would be correct, but it's us!" she pleaded. "We don't keep secrets from each other!"

"Maybe we should," Daria said. She and Melina were my closest friends, maybe tied with Milka. She was tall and thin, her long, straight, dark hair was always pinned up, and her taste in clothes was much better. She wore a simple, goldenrod A-line dress with a bright white-and-brown shawl. She was pretty in an unconventional way. Her nose and ears were a bit large, but that was not uncommon in Polska. The women had strong features, and the men were not at all displeased. "We found out entirely too much about your... encounter with that blank that worked in your family's stables."

"Rudolph?" Melina's eyes took on a distant look. "Such rough hands, but such soft lips."

"I was as surprised as everyone else. I was hoping they could provide me with a comprehensive prospectus on the brand, but it appears to be the first of its kind, as far as they can tell. I know a few things, but I've only had it for a week." The girls' reactions ran the gamut from acceptance to complete disbelief.

"Is it physical, like mine?" Elżbieta asked. She was from a very good family, and because of that, I never complained when she brought along Anna, her younger sister. She was eighteen, like me, though she was eight months older and had gone through her trials the previous year. She touched her water glass with a single fingertip, and the liquid quickly froze solid. As she used her power, I could see the lines of energy flowing from her finger into the cup, and back again. I was fascinated by my ability to almost spy on other wielders as they used their gifts.

"Or is it more mysterious like Milka's precognition?" Anna asked. Both sisters were thin, with long blonde hair. Elżbieta wore a spice-colored halter dress, cut to reveal neither cleavage nor too much thigh. Anna, on the other hand, wore a short, sage-colored wrap dress that was very revealing. She knew that her big sister was their parents' pride and joy, so she compensated by pushing the boundaries of propriety.

I could already tell that I wasn't going to get away without some demonstration. I pushed my chair away from the table.

"Remember, I've only been practicing for a week now. Don't judge me too harshly."

I concentrated, and the glowing webs of energy revealed themselves to me. Without moving any part of my body, except my head to look around, I gathered a large amount of the strings and quickly wove them into what looked like a hammock. At least to me. I knew that they couldn't see anything. I ordered the hammock to slide between my behind and the chair. Being unsubstantial, it was possible to do this without getting up. I lifted upward, and to my friend's eyes, I had begun to levitate. I lifted several feet above my chair until I was able to look down on them. They cheered me with a round of oohs and ahs.

I wanted to try something, so I willed it to happen, and it did. I secured the weave so I wouldn't have to maintain it constantly. Summoning more of the ambient energy in the room, I plucked my hot tea from the table, saucer and all, and had it drift up to my waiting hand. I took a sip, watching for their reaction.

"That's incredible!" Melina said. "Come down, please. I'm getting an inferiority complex."

It took a lot of concentration, but I drifted back to my seat, holding my saucer and cup as if I had never moved an inch. I took a sip, then set my beverage back on the table. In contrast to Melina, the others seemed suitably impressed.

The waiter came, and we placed our orders. I didn't usually like duck, but I was feeling adventurous and went for the canard à l'orange. The others mainly chose clear soups or salads. I also called for a couple of bottles of wine. I was in a celebratory mood.

"Be careful," Milka said. "The dress you just purchased was form-fitting. Too much rich food and wine, and you'll be busting at the seams at the ball next week."

"Father and Stefek are insisting that I begin, or I should say, resume my fencing. I gave it up two years ago, but now that I am an adult, they might have a use for me."

"I thought they were going to ship you off to marry some potential ally?" Elżbieta asked. "Of course, the Ascension Ball is to celebrate your coming of age and passing the trials, but we've all met your mother. No doubt, she has sent out invitations to all of the eligible bachelors, not just in Polska, but in Germania, Eastern Prussia, and Austria."

"They still want me to know how to defend myself."

Milka waved for us all to listen carefully. She made sure no one else was around before speaking. "I'm pretty sure that war is coming. I've seen numerous signs that war with Rus will start in the next few months. Though I'm not sure."

I grasped her hand tightly. "Can you please see my future again? I am scared for my brothers."

Unlike last time, she was agreeable to reading me. Her eyes became glassy, and I could see the webs being drawn to her, clinging to her eyes and head. Her face became a mask of fear and horror. I, too, had suspected that we might have war in our future, but I had been so obsessed with my own concerns that I almost purposely ignored the signs.

"I see bombs dropping on Warszawa, whole neighborhoods on fire! Your brother Stefek is there, leading a squad of channelers and backed by a legion of blanks. They are fighting soldiers in dark maroon uniforms, many wearing gas masks."

"I thought her visions were about the person she is touching?" Anna asked.

"Shhhh, don't break her trance," her big sister scolded.

Milka squeezed harder, and I was ready to pull away; it hurt so much.

"I see you on a battlefield, fighting alongside your brothers with other wielders. Black airships are flying high above, dropping death on our city. You are in the thick of the fighting, surrounded by death and destruction. You are covered in blood…" She released me and slumped back in her chair.

We were all quiet for a full minute.

"I think that's why your father wants you to prepare. These men know something they are not telling us," Melina said.

"They are keeping us ignorant, for our own good," Daria added.

This talk of war with Rus would have been a complete surprise to me, but I remembered my trial, where I was in a Rus colonel's home. The way he treated his wife was an indication of how he would treat my country. House Sobieski was charged with protecting the capital, and we would safeguard it with our lives if the need arose. I had no intention of going to war alongside my brothers, but I needed to be more self-sufficient and learn the limits of my power.

"I don't think any of us have been taken completely by surprise. With the attacks recently, and the Rus ambassador being expelled last month, I think, in the back of our minds, we all can see what is coming," I said to the girls. "Get ready for my party on Saturday. Have a great time, dance, drink, and if you dare, kiss a boy." The tension was broken, and they all giggled. "After that, we need to become stronger. Polska will need her men to protect her."

They all nodded in agreement. I could see the fear in their expressions, and I knew the next few weeks would be a profound change for all of us.

I asked my maid to get me up at the crack of dawn. I knew that she almost always was up at that hour, doing the dozen things necessary to make my day go by pleasantly and smoothly.

Ingrid was an immigrant from Scandinavia. I think she was from the Kingdom of Sweden. She was a large woman, not fat, but tall and sturdy. Her honey blonde hair had been pinned up and tucked in her uniform cap every single time that I had been around her. I had no idea if she had a private life or what she looked like when not on duty. Studying her, I concluded that she was not unattractive, though I doubted most men would be drawn to her strong frame and severe countenance.

"Time to rise, miss," she said. I heard her, but I didn't stir. Damn, it was too early. "Time to awake, miss!" This time, she was more insistent. I wanted to slap her, to make her shut up and let me sleep, but I didn't have the energy, and besides, I'd never hit anyone.

The third time, she skipped the pleasantries and pulled the sheet back, exposing me to the crisp morning air. I wore a full-length, soft cotton nightgown, but it did little to keep a breeze from chilling me to the core. I sat up, grumbling.

"You asked to be awoken at this hour, miss. Time to get out of bed!" Her energy at this hour was annoying at best, and I grumbled again as I took her arm and was led to the water closet.

I took care of my business, then put on a pair of my younger brother's britches. I didn't own pants of my own, and for what I was planning, I would need something more practical than dresses. I put on one of his simple shirts as well. I was a couple of years older than Jurek, but at some point in the last several months, he had caught up with me, and we were about the same size. If my older brothers were any indication, he would get much taller and would fill out in his arms, legs, and torso. The drab brown pants fit well, but the shirt was a bit tight across my chest. It would have to do. I accepted a biscuit from Ingrid before going outside and across the yard to the practice ground.

Father wasn't there, but all three of my brothers were. Stefek and Krystian were already masters of their powers, but

Jurek was still too young. Father had always encouraged them to acquire and master other defensive and offensive skills. They were already hard at work crossing practice swords on a patch of barren ground situated near the gymnasium.

I heard the clack of wood on wood before I rounded the corner. My two older brothers were shirtless, wearing only dark denim pants and rubber-soled shoes. Although my older brother was far more developed in his musculature, I had to admit that they were both impressive specimens. My younger brother stood by the wall, spinning a wooden sword, first in his left hand, then in his right. When I was close, Krystian looked in my direction. Stef smacked him with the broad side of his sword; the sound of wood on skull was surprisingly loud.

"Pay attention!" he admonished. "A half-second distraction and you're dead!" They were both covered in a fine sheen of sweat despite the coolness of the morning. "What are you doing here, Jafra?" he asked me.

"Hey! Are those my pants?" Jurek asked.

"Yes, and your shirt."

Krystian was rubbing the spot on his head where the knot would soon form. "They look better on you. Jurek is growing out of them."

"I'm here to train," I said to their unbelieving faces. "You boys want to keep us helpless women in the dark, so when the Rus invade, we'll be useless and confused. Thank you, but no."

They looked at each other, not sure which course of action to take. Admit that they were preparing for war, or continue the lie and pretend that all was well. I didn't give them the opportunity.

"Father is making you?" Krystian asked.

"Yes. Maybe he's right. When the fighting starts, it won't be in some distant land. It will be here in our country, in this city." They looked dumbfounded. Not by what I was saying, but that I knew so much. I could almost see the gears turning in their simple heads, trying to devise a lie that would put me at ease and get me out of their private space.

It took a while, but Jurek was feeling bold this morning. "Not sure where you got your information. Can you tell the future now?" he asked.

After a brief pause, Krystian said, "Milka. I told you how questionable her visions are."

"She saw me, and the two of you." I pointed at my older brothers. "We were fighting in the streets of Warszawa. Not only soldiers, but women and children were dying by the score. The same blood runs in all our veins. I have a lot to live for, just like you."

"I'm already stronger than you," Jurek said, grinning like an idiot. "How much do you really think you'll add to our defense?" My younger brother, mocking me?

I summoned the energy around us and wrapped it around my little brother. The bands that were invisible to him bound him tightly. I sent him shooting up into the air until he was twenty feet above us, his legs kicking wildly. I bound his legs as well, then sealed his mouth. He looked at me angrily, but my older brothers broke up laughing.

After at least a minute, Stefek interceded. "I think he's learned his lesson, little sister."

I lowered him gently until his feet were safely on the ground, then I released him. He grumbled and rubbed at his arms, the ghost of his bonds still haunting him. Jurek was fifteen, but yes, he was getting taller and broader every day. His short brown hair was a jumbled mess, as usual. His noble features were more like mine and my mother's than like my father's.

"Ok, maybe you can be helpful."

"Jurek, get a practice sword for your older sister. Show her the basic stances." The thought of being a teacher appealed to him very much. With enthusiasm, he rushed to get me a practice sword.

"How long?" I asked. They had lost the desire to lie to me and considered my question.

"Hard to say," Krystian responded. "Father's spies are doing their best to gather information, but in the end, if the tsar orders it, they will march on us. No troops have been assembled, but we all are convinced that his ego will make a conflict inevitable."

"Conflict?" Stefek coughed out the word. "War. War is coming, and it will be here before winter."

# Chapter 9

I wanted to go to the ball with my friends, but Mother insisted that I go with her and Father. We took a ground car to the airship station, which was located near the transportation hub in Lomianki, west of the Vistula River.

We didn't all go out together very often, so I was delighted when I saw them come downstairs in their finest. Father wore his dress uniform, complete with all his medals and awards. His jacket fell to mid-thigh and was form-fitting, emphasizing his broad, flat chest. The dark green brought attention to the numerous gray hairs, but I thought that he still looked dashing. The gold brocade and crisp folds gave him the look of a soldier awaiting inspection. He had a sword at his hip, held by a black, patent leather baldric that matched his knee-high boots. He was as tall as Krystian, and shorter than Stefek, but he cast a very long shadow.

Mother was a stark contrast to my father. Where he was hard lines and military precision, she was flowing with an ephemeral aura about her. Her midnight black hair was set in a tight chignon, with silver cords braided into it. Her earrings had three layers of ice-blue, oval-shaped diamonds that grew in size; the bottom one was the size of a peach pit. The settings and chains suspending them were made of brilliant platinum, shining nearly as bright as the gems they held. Her necklace was made of the same translucent, pale-blue diamond. The platinum rolo chain featured blue diamonds at intervals of a few inches, from the collarbone to the massive stone pendant.

Mother's milk-white, off-the-shoulder gown exposed her shoulders and more bosom than I was accustomed to seeing from her. The entire bodice was covered in delicate lace, meticulously set with small pearls. Her sheer sleeves featured lace appliques, as did her cape and the drapes that fell from her shoulders. The slim waist belied the fact that she had given birth to five children. Damn, she still looks incredible!

My older brothers were arriving later: Stefek with his wife, and Krystian alone. My younger siblings were grousing because they weren't invited. These events were strictly for adults, and this would be my first.

My Ascension Ball would begin in just over an hour. It was, in fact, my first ball of any kind. Somewhere along the way, I realized how sheltered my life had been. We all had private tutors, and my only classmates were my cousins and siblings. I had seen a life being taken before getting my first kiss. That seemed terrible and wrong. This was a celebration of my ascension, but there would be boys there! Well, men. Some of them might look like boys, and all of them tended to act like boys, but I would be foolish to forget that they were men.

And I was a woman. I'd had a woman's body for a couple of years now, but now I was old enough to marry, to own land, to receive a brand.

My mother was standing there on Father's arm, looking as beautiful and sexy as her portraits on various walls in our mansion. I felt inadequate next to her. I stole a look in the full-length mirror in the corner of the dressing room. I was shocked. It was still me, but I looked… different. My long black hair, which normally had sweeping waves, had been curled by my maid and another girl she had brought along. They called it a Gdańsk-style up-do. Some of the hair on the sides was loosely braided, brought around to the back, and held in place with a jade comb. The rest formed long waves of ringlets.

I felt like white was a very mature color for a woman to wear, and wearing black would make a strong statement that I didn't fully understand. I was an adult, but it felt like a night for a happy, youthful color. My dress was A-line, with a deep V-neck with ruffles, and the torso fit like a glove. The silk material was a bright lavender rose color, with layers of fuchsia and mauve organza. I presented a much simpler display, but it was colorful and vibrant.

My earrings were not as grand as my mother's; instead, they were simple emeralds, the size of a pea, set in gold and held by a gold chain. I had a small diamond-studded bracelet, a gift from my oldest brother, and two silver rings I had purchased for myself over the years.

"Almost time to go, dear child, but your father has a gift for you," Mother said.

A young officer in full dress uniform handed my father a small box. He grumbled something unintelligible and took a step forward. Opening the box, he looked in and then fished out the gift. He held forth a necklace with an enormous emerald set in gold.

"It's beautiful, Father! You remembered my birthstone! Thank you so much!" I smiled widely, knowing that he was seeing the gift for the first time. "Could you put it on me, please?"

I saw the tiniest bit of emotion on his stolid face after putting the necklace on me and turning me back to see how it looked. I thanked them both, and we piled into the elevator. Four glass elevators were located on the outside of the docking tower at the airship hub. We got into the glass-covered cars, along with our security people, including my men, Kazuch and Urban. Steam engines ran the elevators, and somewhere, there were cables and counterweights, but from the passenger's point of view, it all seemed very magical.

Five hundred feet went by too quickly. I barely got to see the city, with its broad streets and grand architecture, which had been maintained for centuries before the comet. When we reached the top floor, the door opened to the sky-dock. Stewards in crisp tan uniforms met us and ushered us aboard the Perła Lechii, or Pearl of Lechia. I had been on the family airship and even a yacht, once, but the Pearl was a thing to behold. The ship was twice as long as a standard football pitch, and almost as wide as one. The aft of the ship had five decks, complete with state rooms, kitchens, and an indoor ballroom in case of inclement weather. As the sun was setting, lights came on all around the perimeter of the main deck. There must have been around a hundred leafless trees in pots bolted to the deck, each decorated with a cloud of white lights and different-colored cloth to diffuse the light.

As we mounted the craft, a full band began playing at the center of the wide-open main deck, surrounded by a dance floor that was a hundred feet on a side. There was a large bar and tables where the upper decks met the main deck. A dozen bartenders were busily concocting the most exotic cocktails and pouring ales and beers as expeditiously as possible. A tall, thin steward extended an elbow for me and guided us to a raised platform where we could look out over the massive event.

I knew maybe a hundred of the attendees. The other thousand were guests of my parents. As the highest-ranking lord next to his highness, Oskar Sobieski was a man of significant influence. I would guess that many of the older couples came for the free food and liquor, and to cozy up to their lord. All of the major families were in attendance, many of whom I was familiar with, and many of whom I was not.

On the occasion of my ascension, during a party to recognize and honor me, I would have thought that I would be the center of attention. I was wrong. What followed was a parade of family heads that sauntered by to wish me well, then to ignore me while fawning over Lord Sobieski, trying to gain his favor.

Lord Potocki, his wife, and son were among the first to pay their respects. All I remembered of the man was that he was obese and sweaty, even though it was quite cool out. I remembered even less about his wife. I did remember the son, though.

Tadeusz Potocki was over six feet tall and had an athletic physique. His sandy hair was cut mid-length and tousled to perfection. He walked the line between disheveled and stylish, and it was clear from the way he carried himself that he knew it. The father kissed my hand, said a kind word, then moved over to center himself in front of my father. Lady Potocki curtseyed and offered a polite greeting. I think. Then joined her husband.

Tadeusz took my hand and held my fingers lightly in his soft yet firm grip. He laid a kiss on my fingers, his ruby lips pressed lightly against my skin. All the while, he maintained eye contact with me. Of the three of them, he was the only one who seemed the least bit interested in me.

"Congratulations, Jafra. If I may be so forward…" His smile was warm, if not well-practiced. "This is quite the event. Mine was two years ago, and somewhat smaller."

"I'm glad that you could come," I replied. His eyes were a very light blue, the color of my mother's diamonds. "I hope we can chat a bit later."

"Perhaps you'll even save a dance for me?" His confidence was very attractive.

"Perhaps I shall."

They moved on, and moments later, the next of the supplicants arrived. The pattern had probably been established generations ago. Lip service to the guest of honor, then witty conversations mixed with subtle requests for a future audience with the lord.

By virtue of who my father was, I had become a hot commodity. The families with age-appropriate, unmarried sons were approaching and forming an actual queue. The next two were completely forgettable. I honestly had no recollection of them at all.

A very handsome couple eventually stepped before me; the gentleman was in a perfectly pressed black uniform, devoid of medals or excessive ornamentation. His silver brocade complemented the tight jacket and silver buttons. His shoes were polished to a mirror-like finish, and his cane was long and thin, with a boar's head carved on the crook. I estimated that he was a few years my father's senior, but he was an exceptionally handsome man. As he kissed my hand, I could see streaks of silver in his short, wavy, dark hair. He had a short-cropped beard and mustache, and the hand that held mine was adorned with an enormous gold ring bearing the signet of House Poniatowski.

"Congratulations are in order, Miss Sobieski." His voice was strong, yet suave.

"Thank you, your highness," I replied as I curtseyed. I had met the king a few years ago, but I was now seeing him up close through new eyes.

He stepped gracefully to the side to take my mother's hand. She was unusually bubbly at the attention she was receiving from our sovereign.

I shook hands with the queen, who was following right behind her husband. The woman was gorgeous; she put both my mother and me to shame. She wore a simple, black trumpet dress. Her jewelry was minimalistic—diamond studs in her ears and an old brooch with the profile of an elegant woman carved from ivory, surrounded by pewter and pearls. She was my height, and her figure was thinner than mine. Her boyishly short hair was a warm shade of sandy blonde that enhanced the bottomless depth of her deep blue eyes. I knew her as a kind woman, and I knew Mother quite liked her, but her expression as I greeted her gave me pause. It felt like she had a secret, and I was somehow a part of it.

"That's such a lovely piece," I said, pointing to her brooch with my eyes.

She touched it with her long, thin fingers and smiled demurely. "How kind of you, my dear. I quite like your pendant. I saw your father give it to you earlier. It matches your earrings. Truly a spectacular present for our country's newest wielder, and might I add, a lovely young woman." That smile. Something was going on, I was certain of it.

She dragged a young man over; he was probably twenty, if I had to guess. He was almost as tall as Stefek and muscular. Not like Adonis; he had more of a swimmer's body. His hair was lighter even than his mother's, the color of shimmering sand on a hot summer's day. His features were more angular than hers, and he had gotten the sharp nose and high cheeks from his father. He might have come off lanky, if not for the self-assured way that he carried himself. He was young, but he was no stranger to being amongst the rich and powerful.

"Jafra, darling, this is my first son, Stanisław. He's just returned from a year abroad in the United Kingdom," she said proudly. "He was studying International Relations at Oxford."

He took my hand and kissed the fingers with a familiar flourish. As he did, he looked into my eyes with his bright, sky-blue eyes; somehow, they were both dark and bright at the same time.

"Technically, I was in England. I had a flat in London for the weekends and breaks. Have you ever been? To England, that is?"

"I have not gone abroad, your grace." I saw the look in the queen's eyes, then turned to see a similar expression on my mother's face. A conspiracy! "If you would honor me with stories of your travels, I would be truly grateful." Both women gave an approving look without moving their faces or changing their demeanor.

"Only if you promise me a dance, Lady Sobieski." He bowed with respect. I'm sure that his asking was as much to please his mother as it was a genuine desire to dance with me. I didn't care. He was rich and very, very handsome!

# Chapter 10

The parade of well-wishers seemed interminable, stretching to the edge of the platform. When the last of them had shaken or kissed my hand, and I had cheerfully greeted them and made polite conversation, I was exhausted. My parents were chatting away, no doubt planning my future.

"That looked like fun." I turned my head at the sound of Krystian's voice. "Mine was nothing like this. Mother went all out." My brother looked especially dashing in his forest green uniform. Of all of us, he was usually the least put together, but tonight, for me, he was uncommonly distinguished.

"Don't you mean Father? He's out the money for this soiree."

"The pension and rents come in under his name, but once they are in our accounts, he has no idea how the money is invested, saved, or spent. Mother is the financial head of our family. You might be asked to do the same, should you get married any time soon." He turned his head to the swath of eligible bachelors that stretched from the bar past the dance floor. "Let me escort you to a table that's been reserved for us."

He bent his arm, and I took his elbow as we walked through the crowd to a large round table on the far edge of the dance floor. A silver bucket of ice sat in the center of the table, where several bottles of the finest champagne were chilling. Elegant crystal flutes were stacked in a pyramid next to the chiller, and plates of fruit and cheeses were oriented strategically around the table.

Krys whispered in my ear, "I would dance with you, but you should dance with Father first." He smiled proudly at me. "It will take some time for him and Mother to get here. Eat and have a drink or two. After the father-daughter dance, you won't be sitting for a while." He poured each of us a drink, then downed his in a gulp.

I took a seat and scanned the crowd. The older folks were mingling near the grandstand, taking advantage of the open bar. The dance floor was vacant, waiting for me to have the first dance. Everyone between my table and the dance floor was between eighteen and thirty, including a lot of eligible men in their early twenties. I saw Stanisław in the center of a pack of young men, all of them well-bred and well-dressed. These were men who had been brought up in privilege and had never lacked for anything. Each of them would be a fine choice for a husband, though the first sons had the advantage of inheritance.

Tadeusz was in another group on the other side of the band. He was in a heated conversation with Bazyli and Piotr. Both men were from lesser noble houses, but all were young and athletic. They drank and scanned the crowd, no doubt comparing and contrasting the women present. I caught them looking directly at me on more than one occasion. Maybe I should have felt objectified, and I would never admit it, even to my girlfriends, but the attention was like oxygen to me.

Few of them had experienced combat, even though every one of them wore a uniform that represented their House. One exception was Krystian. He was still only twenty-one, but he had killed men in defense of our city. I had seen both of my brothers take a life. He was a second son, so his Ascension Ball had been a much smaller affair. Or so I'm told.

With nothing to lose and no burning desire to be tied down, he spent his off-duty time enjoying his life to the fullest. He had only left our table minutes ago, and young women already surrounded him—unmarried ladies who were open to marrying into the right house. I watched as he whispered into a lovely blonde woman's ear, and she responded with a very feminine giggle. Her green eyes flashed, and a rosy color touched her cheeks.

My parents finally arrived at our table with Stefek and his wife, Iza. Stefek was heir to the second-most prestigious family in all of Polska; his wife, naturally, had to be stunning. Her long, brown hair flowed like a caramel wave across her left shoulder. Her smile was wide, with perfect white teeth and lips the color of winter cherries. Her pale skin was flawless, and her hourglass figure was head-turning.

Father planted himself in front of me and held out his open hand. "On this day of celebration for my oldest daughter becoming an adult and earning her signet, I want to be the first to dance with you. Someday, you will marry and leave the protection of my roof, but until then, you will be my treasured daughter."

"It is my honor, Father," I said. I loved my father, but at this moment, I felt closer to him than at any time I could remember since entering my teen years.

I floated to my feet and, holding his hand, we made our way to the center of the square. He held my right hand in his left and placed his right hand on my hip. My left hand lay on his right shoulder, and we stood still, really looking at each other for the first time in a long time. A wide smile broke my stoic demeanor, and he couldn't help but almost smile.

The thousand-plus guests fell silent, and even the whistle of the wind ceased for the moment. The orchestra began, and we exploded into motion. I had taken years of dance, and to my great surprise, Father was light on his feet. This must have contributed to his winning Mother's heart. Normally stiff and unbending in all things, he was fluid and graceful as he whisked me around like two feathers caught in a zephyr. I hadn't danced in weeks, and the exhilaration I felt was indescribable. I knew that all eyes were on us, were on me, and it only made it all the more wonderful!

When the waltz was done, Krystian was there to scoop me up. He wasn't half the dancer that our father was, but I enjoyed every second.

"Shouldn't you be dancing with some of those pretty girls I saw you speaking with?"

"Me? I'm the backup son. No hurry. What about you? There are plenty of suitors here. Brought along by mothers seeking to make powerful connections."

I saw an index finger tap Krystian on the shoulder. He jerked his head at the touch, caught by surprise. Behind him was Tadeusz Potocki.

"May I cut in?" he asked.

Krystian smiled and stepped out of my embrace. Tadeusz gave a slight bow, then assumed the position for the waltz. He smiled as we effortlessly fell into the rhythm of the music. He couldn't match my father, but he was a better dancer than my brother.

We rotated around each other, around the dance floor, and my nervousness was rapidly abating. I hadn't danced with a boy before, only my dance instructors and my brothers. This was the same, essentially, but different. Was he dancing with me because he just loved to dance? There were now over a hundred couples on the floor. Was he dancing with me because his parents were interested in making a connection with my family through marriage to me? Or did he look at me and see a desirable woman? A woman he wanted to hold in his arms, to touch, to ride the waves of emotion in the plaintive melody that was currently playing? I was conscious of his hand on my waist; it felt hot, even through layers of silk.

"You're an excellent dancer," he said near my ear. The music was loud, and the wind at this altitude was like a throbbing moan.

"As are you. Have you taken classes?"

"Not really. I am a bit of an athlete, so physical challenges are easy for me." He looked to see what my reaction would be. I didn't say anything, so he continued, "I was in the university football club and the rugby league. I still try to stay in shape."

We weren't dancing that close, but his arms felt strong, practically lifting me through the turns. He had a strong cologne that tickled my nose. I felt like it was too much, but the scent was pleasant, and I breathed it in contentedly. He went on to tell me about his education, the business his family conducted, and some of the plans he had made for his future. I didn't get many opportunities to contribute to the conversation, but that was ok. I found his enthusiasm to be infectious. The song ended, and he ushered me back to my table.

I was only able to get in a quick sip of my champagne before the next young man approached. He barely got out the invitation to dance before my mother was pulling me to my feet and thrusting me into Stanisław's outstretched arms.

We walked to the center of the floor, and other couples made way for us. The band had paused while we attained our spot, then began again with a flourish. The notes carried us on the wings of eagles as we glided around the floor. I may have been a poor judge of such things, but he seemed to be nearly perfect in his execution of the more complex turns and glides. After a particularly flamboyant spin, he pulled me close until our bodies were pressed together for a single, heavenly moment. I could feel his firm body against mine, lean and muscular, shaped like a parallelogram with broad shoulders and a narrow waist. His chest was wide and flat, and if I had to guess, made of stone. All the men wore expensive colognes, but beneath the notes of citrus and herbs, cinnamon, and black pepper, he had a more animal-like scent. He was perspiring, and his body gave off a natural musk that was almost imperceptible but stirred chemical reactions in me. I wanted him to crush himself against me so that I could feel the heat of his body, smell his maleness, to feel just a little out of control.

Unfortunately, he was a true gentleman, and though we collided for a second here, half a second there, we never were pressed together before the song was complete. Taking my hand, we drifted back to my table. His hand was as strong as Tadeusz's but was rougher, more accustomed to swinging a sword, or maybe even a work hammer. I enjoyed the contrast between his large hands, which were made for and used to doing work, and my hands, which were delicate and small, made for more feminine pursuits.

Before I could even consider sitting, I was propositioned to dance with Piotr… something. This was a party in my honor, but it was also an opportunity for House Sobieski to showcase our wealth and stature. This was probably even more important to my Father and Stefek than to me. I didn't think that rejecting any offers was an option, so one after the other, I danced with so many, many young men.

They blended in my mind; they were so alike. With a few exceptions, they were uniformly tall, thin, and well-built. They all had luscious mops of hair, some with well-trimmed beards, and eyes that penetrated to the soul. All were sons of rich and powerful fathers, men born to wealth and position, who would be handed the keys to their individual castles. In a couple of cases, they lived in real castles!

I danced a polonaise with Kazimierz Leszczyński, a cousin of the king from Kraków. He was more formal than the rest; his footwork was flawless, and his suit was exemplary. I danced with brothers, first Antoni Zamoyski and then his younger brother, Jan. They were both in expensive, well-tailored suits, but neither of them had the overwhelming arrogance and pride that the others displayed. Of all my partners, they seemed the least concerned with winning my hand, and maybe the only ones on the dance floor, except my brother Krystian, who was there for the fun of it. I danced with Józef Sapieha. His family was not noble; they had no brands, but they were prosperous and well-connected. His father and my father were close friends, and I learned later that they golfed on a fairly regular basis.

As not every boy was able to initiate a compelling conversation, I was able to survey my competition. I saw dozens of daughters from noble and royal families. There was Katarzyna Czartoryska, a first cousin of Stanisław. I wouldn't go so far as to say that she was a plain-looking girl, but she would not inspire many love sonnets. Her dress, though made of the finest materials, was influenced by the Rus styles that were never in fashion in Warszawa.

I shared a flashing smile with my friends, Elżbieta and Anna Ostrogski. They were each on the arms of very handsome gentlemen, and they seemed to be having the time of their lives. Helena Radziwiłł was on the sidelines, waiting for a partner, and appeared to have had a few too many glasses of wine.

I was surprised when I saw my brother dancing with Stanisław's younger sister Jadwiga Poniatowski, who was my age. The genes in that family were dominant. She was every bit as beautiful as he was. Her long, blonde hair had incredible volume and a natural-looking wave. Her figure was nearly as voluptuous as mine, and her face was taken directly from a Michelangelo bust. If I were to give Stanisław serious consideration, I would be glad that she would not be a possible competitor.

# Chapter 11

The party had been going on for a couple of hours and showed no signs of slowing down. I had been sitting for only about two minutes when a man I didn't recognize approached. I had met most of the more prominent guests at the outset, and I would have remembered him. He was one of the few men on the whole ship who wasn't wearing either a military uniform or a ship's crew uniform. Instead, he wore a dark blue frock coat over a cream-colored shirt, a brilliant white cravat, and a dark green vest. He tipped his black felt hat, then handed it to his manservant, and dropped his leather gloves and copper-colored goggles into the hat.

"I apologize for my tardiness, Lady Sobieski. I was in the radio cabin communicating with my father, who sends his regards, about some skirmishes on the border." His smile was unapologetic.

"I'm sorry, sir. I don't believe that we've been introduced," I said.

"Jaroslav Záhoř, milady. My father is Oldřich Záhoř, the High King of the Bohemian Empire. Like you, we've had an outbreak of rabble-rousers, radical anarchists. I spend a lot of time working with a special squad to neutralize them, but I was sent to represent the kingdom." He accepted a full glass of whiskey from a server and downed it before returning the glass.

"My father has wandered off somewhere, if you need me to have someone find him," I offered.

"I understand that your king is here. I'll try to pay my respects and pass him a directive from my father later. My main reason for coming was to honor and congratulate you.

Our fathers fought together in the Ottoman wars, over ten years ago now. He saved my father's life, and that's a debt that house Záhoř will never forget. I was too young to attend your oldest brother's ascension, but I did attend your brother Krystian's ball. I was only nineteen then, and not allowed to speak." He chuckled at his joke.

"On behalf of House Sobieski, welcome."

"Your heartfelt greeting is appreciated, but I would prefer a dance." His short, straight hair was wild and white as milk. He was a year older than Krystian, and he looked youthful, but the color of his hair was peculiar, to say the least. His strong, deeply-tanned features were not hidden by facial hair; he had prominent ears, a long nose, and brown eyes the color of oiled leather. His smile was wide, with teeth as white as pearls, and a three-inch scar that started at his high cheekbone on the left side and almost touched his ear.

Krystian was nearby, and he gave me a look that may have been meant to be a warning, but I wasn't sure. Tonight, 'no' was not in my vocabulary. He took my proffered hand and led me out on the floor. It was not as crowded as it had been earlier, and we could hear each other a bit more easily. He held me close, even though the music was a more formal piece.

"Thank you for dancing with me," he said. "Your brother referred to you as a cute kid, but I think he was intentionally underselling your attributes. A sensible man could find many words to describe you, but cute would not come to mind."

I wasn't sure how this would go, but I was interested in playing along. "So, I'm not cute?"

"No, milady. You are not cute," he said calmly. "Cute is the word a brother uses to describe a family member, one he doesn't see for who she is."

I leaned back to look into those deep, brown eyes.

"You may have just turned eighteen in the last week, but I look at you, and you didn't get this figure overnight. A lot of the men who came to honor you did so because of your last name. If they're smart, if they enjoy the company of women, they will see what I see."

"Which is?" I thought that I now knew where this conversation was going, but I wanted to continue the game.

"Are you fishing for compliments?" he asked. "In that, all women are the same." I didn't care for that statement, even if there was a grain of truth in it. "It doesn't matter to me who your father is. I'm a prince. I'm not interested in how much money you have. I am richer than Midas, or at least I will be when I become king. My interest in you, now that I've met you, now that I have your body pressed against mine, is purely prurient."

I looked at him, clearly confused.

"Lascivious, lewd, ribald, risqué, indecent… need I go on?" He smiled wickedly at me, and his eyes were filled with something, some quality that I was not familiar with. I was too mesmerized by his strange and blunt way of speaking, and I hadn't noticed that we were indeed slow dancing. My chest was crushed against his, his hand was at my waist, though edging lower with each passing minute. Our lower bodies touched, and I dreaded speculating exactly which part of him was grinding against which part of me.

"We've just met. You overstep, Your Grace." I was ready to do the unthinkable: leave in the middle of a dance and walk off. He wants to fuck me. I may still be a virgin, but I get that. I've had my share of men, including my brother's friends, look me over. Hungry eyes that were oblivious to our relative stations. But to say it to me on our first meeting? What a pig!

"I'm sorry that you feel that way." That was not an apology at all. "From what I've heard about you from Krystian and the few minutes that I've known you, you seem like a person who appreciates being told the truth. Not half-truths, nor euphemisms. As you can already tell, I'm a very blunt, plain-speaking person."

I saw an index finger tap his shoulder. He ignored it as we continued to drift slowly about the dance floor. A whole hand of fingers appeared, firmly tapping on his left shoulder. While turning, I saw that it was Stanisław, attempting to cut in. My partner continued to ignore him.

Jaroslav and I were now close enough that I could swear that I felt his heartbeat through my chest. I could smell his natural scent; he wore no perfume. We were close enough that he could speak into my ear, and no one else would be able to hear. Jaroslav was able to see who was disturbing our tête-à-tête, but he didn't seem to care.

"You've had the lady's company for quite a while now. Pardon me if I cut in," Stanisław said, his confidence tinged with anger. I suppose that if you're a prince, you're not required to use common courtesies when addressing other princes.

"When this song is over, I'll escort the lady back to her table. You can go now." He turned his attention back to me as if the heir to the Polska throne wasn't standing behind him, fuming.

"Are you sure that it's wise to make an enemy of the future king of this country?"

"I'm enjoying having my arms around you far too much." His smile was threatening to turn into outright laughter. "That pretty boy works on his polo game, or lawn darts, whatever the hell your royals do. Croquet? Like your brothers, I am risking my life to fight the terrorists, who I think are really just advanced teams from Rus. I am a serious person, and when I have my sights set on a goal, winning is the only option."

"Am I now a goal of yours?" I asked. This man was so strange, and yet I couldn't tell if I hated him or was intrigued.

"You are, and I will have you." Strangely, after claiming me without asking my opinion on the subject, he continued to dance. The song was nearly over, and I was anxious to get back to my parents' table.

All of my thoughts went up in smoke. Sirens sounded, and alarms mounted on the rear deck were ringing. I heard an explosion and felt the entire airship shake. At the far end of the main deck, I saw about ten small airships land. Each one disgorged a dozen men wearing assault uniforms. They carried axes and pistols, while some also had swords or wooden clubs. There were a few women among them, but the majority were men between twenty and forty years old. They had no insignia on their tight black jackets, but they did have many pockets for carrying items I couldn't identify. All of them wore kerchiefs across the lower halves of their faces, heightening their intimidating presence.

The ship's security met them, but the speed of their attack and the violence they used made short work of our defenders. I shook with fear, not sure what to do, but Jaroslav grasped my arm in a vise-like grip and hustled me back to my family's table. It was far firmer than the hold he had on me while we were dancing. More than when we embraced, our bodies crushed together.

When we reached my table, he kissed me full on the mouth, his hot lips on mine, his tongue reaching into my mouth and tangling with my tongue. His hand held me by the back of my neck, and his other hand squeezed my hip tightly as he ravaged me with his kiss. I felt warm all over, lightheaded. Then he broke contact.

"Stay here with your papa. I need to go kill some men." His smile told me that he was now truly in his element. I could see the Abyrinth dancing on his skin, growing in brilliance as he ran towards the invaders. The ship shifted, and some of the furniture slid to one side; I saw an older woman tumble over the edge and into space.

My brothers and father all had their swords out, and they glowed with power, waiting to be released. Father stood only a few inches taller than I was, but he looked down on me, and I felt like I was in the shadow of a giant. His steel-like reserve had become even more fixed.

He laid a hand on my shoulder, meeting my frightened stare. "Take your mother into the cabins and wait. We'll deal with this assassination attempt."

I never disobeyed my father, and I wasn't going to start now. Holding the edge of my skirt, I took her hand, and we headed for the cabins at a sprint. She had a concerned look on her face, but said nothing until we got to the 'safety' of the superstructure at the rear of the ship. People were running everywhere, and full panic had set in on the ship. There were the sounds of screaming and dying. The wind seemed to be battering us now, roaring over our heads and pulling at the crew and passengers alike. I realized that we were rapidly losing altitude.

"Stay back here with me!" she yelled over the din. Mother had a brave face on, but I could tell that she was even more scared than I was. She was not accessing her power; hers was not an ability with any offensive potential. Was mine offensive?

The structure shot up five stories, and inside were the kitchens, rooms, but most importantly, the flight deck. Inside, a handful of channelers harnessed their connection to Abyrinth and used it to power the massive ship. We were slowly falling, and I feared that, aside from dozens of terrorists attacking the partygoers, they had also launched a second wave of attacks at the crew. If they could crash the ship, it would take out much of the nobility in Polska and in Europa. When I learned that I was correct, it gave me no satisfaction.

A group of black-clad men poured out of the double doors, weapons in hand. When they laid their eyes on two noble ladies, they saw an easy target. The one in front had a machete in his hand and madness in his eyes. Short black hair stuck up like bristles on a worn-out brush. He was large, like an ape, much larger than my brother Stefek, both in height and build. They had no aura around them. They must have had channelers to make their landing ships fly, but all of these foot soldiers were blanks.

He swung his blade at my mother, but it stopped in mid-swing. I had gathered the flows of the energy that were ever-present and wrapped them around his machete and his arm. Almost casually, I squeezed the strands and snapped his arm. The man fell to his knees, holding his broken arm and screaming in agony.

The men behind him had no idea what had happened, so they continued to run at us. I wove a wall between us and watched as they crashed face-first into it. Mother couldn't see the flows either, but she saw my concentration and realized I was the one holding the attackers at bay.

"You're doing this, Jafra?" she asked. She looked concerned and reached out to touch me.

"Not now, Mother!" I said, perhaps too harshly. We were near the railing, and I had a thought. I sent out tentacles, not unlike an octopus's, that wrapped around the waist of each man. I lifted them into the air and carried them over until they hung in the air, twenty feet away from the safety of the main deck. They squirmed, their legs kicking frantically back and forth, but they were firmly in my control.

They tried to kill me; they wanted to kill my mother. Not only did I have no sympathy for them, but I felt... pleasure, when I released them.

Their screams eventually became lost in the thin, misty air, and we were still too high up for us to hear them hit the ground.

I turned to see a very different look on Mother's face. A look I'd never seen before, something I would have never thought to be directed at me. She had a layer of shock; I would have expected that. There was also a respect, some pride, and more than a little fear.

"I know your father and your brothers do that sort of thing. I know that sometimes it's necessary, but I never

expected it from my baby girl." She didn't look angry, more...
disappointed.

"I saved our lives." That was all the explanation I
thought my actions warranted.

"Yes. Thank God you were given the power to kill...
to save our lives." She looked sad.

"Mother. Go inside and see if there is anyone that you
can heal." She nodded and, for the first time in our
relationship, followed my orders. She was a very potent healer.
If the channelers weren't dead, there would be a good chance
she could bring them back from the brink.

# Chapter 12

Now was not the time to hide, to play the delicate flower. People were dying, and I wasn't helpless! Against my father's wishes, I returned to the madness at the other end of the ship.

I thought even more ships had arrived because the chaos was not possible with only a hundred invaders. As I got closer to the action, I almost stumbled across the body of Zofia Lubomirski. I didn't know her that well; she was more of an acquaintance of my brother than of mine. I neither liked nor disliked her, but she certainly didn't deserve to have her life end at my party, with a gaping hole in her forehead.

I saw my father briefly use his power once. To show Jurek and me what it was. That was several years ago, and I had forgotten how powerful he was. He was in the heat of battle, shoulder to shoulder with his sons. Father could turn his body into flexible steel. He was bulletproof, stab-proof, nearly invincible. He could only stay in that state for a few minutes before needing to recharge, but when his power was active, he was unstoppable. Shots rang off his metallic hide, and another terrorist tried slashing him, only to see his blade shatter. Father went without his sword and instead punched the invaders with fists that hit like sledgehammers. I watched as he caved in the skull of a man who was trying to shoot him. The man next to him died as a steel-hard fist pushed through his sternum and exploded out of his back.

Stefek was equally deadly, perhaps even more so. His razor-sharp blade found vital spots on his opponents one after the other. By the time I arrived, he was surrounded by dead blanks, and his fine coat was soaked from collar to cuff in the blood of the invaders. My brother was a perfect killing machine. Precise and practiced with his power. I believe that he would have been nearly as deadly without the ability to pause time, but using his power, he was able to fight with little chance of being countered.

Krystian and a boy named Kazimierz Leszczyński worked together, positioning themselves in front of the women and the older nobles. My brother created thorny obstacles that penned in the terrorists, making it impossible for them to move forward or backward without skewering themselves on his metal spikes.

Kazimierz was able to manipulate electricity. Not full-on lightning bolts, but smaller versions. I could see the Abyrinth coalesce around him, and he would channel it as a bolt of energy that would instantly electrocute anyone it touched. Krystian would trap them, and he would fry them. They seemed to work together like a well-oiled machine.

I could see the energy surrounding all of the wielders. The blanks were just that, blanks in the canvas of energy that I could now perceive. My family, like the other nobles, each had lines of power that passed into and out of them as they used their special abilities. When Father's energy level dropped to near zero, he reverted to flesh and blood. He retreated from the front lines and saw me standing there. I couldn't tell if he was relieved or angered to see me standing there, so close to the action.

"Where is your mother?" he demanded.

"She went inside to see if she could heal any of the crew. We're falling."

He was breathing hard, but he looked around at the carnage, the dead and dying all around us, and he could feel the dangerous tilt to the ship's deck. He looked from side to side, evaluating how the battle was going, and then I could almost see the gears in his mind turning. For the first time in my life, I saw indecision on his face. Win or lose, if we were going to crash, we would all die anyway. Stefek came running up.

"We got help from Stanisław and the other would-be suitors. They are cleaning up now," he reported.

"I can see that. Push their ships off the side. See if that will slow our descent!" Father ordered.

He ran off, and I followed behind. The terrorists were foolish to attack a ship with so many wielders on it. Even with the hundreds of fighters they brought, there was never a chance that they would be able to kill the king or his heir.

The cost to us was still very high. I saw a crewman who had been shot many times. He lay next to the rail with his dead eyes staring off towards the capital.

Then I saw a dress that looked familiar, and when I got close, my worst fear was realized. It was Daria. I was sure, even though her head was missing. I looked around and saw that it had rolled a dozen feet away and was lodged beneath a dead terrorist.

I don't know what was stronger, my reaction to the horrors of the last half hour, or the anger I felt. These attacks were meant to soften us up, to inflict as much damage to both our noble class and to the psyche of the Polish people. Thoughts of finding a nice man, marrying, and having children all seemed distant and unimportant now. They had tried to kill my mother, they killed one of my best friends, and if they could, they would kill us all and take our country. I was not going to sit idly by while my countrymen were killed and subjugated. It would be better to die than to become a slave to the Rus.

I was seething as I stomped to where my brothers were working with the other young men to get the enemy airships off the deck of the cruise ship. I could see the streams of Abyrinth all around, and I could feel it coursing through me.

"Stand back!" I yelled above the howling wind. "Get back, now!"

"You shouldn't be here, Jafra!" Stefek shouted.

I wrapped him in cords of energy and pulled him to the side. His eyes went wide as he realized that his little sister was manhandling him.

"Step back!" I yelled.

"Everyone, get back!" Stef screamed at the young men trying to muscle the landing craft. He turned to me and nodded. Stefek has a very commanding way about him; even the prince heir heeded his command.

I released my brother, then gathered all the Abyrinth I could. There was no physical strain on me, just the strain to gather enough energy to move the mass of the ships. They couldn't see it, but to me, there was a vast cache of energy around us that I imagined forming a giant hand.

That invisible hand contacted the first ship and, like a giant child, swept it over the edge of the cruise ship's deck. The landing craft fell away into the night, far below. It wasn't easy, but it wasn't as impossible as I had thought, even a day before I got my brand. I completed the same process with the next few ships until the deck was clear of the invaders' vessels.

I'd thought there was no physical toll, but when I was done, I realized that I was sweating profusely. I examined myself, and I wasn't sure that there would be any saving of this beautiful gown.

No. Completely trashed.

"Jafra!"

I looked up to see Milka standing a few feet away. She looked more disheveled than I did. Her hair was a complete mess, her dress was torn in a dozen places, and she had a blood stain that covered the whole body and the lower part of her dress. She had a strange expression. I wasn't sure what was wrong.

"Are you alright?" I asked her. I walked over to where she was waiting with Elżbieta and Anna.

"No. I'm not alright." She looked shell-shocked. "That was the most incredible thing I've ever seen!" She practically threw herself on me, held me close, and began crying and hyperventilating. As I held her, I felt a sinking feeling. Like falling.

"We're still going down!" someone yelled.

I saw Stefek and Father a few feet away; they were shouting and moving their arms frantically. The evil men were dead, but something was still wrong.

Then the ship tilted again, and everyone started sliding to the port side of the deck. Dead bodies began falling, and then the party guests were also sliding towards oblivion. I felt myself sliding out of control until I caught the railing. Most people were able to grab hold of one of the secured fixtures, but several were heading hopelessly towards the railing. Thirty feet away from me, I saw Krystian and his friend Jaroslav rolling head over heels, right before going over the edge.

I screamed as I had never screamed before in my life. It was instinct; my power reached out and wrapped both men in energy tentacles, hauling them back on board. If the ship tilted any more, it would dump us all to the ground, then crush us when it finally crashed.

In the air, there was power to be had, power to tap. I summoned it to me as much as I could. I filled myself to the brim, then filled some more. I felt like I was glowing, almost as if I could fly.

Focusing on the ship, I put a giant hand underneath and gently supported the vessel until it was level. I could hear people shouting, and the wind at the railing felt like hurricane-force winds. With my power, I could lift things infinitely heavier than what I could lift with my muscles, but I was wrong that it took no physical effort. I strained; the hand I had fashioned grew larger, large enough to support the entire cruise ship. I felt gravity trying to defy me, trying to defeat me. I would not have it!

The rate at which we were falling decreased, but we were still falling. I could now clearly see features on the ground. We were over farmland, but I could make out churches, barns, and a whole town not a mile to the south. Seconds ago, I felt like a dam that was full to bursting, but now I felt like a pitcher with a hole near the bottom. I was emptying at an alarming rate.

I pulled Abyrinth from all around me. It flowed in from the air around us, and more flowed in from God only knows where. I greedily sucked it in and instantly released it into my ghostly construction.

I didn't need to look down; the ground was rushing up at us, and I was anticipating our end. With every ounce of my strength, my concentration, my very breath, I held up the ship. Closer, the ground was so close now.

I. Have. To. Give. Every. Thing. I. have.

My vision went black as I passed out.


"Wake up!"

I heard my mother's voice. I felt her hands on me, and I could feel her healing.

"You're ok, child." My father's voice.

I pried open my eyes, and the light of a new morning almost blinded me. If I thought that I was covered in sweat before, I had no idea what that meant. I was soaked. Completely soaked.

Mother dabbed at my nose with a handkerchief, and when she pulled it back, there was a sizable spot of blood on it.

I'm not dead. We're not dead.

I was helped to a sitting position. I was surrounded by my family, my girlfriends, and about a hundred other people. The king himself held out his hand to help me to my feet. He looked relieved, even kinder than when we had spoken hours earlier. "That was an incredible display, Lady Sobieski. In all my years, I've never seen a wielder harness such raw energy. Your father told me about your brand, but none of us had any idea how powerful you are," the king remarked.

"What happened?" I was still very dazed. All eyes were on me, and they were smiling, so I felt a  little better.

Milka took my hand. "We were falling towards certain death for everyone. You slowed our descent to almost a stop, only a few feet from the ground!"

Krystian was smiling at me. "You saved a thousand of Polska's most influential people. I guess Cousin Milka was right about how strong your gift would be."

"I still don't know how I did it. I felt so… empty."

"That's the strange part. You drained all of us to make it happen."

# Chapter 13

I spent most of the following week in bed, resting and hiding from people. I eventually felt well enough to get off my ass and go outside.

Since Jurek was growing like a weed, I appropriated several pairs of his pants and a half dozen of his light shirts. I made my way down to where the boys were practicing. I got a decidedly different greeting since the first time I'd gone down there.

"Finally out of bed?" Krystian asked. "It's about time you stopped malingering."

Stefek showed me more respect in his manner. I found it unnerving. "Are you sure you even need hand-to-hand training? Mother said you snapped a guy's arm, then threw the lot of them over the side of the ship."

"I've heard you and Father say a million times that you can't always count on your power to save you. Train like you're a blank and have no special skills." I fetched a wooden training sword.

"Excellent advice, if I do say so myself." He indicated for Krystian to sit. Meeting me in an open lane, he assumed the first position. Last time, I hadn't sparred at all; I only worked on stances with Jurek. "When training with us, remember, you can't use your powers. For the next two hours, we're just like blanks."

"Two hours?" I whined. The sound made even me cringe. "I mean, yes, teacher!"

And for the next two hours, my brothers took turns teaching me and beating the crap out of me. I may have learned something, but all I remembered was the bruises.

When we returned to the house, Mother was waiting in the family dining room. She waved me over, giving me a sniff and a disappointed look as I sat down. "Jafra, dear, I have excellent news!"

I love my mother, but something about her bright, cheery approach made me feel very suspicious. "Well, I do like getting good news." I accepted tea and biscuits from the maid.

"I've been meeting with some of the most prestigious families in the country." I totally saw this coming. "I have gotten literally dozens of inquiries, and at least a dozen actual requests for negotiations. Best of all, I have made a date for you!"

I hadn't begun dating yet, and I should have been more excited, but the thought of my mother choosing who I would go out with bothered me. I knew that she had my best interests in mind, but she was also responsible for making the best connections for the good of the family. Still, her marriage to my father had been arranged, so maybe it would work out.

"That sounds great!" I was good at feigning enthusiasm. "Um, who will I be going out with?"

"I'll let you guess," she said. Her joy was palpable.

"Give me a clue?"

"Only the most eligible bachelor in the country." She was teeming with excitement.

"I can't date my brother!" I said to Krystian, who was at the counter fixing his own sandwich.

"I have to draw the line somewhere," he said before taking a massive bite of his snack.

"No! You kids, stop fooling around. This is serious!"

"Ok, so, the second most desired man in Polska… Stanisław Poniatowski?"

"Prince Stanisław Poniatowski," she corrected. "I was already in negotiations with his mother, and after meeting you at the ball, the prince is quite taken with you."

"With me, or with my brand?" I asked.

"Probably with your boobs," Krystian added. Mother gave him a withering look.

"Whether it's your name, your power, or your… looks" she gave him another hard look "it would be a beneficial match all around. If I'm honest, he is a rather handsome young man. You could do much worse. Yes, much worse indeed." She must have been contemplating some of the men she'd already eliminated.

I thought back to meeting Stanisław at the party. Our families were familiar with each other, and we had met, but his change during his studies abroad had been considerable. I didn't clearly remember him from before, but now, he was about perfect. I wasn't sure what type of man interested me, but his Greek god looks were extremely appealing. Even through his formal uniform, I could tell that he had an incredible body. That golden hair, the lose-yourself-in-them blue eyes? I think Mother gave me the best gift ever.

"For you, Mother? I'll give it a try." Ahhh, the sacrifices that I make.

I hadn't seen Aunt Bronisława for a long time, more than three years. She had been traveling abroad, but luckily, she was in town in time to be my chaperone.

If anyone were going to protect my chastity, it would be her. My mother's sister was not what you would call a handsome woman. I was so grateful that all the good genes were passed down through my mother, because she got a very mixed bag. She had dark hair like my mother's, but her fine, thinning hair was rapidly turning gray. She had to pin it down to keep it from floating away. She was four years my mother's senior, but looked like she could be my grandmother. She was nearly as tall as I was, but she wore so many layers, only her doctor knew if she had any figure. Her clothes were high quality; the sister had come from a very good family down south, but the style was not and never had been in fashion. Her spectacles were perched on the tip of her long, thin nose, exposing the dark circles and bags around her eyes.

I wouldn't say that I knew her well, so I hadn't really formed any opinions of her. I knew that a chaperone would be necessary, but I still didn't like the idea. By now, the strength of my brand was common knowledge, and any boy who tried something too forward would be picked up and tossed in the nearest rubbish heap. To be honest, the idea of Stanisław sneaking a kiss didn't bother me at all. I might have even encouraged it if that wouldn't have gotten me in huge trouble at home.

Only a week later, we went on our initial date. My first.

The executive limousine was let through the front gates of our estate and hovered down the long, cobbled driveway, lined with blossoming peach trees. The front of the mansion had wide marble stairs and thick marble columns on the façade. The main house was three stories, with east and west wings surrounding the front gardens and fountain.

The fountain was one of the best in Warszawa. It was oval, with ten-foot-tall stone statues of women in Greek-style togas, a single breast exposed, their curly hair braided into crowns. For all eternity, they would stand on a small island in the fountain, pouring out water from large copper pitchers.

The gardens behind the house were also quite spectacular; the garden in the front was smaller, with the usual roses, tulips, and daffodils.

Our house had fourteen bedrooms and a dozen smaller chambers for the servants. We had two kitchens, one for everyday use and a larger one for entertaining. We had a ballroom, although it paled in comparison to the one on the airship. There was a library and a study for each of my parents. We had a small salon, our own chapel, trophy room, armory, a gallery where we displayed some of the country's best artworks, a conservatory, and scads of pantries, closets, and other storage areas too numerous to detail here.

The prince's car was truly a marvel. It was made from hammered copper and brass, and longer than our limousine by half again, with a spacious rear cabin, with red velvet, padded couches. It had lights and horns up front by the channeler, and overall, a very sleek design.

He was admitted to the house and was escorted through the entry foyer and into Father's drawing room. He was offered tea while I was putting the finishing touches on my hair and makeup. Aunt Bronisława came down first to sit with him, and I was to wait until called. She entered the tea room as if this were her house; I felt like her pride felt misplaced when addressing the future king.

My hair was curled and loosely braided, and my makeup was on point, with rosy cheeks, candy-apple red lipstick, and a hint of azure on my eyelids. I had on a maroon A-Line cocktail dress with black lace over the shoulders and across the modest cleavage. Unlike my Ascension Ball dress, this dress had a high waist and a fluid skirt that billowed past knee length. It showed my curves without being ostentatious. My open-toe shoes had three-inch heels with a black and silver floral pattern. I finished with a light touch of a perfume given to me by Elżbieta, featuring notes of vanilla, lilac, and citrus. I won't waste time on false humility; I looked impeccable. I looked hot!

So, what the hell is taking so long?

My first date ever, and I was in the hallway waiting to be summoned to a room in my own house! Unacceptable. Auntie can be a bit of a talker.

I edged close to the open door, and I could hear the sounds of a spirited debate. It seemed that she'd forgotten that she was a third wheel and had put herself at the forefront of my date. Time to put an end to this.

I took a deep breath, lifted my chest, and glided into the room.

My aunt was sitting in the overstuffed wingback chair. She was ready to go, a white bonnet on her head and her fan moving in time with her conversation. The more animated she got, the faster the fan would wave. Dear sweet Stanisław was taking it like a true champion. Not cowed, but still very respectful. Score one point for the prince!

He deserved saving, so I entered the room before being summoned. He looked up and showed me the same radiant smile that I remembered from the ball. The distraction had interrupted Auntie's flow; she was paused with her closed fan extended from her upraised hand. Before I could address them, he stood to greet me.

"Lady Sobieski, you are truly a vision to behold."

Maybe I was, but he was the embodiment of a hero from Roman myth. Tall and strong from head to boot, his body was sculpted like the David; his lengthy, flat torso had not an ounce of fat. With his curly, dirty blonde locks, noble features, and sky-blue eyes, he treaded the line between feminine beauty and masculine strength.

We both stepped down from the formal dress at the ball. He wore a simple suit, opting not to go in his family's uniform. He wore a black coat and trousers with a crisp, ruffled white shirt. His only jewelry was his family signet ring, and unlike the men that surrounded me, he wasn't armed. At least not tonight.

"Please call me Jafra, Your Grace," I said, making a respectful curtsey. Out of the corner of my eye, I tried to see what body part he was focused on, and to my surprise and delight, his gaze stayed locked on mine. Another good sign? I was looking pretty hot, so it would have been ok for him to ogle me a little.

"My friends call me Stan. I would like you to consider yourself part of that elite group." He was so pretty that even what might be considered an arrogant statement came across as charming.

"Thank you, Stan. I trust dear Aunt Bronisława entertained you?" I gave him a grin that conveyed my apologies.

"Yes, we've had a delightful conversation. It's good that you are ready; we have an eight o'clock reservation." He stood and addressed my aunt. "Are you ready to go, madam?"

Auntie didn't like being interrupted, but she must have remembered her role in tonight's excursion. She smiled warmly and nodded in agreement.

He ushered us out, then let us lead him back to the main entrance. "I won't tell you where we're going, but let's just hope you like food from the Orient."


The restaurant seemed garish to me. Every surface was covered in bright red or gold. It was painful to look at it for too long. The place was packed with diners, but we were taken to a private room off to the side. The three of us were seated at a large round table that could easily accommodate ten people. There was a second round table in the center of the table that rotated easily if you gave it a push.

I hadn't been too familiar with Oriental food, but I found it to be delicious. If we were married, I would insist that we eat it every month, or at least a few times a year. All of the servers were Orientals, maybe from Cathay. The men were of short stature and had a very severe appearance. The women had long black hair like mine and were petite with beautiful, delicate features.

We ordered a dozen dishes, and instead of potatoes, they were served with rice. Some of the dishes were very spicy, others had a sweetness to them. We sampled fish and fowl, land creatures, and odd creatures from the depths of the sea. In Polska, we are accustomed to heavier dishes, with rich, creamy sauces. This cuisine was lighter, oilier, and seasoned with garlic and a thin, black, salty sauce. I didn't like every dish, but the experience of trying them was phenomenal. I even think the wine was made of rice. I didn't care for it and only had a few sips.

Stanisław must have carefully planned our evening. With instructions to his driver, we next headed to Ogród Ciszy, also known as The Garden of Silence. The entrance to the park was well-lit, but the clearing had half a dozen trails leading in every direction. One went through an open field with professionally manicured gardens. There was a trail that wound around a small lake, and another trail went straight into a stretch of woods.

Against my aunt's grumbling complaints, we took the forest trail. There were lit lanterns along the path, but the sun had set hours ago, and the long stretches between lanterns were very dark.

We walked side by side, and our keeper followed about twenty feet behind. I don't know how he arranged it, but the weather was perfect. It was dark, but above us, the heavens were spread out like a blanket of diamonds. It was generally warm, but intermittently, a cool breeze would sweep over us. I longed for him to put his arm around me. Why? I had only spent a few hours with Stanisław, but I was already imagining what it would be like to be in a romantic relationship with him. I couldn't believe that my first kiss ever was with that cretin from Bohemia. I want to forget it ever happened, and have my first kiss come from my prince!

He must have been thinking the same thing. As we walked, he casually reached out his hand and took mine. It felt so good. His hand was larger and warmer, while my hands always seemed to be cold. He gripped it, his long fingers almost wrapping around mine and squeezing, but not too tightly. I felt like my heart was going to pound its way through my chest. It lasted for almost five seconds.

"Stop!" she barked. "No holding hands!"

As of then, instead of her being out of range to hear our conversation, she was close enough that I could smell the medication she rubbed on her neck. We weren't saying anything particularly scandalous. For the most part, he told me about life in his father's castle. He spoke about how, after the debacle on the airship, he had taken up fencing and self-defense. He talked about admiring my older brothers and how they were at the vanguard when the fighting began.

I spoke very little about myself and instead complimented his courage at the ball and his parents' kindness to me. He graciously accepted my praise and told me about his plans to rule when he would eventually take the throne. He had so many ideas, like how to modernize our country and protect us against threats from abroad.

I knew the potency of my brand had worked in my mother's favor when arranging the date, but to my surprise, he didn't bring it up at all. I decided not to mention it either. Having a woman be so much stronger than you is not a situation that most men are agreeable with.

"Are you going to university?" he finally asked. I looked up into those eyes and almost forgot that he was speaking to me.

"There is an excellent art institute in Gdańsk. I love painting, and my tutor says that I have genuine talent. I want to learn more about art and art history."

"I don't know if it is proper to ask… but are you meeting with other potential suitors?" He had a strange look, as if he either knew the answer already or was expecting a specific response. It felt like a test, and it made me uneasy.

"Not to my knowledge, Your Grace," I replied. The romantic glow that I was floating in had dissipated, and I was again aware that this was more of an interview than a simple night on the town. "This is my first date ever. I don't know if my mother has planned any other dates. I know she feels that we are a good match. Not that it matters, but I find that I like you very much."

He could see the change in my mood. "I was wrong to ask such a personal question. I guess one of my failings is that I can get jealous." He flashed his porcelain-white teeth, his smile sheepish, conveying regret. "We barely know each other, but I already feel at ease with you, and I enjoy talking with you." He lifted my chin with his forefinger and looked deep into my eyes. "I need to get you home soon, but honor me with a goodnight kiss." He leaned in, his luscious lips pursed.

"Stanisław, I'm sorry," I held out my hands to stop his advance. "It's too soon." I gave him my most cheerful smile, trying to convey that I wasn't rejecting him specifically, but I had standards that I needed to follow. I was hoping he would value my purity and be willing to wait.

Instead, something flashed across his face that I didn't expect. Annoyance.

"Too soon? I have to admit that I'm confused. I saw you kissing that Bohemian prince at your Ascension Ball." His expression was flat, accusing.

I was taken aback, stunned into temporary silence. I felt like I had been called a whore in front of the whole world.

I couldn't help the tears that welled up and began rolling down my cheeks.

"I didn't kiss him! He kissed me! In the chaos that erupted, he took me back to our table, then kissed me without permission. Without permission!" I was extremely adamant about that last part. "Whatever you saw or thought you saw, I have yet to kiss a man. I am saving myself, every intimacy, for the man who will make me his wife!"

There was almost a cruelty in the way he stood there, looking down at me. I could sense the thoughts rushing through his mind at a mile a minute. Then it changed. Like the flicking of a switch, he changed from whatever dark place he had gone to, and was back to his suave, likeable self.

"That's good to know. I'm sorry that you had to deal with a cad like that." We headed back to his limousine. "It's getting late. I'll see you home."

We walked in silence, and I couldn't help thinking that I was not understanding something. He sounded like nothing was wrong, but his eyes seemed cold. How could he be upset about something that I had no control over? I had been taken advantage of. And besides, I was raised properly, and I wasn't going to kiss any man on the first date.

At my front door, he held the door for both Auntie and me. He was polite and gentlemanly as a prince should be. After some brief small talk, he whooshed off into the night. Auntie said her goodbyes before heading upstairs. No doubt, Mother would be speaking with the queen, if not tonight, tomorrow. I only hoped to find out where I stood with Stanisław.

# Chapter 14

I look pretty good if I do say so myself, Krystian thought. Hair is getting long; if I don't cut it soon, Mother will have me whipped. He laughed at the idea. His wavy dark locks touched his shoulders. Where his brother tried to look older, due to his eventual rise to the title of Lord Sobieski, protector of Warszawa, Krystian was always clean-shaven and looked like what he was: a young man still in his early twenties. A young, wealthy man!

He decided to go with a classic. Looking in the mirror, he saw his crisp, white linen shirt with a high standing collar, fastened with a silver pin at the throat. Over that, he wore a dark silk cravat, knotted and tucked into the charcoal grey, double-breasted waistcoat. The worsted wool trousers were thin, the fabric starched and pressed to present a perfect crease. His shoes were polished, black leather with a narrow cuff that reached mid-thigh. Satisfied with his look, he donned the last item, a tailored charcoal grey frock coat made of the finest wool, fitted close at the waist and flaring slightly at the hips.

The princess deserves only the best, and in lieu of that, she can have me for now.

With a skip in his step, he bounced out to the garage. His sports car was a very expensive toy, but he worked hard, and since he had no wife to shower with gifts, he had given this one to himself. He saw the car every day that he was in town, but he still stopped to admire it. It was a late-model Mercedes with a high-gloss, candy-apple red finish. The coup ran on steam packs, but could also be propelled by directed Abyrinth. The low profile at the front and the polished brass steam circuits at the back gave it a very futuristic look.

Jumping in, he gunned the accelerator and roared off the property and onto the roads that led to the highway. Once on the main thoroughfare, he was able to go at speeds that would make most drivers tremble in fear.

The Sobieski estate was not too far from the palace, and he made it in record time. He didn't need to drive like a bat out of hell, but that was the way he lived his life.

Pulling up to the front steps, he was met by guards at the front door who allowed him in, where a footman ran off to notify the princess that her date had arrived. He was ushered to a waiting room located off the main foyer.

What the hell is that racket? There was the sound of a party and loud music coming from one of the smaller ballrooms down the main corridor. He'd been to the palace with his father on a few occasions, so he somewhat knew his way around. He didn't have to be sneaky; half a dozen voices were coming from the room down the hall on the left, and they were shouting and laughing at the top of their voices. When he reached the door, he stood still, silent, watching.

He knew two of the three guys, and none of the women. There was the rich kid, Józef Sapieha, the future king, Stanisław Poniatowski, and some other twenty-something man who looked vaguely familiar. He could tell that the four ladies in the room were not wielders or channelers because they were all topless, and they had no brands on their backs. Empty wine and whiskey bottles and clothes littered the floor and furniture. He stood there watching the fun and games when he felt a hand on his shoulder.

"Getting any ideas, watching my brother and his friends?"

Krystian backed away from the open door, taking Jadwiga with him. "It does look like they're having a good time."

"You want to join them? My brother likes you. I'm sure they'll welcome you to the party."

He looked her over from head to toe, then back again. With a wry smile, he whispered, "I didn't come over to play games with boys. I have an engagement with a vibrant, enticing woman."

She tried to smile coyly, but it came out more seductive than shy. She took his hand and led him to the door. He let her walk a step ahead so he could inspect her one more time. Her silver wrap dress fit like a second skin, hinting at cleavage and ending a few inches above the knee. Her long blonde hair was full and almost reached her ample derriere. She was a daughter; daughters didn't carry on the family name, and he was the second son of a prominent family. It might work, he thought.

Outside, he held the door for her, then got in the driver's side. Pushing his energy into the drive system, he got the car to coast noiselessly down the drive and out the gate. He gave her the occasional glance before returning his eyes to the road.

"Where are we going?"

"That way," he said, pointing in the direction they were traveling.

"No hints?" She pretended to be disappointed, her slight grin giving her away. "What if I don't like where we're going?"

"No chance of that, Princess."

They drove in silence for a few minutes, both of them taking in the beauty of Warszawa at night. The shining lights, the stunning architecture.

Soon they came to the Gnojna Góra, the view terrace near Old Town. She got out before he could get her door, so they met at the boot. He opened it to reveal an actual wicker basket and a large, fluffy-looking blanket. Scooping up the items, he took her hand and led her down a trail to an open spot where they could see both the Vistula River and the city skyline.

"You're a man of means going out with a woman of even greater means, and you take me on a date that costs you nothing? A high-risk strategy."

"A high-risk strategy would be taking you rock climbing or skiing. Would spending a small fortune impress you?" He smiled the smile of a man who already knew the answer to his question.

"No." She helped him spread the blanket, then he opened the basket and began removing the contents. Two bottles of wine, sandwiches, fresh fruit, cheese, and sweet bread.

"Two bottles of wine? Trying to get me drunk?"

"Of course. I'll drink a little myself," he said, uncorking a bottle.

She was shocked when he almost put the bottle to his lips to drink. Laughing, he pulled out two wine glasses and poured each of them a substantial amount of a dark red. He pulled out paper plates and divided a large sandwich, giving each of them a half. The sandwich was a work of art. The thick slices of artisan sourdough were golden and crisp at the edges, soft in the center, and lightly brushed with garlic butter. The smell that hit first was the smoky, crisp bacon, cut in thick slices and topped with grilled zucchini ribbons, caramelized red onions, bright red tomato slices, and a handful of fresh spinach and avocado slices. Over it was drizzled a generous smear of roasted garlic aioli.

"That's one hell of a sandwich, Lord Sobieski. Did you make this for me?"

Laughing, he corrected, "First off, it's for us, and no, in what world am I making a sandwich like this?" He gestured that she should take a bite. "I can fix that car over there, but I can't fix a sandwich."

They ate and chatted, enjoying their repast and each other's company.

"So, you hate my sister?"

She looked at him, surprised by the change of mood. "Hate is a strong word." She thought for a moment or two. "If I'm being honest—and you deserve that—I guess I envy her." This surprised Krystian. "She's still a child, but her body is amazing, pretty face, nice hair, not completely terrible to talk to, but the brand! My brand is cool. I can become a ghost, pass through walls, and not get shot. All very cool stuff. But her powers are probably the strongest in Polska. I appreciate her saving everyone at her ball, but being able to siphon all the Abyrinth from those around her? If she did that to me while I was phasing through a wall? Dead!"

"She got lucky. Mine is ok, but there's so much more to life than using powers that the vast majority of our countrymen can't have. I haven't used my powers all day."

"Neither have I. Everyone is so tense right now. Father is meeting with foreign envoys almost daily, trying to put together an alliance to counter Rus aggression. For me, a girl? Not much is expected, so I meet those expectations." She ran her fingers down his arm, feeling the strong body beneath. "Are you going to fight?"

"Whether I want to or not, it's expected of me. I'm already technically in the army. I fear the need to be full-time in the service is coming soon. Brother and I train daily, getting strong and sharpening our sword skills and our boxing and grappling."

"Grappling? Two sweaty men rolling around on the ground? Sounds delightful." Her smile was far from innocent.

"I could show you a few moves," he offered. Leaning over, their lips met, and he kissed her, more with hunger than romantic passion. He wanted to kiss a beautiful woman, and she was right in front of him. They continued kissing, his hand feeling the bare skin of her arms and upper back. She melted into his touch, letting pleasure soak into her being. Eventually, they came up for air. "Do you think it's weird that you and I are… well, and that your brother might eventually marry my sister?"

"What do you think we are…?" she asked.

Sitting up, he pulled off his jacket and laid it aside, then his vest and cravat, never breaking eye contact. "Let's not catalog it or give a name we might regret later. I plan to get you out of that dress and then find out how compatible we are." His look was that of the wolf, appraising the flavor of a sheep just before taking the first bite.

"You're going to show me some wrestling moves?"

"Not the same ones I use with my brother, but yes."

# Chapter 15

A message arrived for me the day after my date. It was a folded leather envelope with a heavy wax seal. Usually, a signet ring would have been pressed into the wax, providing a clue to its origin. The seal on the message was blank, and I couldn't imagine who it might be from. I was alone in the library, so I broke the seal and began reading.

*Jafra—*

*News of the display at your ball is country-wide, if not world-wide, by now. What an incredible show of power. Even though I've read about the strength of the prime brands, it still amazes me what you can do.*

*Now that your secret is out, you will be sought out, not only by suitors and sycophants, but by those who would try to harm or control you. Just as I asked you to help me find the other members of your Triumvirate, they may now be looking for you as well. Neither of us knows if they are good and kind people like yourself. They might be ne'er-do-wells or outright villains.*

*The attack on your Ascension Ball was the most recent and audacious assault on our way of life. Trust me, this is only the beginning; the raids will continue and become more numerous. My sources tell me that the Rus are already massing their forces to march on Polska. The nobles have better information, but the ordinary people have no idea how close an invasion is. Only by unleashing the power of the stones can we hope to match them. Rus is five times our size, and they have many hundreds of wielders. Meet me at the air races this Sunday. If you agree that we need to do everything possible to push back the invaders, I would like to ask you to join our organization covertly. I won't pressure you, but know that we desperately need your help. Come alone. We'll be in a public place, and you will be as safe as possible.*

*Hedwig*

She couldn't possibly know what I saw in my trials. I didn't tell anyone about my treatment at the Rus lord's hands. More importantly, they were on the verge of invading my country. If they invaded, they would be attacking here, at the capital. With all of the personal things going on in my life, I hadn't thought too carefully about the rash of terrorist attacks. After my ball, I couldn't avoid it.

She was right. I could feel it in my soul. The Rus were coming, and probably sooner than later. She was also right about our chances. Rus is so much larger than my beloved Polska. It was only natural that they would have ten times our number of wielders. We would need some unfair advantage. If we had all three of the prime brands, they might turn the tide of battle.

I wasn't sure who to trust. The king and all his lords, including my father, were hiding the secret of the century, that these fantastic powers we had were not due to our bloodlines, but because we denied access to the masses.

I understood why they might have restricted access to the stones. The blanks and even the channelers couldn't be trusted with some of the abilities that we nobles wielded. If everyone won the lottery, there would be widespread chaos. Maybe we were restricting who could attain powers to protect the masses from themselves.

There was much truth in what Hedwig said, but I still didn't fully trust her. She saved me from kidnappers, but I was still wary of her. I went back and forth, but ultimately decided to meet.

It was the Wednesday after the ball, and a bouquet arrived with a card for me. Calling it a bouquet was truly not doing it justice. The crystal vase that it came in was as large as a mixing bowl, and the variety was insane. There were Black Baccara roses, whose deep crimson, velvety petals were almost black. In contrast, there were white peonies with lush blooms and a heavenly scent, symbolizing pure intentions. Interspersed among the blooms were blue delphiniums. The royal blue was calming, while the white orchid sprays and delicate lily of the valley rounded out the presentation, giving it a regal signature.

It must have been from Stanisław. A signal that he did not mind my withholding my kiss until we knew each other better. I had wanted to kiss him, and part of me regretted not giving in to my animal urges. His smell, the thick golden hair, how he was so tall and firm like an athlete... Damn you, Auntie! I would not have objected to being held in those strong arms, held against his broad, muscular chest.

I picked up the card with great anticipation. There was a sealed note clipped to a wooden rod sticking in the bundle of stems. The outside had my name, Lady Jafra Sobieski, in elegant calligraphy.

The seal was not immediately familiar to me, and that surprised me. I, of course, knew the king's seal, which would be the same as his son's.

I broke the seal and unfolded the card. The script inside was also done in perfect handwriting, most likely dictated to a woman, as men rarely wrote so perfectly.

Needless to say, I wasn't expecting to hear from the Bohemian. I thought he would steal a kiss and be happy with his conquest. He spoke about wanting me, but every girl has been fed honeyed words by a lecherous older man. I had no intention of falling for flattery, and I was not so naive that my knees would get weak at a man's touch.

I thought about his touch. That evening, I had danced with two dozen men, each of them allowing daylight between us. The Bohemian held me tightly, pressing his powerful frame to mine. His hand held my waist tight; it was strong and warm, and I could feel it even through my ball gown. My breasts were pressed against his chest, and his mouth was near my ear. His breath had been hot and yet… sweet-smelling. His kiss was rushed, but it had been my first, and despite telling

Stanisław that it didn't count, it had shocked and thrilled me. I close my eyes and let my memories drift back to those ten seconds of his mouth on mine, his tongue on my lips, dipping inside to touch my tongue. At the time, I had been stunned into immobility, but each time I relived it, I felt a chill that started in my throat, flowed like hot honey through my chest, and pooled in my loins.

My mother came into the drawing room and gasped at the size and beauty of the flowers. Even when we were at home, neither entertaining nor planning to go out, she was dressed exquisitely. As usual, she wore a floor-length white dress with lace on the bodice and wide sleeves. I'm not sure why she put on her everyday diamonds, but she was always ready to go out at a moment's notice.

"Oh, my!" she said. "These are beautiful! Who are they from, dear?"

"Prince Jaroslav Záhoř." I held up the card.

"What a coincidence," she replied. "I got flowers from Queen Seraphina Záhoř." She ran her eyes over my bouquet again. "Though not as grand as these."

"The Queen of Bohemia sent you flowers?" Of course, that was not a coincidence. "I assume there was a letter?"

"As a matter of fact, there was!" Her display of surprise was not even a little bit convincing.

"Please enlighten me, Mother. I assume you sought me out?"

"As you know, I've been in talks with most of the better families in Polska. I am still waiting for a reply from our queen, when I got a lovely bouquet and letter from Queen

Záhoř of Bohemia. I hadn't yet spoken with any of the royalty in our neighboring counties, but Bohemia is right on our western border. Not too far." She smiled innocently.

"What is she proposing?" As if I didn't already know.

"This is the first year for them; they are sponsoring a ship in the airship races this Sunday. She has a son—"

"We've met."

"Everyone is going anyway. Our ship is favored to win, or at least, that's what your father says." She gave me the sweetest smile. My mother was quite the charmer. "She thought that you and…"

"Jaroslav," I supplied.

"Yes, that you and Jaroslav could sit for tea in their private box and really get to know one another."

Her approaching me was a courtesy. I knew the way these things went, and the date had already been set in stone. If I were to refuse this meeting, I would see the other side of my mother that was generally reserved for the boys.

"He's the boy who kissed me before running off to fight the invaders."

"I know." She looked truly regretful. "Everyone saw."

"That was my very first kiss. I wanted to save it for someone special. Someone like Stanisław." I'm sure that my face took on that dreamy quality that I sometimes got when I got lost in my fantasies.

"I've yet to hear back from the queen, and each passing day makes the match less likely. Your aunt said that you were a perfect lady, and towards the end of the night, when the prince tried to kiss you, you rightly rebuffed him. You did the proper thing, but men can be very impulsive, very sensitive. If he was looking for a lover instead of a wife, he approached the wrong girl!"

"Since I will be there anyway, I will meet with this foreign prince. I just hope he can keep his hands to himself."


I not only trained with swords, but I also asked my brothers to teach me to shoot. More than anyone around me, I knew that war was coming. My power was ridiculously strong, but I needed to be able to protect myself, even if I wasn't able to manipulate Abyrinth. I didn't want to have a weak body, so when the boys went running, I would join them. At first, I couldn't keep up with them, not even my little brother Jurek. They had been training for a long, long time, and on my first day, I went about a mile before falling to the ground, gasping for air. Every day, I joined them early in the morning while it was still cool, and we ran. I improved each day, but I knew it would take months before I would be able to match their pace.

I had spent way too much time learning stances and holding my sword out at arm's length. They didn't look too heavy when my brothers were swinging them around, but when you stand straight and hold a sword out, it gets heavy very quickly. Eventually, they allowed Jurek to start sparring with me. We moved so slowly that it seemed comical, but they all told me it was necessary to build proper technique and muscle memory.

Between running and training, I felt tired all the time. I found myself eating more than usual and actually losing weight. I thought I looked pretty good before, but the fat reduction and the increase in muscle were giving my curves less of a soft look and more of an angular and tight appearance.

"Looking good, little sister," Krystian said. I was crossing swords with Jurek. He had been told by Mother to avoid leaving bruises and welts on my head and shoulders, as I had a date the next day. She could heal even grievous wounds, but if I were to get a bruise on my face, there still might be a yellow stain for a day or two, and that was not attractive to anyone.

"Thanks, big brother. Are you working with the race team?"

"Unfortunately, no. My military responsibilities have been intense lately, and I don't have time to devote to hobbies like racing. I am planning to take a date to the Sky Leviathan Derby."

"Oh? Who's the lucky girl?"

"I'm going with Anna," he said casually.

"Anna Ostrogski? My friend Anna?" I did not see that coming.

"You have hot friends. I prefer girls who are a few years younger and from a good family."

"Well, don't get pervy with her. She and Elżbieta are a package deal. If you scare her away, I will lose both as friends, and if that happens, I will literally murder you!"

"I'll try, but I'm pretty irresistible. If she starts kissing me and rubbing against me… I'm hardly to blame." He waved a long lock of hair away from his eyes.

"I've warned you. Don't lose me any friends!"

"As a second son, I don't have the benefit of getting set up on dates. You're going on your second date at the races, and it will be with your second prince. Apparently, there aren't any kings available."

I was done for the day and made to stomp off. "Don't fuck this up!" I yelled as I walked to the house.

# Chapter 16

As usual, I traveled with my parents, and for an event like this, we brought Jurek and my younger sister, Dominika. She was eleven and looked like a much smaller version of our mother. She was under five feet tall and weighed about eighty pounds. She was yet to blossom, and that was fine with everyone. Jurek was starting to realize that girls existed, and I was in the prime of female health and beauty.

We took the larger limousine to the racetrack, with enough room for the whole family, the driver, and a dozen guards. I was accustomed to traveling with my two men, but after the recent violence, everyone had tightened their security measures.

The race field was located to the north of the city, where there was ample room to fly without conflicting with regular air traffic. An enormous oval stadium, once used for many sporting events, including the football championships a few years ago, was now configured for the air races. In the open area in the center, there were a dozen towers that reached up two hundred and fifty feet in the air. Moored to each was an airship that was sponsored by either a noble family or some giant corporation. Everyone, including us, was dressed in their Sunday finest. We were escorted by our security detail to our private box located at the top of the large bowl, directly in the back.

Bulletproof glass could be slid into place, but today we opted for open air. It was nearly perfect weather, not a cloud in the sky. Mother wore white, but I wore a mid-length, light green and white floral print dress, with spaghetti straps and a corset. Dominika wore a poofy pink dress and pink patent leather shoes. We all wore wide-brimmed round hats, their style patterned after the Kentucky Derby over in the American colonies.

"Mother, should I place a bet on the race?" I asked. Everyone in the stands was placing wagers, guessing which ship would be the fastest over the course. Men were eating large, greasy sandwiches with peppers and onions falling out of them. They swilled dark beers and smoked fat, stinky cigars. The nobility sat in their private boxes, but the channelers and the blanks filled the stands and were having the time of their lives.

"We can't bet on the race. We have a ship, and that would be against race regulations."

They only had the big race once a year, and now that I was an adult, I wanted to try it all. I was ready to smoke, drink, and lose money on an ill-thought-out wager. I was ready to repel this prince if he tried to grab and kiss me again. I would bend his nose, even if it did cause an international incident. I didn't usually get my entertainment from sports and other manly pursuits, but I was excited to see our ship, the Smok Mazowiecki, or Mazovian Dragon. When they announced the countdown to the preliminary sprint races, I took my seat with the other ladies to sip wine and daintily eat from a cheese and fruit plate.

The ships above our heads were moored at the lower docks, only fifty feet in the air. They were no bigger than our limousine and only had room for the pilot. The rest was engine. Our ship was racing in the main attraction, so for the half dozen preliminary races, we were spectators like everyone else.

A single channeler piloted each ship; eight of them were men, and to my surprise, four were women. I decided to support my fellow women and chose ship number seven as my favorite. Her craft was sleek, unlike the car we came in. It was aerodynamic, with the front forming a pointed cone, and the windscreen angled sharply to allow air to flow over the top.

Most airships relied solely on the power of the channeler to both lift and fly forward. As such, most airships were blunt, shaped like a flattened potato, but old number seven had wings like a bird, extending perpendicular to the line of the craft. I read in the program that she claimed the wings added lift, freeing up much of the energy she would have used and allowing her to put more into forward propulsion. The ship had smaller wings in the back for turning, and a fin like a shark at the very rear. The ship looked ridiculous, but I placed a bet for a hundred złoty from my birthday money, since I could afford to lose it.

When I got back to our box where Mother was waiting for me, her good humor was gone. "Where have you been, Jafra?"

"I had to visit the ladies," I replied.

"These gentlemen," she explained, indicating to well-armed men in Bohemian livery, "have come to escort you to the prince's box. Aunt Bronisława will, of course, go with you."

"Alright," I said, seeing the severe woman standing behind the guards. "Let's go!"

We went about half a dozen suites to the right of ours, passing the owner of Polska Airwerx, a very affluent family. We passed the Ostrogski family suite, and Elżbieta waved, but Anna was huddled in the corner with Krystian, and they didn't notice me.

The king's box was quite large, almost double the size of our family's. The king was chatting with some men I didn't know, and the queen was having tea and visiting with a flock of ladies. Stanisław was there with five or six other boys. They were having a grand old time, each of them with a large beer stein in their hands. I hoped that I might make it past them without being noticed, but no such luck. The prince caught sight of me and did a double-take. He wasn't so ill-bred as to call out, but the look on his face was a mixture of shock, disbelief, and annoyance. I pretended not to notice them and continued to the next box, where Jaroslav, his mother, and a handful of other people were preparing for the race. The guards stayed at the doorway as I entered.

Jaroslav stood and took my hand as I carefully crossed the threshold. The queen rose as well and held out her hand for me to take.

"Thank you for accepting our invitation." He looked at his mother sideways, like he wanted credit for saying it correctly. "I would like to introduce you to my mother, Queen of Bohemia, Seraphina Záhoř. Father had other obligations and couldn't be present today."

I looked at Jaroslav, and I could barely recognize him. He had the same height, the same musculature, and he was tanned from being outside, but there were differences from the man I had met at my ball. The evening we had met, his hair had been white as snow; now it was the rich brown color of coffee beans. The only other change was the way he carried himself. At the ball, he was suave and supremely confident. The man who now kissed my hand was reserved, cultured, and self-effacing.

I was confused and wanted some answers, but I had to sit for an interview with his mother first. She was on the plump side, with rosy cheeks and bright grey eyes. Everything about her was rounded: her cheeks, chin, nose, and body. She wore an expensive silk dress that downplayed her flaws, giving her a lovely overall appearance. She exuded charm and care, as any mother should, and I instantly found her to be delightful.

As much as I enjoyed speaking with her, it was most certainly an interrogation. I detailed my plans to attend university; we talked about my family and their holdings; and, lastly, we discussed my brand. It had become an open secret that I could see and manipulate Abyrinth. She asked many questions I could only partially answer. In the end, she seemed satisfied.

"Dear, I apologize for so many questions, but Jaroslav was quite taken with you, and your mother seems so pleasant, but nothing can replace a conversation between two people. I would be remiss if I didn't thank you for saving my son's life. Not only is he the heir to our throne, but he is a good and kind son. We task him with so much in the defense of Bohemia and our citizens. He never complains or hints that he is unwilling to make any sacrifices. I have already monopolized too much of your time. Please sit with Jaroslav; the race is about to begin."

I bowed respectfully. "Thank you, Your Grace."

I took the seat near Jaroslav. He had stood far enough away so it would not appear as if he were eavesdropping. With a nervous smile, he sat next to me. We sat quietly for almost a minute. A long, uncomfortable minute.

"Did you place any wager on any of the races?" I asked, breaking the silence.

"No… Jafra. I'm not really a betting man. I guess I hate the idea of losing money more than I would enjoy the thrill of winning it."

"Oh! They're starting!" I pointed at the countdown clock. The old clock had brass hands that were ticking down towards zero. Steam hissed from the pipes, and gears were visible through the face of the device.

When the clock hand hit zero, a steam whistle sounded, a loud, piercing blast that echoed throughout the stadium. Airships were generally slow to start, even the smaller ones. The dozen ships lurched away from the mooring stands, slowly picking up speed as their momentum built. I saw that number seven pulled ahead, its wings adding lift and making it easier for the driver to create forward motion. She separated from the pack and began to leave them behind. After a couple of hundred yards, she was zooming down the course at twice the speed of the others. She reached the far end of the oval and turned left, following the track and heading back to the stands where tens of thousands were watching the spectacle. She crossed the halfway point just as the other ships were coming at it from the start line.

I turned to the prince. "How many circuits do they make?"

"Five. At this rate, number seven will finish, and the others will only be on lap two or three."

He was astute. I guessed the same, and it was happening before our eyes. I could see the weaves of energy both lifting and propelling the other ships forward. Number seven only had energy, pushing it through the sky. When she passed our box, she was close enough that I could see the energy wasn't flowing over and under the surface of the long, rounded wings. I could tell that no energy was required to keep it aloft; the air was pushing up on the wings, providing lift. Mentally, I was already counting my money.

Number seven was starting its third circuit, only the second circuit for the rest of the flyers. That's when things got ugly. A dull, pewter-colored ship, shaped like a cucumber, passed above her left wing as she was on the right. The ship, number four, dropped abruptly, and its weight broke off the left wing, snapping it in half like a cracker. The other wing still provided lift, and number seven began to corkscrew through the air. She began to reduce her altitude until she was right side up a few feet off the ground and let the ship fall the rest of the way.

The crowd was up in arms, including me. I yelled about the unfairness of it all, and not just because I lost my bet. Number four was disqualified, and after what now seemed like an eternity, number eleven was the eventual winner. There was a loud chorus of boos as the trophy was awarded.

"Boo!" I yelled, not caring how I looked.

"An unfortunate ending," Jaroslav said, smiling at me with genuine amusement.

"Damn cheater! She was going to win!"

"Giving the ship a lifting surface was genius. I would bet anything that it becomes the standard overnight."

"I wouldn't bet on it. I just lost my birthday money!"

"Betting? I doubt your mother would approve." His smile this time was wide and unabashed.

He was different than the night before, but still, I found him to be intriguing. It was going to take the better part of an hour for the larger craft to jockey into position, so we took the opportunity to really talk. He asked me about myself, including my school, family, interests, and travel experiences. He was a good listener and never once tried to cut in with his own stories. Finally, I had to pry some out of him. He'd graduated a few years ago and attended university for two years before having to drop out to protect the realm. He was young and had been in the service of the Bohemian special forces unit, the Vlci Temna, or Wolves of the Dark.

"That sounds dangerous," I said. He seemed so meek; it was hard to believe he was such a badass.

"Yes, it's pretty dangerous. I've been wounded a couple of times. Thankfully, nothing too serious." There was no boasting in his manner. He had sacrificed a life of leisure, as my brothers had, to be at the forefront of his country's defense. The next race was about to begin, and I had to know something. The one thing that had been driving me crazy ever since entering his family's luxury suite.

"I have been having a lovely time, and I don't want to be rude…"

"But…"

"You seem like a very different person from the one I met at the ball." I stared into his eyes to see if there would be a flash of anger, but he gave more of a self-conscious expression. "You dyed your hair. Don't get me wrong, I like it both ways!"

"I didn't dye my hair," he said flatly.

"And you seem… what's a delicate way that I can say this? More gentlemanly?"

"It's part of my brand. I bear the Trojvlk."

We had been speaking Polish this whole time. "I'm sorry, my knowledge of Bohemian is very limited."

"It refers to three wolves. My power cycles me between three phases, one of which is as I am today. This is how I've been since birth. The person you met at your ball is my intermediate phase. He knows what I know, he is… a part of me, but he has his own personality."

"He says and does things that you want to do, but are too controlled to do?"

This made him blush a dark red. "I guess that's a fair statement."

"What about your third state? What is that?

His face became hard, and he took on a somber countenance. "You don't want to know about that. The third wolf is the one I save for my enemies." He looked at me, his gaze passing through me and stretching back for a thousand miles. "And for those I care about. Those I am pledged to protect." We sat in silence for what felt like an eternity.

"Your middle state is a bit aggressive. Are you able to control it?"

"Aggressive, yes. I like to think of him as honest." He looked me in the eyes for the first time since going down this road. "I've liked you since the first time I saw you. We are the same person after all. What he sees, I see, and after talking with you, I know so much more. He saw your face, which, like Helen's, could launch a thousand ships. He saw the figure, which even under layers and layers of silk and lace, and thought you were incredible." His eyes took the quickest of scans. "Yes, you have an incredible figure."

I leaned in to avoid my aunt or his mother hearing. "So is that all I am? Large breasts, long legs?" I asked, knowing that I was putting him on the spot.

"Well, you have a near-perfect behind, if we're being honest." He looked at me with a twinkle in his eye.

"Near-perfect?" I feigned outrage.

"I haven't seen it, and you ladies wear more layers than an onion." He was doing well, and we both knew it. He soldiered on. "You're funny, you have a sense of humor. I like that in anyone, but especially in you. I know you're smart. Mother pulled your school records. Funny how easy it is for a queen to get information. You bet on air races." He paused. "You are learning to fight with sword and pistol?"

"We both know which way the wind blows. Rus has been sending raiding parties into Polska for the last year. I wouldn't be surprised if they were doing it to test our defenses."

He didn't hesitate. "They are. Not just at your party, I've spilled Rus blood."

"I threw some men over the side." He was shocked at the news. "They were attacking Mother and me, and pushing them was child's play compared to pushing their ships over the edge of the deck."

"I see in you a woman who is willing to risk everything, including her life, to perform her duty to her house and her country. Many of us nobles pay lip service to such ideals, but your brothers are constantly risking their lives to protect your people. Knowing that you risk your station in life and the comforts that it provides for a life of service? That means a great deal to me."

"I defended myself, my mother, and the people who were attacked the air cruiser, but I don't plan to go off to war. I'm a girl, and I don't know anything about war. I wish that no one had to go to war. Not my brothers, not my countrymen… and not you either. You're too young to be tasked with risking your life and killing men."

"I hope that they don't call on you to join the army, but we may all have to decide what to do, and very soon. Some will flee, the old, the children, many of the women. As they should. Many others will either join the military voluntarily, and when your king runs out of new recruits, he'll draft the unwilling. I pray that doesn't include you. I'm growing quite fond of you."

We sat looking at each other for what felt like the longest minute of my life. I felt we had connected in a meaningful way. We had gone beyond the small talk of a first date and gotten to the really important things.

"I'm still not going to let you kiss me," I said, a slight smile on my blood-red lips.

He smiled. "I wasn't going to try. I'm not that guy. Right now."

The horn sounded to announce the countdown for the main attraction. Six heavy ships were lined up, ready to blaze a trail to victory for their house or corporate sponsor. The Mazovian Dragon was a large ship with a steel frame and treated canvas panels, with bright orange and red flames painted from stem to stern. There was a dragon's head cast in steel and coated in bronze as the masthead. She was twenty feet wide and forty feet long. Two sets of steam-powered propellers, located equidistant on the ship's long axis, held her aloft, while side-mounted steam props on either side moved her forward. These large yachts could sail by Abyrinth, and a crew of four channelers was always on duty to take over, but there was a certain romance to watching these steaming tea kettles amble through the sky.

"So, they fly to Radom and back? One lap and whoever crosses the finish line wins?" he asked.

"Yes. Once they get out of sight, we have nothing to do for over an hour until they get back."

"I'm sorry, but that sounds rather boring."

"It is." I smiled. "It gives everyone time to place their bets, have some drinks, and even order a three-course meal for the private suite owners. Yours should be arriving within minutes." My smile widened. He was an actual prince, but he had very little experience being rich and pampered. "I should be getting back to my parents. I eat every dinner with them, and my younger siblings are probably driving them crazy by now."

I saw some of the light go out of him, but he maintained his composure.

"Of course. I don't want to show my hand too much, but I want to spend even more time with you." He took my hand and kissed the fingers with his eyes averted.

"I'll tell my mother of your desires, and of my... agreement."

He looked up with a warm smile. He was swarthier than the men in my family, more so than most of the nobles in Polska. Still, the dimple in his left cheek, the smile lines that framed his soft lips, and that radiant grin only made him all the more appealing. I could tell that he wanted to pull me in for a hug; the elated energy around him was evident, even without my power, but Auntie was hovering now, and the date was officially over. I paused to offer my regards to the queen, and then we returned to where my family was watching the races.

When we passed the Poniatowski's box, Stanisław was still there with his friend, but now they were joined by several young ladies. I didn't want to stare or even be seen to look in that direction, but I was working my peripheral vision to its utmost. I didn't recognize any of them, and then it struck me. There was no power signature around them. Any wielder or even a channeler will have a halo of power on the surface of their skin and in the air near them. The girls they were entertaining were blanks. No doubt they would be quite grateful to be able to watch the races in such luxury. How would they express that gratitude? I could speculate, but it was not any of my business. Food for thought.

"How was it, dear?"

"Lovely, Mother. I had the best time."

# Chapter 17

I needed to visit the ladies' room, so I excused myself and headed away from the private suites and back away from the track. My guards walked a few steps behind, then waited outside while I went in to refresh. As I sat, I thought about how charming the Bohemian had been, and how my own prince might be engaging in lewd behavior, even now. I had so many emotions swirling around, but the one that eventually won out was… anger. That damn cheater made me lose one hundred złoty!

I heard a knock on the partition between toilet stalls. I thought it queer, but decided to ignore it. I came again, two distinct knocks.

"Jafra." It was not a question. I knew the voice.

"Hedwig?"

"I'm glad you could make it." There was a long pause. "I realize that you have little time before your men think you are in trouble and come storming in here. Have you considered my offer?"

"To join your revolution? To be part of your secret cabal?"

"Like a snowball rolling down a mountain, the rate at which the developments I told you about will occur is increasing. Attacks like the one at your ball will become more frequent. Bloodier. My coterie seeks out the prime brands to give us the edge over the Rus. When we have that level of power, we can seize control of the stones and open up their power for everyone."

"You haven't been forthcoming with me," I replied. I had been thinking about this a lot lately. "I am supposed to help you find the other primes, but you claim that you don't know what they are?" She was silent, probably thinking up a convincing lie. "Tell me what they are, or I think we're done. Forever."

This time, she waited even longer.

"We have very limited information on them. They do not appear in the official records, but the stone in Germania has all of the brands etched into a plate of some unknown metal. The plaque is affixed to the back of the cave, and three brands sit highest of all. Yours, the Abyrinth Embermark, is one of them; it represents the control of energy. The second one is called Chronovore Emberrift. The design is of a clock, flanked by gears, all suspended over wild tendrils of power. We know that it has something to do with time, maybe similar to your brother's Chronoburst. The last one is called Omniport Gatefold. It depicts an arch, radiating lines in every direction, and again, suspended over tendrils of power."

"I know that my brand is unique and very powerful, but there are two other brands out there with fantastic power? It seems very hard to believe. How can I believe you're not making this all up? To what end, I can't begin to imagine."

"You can do your own research. Ask someone who will have access to knowledge that even most nobles are not privy to. Your father might know. The king would for sure. There might be plaques in every chamber where the stones are. Just be careful. If you ask too many questions, reveal even a hint of what I've told you just now, you will be putting yourself in jeopardy."

"I'll ask a few people I know, very cautiously. If I come up with nothing, I hope to never see you again."

"You'd be surprised at the number of secrets that are being held by those in power. Great men will go to any lengths to preserve their power."

# Chapter 18

It was past midnight when Krystian returned home. Recently, both of my older brothers started going on missions, sometimes for a week at a time. We never knew where the battle was until they got back, and sometimes, not even then.

Stef was with him, and they were both pretty fucked up. They were bleeding from multiple wounds, and a few looked serious. They could have gone to a hospital, but Mother's healing was exponentially superior to any blank medical facility.

"You've looked better," I said to the boys. "I'll get Mother."

As she was tending to their various injuries, Father poured each of them a drink and made one for himself.

"I would like one, Father," I said to everyone's astonishment. They sat around the kitchen table as they had on several occasions that I could remember, getting treatment from Mother and giving Father the details of what happened out in the field. "I'm old enough. And before you try to send me out of the room, I'll remind you that I'm an adult now, with a damn powerful brand."

"Language!" Mother said, not looking up.

"Sorry, Mother."

"She's right. After tonight, I'm not convinced that we can shield anyone from what's coming."

I was in shock. I had always been closest to Krystian, but it was Stefek who was advocating for me. Perhaps he saw my dedication to learning how to fight and defend myself, and that is what swayed him.

"Alright," Krystian said, "but let me tell the story. You suck at storytelling."

"You do, dear," Mother said as she worked on a bullet hole in Stefek's arm.

Father handed me a straight whiskey in a clear, lead crystal tumbler. Knowing my father, it was the best of the best, but it burned my mouth, blazed its way down my throat, and simmered in my stomach. They all looked at me expectantly, my brothers trying—and failing—to conceal their amusement.

"Smooth," I gasped.

"Anyway, Stef and I were informed that there was an active incursion on the Biała Ruś border. Three hundred blanks and an unknown number of channelers. We practically ran to the base and got the battalion geared up. We had twenty mechs, ten tanks, and some artillery pieces." He winced as Mother twisted and turned his limbs, looking for more holes.

"Get to the part!" Stef said before downing his drink.

"Ok, skip ahead. We made our way to the border across from Brest as quickly as possible. That's where they were leaking across. When we got there, all of the smaller villages had been leveled. Bodies littered the ground, men, women, and even children. I saw a young girl, maybe a year younger than Dominika. It was hard to tell her exact age because Rus boots had crushed her head." The memory visibly shook him. "They had tanks. That was a first. Every incursion on our soil, including the one at your ball, had been just a group of radicals and their transportation. This time, they had armored personnel carriers, six tanks, and a few mechs."

This was a different story than their usual interceptions. From Milka's visions and my trial, I should have expected that things would escalate.

"They saw us before we saw them. When we arrived at the village, shots rang out, and our driver was killed before we even knew we were in the combat zone. A few more shots, then all hell broke loose. Stef and I were both yelling to have the men take cover, but when they brought out the big guns, things went south quickly."

Stef had belted another shot of whiskey before adding to the story. "One of our personnel carriers rounded a corner and took a point-blank round from one of their tanks. It penetrated, and once inside, ricocheted around the interior, liquifying everyone inside."

Krystian took back over. "I called Stef to get me over there. He held my hand, and we were able to time jump for long enough that I could reach the tank. It's hard to warp metal that thick, but I was able to pinch the end of the tank's main gun barrel. Just a fraction, but enough to cause their next round to explode inside the barrel."

"The tanks rolled in minutes after our troop transports were on the scene," Stef said. He accepted a sandwich from Mother and took a big bite. Through a mouth full of food, he went on with the story. "I ordered the tanks to focus on one of their tanks at a time, and I sent a couple around the corner to attempt a flanking maneuver. I had four steam-Panzers hammering their lead T-47 Rasputin. They bounced shells off of each other for minutes until my lead Panzer was able to attack from behind. A direct hit to the cooling manifold on the back side, and she was dead in the water."

The tanks were too heavy to run on Abyrinth only, and most were new-wave steam-powered. The Rus tanks had tracks that were sloped at the rear and ran around a large front axle. The main gun fired a myriad of specialized rounds. The turret could swivel three hundred and sixty degrees, targeting enemies well over a mile away, but accurately for three-quarters of a mile.

"I neutralized the main gun on another tank, but I didn't see the mech coming." Mechs were armored suits worn by channelers to give them protection and strength. They utilized the new-wave steam, which allowed their hydraulics to be powered using much more compact power sources. Even with this advanced technology, the mechs were twenty feet tall and about fifteen feet wide at the shoulder. The newer ones had large, bulbous bodies, with long arms that looked like steel girders. They usually had small cannons or high-powered machine guns on their shoulders. They were not as heavily armored or armed as the tanks, but they were very versatile.

"Were you wearing your armor?" I asked. I don't know why I was afraid for them. They were home now, alive, if not worse for the confrontation. Most troops these days, including wielders and channelers, wear suits that accentuate their bodies. Metal attachments ran along the arms and legs to increase the wearer's strength, with metal plates to protect joints and vital organs.

"Yes, second mother!" he said, laughing at me. "They don't provide full protection, as you can see. The Rus mechs had machine guns, and I caught a round to the actuator on my left arm. Ripped it apart, and I got shrapnel in the bicep and triceps."

"An inch to either side and it would have torn through the bone, and possibly ripped your arm clean off," Mother scolded as she continued applying her healing ability. I watched as tight weaves of energy passed from her hands to the wounds on her son's arm.

"There were train tracks nearby, so I warped them, turning them into an impassable coil of spikes. Their soldiers weren't able to pass, but the mechs were able to shoot through them and eventually stomp them down. They did nothing to stop the tanks." Stef was finally finished with his sandwich. "I was leading the boys of the fifth, and we ran out to meet the enemy. We took heavy losses, but we were able to push them back and set them on their heels."

"I hate to admit it, but big brother was a force to be reckoned with out there. He bounced from man to man, pushing his sword through their throats and moving to the next. I personally saw him kill a half dozen of the invaders, and from the bodies left behind, I know that he killed over twenty just by himself."

I remember the one time, not too long ago, when I saw my brothers in action. They had always been such sweet boys, but that day, they killed without remorse. As they spoke about their battle earlier, I could picture it all in my head. Stefek used his Chronoburst to perfection, as deftly as a magician or a juggler. His ability with a sword, though, was something to marvel at.

Even if he were a blank, God forbid, he would be a dangerous man. I'd been to some of his matches where nobles and other elite swordsmen would test their skill, and he was always the top performer. He could beat a ranked contender in seconds, and champion-level opponents didn't take much longer to defeat. When I saw him on the streets, fighting for our citizens, he was brutal. Still controlled, measured, but instead of scoring points, he punctured organs, cleaving hearts in twain.

My eyes glazed over as they recounted the day's events. I could see in my mind's eye Stefek disappearing, then reappearing a dozen feet away, his sword point projecting from the back of a dirty Rus' neck. I could imagine him reappearing, standing next to an enemy with his sword pushed up under their armor and enhancements, tearing through heart and lungs, killing a man while plotting his next time jump. Could he kill a score of men? Two score? He was only limited by his energy, and his well of energy was deep.

The energy expended to supply us with our powers was not infinite, and most people never got to the point where it would run dry. Stef said something, and it caught my attention.

"I haven't been drained in a long time. A couple of times in training, I would practice so hard and for so long that I would expend everything. Today was the first time I was in combat and used every scrap of my reserves. I had picked out my next victim, and when I reached for it, it wasn't there."

"That's terrifying," I said. "If you were too far behind their lines, you might not have gotten back to us."

He patted his sword that he'd set on the counter. "I can carve them up, with or without my brand, but it made more sense to pull the blaster. Krys had caught up to me, and together, we shot our way back to our front line."

They talked on and on for a while, telling every gruesome detail of the battle. When they began winding down, I was starting to feel queasy, and the whiskey didn't help any. So much blood, so much death. They didn't seem all that bothered by what they had done, even though I completely agreed that it had been necessary. Father was living vicariously through his sons, getting excited with each description of tanks exploding, of mechs being blown to bits. Mother seemed to take it all in stride.

"I'm sorry that you had to go through that," I said, catching them all by surprise.

"What do you mean, Jafra?" Krystian asked.

"You did your duty, you protected the homeland, but this fighting sounds horrible. The men who sent those young boys to attack us are evil. Truly evil. They deserve to have their heads on spikes, and even I would be for that. But how many men, boys really, did you kill today? Some of them were bad too, got what they deserved, I'm sure. But I bet a majority of them were sent, forced to come here to fight us and steal our land so that some Rus warlord can grow richer." At this point, tears filled my eyes and started leaking down my cheeks.

"What is your suggestion, little sister?" Stefek asked, not unkindly.

"I don't have one." They looked at me, and I think they all understood.

Smaller raids continued along our eastern borders with Galacia and Biała Ruś. None were as extensive as the ones my brothers were sent to quash, but they were violent. A dozen men, and sometimes they would have women with them, would cross the border, and when they came upon a small village, they would go house to house. They would wake a family, sleeping in their beds, and do the unspeakable. Men hung from trees in their front yards, and women were brutalized and raped in front of their families before being shot and their bodies left on the ground.

The people were afraid and were demanding protection. Most of the cities in the east were fleeing west. The call for the king to formally declare war was loud and growing in pitch every day. Father was away a lot over the next few weeks, meeting often with the king and the other lords whom he relied on for counsel. My brothers continued to train and, when called on, to rush to the border to repel invaders.

# Chapter 19

Over time, I continued to train in sword and pistol, trying to learn as quickly as possible before the inevitable invasion. I was weak at the sword; it took more physical strength than I was capable of, at least as strong as I was at that time.

I was surprised that I was a natural with a pistol. A rifle was too heavy and awkward for me, but a pistol was lighter and easier to aim. I was fair from a distance, and deadly within fifty feet. I continued training with my brand, becoming adept at manipulating multiple weaves simultaneously. I practiced on my own, not wanting the others to distract me. No one could teach you how to use your special talent, so I felt there was no need for Stefek, especially, to tell me how to control my power.

I was finishing up a sparring session with Krystian when he said he was going to town to pick up the daily dispatches. In these troubled times, we used only non-electronic means of communication, fearing spies might intercept them.

"I'll go with you," I said, wiping the sweat from my brow. I wore simple britches; mine were taken from Jurek, who no longer fit them. I had on a simple bra to keep the girls from falling out of the plain white cotton shirt.

"I'm leaving right now. Are you ready to go?" He gave me that expectant look. "Really ready to go?"

I didn't have my purse or wallet, but if we needed to buy anything, like lunch, big brother could pay. I nodded and pulled on a light jacket that I had also procured from my younger brother. On a whim, I tucked a small pulse pistol in my waistband and followed him to the garage. I always had security and a driver, but the men in our family were very insistent that they do the driving, and when in town, they rejected the need for security.

It was pretty nice, just jumping into my brother's coup and taking off. Unlike Stefek, who was married, Krystian was a bit of a playboy, opting to drive a sleek, bright red hovercar. It hovered about six inches above the ground when under power and had a low profile. The front was long and flat, narrow, with a small, round grille and bright, circular headlights. The sides had tubes and valves, mechanical bits that I didn't understand, and a large motivator wheel at the rear, all made of shining copper and brass. The windscreen was only a few inches high, and on a sunny day like this, we traveled with the top down.

"I'm surprised that you would go out like this."

"What do you mean?"

"Pants, shirt, and jacket. If not for the hair, and the… you know… I'd say you looked like a boy."

"Are you referring to my boobs? I haven't been mistaken for a boy for several years now."

"Well, if one of the many beaus that are after you sees you like this, you might scare some of them away." He smiled. Krystian always loved to pick on me.

"If they're scared away that easily, they're not worth having."

"You have a point, dear sister."

"So tell me, what the hell is taking the king so long to declare war?"

He was a bit startled by my blunt question, but recovered with his usual good humor. "Straight to it, eh? Father goes to the strategy meetings, not Stef or me."

"That's an evasion. You know more than you say, or at least, you suspect more than you are willing to say. We are at war already in all but name."

"If we go to war, our father will be a commanding general, and both of your older brothers will be on the front lines. Are you ready for that?"

"How is it different from what we have now? Weeks ago, you came home with a fractured arm, a gunshot wound, and were bruised from head to toe. Same for Stef. You've taken lives, led men in battle, and suffered wounds for your country. We are already at war, but in this war, they are harassing us, and we take their abuse."

"We should invade Rus? They, and their allies, are ten times our size, both in land size and population." He stopped the car when we reached the royal post office. "This war will take place in our country; there's no avoiding that. The best we can hope to do is to keep repelling them. Make the conquest of Polska so costly that they choose to shop elsewhere."

I looked around at the city street. Usually bustling, the crowd was a shadow of what it usually was. People were moving quickly, with their heads down and holding their children tightly. There was an air of tension in our city, and I suspected, in all of Polska. We knew that we were no longer safe. Not in our city streets, not in our homes.

"The people are scared," I said, and he couldn't deny it. "It might be better just to get this started. Their dragging it on, chipping away at the border, is like a slow torture. I don't want war. I fear for you and all the men of our country, but since it is inevitable, the waiting is worse."

"I can't really disagree, though my official opinion varies." He got up and jumped over the closed door. The stored energy kept the car hovering. "You don't have any ID, so wait here. I will probably be about half an hour." He crossed the wide sidewalk and entered the old building.

The government building was hundreds of years old, a relic from before the comet. Like all of the buildings along this cobbled road, it was connected to all the other buildings. They formed a massive structure spanning the entire block. There were hundreds of windows with outdated stonework around the frames. The fifth-story roof was a cluster of chimneys and antennas, with a decorative spire at its center, rising another story.

So I was stuck in a boring part of town. There weren't many people walking around, a few who looked like bureaucrats, part of the administrative machine. Even more than people in other sections of the city, they looked beaten down. Perhaps they were more in touch with the coming unpleasantness than the average citizen.

I was bored, and there was nothing to do. That is, until I saw a little boy walking by himself down the sidewalk, coming in my direction. When he got closer, I could see the lost expression on his face. He was four, maybe five years old. His dark hair was tousled, and his face had dirt with streaks made by flowing tears. I got out of the car and put myself in his path.

"Hey, buddy, are you lost?" I was good with children; I helped to raise Jurek and Dominika.

His tears intensified, and all he could do was nod his head. It took some work, but I eventually got his name. Piotr. He was shopping with his grandmother and somehow got lost.

"Ok, I will try to help you find your grandmother. Stop crying, it's time to be brave!" After wiping his nose on his sleeve, he felt a little better. I took his tiny hand in mine, and we started walking back the way he came from. She had to be in that direction. When we reached the end of the block, I asked him from which direction he had come. He pointed to the left, and I nodded as we turned down a dusty street lined with small stores and markets. There were more people on the smaller side streets, but they, too, were walking around, carrying the weight of impending doom on their shoulders.

I had been in the government district before, and I had been to the arts and fashion districts many times. However, I had never been in this part of the city before. There were more people on this street compared to the more affluent areas, and they were doing a million different things.

There were hawkers selling fish that were brought in from the coast. Women were selling every manner of fruit and vegetable from low wooden stands, apples, peaches, plums, and pears piled in big pyramids. Bags of onions and potatoes were arranged on a large wooden table for easy access by the hundreds of shoppers. Further down, there were shops selling meat. Inside the open windows were men with huge arms and bloody aprons, carving off steaks and chops as they were ordered. They would take the cuts of beef, lamb, venison, and turkey, wrap them in waxed paper, and hand them over the counter to waiting customers. Other stands were cooking food for immediate consumption. Some were grilling pork on skewers over small coal braziers, coating it with what smelled like a sweet, tangy sauce, then handing it to hungry workers.

Further down were shops of every variety. I passed cobblers hard at work resoling work boots. I saw a young woman, my age or younger, putting loaves of fresh bread in the window to cool. I saw a fromager cutting into a huge wheel of Parmesan, and a vintner rolling out kegs of his latest wine lots. Everyone, including the customers, was working hard. I heard a lot of friendly chatter, but everyone seemed to have an endless list of tasks and was in a constant state of motion.

One thing that eventually caught my attention was the lack of Abyrinth. I had become insensitive to the energy that floated everywhere and congregated on wielders and channelers. Everyone in my life, except the servants, was able to use the energy for powering machines or wielding the power of a brand. Everyone on this street was a blank. My maid was the only blank that I can say that I truly knew. Being able to wield was very new to me, but even so, the thought of not having power was so alien to me that I actually shuddered at the thought. I wanted to pity these people, but as I observed them going about their day, they didn't strike me as people who needed or wanted my pity. They seemed perfectly content with their lot in life.

They may not have had any superpowers, but the vast majority of the city, in fact, the whole world, were blanks. People with no special abilities, save the blessing of life from God. I realized that everything I used in my daily life, every scrap of clothing that I wore, every morsel of food I ingested, was touched by their hands. They were the engine that powered our society, allowing my family to enjoy such wealth and status. What surprised me the most? They seemed happy. Not laughing like imbeciles, just happy.

"Piotr!" I heard from across the street. A woman my mother's age came barreling across the street, traffic be damned. She wore a very simple dress, just below knee length, in light amber with a simple floral design. She had brown leather flats on and a wide-brimmed straw hat with a red ribbon. She was on the heavy side, with brown hair that was streaked with grey, and a face that was not unpleasant, but by no means attractive. Her rounded features were stretched with worry. "Where have you been, boy?" She had found him, but her voice was still thick with fear and panic.

"Nana!" he yelled. He pulled away from me and ran to her, also heedless of any passing cars. He looked heavy, but she scooped him up and held him close to her sizable, pillow-like breasts. She didn't quite cry, but I could see her relief in her eyes as they welled up and her face turned bright red. After a long, cleansing embrace, she set him back on his feet. She held his hand in a death-grip and gave me a long, appraising look before walking over to where I was standing.

"You found my Piotr?" she asked. I felt like her question carried a lot of accusation.

"I did. He was walking alone on Hightower Street," I pointed to the main street where the government builders were located.

"Why on earth would he be so far? There's nothing on that street to attract a young boy." Now I definitely detected an accusation.

"How would I know?" I replied, already angry. "If he were properly supervised, he wouldn't have strayed so far." Was that mean? Yes, but I didn't care.

"Why, I never!" she sputtered. If possible, she turned even redder. "You, dressed up like a boy, sassing me? I ought to box your ears!"

"Try it, and I'll put you on your fat ass," I replied, feeling confident enough in my fighting skills to fight against an overweight, much older woman. Onlookers were starting to gather. Apparently, when there was any kind of confrontation, they saw it as free entertainment.

"What's going on here?" a man's voice came from behind the crowd. A tall, sturdy man pushed his way through the crowd. When they saw his policeman's uniform, they ceded ground to him. His coat and pants were clean and pressed, but were made from a rough, dark blue wool. His belt buckle and buttons were brass-plated, and his thick, black leather shoes were polished to a mirror finish. The hat he wore was tall and curved like an upside-down wine glass, with a brass medallion on the front. The emblem was familiar to me, as it was our family crest.

"This girl was walking with my grandson, who had gone missing. When I questioned her about it, she was most disrespectful!" the grandmother blubbered.

"What say you, miss?" the policeman asked. He looked me up and down with a skeptical eye. It was his place to be neutral, but I could see that he didn't like the way I was dressed.

"I was walking on Hightower Street, where I encountered this sad, lost boy." I pointed at Piotr. "As any good Christian would do, I wasn't going to let him become even more lost. He remembered coming from this street, and we walked together until this large woman saw us. He was happy to be reunited, and that should have been the end of it."

"Do you see!" The grandmother was getting madder and more confident in her position. "Disrespectful!"

"Assuming you didn't steal the child in the first place."
Is he freaking kidding? "You have performed a commendable
action by returning the boy. It's not against the law, but you
should never be disrespectful to your betters," he said in a
scolding, fatherly tone.

"Betters?" I was incredulous. "This fat lump of a
woman? Who can't keep tabs on a single child entrusted to
her care?" I actually stamped my foot.

"This is exactly what I was talking about, young lady!
I may need to take you in. Show me some ID!" he demanded.
I could see that he was starting to get angry, blood rushing to
his face.

Damn it. I'd rushed out of the house without my
purse. "I-I don't have any identification on me."

"What is your name? You're going to come with me!"
He grabbed me roughly by the collar, pulling me off-balance.
I think he saw a glimpse of my brand, and I could feel him
stiffen. "What is your name, miss?" His tone had changed. He
was now afraid, as he should be.

"Her name is Jafra. Lady Jafra Sobieski," Krystian
said. The crowd parted like the Red Sea before him. His sporty
hover car waited in the middle of the street a few feet away.
Feeling like a blank myself, I saw him the way they did. He
seemed to be a dozen feet tall. His uniform was clean and
crisp, his brass was gleaming, and his long hair was tied back
in a tight ponytail. "Officer, is my sister causing a problem?"

The officer was stunned; he looked at my brother as
if he were our father. Indeed, he carried much the same
authority. "No, Lord Sobieski. There's no problem." The
uniform alone caused people to get out of his way. When they
heard the name, they retreated even further.

"That's good. She has the strongest brand in centuries, maybe ever. If you were to treat her harshly, I fear that I would be tasked with saving you."

The man was shaken, but I gave him credit for straightening up to answer Krystian. "As I said, milord, no problem here. She has no identification and is dressed so strangely… but there's no problem."

"Good to hear." He slowly cast his gaze around the circle of onlookers until he came to the grandmother. "It's unwise to judge people by the way they dress and make unsubstantiated assumptions." He gave the woman a withering look. "And it is a crime to accuse another citizen of a serious criminal action without the slightest scintilla of proof."

"Let's go, brother. I've done my good deed for the day and have lived to regret it."

# Chapter 20

I was in a mood. I felt very negative, and I needed an outlet. Luckily, I was able to indulge in one of my favorite activities. Shopping! I coaxed Milka into going with me. She always liked our little outings, but after the last time when the terrorists were attacking the government district downtown, she was a little hesitant.

"Don't worry!" I told her as we were driven to the garment district. "If we stop shopping, we're letting the bad guys win."

She looked at me skeptically. "And you're going to another ball?"

"Yes, we are. This is the biggest event of the year, and we have to be there. Tell you what, I think your blood sugar is low; let's get some lunch first." That brightened her mood. It sounded good to me, too; perhaps hunger was making me feel grouchy. I told the driver to stop at a nice homestyle restaurant.

The place was quiet and meant for the middle class. We weren't dressed in our finest, and no one who didn't see us get out of a chauffeured limousine would know that we were nobility. We got a small table near the window and enjoyed the sun shining in. It was a lovely day, and we both wanted to start enjoying things again.

When the waitress came, I ordered a quiche and a cup of hot tea. As Milka ordered, I sat watching, trying not to let my mouth hang open.

"I want to start with kotlet schabowy, a plate of pierogi—"

"Pork or chicken?" the waitress asked.

"Pork, please. Come back when we finish so that we can see your dessert menu." She smiled up at the woman as she handed back her menu.

"Milka…"

"Yes?" she asked, with a wary scowl.

"That's a lot of food. You are already looking a little…"

"Fat? Were you going to call me fat?"

I was ashamed and dropped my eyes.

"You would call an expectant mother fat?"

My eyes shot up to see the broad smile on her beautiful, kindly face. "Milka! That's so wonderful! Um, how long…"

"I'm only a few months right now. The doctor says that it will grow quickly during the second trimester. I'm starving because my child is eating all of my food!"

I jumped up and gave her a big hug. It lasted for several seconds because I was truly happy for her. We had been hungry and out of sorts, but now both of us were beaming with joy.

"I wish we were sisters. I would love to be an aunt," I said.

"I'm sure Stefek and his wife are going to have a kid any day now."

"No, I want to be an aunt to your son or daughter. I really love you, cousin."

"I love you too." She looked around, scanning the restaurant. "Now where's my food?"

We ate and made small talk for an hour when a homeless waif approached our table. He was about ten, dirty with disheveled hair, clothes that were ripped, and no shoes. He went from table to table, asking for coins or food, whatever they would give. Some people shooed him away, no compassion in their hearts. Many of them gave him leftover bread, and several reached into their purses and gave him coins. He came to our table.

"Miss, could you please spare a bit of bread, a coin or two?" I looked in his large brown eyes, and I saw sadness as I'd never seen before. I looked into the face of a ten-year-old who had given up on hope.

"Do you have a family?" I asked him

"I have Mother and two sisters," he said. "After Father died, I'm now the man of the house."

Milka leaned over to talk to the boy. "How did your father die?"

"He worked in a factory, making steam engine battery packs. They had a big explosion, and seven men died, including my Pa." It looked like he'd told the story a hundred times. He presented the facts, but instead of displaying sadness, he looked dead inside.

I remembered hearing about the accident, so I hoped that I wasn't being scammed. He looked skinny, underfed. I called over a waiter.

"Is this boy bothering you, miss? I'll roust him out immediately!"

"You know this boy?" I asked.

"Yes, miss. He comes in pretty much every day since his Da passed. Always begging and sometimes bothering the customers."

"He's not bothering us at all. Set him up with a week's worth of bread, a large pot of stew, and two dozen of these delicious pierogis. Put it on my bill."

The man's face lit up, and I saw the empathy that he had for the tyke. It was a large order that would help the proprietor but would also really help the boy's family. "That's a wonderful thing to do, young miss. Are you always so generous?"

"I wish that I were, but I don't really get out that much. This is in honor of my cousin's announcement of a child on the way."

"Congratulations!" he said, looking at Milka. "I will get the generous benefactor and the expectant mother a complimentary piece of my wife's world-famous paczki. Today's deep-fried doughnut is filled with fresh peaches."

"Mmmm, that sounds good!" Milka said, almost salivating.

"Are you hungry already?" I asked her. "You're eating for two, not twenty." I turned to the owner. "Are there many children like this? People who are without food, without a warm place to sleep?"

"You must lead a very sheltered life, miss. Stories like this boy's are relatively common these days. The economy fluctuates, and those on the bubble are the most at risk. If you were to travel a few blocks south, and I highly recommend that you do not, you would see men and sometimes women living on the street. They camp under trees or bridges. It's not so bad in the warmer months, but many of them freeze in the winter."

I hadn't really thought about poverty. We were so wealthy that I hardly thought about money. Whenever I wanted or needed something, it magically appeared. Here was a boy who spent every day of his life begging for money and scraps to feed his family for the day. I was going to help them for a week, but then he would be back on the street. I couldn't do more; I was unable to provide a long-term solution for this child. Even if I supported this boy and his mother and siblings, according to the restaurant owner, there were thousands of people in need. Some were worse off than this stick-thin boy. I called them blanks and never really thought of them as living, breathing people. I felt sad for the boy, but the shame I felt was much worse. If I were to become queen, I would make it a point to care for the less fortunate.

On the drive home, I thought about my country, about its people. All of its people. My cousin Milka was sitting next to me, and her child would be born into privilege. Her husband didn't have a fraction of my family's wealth, and yet they would be more than comfortable for their whole lives. Her son would never have to beg for bread. Aside from the money that we held, as nobles, we were also given the gift of a brand. A permanent conduit to Abyrinth that allowed us to do miraculous things. Blanks led very simple lives. They worked every day until they were old and grey, and with luck, they had good children who would take them in and care for them until death.

I began to wonder, if all people are equal in the eyes of God, then shouldn't they be more equal here in the mortal realm?

I began to see the point that Hedwig was trying to make. Maybe if we allowed unfettered access to the Abyrinth's Fire, then many blanks could become channelers or even wielders. It sounds like it could be a disaster, but then again, I'm only eighteen, and what do I know?

Hedwig didn't instill complete confidence in what she said, but she acknowledged that I would be skeptical. I would listen to her and decide soon if I was going to help her with her vision of expanding the number of people who could attain powers.

# Chapter 21

After the debacle at my Ascension Ball, I was sure that my appetite for balls was quenched for life, but that was not the case. It had only been weeks since I had thrown men off the deck of the Perła Lechii to fall to their deaths. The massive airship had been a unique and, from what I was told, a very expensive venue for my coming-out ball, but you couldn't pay me a million złoty to ride one again. Luckily, the Warszawa Council of Nobles had more sense. The Studniówka, or Autumn Ball, was a week away, and I was ready to get out and mingle again.

I believed that there were multiple invitations for outings with some of the most eligible gentlemen in the capital. Still, my mother was in complete control, and I only heard about a few that seemed to fit her grand design for my future.

Milka, Elżbieta, Anna, and Melina had all come to my house to shop for dresses. We were sitting around in the larger drawing room, sipping hot tea and dining on small, sweet cakes. The scents of cinnamon and chamomile, along with the laughter of my friends, had me in the frame of mind to get back into the socializing that my peers were engaging in. The lack of our friend Daria was a dark cloud that hung over our happiness.

My mother entered the room on the maid's heels. The maid had another platter with deviled eggs, mini quiches, jam-filled biscuits, marzipan petits fours, and many other glazed pastries. The young woman silently entered the room, set the trays on the round glass coffee table, then carried the used dishes to the kitchen.

"I hope you ladies can control yourselves. No man wants a fat wife, at least not until long after the wedding."

"Aunt Roksana, that's dated thinking! We, women, have the same rights as men do to enjoy our lives," Milka said.

"I don't know where you got this new philosophy, but men have never changed. They don't care about your education or the power of your brand. At first, all they want is a pretty face and a tight, shapely body. Give them a few children, especially a son or two, and then they'll forgive your lapses."

"Well, I want a cute boy," Anna said, her eyes dreamy with the thought.

"No boys for me," Elżbieta said. "I need a man. I don't like men my own age. I think the perfect husband for me will be older, maybe even as old as twenty-five."

"Twenty-five?" Mother asked. "That's positively ancient!" She looked over at me with a shrewd expression. "How about my own daughter? Do you dream of a young prince?" The girls all oohed and aahed. "Or a mature man in his mid-twenties?"

"Are you saying that I have some input into my match?" I asked hopefully.

"No." She smiled, then turned and left the room.


The dressmaker brought literally a hundred gowns. There was such an uptick in violence lately, especially in the city, that my parents thought it would be more fun to have us shop at home. After the first twenty gowns had been evaluated to mixed reviews, a bottle of wine was brought in by the maid.

I don't know if switching from tea to wine improved our ability to pick the best dresses for the upcoming dance, but it certainly made it more fun. By the time we had all selected a dress and had been fitted for alterations, we were pretty drunk.

My parents were not against me having a drink, and when I was at home, they let me have more than one. I would never let Mother know that I'd had four glasses, even though I had seen her at the Christmas party last year matching Father drink for drink.

"I've had too much," Anna said; she looked half in the bag.

"Not too much, but a lot," Elżbieta said. Her pale face was bright red, and her glassy eyes gave her a very cheerful appearance.

"Stay the night!" I suggested. "If you're not going anywhere, we can maybe have another glass, and we can share stories until the wee hours."

"Maybe your mom is right," Melina said. "We've eaten like a million calories in the last six hours, and with all the wine on top, I'm feeling bloated." She looked drunk.

"I don't know if I'll be able to find a dress to fit my new shape. My husband says he likes how round and full my butt has gotten, but I don't imagine he'd complain if it got back to where it was when we met." Milka's gaze went to nothing in particular, and she had a wistful look. "He couldn't keep his hands off it when we were courting."

"Oh my!" I said aloud. I was shocked. "Is that how you got pregnant?"

She shot me an evil look. "I told you that in confidence."

Elżbieta cut in, "We were talking about it before coming over. We guessed that you were expecting. You're glowing, dear!" They didn't mention that she was starting to show, and that she ate like a horse.

"He touched you before the wedding?" Anna asked, changing the subject. She leaned in, afraid that she might miss some sordid detail.

"You're the only one here that's married. Tell us… what to expect," Elżbieta said before pouring Milka another glass of iced tea. Another sign of her condition.

"So… how far did you let him go before the wedding?" I asked.

"First off, nothing in the first meeting. We didn't have a chaperone, but I was raised to be a good girl. That didn't last too long, but on the first date, I was very controlled." She smiled the smile of a person who had secret, precious knowledge that the rest of us did not have, but desperately wanted.

Melina was getting anxious. "Go on."

"He looked at me the whole time like a love-struck puppy. On anyone else, it would have been off-putting, but he's so handsome that I was blind to his awkwardness. He wanted to kiss me that first night, he wanted to hold my hand, but I held on and resisted." She drank from her cup, stretching out her oration as she took center stage. "Though I gave him no physical contact, I poured on the seduction. I batted my eyes." She showed us a sample. Not bad. "I gave him my best smile." She did have excellent teeth. "I found reasons to push out my chest, letting him imagine what might lie beneath my bodice. He tried to hide it, but I could sense his eyes on me, examining every curve, every bend. His request for a second date came within days, and we went to the arboretum to see the summer blossoms.”

“Flowers? Tell us the good stuff!” Anna pleaded. I was enraptured, sipping steadily as she told the story.

“Relax. We have all night. So, there is a fine line between flirty teasing and being a cock tease.” Her rough language took us all by surprise. “Men like a challenge; they rarely respect a woman who quickly gives in to their demands. On the other hand, if you make them wait too long, they may lose interest, and once that happens, there is no going back.”

She sipped her tea while thinking, then met our eyes again. “You can only go on so many dates without showing your interest before they lose hope and move on.” Turning to me, she asked, “Do you remember when I went out with that duke’s son a couple of years ago? I wouldn’t kiss for the first two dates, and sadly, there was never the offer of a third. Anyway, I had that in mind, so when he reached for my hand, I let him take it. I gave him a shy look, but truthfully, I enjoyed it as much as he did. We walked and looked at flowers, talking about anything and everything, and holding hands the entire time. His hand got sweaty, but I didn’t care.”

“When did you kiss?” I couldn’t help myself. I wanted to know how badly I’d handled the situation with Stanisław.

“Third date. One innocent, but passionate kiss at the end of the date. I was ready to board my hover car when he pulled me to him, leaned in, and it was pure instinct when I met him halfway. No tongue or anything, but his lips on mine sent electric shocks throughout my body. Even to my lady parts.” We all gasped at her bold description.

“If you had a chaperone, you wouldn’t have been able to do anything,” I said, suddenly frustrated and disappointed that Auntie had been on my first date. Should I have let Stanisław kiss me? Was I having regrets?

"I wouldn't have had my first kiss. And what we did on the fifth date would not have happened."

This time, Elżbieta was pouring the wine. She was sweating and flushed, and I don't think it was due to the alcohol. We all drank.

"The fourth date, I could tell that all he wanted was to kiss me again, and that's what I wanted too. Once you take things to the next level, you can never go back. Kissing was now on the menu, and he was ready for a double portion. We had a nice lunch by the river, then walked on the boardwalk for some time. He suggested we go to the cinema, and I agreed. When we were in the privacy of his limousine, he put his hand to my cheek and pulled me to him. He kissed me, not like the first kiss, timid and begging, but bold and hungry. His lips on mine made me dizzy. We kissed, our lips not parting for minutes at a time. My mind went blank, all I could do was to surrender to the exquisite pleasure of his mouth on mine, his tongue flicking against mine. He made me so wet, I would have to douche thoroughly when I got back home."

"I know what you mean," I said. The alcohol was starting to get to me. "Just hearing about it is making me lightheaded and filling me with fire!"

"So he reached for my breast, trying to cup it in his hand while my mind was on his kissing attack." We were all surprised at how forthcoming she was. I knew that she was married, but the idea of what she'd done with a man never truly occurred to me. Not the details.

"I pushed him away. We kissed for a while, and then he tried again. So I pushed him away again. Not angrily, more like the scolding a mother does to her naughty son. The fourth date was very similar. On the fifth date, I was so aroused that I let him touch my chest. When he cupped my breast, I let him. We kissed, and my arms were around his neck. He kneaded my left tit for a long time, until we came up for air. When we leaned back from each other, I saw a look on his face."

She was loving this, and we let her keep the spotlight. "On his face was victory. There was joy, discovery, and satisfaction. I could tell that even though he wanted everything, what he'd received would carry him over for that day and days to come. I had enjoyed it too. When he saw that I was a willing participant, he reached out to hold my right breast. Then he held them both. I watched his face as he watched his own hands. He looked like he was watching someone else perform this intimate act. He asked to see them, and of course, I said no, but he wasn't too upset. He'd already won a major victory and would certainly take care of himself when he got home, using my tits for inspiration."

"Ugh! Gross!" Anna groaned.

"It's what they do. All of them." She looked around the circle at the rest of us. "Every man does it. Your brothers, your fathers, every one of them is an animal at their core."

"I wouldn't mind…" Elżbieta started. "It might be interesting to see one of them doing it."

"Really? Why would you want to see that?" her younger sister asked.

"It's weird the first time, but it's hot!" Milka was thrilled to be the only one of us with any firsthand information.

"Which date did you get to witness this… performance?" I asked. I was both excited and worried about what would be expected of me in the near future.

Milka laughed lightheartedly, "Oh no! His member did not make an appearance until the wedding night."

Elżbieta whispered, "Didn't you want to see it before? Make sure that it's not too large, or too small?"

"I fell in love with him, and my parents approved the match, so it didn't matter." Her smile was peculiar. I couldn't decipher what coded message she was trying to pass.

"Well?" Anna asked. "Is it…" She held her hands vertically and moved them closer together, then farther apart. Milka laughed, then we all joined her.

"I'm quite satisfied with my husband. In every regard." She did look happy.

# Chapter 22

My parents were otherwise occupied, so I was to attend the autumn ball with Krystian. Even though we would separate when we entered the ballroom, he was responsible for making sure I was on my best behavior and that no one would try to take liberties with me. Per mutual agreement, we split the second we were announced. He headed towards a pack of his fellow hounds, and I to my gaggle of hens.

The Studniówka was being held at the Sala Balowa Wilanów, the royal palace where King Poniatowski, his queen, and their children, Stanisław and Jadwiga, lived. There would probably never be another ball on the deck of an airship again.

The palace estates were extensive, dwarfing our own by a factor of three. I had never gotten the full tour, but I heard they had miles of fields and forests where the king and his sons hunted deer, elk, and boar. The ballroom was in a separate wing of the house, and servants with light sticks were stationed in the driveway, directing cars to the event entrance. We waited in a short queue as each hover car pulled in front of the main entrance and disgorged its passengers.

It was undoubtedly a high-class affair, but the vibe was very different from my Ascension Ball. The men were primarily dressed in suits, opting not to wear the military uniforms of their respective houses. The women went all out. I had picked out a fancy ball gown and spent most of my monthly allowance on it. My dress was floor length, of course, but without a petticoat. It was a dark burgundy with gold corset appliqué ruffles. The sleeves were puffy along the forearm, and long, cream-colored ruffles began at the base of the corset and flowed down each hip, reaching to the hem of the dress. The neckline was deeper than I was accustomed to, but the presentation was... exceptional.

I had my jet-black hair piled high on my head in a French twist updo held with ruby-encrusted silver pins. Mother had helped me with my makeup while Dominika ran around asking questions and generally being annoying. I'd borrowed perfume, giving my scent essences of jasmine, sandalwood, vanilla, and white musk.

All eyes were on me the moment I exited my car. The valet took a furtive peek, the doorman smiled as his eyes did a subtle scan of my dress, pausing for half a second on the gem between my breasts. The enormous chasm of status between us didn't stop them from having animal urges in my direction.

The boys inside were equally titillated, each kissing my hand as I entered, and taking not-so-subtle scans of my body. The attention was intoxicating, but I drifted off to join my girlfriends before people started talking. The girls met me with a mixture of acceptance as one of their own and a few envious stares. You would think that having other girls hate me would bother me. Quite the opposite; it filled me with an immense feeling of satisfaction.

"Quite the selection this year," said Marianna Kowalska, one of the girls on the welcoming committee for the university I was considering attending. I had met her a few times over the years and thought that she was nice, if not a bit snarky for my taste. She was a couple of inches shorter than I, though her high heels brought her close to my height. She was thicker, and her face was too round to be called attractive, but her rosy cheeks helped to give her a merry appearance at first glance. "Every man worth kissing is going to be here tonight."

Aniela Tarnowska joined in on the fun. "Your brother Krystian is looking pretty good. Very kissable!" She was as tall as I was, and very thin with elegant features and wide brown eyes that shone like caramel diamonds. She was wearing a pale-blue empire-waist dress that accentuated both her lankiness and her lack of a bust. I'm not even sure what she was thinking when she made that choice.

"I don't kiss on the first date," I said to a potpourri of expressions. Some were in strong agreement, several were neutral, and a couple were clearly not in agreement with me.

"So we've heard," Marianna said to the snickers of several of the girls present. Elżbieta and Anna were there, looking like they had a secret. I hadn't told them anything about my dates, at least not the disappointment in Stanisław's formal parting after our date. Helena Radziwiłł, along with Milena, looked utterly clueless.

Then I focused on Jadwiga Poniatowski, Stanisław's sister. She was as beautiful as he was, damn her. She was as tall as I was. Her long blond hair was combed to look like a sheet of gold, cascading down her strong shoulders and toned back. Like everyone in her family, her features had that Roman perfection. She was a fencing master at the university, a member of the tennis team, and a long-distance runner. Her curves were not as pronounced as mine, but she had that athletic look that many men found appealing. I knew from the smirk on her small mouth that she was the source of the gossip against me.

"What exactly is it that you heard?" I asked Marianna. "If someone is speaking out of pocket about me, I should not only hear it… but I should like to know the source of your information is. My reputation is intact, and as ladies of the court, it is important that we don't sink into the gutter."

Marianna looked suddenly petrified. It was fine to poke fun at me when she thought I would back down, as many of her classmates did, but I was a Sobieski, and my last name was second only to the king's.

Jadwiga came to her rescue. "It was me, Jafra. My brother told me about the date you went on. All he wanted was a little kiss, and you were too good to kiss the crown prince of Polska."

What the hell was she playing at? If rumors were true, she'd kissed quite a few boys, and God knew what else she'd done with them. She was trying to influence our group, bring them over to the dark side.

"If he were to become my husband, then he could have everything. Unlike some, who will remain nameless, I am saving my best for whoever becomes my mate."

She turned red with anger, and I could see the lines of energy bubbling on the surface of her skin. What is her power again? I couldn't remember.

She took a step closer, trying to be menacing. We were pretty equally matched if it came to a fist fight, and if she wanted to use our powers, she was outclassed. I was feeling stronger each day using Abyrinth Embermark, and what Hedwig had said was true: I was more powerful than any wielder in an age.

"Saving your best?" she asked, steam issuing from her ears. "What about that Bohemian? All of us saw you kissing him! He gets your best, but my brother does not?" Her body was tense; she was seconds away from exploding. Wind! That's it, she can create and control gusts of wind.

"Prince Záhoř? He kissed me. I did not reciprocate. I met with him at the airship races, and he has since apologized."

"I was nearby," Elżbieta said. "Jafra was taken by complete surprise. He stole a kiss, then ran off to help fight the Rus mercenaries." She paused to look around. "That was right before Jafra saved all of us by stopping the airship from crashing to the ground."

"That was incredible," Aniela said. "With all this talk about kissing boys, I almost forgot how powerful your brand is."

The tide was not going her way, and Jadwiga made a visible effort to calm herself. She was about to say something when her brother approached our group. Stanisław stalked over to us, confident and masculine. His hair was perfect, his face as smooth as marble, and the dark black suit he wore fit him like a second skin. He smiled at his sister, gave the others a cursory look, then came to stand directly in front of me. Taking my hand, he kissed my fingers.

"I apologize for eavesdropping, but as I passed, I couldn't help but hear a snippet of what you lovely ladies were talking about." Focusing on me, meeting my eyes with his, he started, "I mostly want to apologize to you, dear Jafra. I'm a young man with a young man's raging hormones, and you were entirely correct to deny me. In my frustration, I may have vented to my younger sister. Again, I was wrong in that. If she has shared our confidence, I'm certain that she'll apologize for any harm her words have caused you or your reputation." He gave Jadwiga a murderous look.

"You're quite right... brother. After getting additional testimony from these ladies present, I will admit that my words were rash and ill-thought-out. I am sorry, Jafra." She gave a very slight bow, and though her face was smiling, her eyes were not.

"You have every right to deny me, but it would heal my pride if you would consent to dance with me?" He held his hand out to me, and the sincerity in his deep blue eyes, the crinkle around his smiling mouth, teeth like pearls… I had no choice but to accept.

"I would be honored, Your Majesty."

We drifted out onto the dance floor, where a few dozen couples were already tripping the light fantastic. The floor was stained and polished oak, every bit as large as the one on the airship. Two feet in diameter, granite columns ringed the massive room, holding up the twenty-foot-high vaulted ceiling. From the curtain rods to the door handles, all of the fixtures in the room were gold, and the floor-to-ceiling curtains were made from lilac velvet. Twelve crystal chandeliers, each ten feet in diameter, filled the room with a bright glow that reflected off the gems hanging from every female's ear and necklace. Dozens of waiters and waitresses zipped around the periphery of the room, bringing delicious hors d'oeuvres and flutes of champagne and taking away the empty plates and glasses. A band of nearly thirty musicians was on a raised stage on one side of the room, playing both classical pieces and Polish favorites. We danced for three songs before he suggested we take a break. He was sweating, and the manly scent seemed to stir something in me. He took my hand and led me to a table where his parents were sitting.

"Champagne?" he asked, reaching for a chilled bottle sitting in ice on a stand near the table.

"Water, please."

He nodded and poured from a nearby pitcher. "You dance divinely. We only had one dance at my party, and I forgot how skillful you are."

The flattery made him smile as he handed me the glass. I turned to his parents, gushing, "Thank you for hosting this event, Your Majesties. This is the most exquisite venue I've seen or even heard of!" I blotted at the sweat on my forehead. I wanted to do the same to my cleavage, but I couldn't in front of the king.

"Jafra, darling. How is your mother?" the queen asked. "Such a lovely woman."

"Splendid, Your Majesty." I sipped demurely at my water.

"I wanted to thank you personally for what you did at your Ascension Ball. I know those radicals would have been happy with killing the majority of our nobility, but I also believe that they were specifically targeting our family. You single-handedly prevented a tragedy of immense proportions, and your country owes you a debt we can never repay."

I bowed. "You are too kind, Your Majesty."

"Nonsense." She patted me affectionately on the back of my hand. "I've been meaning to speak with your mother, and with all of the violence recently, I admit that I've been remiss. Stanisław has said nothing but kind things about you since your outing. He says your beauty is more than skin-deep and that your upbringing is impeccable. I'll be speaking with your mother, but I sincerely hope that both of you will agree to a second outing."

"Again, Your Highness, you are very kind. If I were blessed with such an invitation, I   would be inclined to respond in the affirmative. The prince is truly every woman's ideal." I gave him a warm smile, not too flirtatious in front of his parents.

"My boy has turned out pretty well if I do say so myself. I think his father is quite the catch, though, and despite what you children might think, we are not too old to join in on the festivities!" She grabbed the king's hand and half-led, half-dragged him to the dance floor. When the band saw who was coming out, they picked up in both volume and vigor. When the royal couple hit the floor, it was a signal for everyone to join. In a minute, those hanging on the walls and those relaxing at their tables were compelled to get out and dance.

"Should we join?" I asked. Stanisław watched his parents out on the floor, dancing with power and grace, and a joie de vivre. He looked content. Happy.

"Not yet. We have all night." He gave me a look that was difficult to describe. I had thought he was mad at me because of how our date ended. My meeting with the Bohemian at the races, in front of all of his friends and their female companions, didn't help either. Yet, he seemed to have made peace with it, and he was in a good place.

"Now that you are back from studying abroad, are you planning to join the Wojsko Królewskie—the Royal Army?"

"Father asked me to join the service when I first returned, but I had already decided. I have no desire to harm anyone, but I'll be king eventually, and it's a king's foremost responsibility to put himself between the people and those who would cause them harm." He smiled at me, and his dark blue eyes were brighter than coals in a fire. "Besides, I don't want your brothers to have all the glory."

"I don't know about glory. I remembered Mother healing my brothers at the kitchen table just a few weeks ago after a particularly bloody border skirmish. Their physical wounds were fixable, but I could tell that seeing their men die and having to kill young boys from Rus was taking a toll on them."

"You had to kill at your ball as well. How has that affected you?" he asked, taking my hand in his. He leaned in close, his expensive cologne stinging my nose. There was an undercurrent of perspiration, a subtle musk. His icy blue stare bore into me.

"I pushed them over the edge of the ship. Gone. I didn't have to look at their bodies after falling hundreds of feet to the unforgiving ground. Stefek kills with his sword, and after a battle, he's covered head to toe in the blood of our enemies."

We sat in silence, or relative silence since the band was playing very loudly. I was staring off, not really paying attention, when something caught my eye.

"Stan, do you hire channelers as servers?"

He wasn't expecting a question that was so far off topic. "What? No, of course not." He looked around the room, seeing several hard-working servers scurrying around. "Why do you ask?"

I pointed to an older woman in a server's livery. She was around thirty, with long brown hair held in a tight ponytail. She was carrying an empty tray, and her eyes were actively scanning all around the room. Then I pointed to a man, also in his late twenties or early thirties. He had an empty tray, and he seemed to be concentrating on something.

"My brand is the ability to control Abyrinth. As part of that, I can see the energy that we all radiate. I see it in you, your parents, and almost all of the guests here. We mostly have blanks serving us, and they have no such energy aura. Those two do, and…" I pointed at a third across the room. "Those three are channelers, or possibly even wielders."

"I can't understand why our Chief of Staff would hire channelers. They are infinitely more expensive, and they would serve no purpose as wait staff."

I jumped to my feet. "They wouldn't. They're assassins!" Because of what I had done at my ball, I think that the enemy had their eyes on me.

I felt a knife tear into my side from behind. The pain was excruciating, and fire seemed to course through my veins.

Stanisław had jumped up when I did, but was too slow to see a fourth assassin before she could stab me. Through the fog of pain, I saw him leap into action. Energy flowed to him as he summoned a long blade made of pure Abyrinth.

The blade was two feet long and seemed to project from a ball of light wrapped around his right fist. The blade was wider than his hand at the base and tapered down until it formed a point. He hacked at the hand holding the weapon in my back, and the limb was severed a few inches below the elbow.

Her eyes went wide, either from surprise or pain. Possibly both. He should have subdued her for questioning, but emotion and adrenaline were coursing through him, and reason had gone out the window. He pushed the energy sword through the center of her face and into her brain. ensuring her death and the need for a closed casket.

The woman's actions may have been the catalyst for the start of the attack. The other false servers dropped their empty trays to carry out their mission.

I was wrong. They were not channelers; they were wielders.

I felt a wave of fear, then sickness pass over me, and I saw that I was not alone. Everyone in the room was similarly struck by nausea. The music stopped, and many of the dancers dropped to their knees; some fell on their backs.

The king was a strong man, and that was his undoing. He stood almost erect, holding onto his queen as she swooned. I saw minuscule pockets of energy fly from one of the assassins' hands towards the king. He draped himself over his wife as the energy bullets ripped through his flesh. Blood fountained from multiple wounds as the man continued to fire.

I could see the fog of Abyrinth billowing through the massive building, and I reached for it, pulling the raw energy into myself. I couldn't clear the room, but there was a bubble of clarity centered on me that included Stanisław and everyone within twenty feet. Distance didn't affect my ability, or so it seemed. I formed ropes of energy that sprang from the ground at the shooter's feet and wrapped around him until he was held tighter than a caterpillar in a cocoon.

"Stanisław! I have him bound! Go deal with him!" I yelled.

In seconds, he closed the distance, his energy sword stretching out to the length of a longsword. The man's screams were cut short as his head was removed from his shoulders. Everyone was still reeling from the effects of her mind fog; dozens were retching on their expensive clothes.

He looked back at me, and I pointed to a woman at the edge of the dancefloor, opposite the band. His energy sword melted and flowed into a long spear, with sharp points at both ends. I could tell that this was a weapon he was familiar with, as it flew true, impaling the woman through and through.

The spear glowed, three feet protruding from her ruined chest, three feet sticking out of her back. The spear blinked out of existence as she fell dead. He looked again in my direction, but I waved for him to help his family.

As he rushed to aid the king and queen, I took stock of my situation. I was hurt badly, and I could sense that it was more than just the blade that was still stuck in my side. I felt heat coursing through me, burning its way through my veins, causing my muscles to cramp violently. I had been poisoned. Three wielders were tasked with killing the king and queen. One blank had been sent to neutralize me.

I fell to the floor, dizzy with blood loss and sick from the poison. I had a hard time hearing, and my vision had begun to fade. That's when I saw a familiar face.

"Lady Sobieski, you've been stabbed!" Hedwig said as she helped me to a sitting position.

"There is another wielder assassin," I gasped as the poison was working its way towards my heart.

"Not anymore. This man dressed as a server was about to light the whole floor on fire when your brother pushed a sword blade through his throat. The man died instantly." She eased me up and into my chair. She roughly pried my eye open, staring at it with clinical evaluation. "I don't dare pull the blade from you. A major artery has been severed, and if I remove the dagger, you'll bleed out in less than a minute. Worse off, I think you've been poisoned."

"I've definitely been poisoned. I only have a few minutes left." It was weird hearing myself say such a thing. I was on the brink of death, and I knew it. I had diagnosed my demise and spoke it out loud with a remarkable lack of emotion.

Thoughts of all the things I would miss in my life flickered through my sluggish mind. I wasn't old enough or experienced enough to have the past flash before my eyes. I thought about the kisses I would never have, the caresses, the love that I would never make. My thoughts sailed at light speed into the future. A tall, strong, faceless man who would hold me, his protective arms wrapped around me. I saw children at my feet, running around, calling me 'mother,' laughing and playing, showering my cheeks with kisses. I saw Christmas dinners, reading stories to my children by the fire, music, dancing, and so many other experiences that I would never have.

I thought I was ready to leave this world when a glass was put to my mouth. When the liquid hit my lips, I instinctively drank. It was a dreadful concoction, and I wanted to wretch, but whoever held the glass continued to pour. It was swallow or drown. Someone held me up, and I sat there for a long time with my eyes closed. When I finally regained my senses to some degree, I could see that it was my brother Krystian who had me in his arms. Opening my eyes fully, I saw that there was a circle of concerned onlookers staring at me.

"The king!" I croaked hoarsely.

"Barely surviving," Stanisław said. "We've sent notice to your mother. She is racing here in the fastest car, driven by Lord Sobieski himself." His blue eyes were watery with the depth of his grief. "Once again, you have helped to save my family, Lady Jafra Sobieski. I can never repay the debt my family owes you."

"Are you alright?" Hedwig asked. She was leaning over Krystian's shoulder, looking at me with concern on her face.

"Jafra," my brother said. "This is Lady Rozalia Tarnowski. She gave me an antidote to the poison. The knife wound could have been much worse; luckily, you jumped up just as the assassin struck. The poison surely would have killed you." He turned to her. "Thank you, Lady Rozalia. You saved my sister."

My mind was hazy, but I still had my manners. "Thank you, ma'am. Your assistance was… timely."

Mother's face popped up over Krystian's other shoulder.

"Jafra! You're bleeding!" She reached for me.

"No! Heal the king first!" My brother applied pressure to the wound. The knife had been pulled out when I was unconscious.

"Go!" I yelled, not disrespectfully.

She was gone, and I surveyed the scene. The bodies were already removed, and the real servants were hard at work cleaning up the blood. Leaning on my brother and the woman I knew only as Hedwig on the other side, I limped over to where my mother was working hard to heal our king. People parted to let us get close.

Krystian came up to me, applying a bandage to my wound. He had the attempted murder weapon and turned it around in his free hand, examining it as if he'd never seen a bladed weapon before. He tapped the design carved into the handle, then handed it to me.

I looked at the carving, and it only created more questions. It was not Russian; their weapons were plain, without any insignia. What it resembled was the brands that wielders had affixed to their spines. It looked like oxidized copper, round, with an owl's image. The bird was haunting, evil, its long claws grasping at a withered branch, and twisted branch designs sprouting from the circle.

"This seems to bother you. What do you suppose it means?" I asked.

"Not sure. It's neither Russian nor one of ours. Makes me wonder… exactly who was behind this assassination attempt?" He took the knife back from me. "I'm going to show this to Father, see if he has seen its like before."

Lady Sobieski was a professional, one of the most potent healers in all of Europa. Normally, she was an emotional person who openly expressed feelings of caring, concern, and love. While healing, she became a cold professional. I could see the flows of Abyrinth around her, clouds of energy being drawn in, condensed, and woven into strands of energy. I knew that she couldn't see the energy as I could, but she could sense its presence, and like a master weaver, she harnessed the strings and applied them to the king's many wounds. She could heal burns, broken bones, cuts, scrapes, and minor diseases, but some things were beyond her control. I could tell instantly that he would lose the arm.

Stanisław saw me and took my outstretched hand. He had a look of grim determination on his face, an expression that an hour ago would have seemed beyond a man of his tender age. His hands and the front of his shirt, jacket, and trousers were all coated in both his father's blood and mine.

He pulled me to his chest and embraced me in a tight grip. He kissed me. Not a lustful kiss, not a kiss born of passion. A kiss from a man who almost lost his whole world, and then it was given back to him. For me? It was a kiss that nearly drowned out the pain in my side. I didn't like that it was in front of God and everyone, but it still sent a chill down my spine.

"Hey! I'm still putting pressure on this knife wound!" Krystian shouted.

"I'm sorry. I'm just so grateful that my father is alive. Grateful to you, Jafra Sobieski. And thank God for you, Lady Sobieski. Your healing has brought my father back from the very brink of death!" He released me and stood taller than I've ever seen a man stand. "Good people of Polska. I know my father's heart, and even more important, I know your hearts! We've endured enough insults! We've lived in fear! We've been the innocent victims of enough violence! Enough, I tell you! We've all had enough! If the Rus are too cowardly to declare war, then we will." His voice took on an even loftier timbre. "On behalf of the crown, on behalf of the Polish people, I declare war on Rus!"

No one wanted war, but they cheered my prince. He pumped his arms in the air, and each time, there was a roar. Not the kind you get at a football game or a cricket match, but a feral, animal response to the massive indignities we'd been forced to endure. Life as I knew it, as we all knew it, would change forever.

I was right. Everything changed.

# Chapter 23

I came back from an afternoon of running errands, and as I was about to mount the stairs, I was stopped by my mother. She had a sour look, and I was expecting the worst.

"A British gentleman was looking for you. He stopped by the house. Unannounced."

"That's odd," I replied. It was odd. I didn't know anyone from England.

"When I say he stopped by the house, I mean he somehow passed our front gate and the expensive guards that we employ to stand there every minute of the day, and knocked on the front door." She looked at me. Is she expecting me to excuse the behavior? "Knocked!"

"Very odd indeed. Did he leave a name?"

"That's all you have to say?" She was fit to be tied.

"Mother. You've met this person; I have not. Why are you convinced that I know anything about who this man is or where he came from, or why he's darkened our door?"

"After I told him that you were not at home, he told me that he was staying at the Hotel Europejski, and then he disappeared." I must have given her a look. "I'm not crazy, Jafra Nicola Sobieski!" Oh heck, I was in big trouble. "He was standing in front of me, not ten feet away, and blink! He was gone."

"Ok, Mother. I'll check it out tomorrow. I seriously have no idea what he wanted with me."

"You will not, young lady!" I had rarely seen her this upset. We stood there looking at each other, not speaking. Take Krystian. He's home."

"Yes, ma'am," I said, then took my items upstairs. Why would a stranger from England seek me out? I figured it must be related to my brand. Well, I was fine with waiting until the next day to check it out.


I didn't mind my older brother being my chauffeur and chaperone because he was also my protector. I was dangerous with my power, dangerous to others and to myself. Krystian was more mature, though not by a lot, and much deadlier than people gave him credit for.

We arrived at the hotel, and I approached the front desk. "Jafra Sobieski for Edmund Fletcher. Is he in residence?"

The older lady gave me a once-over, noting the quality of my dress and the cut of Krystian's military-style uniform. I could tell that she gave extra attention to the sword and pistol at his side. We were either rich or noble, and in our case, we were both. She wouldn't have been able to maintain her position if she didn't know how to deal with situations like this. Additionally, our name was well known throughout the capital.

"I'll ring his room, Lady Sobieski. I believe he took his breakfast an hour ago and should still be in."

"Thank you," I said. A concierge escorted us to a sunny nook where we were served tea and pastries. I was halfway through my tea and almost done with my second Piernik. The gingerbread had plum jam and was very fresh.

Several minutes later, a tall, gangly man walked over to speak with the front desk. She pointed at me, and the man thanked her before walking over to us. He was taller even than Stefek and thinner than Krystian. He wore a finely tailored suit that looked like he might have slept in it. Not dirty, but creased with a spider's web of wrinkles. His shock of short blond hair and short, bushy mustache gave him an almost comical aspect. His smile boded well, and Krystian stood to greet him.

"I am Krystian Sobieski. You're Sir Edmund Fletcher, I presume?" He held out his hand. The man took his hand and shook it amiably. I was competent, but Krystian's English was better than mine.

"This is my sister, Lady Jafra Sobieski," he said, introducing me. The man took my hand, kissing the fingers in the style of the Latin Kingdoms.

"So good to meet you," he said emphatically. "May I?" He indicated a seat at our table.

"Please join us," Krystian said, sitting back in his place. "You didn't invite us, but our mother heard you name your hotel, and we took the liberty."

"You gave her quite a start," I said. I got chewed out, so I wasn't going to let this Englishman get away scot-free. "She says that you disappeared before her eyes. I've heard of stranger things happening, but your exit quite flustered her. I was questioned like a murder suspect."

"I'm so very sorry, miss," he apologized. "I sometimes forget how my brand can seem strange to others."

"Is it the Omniport Gatefold, or the Chronovore Emberrift?" I asked. Krystian was perplexed by my question, but the Brit took it in stride.

"The first, miss. I know how it's bad manners in polite society to show a brand or ask to see one, so I've taken the trouble to have a rubbing made." He reached into his billfold and pulled out a sheet of paper. Unfolding it, he held it out for our examination. The one-of-a-kind brand was circular like all the rest, but displayed a doorway over tendrils of Abyrinth with rays of energy surrounding the frame.

"Of course, you know that I carry the Abyrinth Embermark. I think it's the worst-kept secret in Polska."

"Indeed. The worst-kept secret in Europa. That bit with the airship made all the papers. But my information came from another source. I have been contacted by individuals claiming to be part of a secret group, called the"

"Brotherhood of Virtue?" I asked.

"Indeed. They have this ridiculous idea that the stones should be made public, so every ne'er-do-well and villain can obtain powers. Not just amusing powers like your cousin, but very dangerous powers, like your brothers." He nodded at Krystian.

"My brand makes me very dangerous. I would prefer to have a power like my mother's, but such is not my fate. Can you tell me about yours?"

"Of course." He was animated when talking about his ability. "I was told about you by this Brotherhood. They said that your brand allows you to see Abyrinth, that it's all around us all of the time, and you can see it and manipulate it. When you move things, it's not that you are actually lifting a cup or a car, but you are commanding the energy to lift them, like an invisible giant. Your power is the control of energy. My power lies in controlling space. I can travel anywhere in the world, as long as I've been there and can visualize it in my mind." He let that sink in. "When I was told that you weren't at home, I transported myself here. Well, actually, directly to my room."

"That's a very helpful ability, I guess." Hearing it left me underwhelmed.

He stood up and held out his hand. "Let me demonstrate." I stood and took his hand. "Very important. For us prime brands, this only works if you are a willing participant." He turned to Krystian. "Have a spot of lunch. We'll be a little while." And before Krystian could respond, we were gone.

The light change made me cover my eyes with my free hand. When I had adjusted, I saw that we were in the shadow of the Eiffel Tower. I may not have been well-traveled, but I knew that we'd instantly teleported thousands of miles west to the City of Lights.

"Welcome to Paris," he said after releasing my hand.

Paris smelled funny. Different. It was cool in the early morning, and not many people were out and about yet. We walked to the tower, and I placed my hand on the cold steel. It was real. I was really in Paris, Francia.

He held out his hand. I took it, and suddenly we were at the top of the tower.

I peered over the rail to see a vast garden several blocks wide and stretching from the base of the tower for miles into the heart of the city.

"The Champ de Mars, a gift from Louis XVI. Quite lovely, don't you think?"

I couldn't help myself. "It's beautiful. This is an amazing city. It may even put my Warszawa to shame."

I took his hand again, and in the blink of an eye, we were standing in the very center of the Colosseum in Rome. A few staff were working somewhere nearby; it was too early for the tourists.

"I see you believe me now, and you see some of the power of my brand. There is more." He waved his hand in a large circle, and a rift in space formed in the air before us. As he continued to rotate his hand, the circle expanded. In a few seconds, it had expanded to ten feet in diameter, with its bottom touching the dusty ground. Through the portal, I could see my own house, so familiar and comforting to me. We walked through, and just like that, I was home. Again, I took his hand, and in a flash, we were back at the table where Krystian was devouring a sandwich.

"Very powerful," I said, thinking about the myriad of possibilities. He could obviously bounce around the world, avoiding trouble with a thought and using only a small portion of his Abyrinth reserve. He could also move armies from one place to another in as much time as it took them to march, run, or drive through his portals.

"The last of the primes is Chronovore Emberrift. If it's not obvious, it is related to time. I don't know much more than that, but these Brothers of Virtue are looking for him or her as hard as they can. They want to use me, and you, and I doubt it's to spread equality among the masses."

"So, you don't trust them?" I asked. We sat back at the table, my brother looked at us with his face stuffed with a sausage sandwich.

"I trust few people, and that lot least of all. My grandad was a bit of a salesman, and what he knew best was people." I gave him a quizzical look. "Yes, we originally came from humble beginnings. Anyway, he could smell a bullshitter from miles away. I learned from him how to be observant, to pick up on body language, and read between the lines, so to speak. On the few occasions I've spoken to one of them, I get that tingle in the back of my head, like a headache that's looming on the horizon. Can I point to a lie they've told? No. Can I show any evidence that they are anything other than what they claim to be? No. But I still don't like them, and whenever I see one of the buggers, I pop off to Timbuktu."

I understood what he was saying; I had the same sense about the Brotherhood, though my doubt was not as pronounced. "The only one that I've met is a woman who goes by the name Hedwig. At a function, I was introduced to her as Lady Rozalia Tarnowski."

"The one who approached me was an English bloke."

"She saved me from a kidnapping attempt. Apparently, this brand on my back has put a target on my back." I snickered at my own joke.

"Did she? A bit too convenient if you ask me." He accepted a cup of tea, which he sipped.

I had similar reservations about Hedwig being in the right place to save my guards and me, and she was present again with an antidote when I was poisoned at the Autumn Ball. I had a sudden thought. I had been carrying the knife that was pulled from my back since the ball. I had some odd attachment to it.

"Does this mean anything to you?" I asked, showing him the owl insignia on the dagger.

"Rather sinister," he said as he examined the blade, then the handle again. "I'm sorry, I've not seen this design before. What's the significance?"

I told him about being stabbed at the ball with the very knife he held in his hand. He scrutinized it before carefully handing it back to me.

"I think I can understand why this symbol causes you unease. Just seeing it makes me uncomfortable. I will keep my eyes out for this owl symbology. I have some associates that I can trust. I'll make enquiries."

I offered to let him take a rubbing of the design, and he readily agreed. We obtained a blank scrap of paper and a lead pencil, and he made his own copy of the owl.

"Before you go," I said as he stood to leave. "You seem a bit paranoid, though perhaps rightfully so. Why would you seek me out?" It seemed like we should have started with that question, but I had learned so much in a short amount of time.

"Paranoid? Sometimes, they are out to get you." He laughed at his joke. "This Brotherhood group wants to find all three of us, and they seem to think that together, we can be a powerful force, able to open up access to the stones with the overwhelming power of our brands. There are only three of us in the world, and clearly, our brands are immensely powerful. I have met you and found you to be a sincere, if somewhat naïve, young woman. I trust that you won't allow yourself to be a pawn in some game, because the stakes are too high. I'll keep looking for the bearer of the Chronovore Emberrift, and I think that you should as well."

"And if I find him or her?"

"I will have to rely on you to judge that person. To determine if they will help society, or help themself." He took a card from the inner pocket of his suit jacket. "If you need to contact me, feel free to radio my solicitor. He can usually reach me on short notice."

"I am glad to have met you."

"Likewise. Rus is on your doorstep. We may meet again, sooner rather than later." He doffed an imaginary cap. "Pożegnanie, Pani Sobieski."

"Farewell, Lord Fletcher."

He waved to Krystian before blinking away. I had a lot to think about.

# Chapter 24

Both Stefek and Krystian were made colonels in the royal army and were each given a battalion of men. All the young men in the nobility who were old enough to be wielders were expected to serve. It was a trade-off for the wealth and privilege we enjoyed: we should be the first to step forward and fight for Polska. Blanks were conscripted by the tens of thousands, and even if some were unwilling, they were compelled to serve. When the king had recovered, less his right arm, he supported his son's call to war.

I attended a meeting of the Lords to discuss the war plans. I wasn't a participant; my father, Lord Sobieski, participated in the meeting, and I sat in the cheap seats.

Apparently, just saying that we were at war didn't mean we were ready to make war. My brothers had been fighting terrorists whom we attributed to the Rus for months now. Sobieskis already had blood on their hands, and now it was time for others to step up.

Father railed against the other lords, men, and some women from different parts of the country. Those in the north and east did not have to endure masked killers rolling through small villages and committing atrocities. I was proud of the way Father spoke to these men who were supposed to be his equals. He made it very clear that they would have to dig deep into their pockets and give until it hurt. They would also be required to conscript and present thousands of soldiers to the crown for the defense of the state. That would include both blanks and channelers.

The speeches went on for hours, but those who resisted were in a weak position and doomed from the start. Eventually, it wasn't a matter of them participating or not, but to what degree. As important as it was, I admit that I found it extremely dull. I fell asleep for a few minutes until Krystian shook me awake.

"It's wrapping up. You might want to freshen up before you get to see your boyfriend," he said, nodding at Stanisław, who was sitting next to his father, the king. He, along with both of our fathers, was the most outspoken advocate for the immediate activation of our army.

"Perhaps you're right," I said, standing and making my way to the side door. My guards walked with me and stood outside while I conducted my business within. I was on my way back to the council meeting room when Stanisław caught up to me outside.

"Jafra, so good to see you." He leaned in to kiss my cheek. "Your father is quite persuasive, and I think his strong support will help us to carry the day."

"Thank you for your kind words, my liege." We fell into a stroll away from the meeting room, our guards tailing us at a distance.

"It looks like we will get everything we asked for. Your brothers are going to be heading their own battalions and training their soldiers." He had a thoughtful expression, and there was worry behind those light blue eyes. He wore a military uniform, stark white and spotless. His stiff, high collar looked tight and constricting; the tunic had wide lapels and no trim. He wore a dark patent-leather belt that matched the gleam of his shoes. He had no medals and wore no insignia of rank. I wasn't sure what message he was trying to send with his dress.

"You look very handsome in your uniform, my prince."

"Jafra, call me Stan, for God's sake. I have proposed that I serve as Commanding General of our army. The generals will all report to me as I set up a headquarters here in Warszawa."

I was surprised by this. "Not your father? You will be the architect of our nation's defense?"

"Yes. I will coordinate our men and resources from here. I didn't want to say this to the council, but I feel that I can trust you. I fear that we have no chance to win any serious offensive by the Rus army. They greatly outnumber us, and they have more weaponry than we have by far."

"If we can't win, then maybe we shouldn't go to war," I said. It seemed to make sense to me, but he was not pleased at all.

"You of all people should know why we must. You were stabbed by agents of Rus, and you almost died. The truth is, we will fight a war; hell, we're already in one. The difference is that now, it's declared. Instead of letting them make raids on our border cities, we can stand against them with everything we have. Because we are at war, we can levy taxes and conscript soldiers at a much higher rate."

I was surprised by him. I had always had stars in my eyes because of how he looked and acted. He was so pretty, so suave and confident. Now I was seeing another side of him. He had assumed leadership and was doing his best to play with a poor hand of cards. My attraction to him grew as he matured, increasing with each passing day.

"With my family's support, and the support of the other noble houses, maybe we will have a chance. Both of my older brothers are experienced. You should lean on them when you need help."

"I appreciate that, Jafra." We walked quietly for a moment before he turned back to me. "Will you be enlisting?"

"Enlisting?" Was he crazy? "I'm a girl."

"You're a woman now. What you did to save my parents, and, my God, what you did to save us all at your Ascension Ball… You are amazingly, ridiculously powerful. I actually think you could turn the tide of a battle by yourself."

"I really don't know the first thing about fighting and war. I only just started sword training, and my younger brother still kicks my ass. I can't run fast or lift things, and frankly, I would look terrible in a uniform." I ran my fingers up and down his pristine, white lapel. "Although you look very dashing in yours."

"I want you to think about it. I know that it's far outside your comfort zone, but I think you would save hundreds, maybe thousands of lives."

"For you? I'll think about it."


I received a message from Hedwig to meet her at an outdoor café. I decided after meeting with the Englishman that I would look more closely at this Brotherhood of Virtue. I had my men with me, and we arrived precisely at the appointed meeting time.

She had already arrived and appeared to be sitting alone at a table for two off in the corner. She wore a gay dress, bright yellow with white trim, trying to offset the severity of her features. As much as she tried to be pleasant and approachable, I always felt on edge when we met.

"Good afternoon, Jafra dear. Please sit," she said, indicating the other chair.

"Lovely day, isn't it?" I asked. I left my guards with the car, but they were alert and never more than twenty feet from me. I sat and placed the silk napkin on my lap. "I never got to thank you properly for your assistance at the ball. I would surely be dead without your timely intervention."

"Think nothing of it. I would have done the same for anyone." She called over a waitress and ordered tea and small sandwiches for us.

"I still have a souvenir of the attack. A remembrance. Would you like to see?"

"A bit odd, but yes. You've piqued my curiosity."

I reached into my bag and pulled out the dagger, wrapped in a lace handkerchief. I placed it on the table, and she reached over to take it. The poison and my blood had been thoroughly cleaned from the rather ordinary blade. The handle is what caught her attention.

"I feel like that scowling bird is an evil portend," I said as she stared at it.

"Yes, evil indeed." She wrapped it again, then handed it back to me as she scanned the area to see if anyone had seen us. "Show that to no one, other than the few you've already shown it to. It is the symbol of a truly evil cadre of villains. They stabbed a young woman in the back, and they would stop at nothing to achieve their wicked aims."

"You know the name of their group?"

"Yes. They are called the Court of Whispers."

"Odd name. Do you know anything about them, other than they tried to kill the king and stabbed me in the back?"

"I don't really know much about them. They are violent, obviously, and they have enough power to enlist both channelers and even a few wielders. I can't tell you what their motivations are. They are very secretive, and they are in every country in Europa by now."

Everything she said seemed to track with what I had been thinking. This group was not afraid to attack even the most well-protected targets. I would have to talk to Father about them; they were as much of a threat as the Rus.

"This is not why you messaged me," I said, putting away the dagger. "Do you have a lead on the other prime brand wielders?"

"No. We have people looking into one of them, and we think we're close, but nothing concrete yet. Have any of them contacted you? You need to be careful. Whoever they are, they may not share our same values. We don't know the extent of their powers." She smiled at me. "Truthfully, we do not even know the extent of your capabilities. I've seen what you can do, but I wonder if we've only scratched the surface."

"They want me to enlist in the army. The Commanding General himself said that I can save thousands of lives, turn the tide of any battle that I'm in."

"I don't doubt that he's correct. You don't sound very enthusiastic about it."

"I hate bloodshed, and I have no desire to hurt people. What I've done in the past was purely in self-defense. I don't want to be a weapon, even if it's in defense of our country."

I studied her expression for signs that she agreed or disagreed with me, but the way she twisted her mouth, scrunched her eyes, I couldn't determine if she was on my side or thought I was being a cowardly, selfish girl.

"Think if we arm every citizen, including the waiter," she commented, pointing at our server across the room with her sharp chin, "or your maid. The man who sells you vegetables, your hairdresser, all of these people might be able to attain brands and would be gifted with power." She leaned over to speak to me in a near whisper. "I have gotten permission for us to return to the Star Chamber. It's a small window; it would have to be tomorrow at eight in the morning. There is a trial going on at noon, so we would have to be out long before then."

"You would be going with me?" I was surprised that she was taking direct action.

"Yes. We need to explore the chamber. When you go through trials, it's in and out quickly. Everyone is so flustered that they don't look around the room. I can only imagine what we might find."

"You are sure that we won't get in any trouble? I'm not looking to break any laws."

"The leaders who keep tight control of the chambers may not like the idea, but there is no law in writing saying that a wielder can't re-enter the Star Chamber."

"I'm curious to see what's in there. I saw a metal placard behind the stone, but I was too scared to do anything other than start the trial. I'll meet you at Izabelin, and we can walk from there." I was curious not only about what we might find, but also about Hedwig and her real motivations.

After the Night of the Comet, a cave system had erupted in Kampinos National Park. Kazuch walked down into the ravine with me while Urban followed behind. I had no intention of wearing a rubberized suit like the first time; instead, I had on my brother's green shirt and baggy brown pants. I had my hair tied back in a ponytail, and at my guard's suggestion, I had a pulse pistol strapped to my side.

At the bottom of the hill, near the entrance to the cave, Hedwig was waiting. She, too, wore clothing more appropriate for spelunking. I told my men to stay behind and only come in if we had not returned within an hour. After a bit of chatter, we entered, and I took the lead.

"I was scared the first time, but now that I know better, I'm not worried at all."

"We may find nothing," she replied. "I hope we get some clues, like how these magical stones showed up in caves all over the world. Were they here all along, since God made the heavens and the earth? Did they sprout from their entombment only when signaled by the comet? Or did the comet somehow place them in the ground where they created chambers, and a roadmap to the powers they granted?"

I had never given it too much thought. Her theories were interesting, and after she said it, it only made sense that the Star Chambers were not natural occurrences and that some intelligence created and placed them there.

"I assume that they were created for some noble purpose, to give us flawed creatures abilities to rise above and help our fellow man," I postured.

"I agree, Jafra. I pray that this gift that humanity has been given is meant to elevate us, not to sow division in our societies. That is a main reason why the Brotherhood feels that this world would benefit from more heroes, more people who can perform miracles."

We walked quietly for a while. My opinion on blanks, the lower caste of our society, had evolved. I never thought about them much until very recently. I only knew a few by name, and they were our servants and people who worked the lands we managed. It was shameful, but I'd thought of them more like furniture. Something useful and available when you needed it, but not particularly important in the grand scheme of things. After seeing the poor boy begging for food, I realized that every house held people who were living, loving, laughing, and sometimes suffering, and in need of help and compassion.

What had not changed was my reticence at giving out brands willy-nilly. Not everyone had good intentions, and many would use their power to threaten, bully, and intimidate others. Super strength was a blessing in the hands of an honest person. There was no limit to the good they could do. But in the wrong hands? The fiend could force his neighbors to kowtow to him, to give up their accumulated wealth, their women, even their lives. If there were superheroes, it only made sense that there would be supervillains as well.

As it stood, only those of noble birth could be granted a brand and have it activated by Abyrinth's Fire. Was that just an arbitrary way of keeping power in the hands of the well-bred and highly educated? Not all nobles were indeed noble. Take, for example, the Rus. Their army had dozens of wielders and hundreds upon hundreds of channelers. They might think they are killing my people for some higher purpose, but I doubt it. What I saw, and what most Poles saw, was an evil empire led by evil men and women who have taken their gifts and used them for murder and conquest.

"Hedwig?"

"Yes?"

"I hear you talking about this dream of giving power to the people. Everyone would get a brand, and then they would have superhuman abilities. In this scenario, would there be some kind of screening process? I know that some blanks are wonderful people, but some are rotten to the core. If a bad person gets the ability to see in the dark, that's not the same as a bad person getting the ability to start fires with a thought."

"You have a great point. I suppose that we would have to determine who was worthy and who was not."

"Who would make that decision? The Brotherhood of Virtue? The king? I don't want to be the one to pass judgment on my fellow man."

"I think you're getting a bit ahead of yourself. We are a long way from realizing such a future. For now, let's see if there are any undiscovered mysteries down here," she said as I exited the crevice and entered the cave. As always, Abyrinth's Fire sat on its pedestal, shining brightly like a captive star.

The space was just as I remembered it. It looked like it was carved from the surrounding stone, with the waist-high pedestal, the metal placard behind it listing all possible brand designs, and nothing else.

The gem was mounted on a machine that looked unlike any I had ever seen. It was definitely not steam-powered, and when I tried to pour Abyrinth into it remotely, it had no effect.

I placed my hand on the stone, gripping it firmly. Hedwig was going to stop me, but I was too fast. Nothing happened.

"I was afraid you would be sent away to do another trial," she exclaimed. She placed her hand on the stone as I had, then nodded when nothing happened to her.

I had another idea. When she removed her hand, I put mine back and then willed Abyrinth into the stone.

I found myself in a featureless white void. There were no sounds, no people or objects around me, and the only thing I could feel was my own body. I tried to look for Abyrith and found it everywhere! Normally, I would see strings of pure energy floating through the air, smoky energy clinging to channelers and wielders, and clouds of Abyrinth wafting lazily through the air. When I focused on the power, I could see that it filled every inch of the void I was in. It felt smothering, claustrophobic. My heart began to race as anxiety seeped into every pore of my being.

I turned off my perception and returned to the still, featureless, but less terrorizing void. I watched a comet pass the Earth; my perspective was from somewhere deep in space. I saw lights blink on, and I knew they were the locations where the Abyrinth's Fire gems were located. Slowly, they winked awake, as if they were opening their petals to receive the life-giving rays of the sun. The gems were buried underground for hundreds or even thousands of years, and the passing comet brought them to life.

There were no voices, no words; instead, I had images and information that were placed directly into my conscious mind. I saw a column of energy rising from the stone and passing through the cave's roof. The scene panned out to show the beam of light rising upward into the clouds.

The view pulled back, further from the light. I could see all of Warszawa, the city lights twinkling in the darkness. The view continued to pull back and upward. I was high enough to see all of Europa; there were a dozen beams of light coming from Polska, Germania, Britannia, Francia, Italia, Hispania, Bohemia, Scandanavia, Hellas, and Moldavia. As I moved farther and farther from Earth, I could see the lights from other continents: the Orient, Ethiopia, the Americas, Austral, and Europa. They extended into space and wove together to form a single ray of light centered on a spot over the Atlantic Ocean, then traveled off into space to be lost among the billions of stars.

I wondered what it meant. It must have been shown to me for an important reason. Was that energy flowing from the stones to some distant location in space? Or was it energy originating from space and feeding into the gems? I could usually detect not only the presence of Abyrinth, but also from which way it was flowing, but I wasn't able to tell its direction.

Like a meteor, I began to crash into the Earth, dropping at a thousand miles a minute. I didn't strike the ground; instead, I passed through it like a ghost. I went through hundreds of miles of solid earth, then through molten rock that seemed to go on forever. All around me, I could see an ocean of Abyrinth, flowing in channels like currents. There was an unquantifiable amount of energy created in the bowels of our planet. I didn't like where my thoughts were going at that point.

The scene changed, and I saw three brands. My brand focused on energy control; the other two were the primary brands, representing control over time and space. My vision showed them as equals, locked in a circuit that would let them travel through time and space and control enough energy to move mountains. They melded together, forming a singular, all-powerful entity that glowed like a star and was impossible to look at directly. I studied the glowing figure as best I could, and couldn't help thinking, Is this God? God was the master of time and space, and maybe Abyrinth was the physical manifestation of the spirit. I had no idea if my interpretation held any merit, and…

"Jafra, are you ok?" Hedwig asked. Her face was only inches from mine, and as she shook me out of my vision, I thought she was both concerned and perturbed by my distracted state. When I lost the flow of images, I slowly returned to the mundane world.

"Yes, of course. Why do you ask?"

"You drifted off for over a minute, just staring into the void with your hand on Abyrinth's fire." My hand had fallen to my side, but I could still feel the comforting warmth of the stone.

"Sorry, I was trying to infuse it with power, see if it would trigger something. Nothing on the pedestal moved?"

"Nothing." She stepped to the stone and placed her hand on it. She closed her eyes, and I could tell that she was trying to make something happen, anything, but to her, it was inert.

"Damn waste of time," she muttered.

"You're right. Let's head back."

# Chapter 25

Interlude I:

Thousands of Rus troops, along with armor, mechs, and a Goliath, rolled into the town of Braniszów. It was only twenty miles from the Biała Ruś border and was a prime target due to the military base just outside the city boundaries. There were five thousand soldiers there, with a hundred tanks, scores of artillery units, two dozen mechs, and three Goliaths.

They only had three of the Goliaths because they were insanely expensive. They used old-style steam engines to propel the fifty-foot behemoths into battle. Each was the size of a small factory, sitting atop four massive legs that propelled them at a painfully slow pace. Their saving grace was that they were nearly unstoppable, and they carried firepower that was unmatched anywhere.

The Rus colonel was sitting in the observation deck of one of his Goliaths. He was an ugly man in his forties, with salt and pepper hair, and a bushy mustache that was wide and curved around his mouth like a frown. His blue uniform had gold-embroidered trim, and his chest was adorned with ribbons that stood in place of his many medals.

The war machine he rode in could carry a hundred men easily, along with a crew of twenty-five that ran the steamworks and controlled the cannons and Gatling guns. There was no need for channelers on those brutes; they ran on steam and carried massive cannons that fired projectiles powered by conventional explosives. The command cabin was reserved for the pilot and commander, but when the highest-ranking officer in the ninth battalion was aboard, he was given the suite.

Standing around a table covered in maps, he listened to his advisors as they planned out their invasion strategy. He felt a tap on his shoulder and turned around to see that no one was there.

"Major Sokolov, show yourself," the colonel said.

The major was more commonly known by the title bestowed on him by the tsar: Baron Gavriil Sokolov. The officer was invisible, laughing as he blinked into view. He looked at the maps, then pointed. He was taller than his brother, but much thinner. He had brown, almost black hair, pale skin, and a pockmarked face. Unlike his older brother, he wore his uniform casually, not bothering to get it properly tailored, and his medals and tie were nowhere to be seen.

"They have their tanks along this ridge, and one Goliath over here by the river. It's shallow enough for the machine to cross," Gavriil said.

"That's what I suspected. What about the other Goliaths?" The colonel stared at the map.

The major pinpointed all the locations of the defending Polish forces. He'd been out scouting for three hours and had very detailed locations and troop numbers. His brother was the leader, the tactical genius of the family. He was the smart, sneaky one. His invisibility made him an ideal scout and spy. The colonel examined the layout and grunted in dissatisfaction.

"We have more assets, but they're dug in and have a better feel for the terrain." He turned to one of his commanders. "Send word to bring up the blackships."

"Right away, comrade colonel!" a young lieutenant said, running off to the radio room. The order was given, and the airship captains were ordered to move their craft to the front.

The Rus airships were a fearsome sight. The hundred-foot-long ships were torpedo-shaped in the front and had rudders and elevators at the rear. A tower rose above the rear of the superstructure, housing the captain's cabin and the steering controls. Below was a metal section that resembled a ship's keel, but instead of tapering to a point, it had a large capsule attached. The canvas sides of the balloon were painted black and bore the double-headed eagle of the Rus Empire: two eagles facing outward and wearing crowns. Steam poured from their engines, which drove propellers on both sides and at the rear. The ships were glacially slow, but they brought death to those in their path.

The captains were given their targets, and they flew several hundred feet in the cool Polish skies. They could be seen for miles, but the defenders could do little to stop them. Their Goliaths had main guns that could fire on targets several hundred feet away, but their range when firing over forty-five degrees was terrible. The airships were out of their range.

Polish mechs and Goliaths began scattering, but they moved even slower than the airships. When they were over the target, the bomb bay doors opened to deliver their payloads. The Goliaths were so large that they were impossible to miss. High-explosive bombs rained down from the ships to impact on the Polish armament. Nothing was able to survive the devastation as twenty bombers dropped three dozen bombs each. When they were finished, all of the defending Goliaths, mechs, and tanks were destroyed. Hundreds of soldiers were also caught in the maelstrom that ensued. Much of the Polish infantry and cavalry withdrew to the town, but when they realized they would have no support, they abandoned the city and retreated east. Braniszów was left undefended.

"Excellent work, comrade colonel," the captain of the Goliath said. He was an older man, a few inches short of six feet tall, with grey at the temples, in his beard, and mustache. He was a fine Rus soldier from a distinguished family, and he carried himself accordingly.

"Yes, commend the captains on their accuracy." He thought to himself as he stared at the maps again. "We need to send a message to these people. Let them know that this is now Rus, a part of the greater Rus Empire."

"What do you suggest?"

"We attack the city. Send in the tanks first, then the mechs. When we've leveled the place, we send in infantry to clean up."

"Clean up? Your brother has gone in personally and has reported that all of the Polish troops have passed through the city and are fleeing down the highways going eastward."

"Yes, but the people are still there. The citizens. They defy us, so they must pay." He looked at his junior officer with a look that sent shivers down the man's spine. "I want the city cleansed. Leave no building standing. Take no prisoners."

The veteran military officer looked at the colonel, not wanting to believe the order that he'd been given. With as much military professionalism as he could muster, he managed, "Aye, sir. I will convey your orders, and, at your signal, we will commence the attack."

The tanks rolled forward, followed by mechs and Goliaths. Tanks were massively heavy, but they were light enough to use the advanced steam power units. They were heavily armored and were armed with massive cannons that could drop a single-story building with a single shot.

Plowing through the city streets, they shot at anything that moved. Mechs followed in their wake, punching through the walls of stores, workshops, city buildings, and anything that they came across. The Goliaths rained hell down on vast swaths of the city, with incendiary rounds that would explode and level almost any structure.

Braniszów was a thriving city of six thousand, a small community that had existed for over a thousand years. In the span of a few hours, it was flattened. The mounds of rubble were stained red with the blood of her citizens. Major Sokolov didn't have to expend his power of invisibility while scouting out the damage. He climbed over broken cars and buildings that were utterly destroyed. Fires were everywhere, and the only signs of life were his own men, scouring the debris for living Poles. He saw the body of a woman, about his mother's age, lying dead in the corner of a burned-out restaurant. She had her arms around the corpses of a boy and a girl who must have been her grandchildren. He followed his brother's lead and the tsar's orders, but such things still broke his heart.

# Chapter 26

When I heard about the massacre at Braniszów, I got sick to my stomach. I actually threw up. Father read the report to us after the evening meal. Mother begged him not to, but he felt it was important that we know what was happening in our country. My brothers, including Jurek, got angry. Stefek and Krystian were already in the military and would redouble their efforts to hunt down Rus invaders and kill them. Younger brother Jurek demanded to quit school and be inducted into the service immediately. Father, of course, said no.

Stefek turned to me in a lull in the conversation. "Jafra, are you thinking of joining? What you did at the airship was… beyond incredible. Power like yours could turn the tide of a battle, save many lives."

"You stop this minute!" Mother yelled across the table. I had not heard her yell like that in all my eighteen years, and it seemed to catch all of us by surprise. "She is a girl, not a man like you. She's meant for marriage and babies, for keeping a home! I didn't raise a perfect lady so she could get killed or maimed in a war that we can't win!"

Hearing my mother declare that we were doomed hit me harder than all the teeth gnashing and foreboding language spewed by the men. Mother was always the most levelheaded person I knew. It wasn't that she was detached from reality, but she almost always chose the path of positivity and optimism. For her to unequivocally state ours was a lost cause was like hearing a proclamation from almighty God himself.

"Your mother's right. We can't ask your sister to risk her life," Father said directly to Stefek. "I've seen her spar with you boys, and she's not ready. True, her brand could be a game-changer in certain situations, but a brand is only as strong as the person bearing it. She's not bulletproof like me, or able to resist an opponent who can stop time and slit her throat." He turned to face me. "Jafra, I'm forbidding you to join the army. If we can't win a war without you, then maybe it's our fate to be conquered." He was angry at the situation, and I could see the frustration in his eyes. In all of their eyes. Even little Dominika looked both terrified and upset.

"I don't mean to contradict you, Father, but she is an adult. She can make her own decisions." Stefek looked me in the eyes. "As nobles, it's our solemn duty to protect the kingdom, our citizens, even if it means we lose our lives. Are you ready to put on the uniform and fight for Polska?"

The room fell into an unnatural silence. Tempers had already been raised, and each of our faces was red with the depth of our anxiety, fear, and anger. They all meant well; they all had a sense of moral conviction, a certitude of their position's correctness. Their impotent rage was moved from the crimes of our enemy to the question of my decision to do, or not do, what for thousands of years had been the duty of men. To fight and die for the tribe.

"Jafra!" Stefek repeated.

I answered with my gut, my head, and my heart. "No. Father is right, I'm not ready. I can't do what you boys do. Hearing about the massacre of Braniszów makes me sick, makes me hate. But I don't like hating, and I have no desire to take life. Even the life of our enemies."

"You killed the men who attacked you and Mother," Krystian said, speaking for the first time since the debate began. I knew it was coming, so I wasn't surprised by the pointing out of my hypocrisy. I was surprised by who made the point.

"I pushed men over the side of the ship. They were gone, no longer threatening us, and I saw no blood. What you do, oldest brother, is stop time and stab helpless men through the heart. You cut windpipes and let men choke on their own blood. What you do, second-oldest brother, is less violent, but you have come home on multiple occasions wearing other men's blood. You're men, created to protect and, if necessary, kill. Mother and I, and even Dominika, were created to bring life, not to take it." They listened to me, and it felt strange, because as a middle child, I was often ignored. Having overwhelming power made me hard to ignore these days. "I love all of you. I love Polska with every fiber of my being, but I will not take up arms. I will not kill."


It was less than two weeks later when I heard the air raid sirens going off. Both of my brothers had gone to their posts, leading brave Polish men and women into battle. Father was too old to be on the front lines, but he worked closely with the king and the other lords to coordinate our defense. I spent most of my time preparing for classes, so I wasn't really paying attention to current events. The sirens were everywhere in the capital and less so in the countryside. I put on the radio to see what the alert was about.

"…and the incursion is in the small suburb of Warszawa."

I screamed inside my head. What? The Rus have already reached the suburbs of Warszawa? I had to know more.

"What city? Where are they? Damn it all!" I rarely cursed, especially out loud.

The broadcast was on a loop, and they continued to give details about the Black Ships that had slowly approached the city limits before dropping their tens of thousands of pounds of high-explosive bombs. By all accounts, the damage was biblical. Fires were raging throughout the town, and the few estates of noble families were especially targeted.

"Alert! All citizens near Lubrawa, please evacuate immediately! Head west or north. Rus forces are bombing Lubrawa, and ground troops have been spotted moving in from the east. Thousands of soldiers, along with tanks and mechanical walkers, are poised to enter the city as soon as the black airships have completed their bombing runs. Repeat, evacuate Lubrawa."

"Milka!" I screamed. I quickly put on my brother's brown pants and a dark green shirt, then ran to the guardhouse. The guards that weren't manning posts at the gate or on patrol were hovering over the radio. Their expressions were a mix of fear, anger, frustration, and more anger. Urban had left our employ to join the army. My personal security guard was there with a few others.

"Kazuch, get the car ready! Cousin Milka is in grave danger!"

"I know, milady. We've been listening to the reports for the last hour. That whole village is under attack; it's not safe to get anywhere near there."

"We have to go! She needs help. She's so pregnant, she has a hard time walking, much less running. They'll target her house for sure; it's the nicest in that whole town."

"I've been there, miss. I've driven you there probably a hundred times. But I won't be driving you there today." His tone was firm, steeled like his spine.

"Kazuch, she needs me! If she's in danger, I can help!"

"You might be able to help, but there is a much greater chance that you'll be killed. My only job, my sole purpose in life, is to keep you safe." He looked at me as hard as Father did. "I will not be driving you into a war zone."

My emotions had gotten the best of me; I wasn't thinking straight. "Give me the keys! I'll drive myself!"

"First off, you don't know how to drive, and this is not the time to learn. Second, and most important, even if you did know how to drive, I wouldn't allow it." There was no hesitation or indecision in his stance; I knew he meant it.

"Damn it! I'll have Father fire you!"

"No, you won't."

I felt myself begin to crumble. My knees were betraying me, shaking like reeds in a strong wind. He took me into his strong arms, and I cried against his chest. Sobs came out of me like the child I felt like at that moment. He had guarded me since before I could remember. He was always a force in my life, trusted beyond reproach. Next to my father, he was the man I trusted most in the world, and he knew it. As he held me, they kept repeating the news, reports of the devastation of a sizable town outside the downtown area. I feared the worst.

According to later reports, our Army Air Corps had used a small fleet of retrofitted airships to go after the Black Ships. They used the same wings I saw at the airship races, and they were a magnitude faster, turning and diving much faster than the massive bombers. Their pulse weapons tore hundreds of holes in each black ship's hull, letting out the gases that kept them aloft. They crashed to the earth, but not before laying waste to my cousin's hometown.

The battalion that was guarding the king's castle was reassigned along with other units in the nearby bases. Several thousand Polish troops surged into the area and, after a long, bloody battle, pushed them back. They retreated east, but not as far as the border. Their staging area was well within our borders, and even though they were forced to retreat, they still held vast tracts of our land.

It was a full day after the Rus retreated that my father would allow me to enter the area. I apologized to Kazuch, and he graciously accepted. He drove me straight to Ostrogski estate, and I could hardly breathe as we neared the gates that I was so familiar with. We saw smoke for a mile before we came to the heavy gates, now bent back from the entrance. I thought I saw the body of a guard in a nearby hedge, but my driver didn't pause before entering the driveway. Her husband's property was not large, and I could see the burnt-out and still-smoldering remains of her house from the gate. As we drew near, I felt a sense of dread.

I saw them lined up in the driveway in front of the house. Milka, her husband, his parents, and three servants. They were in a line on the ground. Each of them had their head crushed.  It looked like a giant hand had pinched their skulls, and the gray matter within had exploded through the top of their skulls. Adding insult to injury, there was a sword wound through Milka's abdomen. They apparently wanted to kill the child separately from the mother. Blood and gore surrounded them, wetting the soot-covered ground.

My worrying had not been unfounded. I knew instantly when I heard what town was being victimized that I would be losing my cousin and best friend. The blood was dried, so this must have happened a full day earlier. If dear Kazuch had bent to my demands, I still wouldn't have gotten here in time to save them. I would have put him and myself into danger unnecessarily.

"I'm so sorry, dearie," he said, taking my hand.

"Let's go home."

On the way home, I thought about the tragedies my countrymen had suffered. None of it was my fault; I realized that I couldn't stay safely on the sidelines anymore. There were no sidelines, no safe places to live your life in peace. I had been selfish and childish and had forgotten my duty. If a pregnant young woman could be so violently butchered in front of her husband and in her own home, then no one was safe.

In that moment, I resolved to actively join the fight. I would do whatever it took to fight the Rus and push them from our lands. Lastly, I would find the creature that murdered my best friend and kill him as ruthlessly as he killed her.

# Chapter 27

Women were not required to join the military, but many of us did. Some female blanks joined if they had a special skill that was helpful. A lot became doctors and nurses, working behind the lines to support the war effort. There were a lot of wielders, like Milka, who had abilities that didn't translate well to fighting. She had worked in downtown Warszawa, organizing the home front resource drive. Food, fuel, and metals were all being rationed, and she helped with the logistics, getting supplies to where they would be needed. Unlike me, she had answered when our country called. That was, until the Rus brutally murdered her.

Against Lord and Lady Sobieski's objections, I joined the military. I was appointed Kapitan in the Wojsko Królewskie under my brother Stefek. Thankfully, I was not given the responsibility of commanding any soldiers. They respected the strength of my brand, but I was still an eighteen-year-old girl and should not have any authority over hundreds of grown men.

I stood in my room at home, staring at myself in a full-length mirror. I wore a dark green uniform, consistent with our family colors, with gold braids and three gold stars embroidered on the epaulets. The utility jacket was tight across my chest, with a green t-shirt beneath. What was very different for me were the utility pants. There were large pockets with sealing flaps on the thighs, and they tucked into heavy, black boots. My long, raven-black hair was rolled into a tight bun at the back of my head. I tried on the beret with three stars on the front, and even though it was a bit masculine for my taste, I thought I looked cute.

The concession that I made was that I should always be close to Stefek. I could sit in the corner of the tent during his planning meetings, but I was not to speak or contribute in any way. I walked across the field where we were camped and reported to my oldest brother.

"Kapitan Sobieski, reporting as ordered," I said with a crisp salute.

He looked me over, his eyes taking in every detail.

"Kapitan. You wouldn't pass even a mild inspection, but for someone who was a civilian only days ago and has not gone through basic training, you have done well." Kind of a backhanded compliment, but I accepted it with good humor. "Jafra, I have something for you."

He walked over to a footlocker on the ground near his cot. He opened it and withdrew two blue velvet bags. One long and slender, the other small and oblong. He set down the smaller bag, then pulled the drawstring of the longer one. Reaching inside, he pulled out a sword by the grip handle. It had dull brass on the pommel and cross guard. The blade was in a flat black scabbard. He also pulled out a black leather belt with a strap that would loop over my right shoulder.

"I would have loved to give you a gleaming parade sword, but in battle, you don't want to be the one shiny spot in a sea of green." He helped me equip the sword belt, tightening it until I felt squeezed like a corset. He made a motion for me to pull the sword.

"Thank you, Colonel."

I had trained for months with my brothers, smacking each other with wooden training swords. This was a real sword. I drew it slowly from the scabbard, entranced by the gleaming steel blade. My oldest brother was not usually a sentimental man, but I could tell that this weapon had been made especially for me. The length wouldn't have served a man his size, but it was perfectly sized for my hand and reach. I held it before me, staring at the blade like a moth does a flame.

"Attention!" he barked. "En garde!"

I assumed the starting position, just as Jurek had drilled into me.

"Flunge!"

I exploded forward, blade first. My point didn't waver an inch. I was very proud of myself.

"Feint!"

I leapt forward to attack before pulling back into a defensive pose.

"Recover!"

I returned to the en garde position.

"Not terrible, Kapitan. I will give my compliments to our younger brother." I got a rare smile from Stefek. He already had the smaller bag in his hands and pulled at the drawstring. He reached inside and pulled out a pulse pistol. It was engineered for a woman, and it looked small in his large, rough hand. "You may be deadly as hell, but I'd feel better with you being fully armed. You're my favorite sister, and my third favorite sibling." Naturally, I was behind Krystian and Jurek. I could live with that.


Since declaring war a few weeks ago, things had progressed rapidly. Rus soldiers had magically formed a brigade equipped with armor and mechs, and it was very near the Biała Ruś -Polska border. Stefek was the leader of the Fifth Warszawa Regiment, and we were waiting for another full regiment from south of the capital, around Radom and Kielce.

There wasn't enough time.

I heard a commotion in the camp, and when I looked out of my tent, I saw soldiers running every which way. It didn't take a Sherlock Holmes to know that something big was happening. I ducked back inside, slipped into my sword harness, and strapped on my pistol. I ran to my commander's tent to get my orders. Like everyone else in the regiment, I knew what would cause this level of ruckus.

"Colonel! The Rus First Brigade has crossed the border by Brest, and is heading towards Biala Podlaska! They will be at the city outskirts in minutes!"

They had a map of the local area laid out on a fold-up table. Stef was pointing to locations and sending his lieutenants to their various assignments. When they had all been dispatched, he saw me.

"Stay on me! When we engage the enemy, stay behind cover and don't peek your head out!"

He ran towards a steam rover and jumped into the passenger seat. The transport was ugly and utilitarian, dull grey metal and fat rubber tires. It could accommodate ten, including the driver, and looked like the food trays given to prisoners or public school children. I barely fell into the back seat before it went steaming off towards the hills to our south.

The small vehicle was faster than the larger troop transports, and we arrived first on scene. We came upon a ranch on the outskirts of a small village that had the misfortune to be between the border and some larger cities in our country. The main house was already on fire, and a forty-ish-year-old man and his twenty-something-year-old son were lying face down with their hands tied behind their backs. Each had a single shot to the back of the head. There were no women, and it terrified me to think what had become of them.

The driver was a blank, so he carried a regular explosive-based rifle. They all wore sturdy, metal helmets, and I realized that I was wearing my fashionable beret. Stef was right, I really should keep my head down!

The driver was gesticulating towards the barn, a motion that we should follow him. Stef had his sword out and was running after him, pushing his way ahead of the man. They entered the barn, and I decided to follow my brother's instructions and hang back.

A strange effect of Stefek's Chronoburst was that when he stopped time, even for a second or two, it gave him the luxury of making a carefully chosen sword thrust. Pushing a blade entirely through a man's heart, or slitting his throat, he could kill his enemy without him having the ability to cry out in pain as he died. I heard three loud thumps, followed a second later by women screaming.  I took that as my cue to enter.

A Polish farmwoman was on a bale of hay, her legs splayed apart. She was a few years older than me, and though she no doubt led a life full of hard work, she was quite pretty. An older woman huddled in a horse stall with her arms around two younger girls. On the ground were the rapists. Three Rus soldiers, each with cuts to their throats that were so deep, you could see their spines. Stefek stood over the bodies, his breath coming in rapid pants and his eyes wild with bloodlust. I went to the woman and helped her piece together her torn skirts and blouse. Though she was my senior, she clung to me as a child to a mother. I let her weep and held her tighter than I've ever held anyone.

Lieutenant Kowalski came in, saw the butchered bodies on the ground, and didn't give them a second thought. He whispered to Stefek, and they moved out, everyone knowing to follow without being told.

"Pani," I said, offering the common salutation to a slightly older woman. "We have to leave. There are many Rus left to kill." She nodded, still in shock. The sound of gunshots rang out, like large hailstones on a thin metal roof. Loud and jarring. "We will kill all of the soldiers here, and then we will move on to the next ranch and the next, until these bastards are purged from all of Polska. When we have moved on, take them." I pointed at the older woman and the children. "Head towards Warszawa. Do not take the time to bury your men. You will probably be picked up by partisans on the main road. They should help to transport you to a shelter." She nodded again, numbly. "Go with God, pani."

I wanted to stay and comfort her, but I couldn't. Despite not having a command or troops that followed me, I was an officer in the Royal Army. I went to the door and peeked around the corner. It was clear, and I ran towards the sound of gunfire.

Our small group had advanced several hundred feet and was now pinned down behind a hedgerow that ran for hundreds of yards in either direction. There were an unknown number of Rus soldiers hidden in a stand of trees across a hundred yards of open field. There was a sniper camped out in a large oak on the edge of the wood, and he was keeping everyone's heads down.

"I could take them out one by one, but the distance is too far. If I expose myself, they'll mow me down, not counting that damned sniper," Stefek growled. He saw me come up behind him and the lieutenant. "Jafra, you're a damned good shot. Want to give it a try?"

My ability with a sword was nothing to brag about, but I seemed to have a natural affinity for marksmanship. Lieutenant Kowalski unslung a pulse rifle and handed it to me. It was incredibly light compared to the gunpowder-based guns. The hollow wood stock was longer than I found comfortable, but not by too much. The steel barrel was a foot and a half, with front and rear iron sights. The idea was for a channeler or wielder to focus energy into the mechanism of the weapon. It would fire a pulse of pure energy that would strike with the force of a metal round, but without the recoil of a gunpowder weapon.

"I'm better with a pistol," I hedged, but I crawled up until I could rest the barrel of the rifle on a rock set into the hedgerow. A shot rang out as I was getting settled, and I heard a cry of pain from someone to the left of us. I looked over to see one of the soldiers who rode with us holding a bleeding wound on the side of his head. A corpsman was desperately trying to apply a bandage while still maintaining cover. A second shot sounded, and I saw the flash of the muzzle up in the branches of the tree. I squinted, and now I could clearly see the man, branches gathered around him. He lay on a thick branch, looking like a baby bird in a nest.

"I see him!" I whispered.

"Take him out," Stefek said with cold fury in his tone.

I lined up the target in the front sight and the rear sight. I remembered my training; firing a rifle was completely different from firing a pistol. I took a deep breath. Another shot broke the quiet of the field. I heard someone groan in pain. I slowly let out my breath, then, when I had expelled half my lungful of air, I pulled the trigger. The pulse, invisible to everyone else, was launched at the sniper faster than the speed of sound.

My ability let me see the pulse, which was about an inch long and rounded at both ends. To my eyes, it was a glowing projectile that rocketed straight through the chest of the Rus sniper. We could hear his scream from where we huddled, and a second later, we saw him tumble lifelessly to the ground. If he weren't dead already, the fall would have sealed the deal.

Cheering arose from our side when their sniper died, but I wasn't done. I began to focus on the next victim. I didn't know the Rus ranks, but he had a lot of gold thread on his cap, so he died next. I put a pulse through his neck and nearly decapitated him. After I took my third victim, they abandoned their cover and started running deeper into the woods. I got two more before the trees hid them.

"Charge!" Stefek shouted. He led from the front, being the first to cross the field and enter the woods. I let the others go first, and I was the last to enter the deeply-shadowed woods. Stefek was long gone, and the soldiers were disappearing into the trees, leaving me at the edge of the small forest.

I walked over to the first man that I shot, the sniper. The hole through his chest was small, but perfectly placed. He lay in a puddle of his own lifeblood; his limbs twisted unnaturally by the twenty-five-foot fall. He was neither ugly nor beautiful. An average face on a man, only a couple of years older than me. He invaded my country, had Polish blood on his hands, so I should have been elated that he was dead. I wasn't. That was the first time I had to confront the face of a corpse of my creation. I couldn't cry for him. No. I had done what was necessary, and I had no regrets. He wanted to kill me, and worse, he tried to kill my brother and the others. But I felt an emptiness inside of me. A hole that would need filling someday. With what? I had no idea.

The sounds of gunfire and screaming brought me out of my reverie. Gun in hand, I rushed in after my squad. I passed the other bodies that I personally dropped. There was no time to mourn my loss of innocence. I would no doubt take more lives before going to sleep tonight.

They weren't difficult to find. There was a full-scale gunfight going on, and I needed to be careful not to catch a stray bullet or pulse shot. I noticed they had a few channelers as well, which would open up a whole new list of weapons and devices that blank troops couldn't use. A hundred feet in, I could keep following the gunfire, or I could follow the trail of bodies. I saw a lot of young men in Rus uniforms, and to my dismay, several bodies of our soldiers. I could imagine this forest as a quiet, peaceful place when humans weren't running around killing each other. Each dead body was just more loss to heap on the pile of pointless destruction.

I felt hands on me, then I was a dozen feet from where I was standing. I found myself held by Stefek, and we were taking cover behind a wide oak tree.

"Damn it, Jafra! Keep your head on a swivel!" Apparently, a Rus soldier had fired his weapon at me, and instead of going for the shooter, Stefek stopped time to move me out of the bullet's path. "The one that shot at you is really good. He killed two men and injured my lieutenant."

I peered around the trunk of the tree in the direction he was pointing. I got a glimpse of a kid, maybe not even eighteen. He saw me and shot, missing me by an inch or less. I didn't care for people shooting at me, especially when they were trying to shoot me specifically. Hard not to take that personally.

"Give me your knife," I told my older brother and my commander. To his credit, he didn't question me and instead pulled out an eight-inch-long combat knife. I held it in my hands, feeling the weight of the perfectly balanced Damascus steel. The dagger had blades on both sides, and the point was needle-sharp.

I wrapped it in bands of hardened Abyrinth, willing it to hover a foot above my outstretched palm. The men were shocked, and even my brother, who had more than an inkling of my ability, was enthralled.

I made the knife race off to the side, away from our front line. When it was almost out of sight, nearly at the limit of my range, I had it go up at an angle, towards the enemy's position, and at least twenty feet in the air. Shots continued to volley back and forth among our positions in the woods, but our side had slowed considerably because of their crack shot. I pulled a mirror out of my utility pocket and wedged it in the notch of a stick. I could see the kid without having to stick my head up. I maneuvered the knife until it was almost directly over him, then I struck. The cords of Abyrinth snapped like a giant rubber band and launched the knife, point-first, into his neck. I saw the blade sink to the crossbar as blood fountained from his fatal wound. When he dropped to the forest floor, I called out.

"He's down!" I yelled.

"Let's go!" Stefek said, jumping up to lead his men. He had a target in mind, and with a series of short time jumps, he was behind his intended target. To everyone's perception, including mine, he popped up a dozen feet away, then another dozen, and then he was in killing range. He thrust his sword through the man, high up on the chest, and pushed through the length of his abdomen. The man screamed, but my brother was already onto the next opponent.

Lieutenant Kowalski was following in my brother's wake. He was a strong channeler, and he ran while firing a pulse machine gun. He sprayed energy bolts, clearing a path and making the Rus soldiers take cover. We only had a handful of men left, but I didn't think they had more than three or four more in their party. I reached out with my extra sense, and I could see the whisps of energy floating around us. Most of them were blanks, but I saw Colonel Sobieski and the lieutenant glowing like fireflies in the night. And… there was another.

"They have another channeler!" I called out. "Maybe a wielder!"

I shouted loud enough for everyone to hear me. Since they'd lost the element of surprise, there was no reason to hold back. The brush and vines around us began to grow and move like a pit of vipers. Before I knew what to do, both my hands and ankles were being constricted by mutated vines. Another vine was reaching up to wrap around my neck. I could feel the rubbery texture of the plant as it cut off my air supply. I could hear screaming as our other men, who were also trapped, were being slaughtered while being held helpless. I was quickly running out of air, and I was seconds away from panic setting in.

Some new instinct kicked in, a reflex to use my new vision. I saw the vines around my hands, and from the corner of my eye, I could see the one cutting off my airway. They were swathed in the power, and I could see the flow of energy, causing them to contract and tighten.

What the Rus wielder didn't know was that I was the master of Abyrinth.

I drew the energy into myself, causing the vegetation that was binding me to lose its animation. The vines slackened and fell off me, and I rushed towards the source of the wielding.

I entered a clearing to find Stefek being held tightly, his sword on the ground, his face turning purple. A Rus was standing over him, ready to finish my brother's life.

I had developed another instinct in the last month. I pulled my pulse pistol and shot. I put a small, but devastating hole through his face, dropping the man like a rock. There were two Rus soldiers in the same clearing, who were caught by surprise at my bursting onto the scene. I shot each of them in rapid succession, then returned my pistol to its holster with a fluidity that I hadn't earned, but it did look badass.

Stefek was retrieving his sword while looking at the havoc I had wrought. "Little sister, indeed. I know that I'm a good teacher, but that was… exceptional."

# Chapter 28

The main body caught up to us within the hour, but our small force had been decimated. Both Stef and I were bruised, but no worse for wear. Lieutenant Kowalski had been butchered while in the grips of branches; his corpse lay in pieces on the ground.

One soldier had somehow survived. Two enemies lay at his feet as he retched his breakfast into a nearby bush. I understood what he was going through, but my battle fatigue was short-lived. I had attended balls just weeks ago, and now I was a killer.

"Major Kubiak, we really needed you an hour ago. We came on a platoon committing atrocities here, and we stepped in to save the civilians."

"Snipers harassed us on the way. We lost a few men, but were able to give them what all Rus deserve: death!" The man was Stefek's age and the fourth son of a nobleman from Poznań. He would never inherit anything, so he had thrown himself into his military career. He was shy of six feet tall with curly dark hair and a bushy mustache. Even in the heat and having been shot at, he was inspection-ready in his dark green utility uniform and his cap with one embroidered gold star and two gold bars. He was a slight man, but he radiated a manic energy that made me want to get away.

"I wish we could set camp and rest the men, but I think that the Rus main body is near, and we can't be caught flat-footed. Put on a double guard and get our scouts out immediately. Have the rest get food and water, and if we're lucky, a breather for a couple of hours."

He stamped while executing a sharp salute. "Straight away, sir!"

The soldiers kept coming until there were thousands of them in the open space between the ranch houses. Though many were conscripted, I didn't see a boy or man who wasn't ready to die for the motherland. Their attitude and professionalism filled me with pride in my people and my country.

It was getting dark when I saw the scouts head out. Some put on dark face paint and snuck off into the night. I saw a couple of channelers set up with glider-like aircraft, fifteen feet long with twenty-foot wings. The diameter of the ships was just enough for the pilot to lie down and work the steering. The ships were launched from special steam-powered trucks that essentially flung the gliders like a bolt from a crossbow. Once they had some lift, the pilot would use Abyrinth thrusters to gain altitude and to steer. Several were shot into the cloudy, starless sky, and everyone else went back to putting up tents and cooking their evening meal.

I ate dinner in Stefek's tent with the other officers. We reviewed plans to fortify defenses at various locations along this stretch of the border. Most of his command staff were wielders like we were, and a lesser number were simple channelers like the late Lieutenant Kowalski, God rest his soul. None of the officers was going to get much sleep; they would all be waiting for the scouts to return with the enemy's location and precise strength. They were excused, and I remained with my brother at his request.

"I want to scold you, but you saved the day. My power is not suited for the kind of traps we saw today." I glowed at his praise, which all my life had been… infrequent. "You killed your first enemy today. Face-to-face. How are you handling it?"

Things had been so chaotic, I hadn't had the chance to stop and unpack everything. I had felt a deep sadness at the time, but since then, I had been just trying to stay alive. After that first one, I had been forced to kill several more enemy soldiers. I felt fine, but I didn't doubt that it might come back and crush me when I had the time to really think about it.

"I'll deal with it later," I said honestly. "Like you and all these brave men—and yes, women too—I have a job to do. If every Rus soldier has to die to ensure that you and Krystian come back alive? I'm ok with that." We sat quietly, staring into our cups. "The first one affected me. I saw the damage I did to a human body, and it made me sick. Shooting the wielder and the men who butchered your lieutenant? Those gave me pleasure."

"Colonel!" came a voice from outside the tent.

"Enter!" My brother stood to receive the report from a messenger.

The man gave the current location and troop strength of the Rus encampment. Stefek instructed him to gather the command staff for an impromptu meeting. He turned to me. "We'll be leaving an hour before sunrise. Go to your tent and try to sleep." He took me in his arms and gave me a firm hug, even more infrequent than praise from him. He looked me straight in the eyes. "You took lives today, but you saved a lot of lives, including mine and your own."

I shared a tent with two female lieutenants, and we were woken by a female tech sergeant who burst in to tell us the army was ready to move. All three of us had slept in our clothes, knowing we might have to mobilize at a moment's notice. I rubbed the sleep from my eyes and blearily strapped on my sword belt and pistol holster.

"Nice sword," Lieutenant Mazur remarked. I thought I sensed a snippy undertone, but I was too tired to respond in kind.

"Thank you. It was a present from my brother." I picked up my backpack.

"How nice. Skip basic training, get promoted to Kapitan, and get an officer's sword as a gift." She looked like she wanted to take out her frustrations on me. I wasn't having any of it.

"I killed seven Rus soldiers yesterday." I paused. "What have you done?" That shut her up. "I'm a higher rank than you two. You're not supposed to be bitches to my face." With that, I walked out to find Stefek.

It wasn't completely black outside; there was the smallest particle of light starting to form in the east. The sun would be up within the hour, and my brother, along with Colonel Estroski's regiment, was set to converge on the last known location of the enemy. The final group of gliders had returned minutes ago, confirming that the enemy was still camped out in a river valley to the west between our two forces.

With the rest of the regiment around us, I didn't feel as outnumbered as I did yesterday. There were so many men and women, all united behind a single mission: to defend our homeland and expel the invaders.

The plan was to move the tanks forward, along with the mechs. They were supposed to inflict mass casualties on the enemy and soften their defenses. They were to be followed closely by the ground troops, who ultimately would be the ones to run into danger, to kill or be killed.

I still didn't have anyone under my direct command, so I stuck close to Stefek in the command personnel transport. The long, boxy vehicle had wide, rounded tires and was skinned with thick steel plates, painted in woodland camouflage. It could hover over deep water or obstacles, but it was mainly powered by advanced steam engines.

We led the way down into the valley, followed closely by a trio of MK-8 mechs. They, too, were powered by the high-tech steamworks, but they always had a channeler inside, working the cannons and running the multiple weapons platforms. They looked like giant robots, with arms that resembled steel girders and legs that were thick and tall as a one-story house. At twenty-five feet tall, they stomped down the hill like vengeful metal automatons. Armor units were all around us, each trying to get ahead of their commanding officer and protect him from direct contact with the enemy.

I could see small fires in the distance, and there were ten times the number of tents that we had in our camp the previous night. Even with the other regiment coming in from the other side, I doubted that we had as many troops as they did. Their mechs stood vigilant, and they were starting to lumber in our direction. There would be no element of surprise today.

We were cruising along with the smooth ride of a hover vehicle, but then there was the thunderous sound of an explosion followed by a shockwave that threatened to toss us end over end.

"They see my standard and are targeting this vehicle," Stef growled. "Foolish of me not to strip it before we left." He tapped the driver on the shoulder. "Pull out of the way and stop. We're going to attract fire like dry tinder."

We piled out of the vehicle to find that the quiet little valley was rocked by mortar and cannon fire. The mechs pulled ahead, guns blazing as they trotted towards the enemy lines. A mech with a large Z-7 printed on its left breast was nearing the small river that ran down the middle of the trench. The guns on its shoulders were firing an almost constant stream of pulse rounds at a mass of approaching soldiers. They were equipped with body armor similar to what our men wore, but it was no match for the high-caliber pulses. Energy bolts tore through chest plates like they were empty eggshells, and heads that were protected by thick steel helmets were lopped off like wheat before the scythe.

I followed Stefek as he ducked into the shadow of the mech's leg. It gave us at least some cover as we advanced. His ability wasn't practical until we were much closer to the enemy.

The mech was too close to fire on the soldiers around its feet, so it kicked and stomped as they swarmed and attempted to lay explosives.

My brother was a merciless killing machine. His sword was less effective against soldiers with heavy armor, so he pulled two pulse pistols and started blasting his way through the would-be saboteurs. I was a great shot with my right hand. My brother was a decent shot with both hands. Simultaneously. He would fire at two Rus soldiers, hitting them in one of the few exposed areas of their armor, like the face or neck, then disappear. He would reappear three strides away to kill a few more. The invaders were distracted by the tall, hulking man who could seemingly disappear and reappear at will. The distraction allowed me to fire mid-range shots without drawing anyone's attention. I had no problem shooting those sons of bitches in the back.

A Rus mech nearly ran towards us, trying not to stomp on its own men in the process. The weapons a mech carried were devastating against ground troops, but ineffectual against each other. When it was over us, and I was literally in its shadow, Z-7 punched at it, creating a fracture in the plasteel canopy. It was smoked dark, but just like our mechs, there was an operator in there, probably losing their shit. Z-7 punched again, and again, causing the canopy to spiderweb and crack. Rus soldiers carrying satchel bombs were desperately trying to get close enough to affix them to Z-7's legs, but that's what we were for.

A woman about thirty years old rushed in without armor, carrying a small burlap pack with an adjustable strap and a wire hanging out, the end looped. She pulled the loop and was in the process of wedging the bomb in our mech's knee joint. I gathered Abyrinth around her and her satchel and, with minimal effort, lifted her and pressed her against the Rus mech's arm joint. She struggled, tried to throw the bomb away, but I held her in a band of energy that was like coiled steel. When the bomb went off, she was vaporized, and the explosion was powerful enough to rip the arm from the Rus titan. Z-7 continued to pound at the canopy until it shattered, revealing a Rus channeler, a boy who was younger than me.

How could that be? We didn't let anyone face the trials until they were eighteen, and channelers weren't given their blank brand until they were eighteen. For some reason, I thought humans were incapable of being branded before the age of maturity, but I was wrong. Hedwig, or whatever her real name was, was probably correct. The government was purposely holding its citizens back, deciding who could and couldn't receive powerful brands. Controlling who could channel and wield Abyrinth gave them enormous influence. It didn't seem fair, but there was no time to ponder such things in the heat of battle. The boy's face was a mask of fear until Z-7 unloaded five or six pulse blasts, turning his face to a bloody pulp.

I tried to put the horror of what I had just seen out of my mind as I lifted the mech high into the air and then brought it crashing down on a Rus tank that was rolling up to us. I found the screech of rending metal to be quite satisfying, though I doubt our opponents felt the same. I probably should have done something a little more low-key; I had brought attention to myself when my commander specifically wanted me to fly under the radar.

I could almost sense the sniper before he fired.

Not a pulse blast, but a bullet slammed into my arm, making it throb as I cried out in agony.

I kept a cool head. I dropped low, thighs resting on my heels. I pulled at the tear in my uniform sleeve, the material giving way to my adrenaline-fueled strength. The wound was ugly and large, but I could tell that it missed the bone, and I would most likely not lose the arm. It hurt like hell. I've never experienced anything close to it in my eighteen years.

Two sets of hands grabbed me and pulled me back, away from the front lines. I was in a state of shock, so much so that I couldn't even look to see who was pulling me. I knew it was two men; their hands were strong, and they easily got me up and into a small transport. The cart was hovering only, and the driver waited as several more severely injured were loaded next to me. When there was no more room, the long, flat ambulance began moving back to the makeshift headquarters.

I was facing the other direction from where the fighting was still in full swing. The beautiful ravine where cattle would graze during certain parts of the year, where boys might come for a naked swim or to fish… was now a hellscape. The mechs Z-7, along with Z-4 and Z-3, were still active, still terrorizing the enemy soldiers. Three other Polish mechs lay in smoking heaps, twisted metal left as a reminder that our enemy was larger and had more resources than we did.

Our tanks had formed a battery and were exchanging fire with enemy tanks. Everywhere in my field of vision, I saw horrible things. Air that was pure an hour ago was filled with smoke and the smell of burning machines and charred bodies. Mechs, tanks, troop transports, and all types of vehicles were exploded and engulfed in flames.

The worst were the bodies. The dead lay everywhere, on both sides of the shallow river. Boys without heads, torsos with massive holes shot through them. It was nearly impossible to navigate the field without stepping on a severed limb. Legs and arms were everywhere, and blood by the gallon was splattered on every surface. Thankfully, I passed out as the medical transport moved past our troops and into a clearing beyond.

# Chapter 29

Interlude II:

The Nikolaeva sisters walked down the street like they already owned the town. Lublin was not far from the border with Biała Ruś, and the Rus invaders hadn't encountered any resistance until they reached the city's suburbs. It was a long trip from Moscva and they were dying for a bit of fun. The Polish defenders were spread so thinly along the border that wherever the Rus forces chose to breach would be a weak spot. Their whole line was a weak spot.

They crossed a bridge and found themselves on the main road leading into the city, where the defenders had set up their roadblock. Two dozen men or more were lined up shoulder to shoulder in full armor, with riot shields and either rifles or batons.

"How cute," Sofiya said, pointing at the massed troops.

"Pitiful," Irina replied. "Let's get this over with."

Sofiya summoned her ability and released her psychic attack. Everyone in front of her was soon contained within a cone that originated from her and spread out in a triangular shape that encompassed the assembled Poles. Most dropped their weapons, falling screaming to the ground. Some ran around in confusion, unaware of their surroundings and what they were supposed to be doing.

"I never get tired of that," Irina said. She was tall, with platinum-blonde hair like her sister. She had small, delicate features, a small, sharp nose, high cheekbones, and wide, blue eyes. They wore the same dark blue uniform jackets as the soldiers standing behind them, but neither had any rank or unit identification.

She stepped forward two paces, then raised her hands like a penitent in a church revival. Like her sister, she gathered the mysterious power to herself, and with a mental command, she unleashed lightning. Jagged arcs of electricity struck a soldier, passed through him, and jumped to the next in line, then the next, and the next. In seconds, the majority of the Polish defenders were smoking corpses lying in the street.

"I like yours, too, sister. A very final solution to minor inconveniences."

Irina pointed left, down a broad street that was perpendicular to the main street. "You men, take two squads and go that direction. Bring everyone to the town square." She sent a second platoon to the right, and the rest followed the sisters down the street.

Most of the shops weren't even locked; a few had their front doors standing wide open. When the enemy troops were spotted outside town, everyone dropped what they were doing and got out of town any way they could. Lublin was a large town with over a quarter of a million people. Thousands were able to flee, but tens of thousands were trapped with no way to escape. Rus soldiers went building by building, pulling men, women, and children out of their homes and shops and herding them to the large square where festivals were held, and speeches were made.

Major Krystian Sobieski was leading two platoons of men and women in an attempt to defend the city from being taken over. His older brother was leading his own men a few hours to the north, near the capital. He had his own command

and his own assignment. He turned as a scout ran up to him, breathing hard.

After the boy regained his wind, Krystian asked, "What did you find?"

"I saw a few thousand troops blocking off all roads heading east and south. I spoke with the radio operator, and she said that we still control the roads heading west and north, but the noose is tightening quickly."

Krystian's normally cheerful and optimistic face was fraught with worry and doubt. The noose indeed. He had his radio operator send a message to General Poniatowski at the capital, warning him of the dangers they faced and asking for combat units to be reassigned as reinforcements.

One of his kapitans spoke up. "Colonel, what are your orders?"

"There are far too many of them for us to put up a fight and hope to win. Let's retreat west and scoop up any civilians that we find on the way."

He packed up his map and slung his pulse rifle over his shoulder. The officers followed him as he went out to brief their soldiers on the plan. More than a few groused about having to flee and let the Rus take another city, but they wanted to live, and they knew that they were hopelessly outnumbered.

The city streets were empty, with most of the people who lived and worked there having already evacuated east or being stuck on the roads near the far end of town. His force was mostly men, with a handful of women in the ranks. They all had the same grim faces as they increased their pace to quick time, then again to double time. They kept up the hectic pace while still holding their rifles at the ready.

Krystian found the rhythm of their march soothing. He was among eighty-seven souls who were all nearly running, but kept their foot strikes synchronized. Each of them would land their left foot at the same time, and their right foot at the same time. It was music to him and allowed him to think over their situation.

They had fought a skirmish east of town with a force of nearly equal size. Two hundred Rus soldiers against his one hundred ninety-two. His older brother Stefek was a better tactician when it came to large-scale operations. He was promoted to colonel in part for his ability to conduct a war and deploy troops most effectively. Krystian was better at the small scale. Guerilla tactics that a larger army, an army of boys who didn't want to be there, would never be prepared for. He quickly devised a plan that played to those very strengths.

When the Rus had passed through orchards outside town, they had no idea that there would be a Polish soldier in every tree. Their initial volley took out seventy of the invaders before they even knew that hostilities had commenced.

Seeing that they no longer had any advantage, the Rus commander ordered one of his mechs to come to the front. The twenty-foot-tall monstrosity was bulletproof and resistant to pulse rounds. The Poles continued to fire from concealment and picked off more of the enemy, but when a mech came after them, the remainder of their lives could be measured in minutes. Krystian witnessed one of his kapitans being stepped on by the metal brute. He knew that the sound of bones being crunched under a metal boot would stick with him until his dying day.

Keeping a low profile, Krystian worked his way through the rows of apple trees until he was near the bloody leg of the mech. Placing his hands on the smooth, hot metal surface, he willed the steel to melt. The boot that came up to his waist flowed like water, then reformed as a mass of thorny spikes. The mech wasn't able to maintain its balance and crashed face-first into two trees that held it up at a forty-five-degree angle. He scrambled up the body of the mech until he reached the chest panel, which protected the operator. Again, he caused the metal to melt away and drip to the ground. The operator was stunned by losing her safety, but she pulled a pulse pistol from her side and fired.

Krystian tried to duck the shots, but took a hit to his shoulder. The pain was intense, but he was trained since he was five years old to put pain in a little room inside of himself, then to shut and lock the door. With his hand still on the metal surface of the mech, he caused the plate directly over her head to warp and reform into a spike. The metal icicle punched through the top of her head, killing her instantly.

He looked at the wound and decided it was not life-threatening, so he applied a bandage and used the woman's belt to hold it in place. A month ago, he would not have conceived that he would harm a woman. Now, he saw the dead person for what she was: an invader, a conqueror, a murderer. She had killed more than a dozen of his troops, and as he stared at her lifeless corpse, he felt nothing.

Another mech was storming through the orchard, chasing after his people. It knocked down trees as if they were overgrown weeds. The whole time, it was blasting away with its shoulder-mounted rotary cannons. Rounds were striking everywhere at once, or so it seemed. There was no safety in front of the mech, and the sides might be dangerous too. He wanted to try the same trick, to upset the giant's balance, then attack the operator. Unfortunately, this mech had Rus soldiers all around its feet, using the monster as cover.

Hiding behind a tree, he pulled out his pistol, but decided to save his precious power for the mech. He had long ago learned the limits of his ability, and he wasn't going to waste it on regular conscripts. He pulled his sword and circled to catch them from behind. The first man he encountered, he pushed his sword between the man's torso protection and his lower body armor. When he was on the ground, Krystian stomped on his neck. He felt the snap of the spine through his boot, but the sound was lost in the din of the steaming contraption only a few yards away. The man had screamed, but there was screaming and dying all around.

His left arm was nearly useless, but luckily, he was right-handed. One of the soldiers noticed that an enemy was in their midst and turned to fire, but Krystian closed the distance in a single stride and lopped off the man's wrist, letting hand and gun fall to the rich earth. He pushed the point of his blade through his neck and moved to the next. In a minute, he killed four men and had the mech all to himself. The mech was busily raining hell on his troops, and it had no idea what was going on around its metal boots.

With some difficulty, Krystian climbed a tree that was wrapped around the metal monster, and when he reached the back plate that housed the steam engine, he performed his magic. The Abyrinth he controlled melted the metal covering and the exhaust tube. He knew that if the exhaust were blocked, the steam would back up, causing the operator a lot of trouble. As safely and as quickly as possible, he got down from the tree and began to run. It took almost a minute, but with a metal-rending scream, the back of the mech blew out. The metal plate flew off into the mass of trees behind as the mech lurched to a halt and fell forward. The intense pressure and heat of the steam had parboiled the operator where he or she sat.

Ouch. That's got to hurt, he thought to himself.

The Polish troops routed the aggressors, killing or forcing the rest to retreat. His force was more than halved, and they were facing an exponentially higher number of enemies; it was time to get away.

Krystian was able to get a healer to attend to his wound, and though it wasn't half as effective as what his mother could do, he felt immeasurably better. He turned to one of his kapitans.

"You lead the evacuation. Get all of our people out, and as many civilians as you can. This city is lost, but I'm going to stay and spy a little."

The man set out to carry out his orders, and Krystian cautiously made his way towards the sound of marching soldiers and the rumble of cannon fire. The city was not as modern as Warszawa; many of the streets were cobbled, and the shops all had an old-world feel. They were relics of the nineteenth century. He worked his way through dark alleys and side streets until he was near the town square, then climbed a building to get a better view from the roof.

Rus soldiers in camouflage armor, helmets, and riot shields lined the entire square, and they either held batons or pistols. They had the citizens penned in like cattle, and the innocent poles were scared silent. One of the roads that opened into the square had a battle tank blocking the way. A soldier in a leather cap hung out of the turret through an open hatch door. He watched as his commanding colonel marched up and down the square, looking at their hostages with as much hate and revulsion as a man can muster. He was of average size, under six feet tall, with a fit, though not overly impressive, build. He was in his early forties, with strands of grey peppering his shiny black hair. His uniform jacket was dark blue, matching his trousers and peaked cap. His epaulettes were golden, their fringe gilded. The embroidery on his high collar was gold, as were the tassels on his belt and bandolier. He had no beard, but his mustache was thick and wide, and as dark as night in the bottom of a well. He didn't look too old, but one could tell that he had permanent lines on his face from frowning and screaming at people, which was what he was doing when Krystian peered over the edge of the roof.

There was a break in the crowd as a dozen Polish soldiers were pushed through to the open center of the square. Krystian could tell at a distance that they were his men. Each of them had their hands tied behind their backs, and it was evident that most had bruises, and some were bleeding from the nose and mouth. They were lined up and pushed to their knees, some of them barely able to stay erect. For the next half hour, the colonel screamed at them, alternately screaming at the crowd. When he was done, the officer took off his uniform cap and handed it to one of his noncoms, then he proceeded to take off his uniform blouse, shoes, trousers, socks, and lastly, his undershirt.

What the hell is this all about? Krystian thought. This can't be good.

To the amazement of the prisoners, the man's body started expanding. He grew taller and broader; his already strong arms became thick, iron-muscled limbs, and his sturdy legs became oak trees. His chest was as wide as a car's width, and he was taller than two men, nearly a dozen feet tall. His thick hair thinned to leave him with a bald pate, only rough patches of his hair remaining. His normal, unextraordinary features became lumpy, mottled, and grotesque. He let out a mighty roar that shook the ground and rattled nearby windows.

I've seen a lot of brands, but this is new. Krystian thought it might be wise to run, but he needed to know what would happen next.

Starting at the far end of the line, he put his massive, plate-sized hand around the head of one of the Polish soldiers. With a curse in Russian, he squeezed, and the head imploded as an egg would in a regular person's hand. Blood and brain shot from between the fingers, and when he let go, it dripped from the cucumber-sized fingers. He let out a horrible laugh that was echoed by his men. The Polish citizens were understandably horrified, and the sound of weeping and wailing could be heard from both the crowd and some of the soldiers.

He went down the line, executing each of the helpless soldiers. The last in the line was Kapitan Rybak. She was one of his best, a thoroughly professional officer with a spotless pedigree and record. The brute picked her up, holding her upper body with his massive left hand, and then grasped her legs and lower torso with his right. With a sickening twist, he ripped her body in half. With disgust, he threw the dead remains at the crowd. Krystian had seen more than enough.

Coming down from his perch, he almost made it around the corner before being accosted by two Rus soldiers. They leveled their rifles at him, ready to blow him away. Krystian grabbed both of their rifle barrels and caused them to melt. The men instinctively fired, and both weapons exploded, peppering them with jagged bits of steel. They howled in pain, clutching at the shrapnel that had made Swiss cheese of their faces. Krystian seized the one on the right by the lapels of his uniform.

In broken Russian, he demanded, "Who was that officer in the courtyard? The one that becomes like a giant, with giant strength?" He shook the man to make his point.

"The colonel. Colonel Dmitri Sokolov!"

Krystian unsheathed his sword and ran it through both of their hearts. He was not in a forgiving mood. "I'll remember that name."

# Chapter 30

I was taken back to our temporary base camp for healing. There was a scattering of women, but hundreds of our men had been damaged to varying degrees. There were many like me who, after receiving treatment, were able to recover nearly fully. Others were like the king, harmed beyond repair.

There was no healing ability to ease my mind. When I heard news from the front, things did not go well.

Even with both regiments attacking simultaneously from two sides, the Rus battalion was just too much. They had double our number of soldiers, more armor, more mechs, and more ground cannons. More of everything. The battle raged on all day and long into the night, when our remaining forces were able to effect a retreat. Thank God that my brother was among the survivors. It was a crushing defeat, an ill omen for the war. I took a train back to Warszawa. It was a bittersweet return home.

My mother met me at the front door. She held me in her arms, crying on the shoulder of my utilities. She seemed tired, but she was happy to see me home and alive. She was just as pleased to know that her sons were also among the living.

"I'm so relieved to see you, Jafra," Mother said, hugging me again.

"It's good to be home."

She looked at me skeptically, like something was wrong. "Are you hurt, dear?"

"I was shot," I replied.

"Oh! My precious girl!" Her tears flowed again. "Come to the study. I need to check what they did to you." She was the penultimate healer and was highly critical of every other healer's work.

She inspected my bullet wound and studied the patch. "Not the worst that I've seen. Does it hurt?"

"A bit. Not like when it first happened. That hurt like hell."

She laid her hand on the wound and closed her eyes. I could see the strands of energy flowing from her hand into my skin. I could feel her healing power inside me, rerouting nerves, muscles, even skin. It was warm and soothing. After a while, she smiled up at me. "That's better. There will still be a scar, dear. I'm sorry."

I looked at the spot where the bullet had struck me. There was the faintest spot of discoloration. It would only be noticed if one were explicitly looking for it. I had to admit, my mother was an artist.

"Since you have your blouse off, why don't you go upstairs and change into a dress. It will make you feel more like a woman again," she said.

More like a woman? Interesting thought. A couple of months ago, I was attending balls, and the most important thing I could think about was finding a good husband. That girl was still inside me somewhere. I did miss the feel of silk, satin, and chiffon on my skin. My hair hadn't had a proper brushing in weeks, and all of my jewelry was in a box, upstairs in my room. My country may have been the one to declare war, but Rus had been invading us for over a year and was bent on swallowing us whole. I needed to keep the uniform on a bit longer.

"I think I'll rest a bit," I said, heading up the stairs.

"I'll have tea sent up. When you're rested, I can bring you up to date on the local gossip and what have you."

"Gossip?" Suddenly, I wasn't quite so tired. "I can take tea downstairs."

She had that evil smile that mothers get when they know their children too well. She met me in the tea room, and soon, the maid brought in a silver tray with two cups, a steaming pot of tea, and a selection of fresh pastries. She went to pour, but I was quicker. I put two cubes of sugar and a dash of milk, the way she liked it. I fixed my cup next and sat back in a plush, velvet-covered chair.

"That Zamoyski boy," she started.

"Nicolai?" I asked.

"Yes, that's the one. I heard that he was killed in a battle a few miles north of where you and Stefek were. They say he got a laceration on his neck and bled out in seconds."

"That's terrible," I mumbled. He was a friend of my oldest brother, another dedicated patriot. He was a handsome man, as I remember. His family would no doubt be crushed. "What was his brand?" I asked.

"I don't recall. Doesn't matter at this point." She sipped her tea and gave a bitter smile. "Are you at all curious about your friend, Stanisław?" She had that evil grin again.

"Do you mean General Poniatowski?" I harrumphed. "Just like the prince to declare himself Commanding General of the Royal Army. He has about as much military experience as I do. Maybe less, now that I've been through a battle."

"Yes, that's the one. He is staying at the base outside town. You can visit him if you want. I won't even send Aunt Bronisława." She sipped again, trying not to look guilty.

"Are you cooking up something with the queen again? I like him, he's very handsome, but we've technically only had the one date."

"She says that he speaks of you often. In very glowing terms."

"So, am I supposed to take a car over there and beg for his company?"

"No. That wouldn't be appropriate." She thought for a minute. "I'll send word that you are receptive to a visit by the general. I'm sure he'll come around, make the first move and all."

I wanted to argue with her for some reason, but it did sound nice. It was said that our parents usually knew what was good for us, even more than we did. Some of the best and happiest marriages were arranged.

I nodded, and she continued. There was a list of people who'd already been killed, a few engagements, some other news that seemed important to her, but it went in one ear and out the other.


Stanisław arrived by military ground car, and I was surprised to see him step out from the driver's seat. Some men liked to drive their own vehicles. I never learned to drive and had no desire to learn.

He was far above average in his looks, but seeing him step out of the car in his uniform stirred something primal in me. He wore more of a parade uniform than the camouflage uniform that was worn in the field. The coat was dark blue and just covered his upper thighs. The trousers were the same color and were tucked into black knee-high boots, polished to a mirror finish. He wore white gloves and a white leather belt, fastened with a metal buckle bearing his family crest. On his shoulders were epaulets, not the small kind that was on my uniform, but wide and with gold fringe hanging down. His high collar looked like it was choking him, but he showed no discomfort; the sides of the collar were adorned with dragons embroidered in gold thread. Around his neck, he had what looked like a snowflake, made of silver and hanging from a ribbon. He had a few medals on his left breast, though I couldn't imagine what they symbolized, considering he had not yet faced the enemy directly.

"My lady, thank you for having me as your guest," he said with a slight bow. Even though our country was at war, he still gave me a devilish grin.

I didn't feel like a lady of the court. I hadn't for a while. I had been torn on whether to greet him in my military dress uniform, a faint shadow of what he was wearing, or a lady-like dress. In the end, the dress prevailed.

We weren't attending a formal ball or any other official engagement, so I went for a more modern look. Taking inspiration from my mother, I wore a gown of purest white. The bodice was tight, accentuating my thin waist and supporting my ample chest; the floor-length skirt hugged my hips, the dress fitting like the peel of a banana. I finished my look with light makeup, and I wore my emeralds.

"Of course, General Poniatowski," I said, giving him a coy smile that was in opposition to the naughtiness implied by my dress. He looked at me like a starving man looks at a perfectly grilled steak.

"Come on, Jafra. Call me Stan."

My mother came up behind me, looking more like an older sister than the parent of an eighteen-year-old woman. She, too, wore all white, though her attire was far less alluring.

"My prince," she said, curtseying.

"Lady Sobieski." He bowed gallantly. "With your permission, I would like to escort the other Lady Sobieski to dinner and a play at the Teatr Wielki."

She thought for a moment, looking at both of us appraisingly. "You are my prince, and the commanding general of our country's army in time of war, but don't let my daughter's shameful display give you thoughts of acting in an ungentlemanly manner." She was a conservative, almost shy person, but when it came to the art of healing or her family, my mother was a fierce protector.

He looked suitably humbled. "Of course, madam. As beautiful as she is, her reputation is, and will remain, spotless." He bowed deeply.

Stan held the door as I climbed into the passenger side of his coup. For most of my trips by car, I rode in the back. It was invigorating to see the city from this perspective. An hour from here, our army was fighting for their lives. Here in the capital, life was only slightly diminished. The streets were still well-lit, and people were strolling the avenues without a care in the world.

When we reached the Teatr Wielki, the National Opera, a boy was waiting to take the car. When he saw who the driver was, he was shocked. Stan gave him the keys, and another boy opened my door. I was a bit put off by that. As hot as I looked, he got more attention than I did.

I had been to this opera house a number of times, but it looked different somehow. At night, the three levels were well lit behind the rows of stone columns in the bottom and middle sections. It looked like a Roman temple, with long wings on either side of the neoclassical main structure.

He offered me his hand, and I took it. We were led to his family's private box. We watched a superb production of The Barber of Seville, which was their first production put on back in the 1800s. He made witty comments, and I laughed heartily, though in a feminine manner. We drank a little wine, and before I knew it, the play was over.

From there, we went to a small French restaurant that was open late. We were taken to a dark corner. The waiter recited the specials, and my date ordered for both of us. His choices were safe, but suited me very well.

When we returned to the car, the prince drove me home. I felt electric, like I had at Christmas when I was a child. We made more small talk, nothing important, but it was nice. Other than my brothers, I didn't have any male friends, and it was stimulating to have a man to spend time with. The ride home flew by, all too soon for my taste. We walked to my door, and I turned on the first step, not wanting the evening to end.

"I've had a lovely time, Stanisław. It's hard to believe that the war rages on while we attend a delightful play and dine on a fantastic meal."

"Alas, the war is real, even though a lot of the people here don't seem to know it." He took my hand and stared into my eyes. "I heard about what you did at the front under your brother's command. Helping to destroy a mech, then using it to squash a tank? Amazing. I heard you were injured."

"I was shot. Right here." I pointed to where my scar was, though it was hard to locate because it stopped hurting after Mother healed it.

"I see Lady Sobieski's touch here." He touched the spot I had pointed out. "She saved my father's life and eased his suffering. She's truly a treasure to the Polish people."

"Thank you. I'll pass your kind words."

"I hope you know, I didn't want war." He studied my face for a reaction. "I don't know if this is a war that we can win, but they obviously wanted one. Killing civilians, the atrocities they committed on our women, our children… unforgivable. Multiple attempts on the lives of my family, on you…"

I squeezed his hand and met his bright blue eyes. "You were right to declare war. We were already in a state of war, and because it wasn't declared, they kept sending men to stir up trouble and then claim innocence. In the end, it didn't matter. Their expansionist aspirations include swallowing all of Polska."

"This was a magical night, Jafra. I want to see you again. As soon as possible."

"I feel the same, but I'm heading back tomorrow. My leave is over at midnight, and I'm taking the train back south in the morning."

He looked saddened by the news. "I could have you transferred back here, to the command headquarters. I am the Command General, after all."

"You certainly have the authority, but we both know that would be bad. Bad for your credentials as a leader, bad for my reputation as both a soldier and as a lady of the court."

"But..." I stopped him with a kiss. Even though I was on a step above him, I still had to lean up to kiss him. I held his cheeks in my hands, and when our mouths met, it was the sensation that I had always dreamed about. This was my first, real kiss.

I relaxed and leaned back. "I knew that would shut you up, my prince."

"I thought you didn't kiss before marriage." He was truly confused.

"I don't kiss on the first date. This is not our first date, and I really, really like you right now." I felt dizzy, and my confession only made my head swim more. I knew he was more experienced than I, and that wasn't saying much. It seemed like everything that had happened recently had changed him. Matured him.

There was a second of indecision, not even a second, then he dove at me. His left hand caressed my right cheek, his right arm practically scooped me into his strong arms. He kissed me with the kind of passion that all young girls dream about. His lips were soft and yet unyielding. He devoured me with a series of long, drawn-out kisses. I felt the tip of his tongue caressing my lips, parting them. Our tongues met in my mouth, dancing a frantic dance of lust. His arm crushed our bodies together, and I could feel the heat of him through the layers of his thick clothing and my thin gown. I felt his hand drifting downward, and that brought me back to reality. There was the slightest break in the action, and I used it to lean my head back. He was getting overheated, and so was I.

Prince or not, if my father caught us in a compromising situation, it would be the end for both of us.

"That was not my first kiss," he said breathily. "But it is by far the best. I want you, Jafra. Someday I'll be king, and I couldn't find a better queen." He was still breathing heavily, and the light in his eyes shone through the dark shadows of our main entrance. His muscular arm still encircled me, and he gulped air as he tried to calm himself.

"You haven't proposed marriage, and I am neither agreeing nor rejecting such an offer. I will say, you are every woman's dream, including mine." I stepped backward, up a step, and out of his hold. "I like you enough to have you as my first kiss, my only kiss. God willing, you are the only man I will ever choose to kiss. Our parents can talk, but let's make sure that you still have a throne to inherit."

"You are as wise as you are beautiful, Jafra Sobieski. I will win this war if for nothing else than to have you all for myself."

He smiled as he turned and sauntered back to his car. I was helpless, just standing there, watching him get into his car and drive away. I couldn't recall a time in my life when I was as happy as I was at that moment.

# Chapter 31

"Colonel, I think we have another wielder in Beacon Square."

These damned Rus are like cockroaches, Stefek thought. Finding their wielders was much easier when Jafra was here.

Stefek had been a military officer since completing his trials and earning his brand. That had been several years now, and he was a respected senior officer. Theoretically, blanks could advance through the ranks of the military and into senior positions such as major, colonel, and general. However, for the last several hundred years, since the nobles started gaining power, it has been difficult for them to rise very high in the ranks. Stefek Sobieski may have taken the fast path to becoming a staff officer, but no one, no one, doubted his leadership skills and his ferocity on the field of battle.

He wore the same armor that all of his men did, a hardened shell covering him from throat to bread basket. Overlapping plates covered his arms, legs, and groin. His officers, noncoms, and soldiers wore helmets, round on the top and extending down on the sides and back to protect the head and neck. He abstained, wanting his troopers to see him and know that he had no fear. Pistol on his hip and longsword across his back, he jumped into a small hover car and raced off, leading a column of troop transports towards the enemy. He forgot the city's name, but it was one of the larger cities in eastern Polska.

The regiment had been resupplied, and replacement troops had been added to his command. He was the leader of five thousand, mostly men, with some women in roles where they would excel.

His personal driver was a young channeler from the west, her short black hair covered by the bulky combat helmet she seemed never to take off. She drove like a bat out of hell, just the way he liked it. They raced through city streets, bracketed by tall office buildings on both sides of the broad avenue. Most civilians had been evacuated days ago, so there was no traffic and few obstacles. In minutes, they reached Beacon Square, where there were apartment buildings, and on the far side, there were medium-sized single-family houses.

Stefek could smell Rus, and when they had passed through a large park near the river, he smacked Corporal Szymczak on the shoulder and motioned for her to pull over and park. "Bring the boys around. The Rus are only a block over," he told his driver. She ran off to collect the platoon leaders.

Seconds later, a dozen men were fanned out around Stefek. They were all given instructions on where to set up the ambush, then the signal came. They rushed, moving their transports and car-mounted artillery to their appointed locations. Stefek moved forward cautiously until he could hear the clatter of the enemy.

The first squad he found was going house by house, looking for people to kill or capture. Ten of them came upon a small apartment building. Six went in, and four stood bunched up around the front door.

After years of practice, stopping time was a simple matter for the colonel. A reflex. He ran over, seeing the enemy soldiers frozen like mosquitoes in amber. His Chronoburst only lasted a handful of seconds, and to be safe, he moved as fast as he could. With his sword, he slit the throats of all four of the outside guards. Time resumed, and they fell like marionettes that had just had their strings cut.

A platoon led by Lieutenant Rutkowska fell in behind their commanding officer and followed as he entered the building. Stefek moved quickly but with precise control. On the second landing, they encountered a group of men waiting to access the second floor. The man in the rear didn't turn around and yelled something in Russian over his shoulder.

Stefek ran him through, his sword pushing through flesh and around bone until it burst out of the man's sternum. He killed the man next to him the same way, and their screams alerted the rest. Stopping time, he pulled the corpses off their feet and off to the side before impaling two more soldiers. When time resumed, the men already in the hall were rushing back to see what the commotion was. Stefek was carried forward by the press of his men, and they stepped over or on the bodies in their way. When they were in the hall, Lieutenant Rutkowska opened up with a pulse rifle, sending large-caliber pulses into the crowd of Rus soldiers.

Rutkowska is a good man. Too bad he's only a channeler. No noble blood, Stefek thought.

The young officer led the squad down the hall, all of them firing at will. The enemy responded with gunfire, the majority of their rounds ricocheting harmlessly off their armored hides. The armor didn't make one impervious to harm. A soldier a few feet behind the lieutenant fell, a bullet hitting him in the face and tearing through his grey matter. The squad tore through the invading soldiers, only losing one man.

"Good job, lieutenant. Take the men out, and let's continue to our rendezvous point."

The radioman approached. "Sirs, there is a whole platoon of Rus soldiers a block from here. They are tearing through the civilians who refused or were too slow to evacuate."

Hand signals were given, and the men flowed back out onto the main thoroughfare. There were plenty of conscripts in the army, but this unit was composed of highly-trained soldiers who worked together seamlessly. They jogged down the street quickly, guns held chest high, ready to engage any enemy. When they came to the next junction, the lieutenant raised his closed fist in the air, a signal for everyone to halt.

Two of his men pulled round balls from bandoliers on their armor, pulled the pins, and rolled the smoke bombs towards the Rus platoon. A loud, crackling hiss was followed by plumes of green smoke that filled the street, making the soldiers retch. The officer gave the order, and his men rounded the corner and opened fire. The enemy soldiers were a mix: some wore armor, some did not. The fighting would be close to even. The wielders would make the difference; there would be some on both sides.

Stefek worked his way around the edge of the fighting, taking out opponents at close range. He mostly used his sword to conserve his Abyrinth.

A young Rus woman stood behind a wall of her countrymen, casting some spell on the defending Polish troops. He saw by their reaction what her power was. The Stop Coil brand was not common, but he'd seen it before. She was able to use the power to petrify an opponent for several seconds, enough time for her fellows to slaughter them. Her power worked like his, giving the aggressor a distinct advantage. He couldn't kill every enemy on the street, but he could level the playing field for his men.

If Jafra were here, she could pick out every channeler and wielder, and I could pick them off. I've underestimated the value of that aspect of her gift.

He worked his way around her until he was behind her. It took a rapid series of time freezes to get around the cone of her paralysis and avoid a rain of flying projectiles.

He was brought up to hold women on a pedestal, to treat each and every one like she was made of fine china. In war, that all changed. When in time-stop mode, everyone around him appeared frozen in place, even if they were off-balance, seemingly defying gravity. He pulled the blade of his sword across her neck, the blood trapped behind the wound, waiting for time to resume before splashing out. He killed four more men around her before time resumed. He instantly stopped time again and got himself out of danger.

Stefek couldn't see the threads of energy any more than anyone else, except when he met one of his kind. The Chronoburst brand was very rare, but not unique as his sister's. He had met an old duke shortly after passing his trials, who also bore the Chronoburst. Their brands seemed to resonate; he could see a glow around the man, as the man could see the aura around him. It was such an odd, unnerving sensation that it stuck firmly in his memory. Now, he had that feeling again.

He had maneuvered to a second-story window overlooking the tumult in the streets, and near the line where the two armies met, he saw that familiar glowing aura. The Rus had a wielder who could temporarily stop time. It was a devastating power. His own experience told him that the Rus wielder would be cutting down his men by the dozen until his power reserve ran out. It would be very, very dangerous, but he would have to eliminate this threat, and he was possibly the only one on his side who could match the man.

He was too embedded in his troops; he would have to be lured out. If he could detect someone with the same power, the man could detect him as easily. Dueling someone in that crowd would be certain suicide. He had to pull the man towards him, have the fight in relative seclusion.

Stefek saw mini-walkers among the troops. The two-legged, heavily-armored vehicle was blasting at the Polish troops with shoulder-mounted pulse cannons. He knew these units well, as they were standard across Western countries. Their weakness was the battery unit on the underside, towards the back. It was out of sight for enemies directly in front, and if anyone tried to flank the unit to tamper with the battery, the soldiers would take them out. Those rules did not apply to someone who could temporarily freeze time.

Stefek made a series of time jumps until he was underneath the furthest walker. The driver's cabin was eight feet off the ground, suspended by two long, spindly, metallic legs. It was a much smaller version of the mechs with less armor and weapons, but much cheaper, and all governments liked that.

Stefek was able to jump up and attach some of his explosive clay to the panel that covered the battery unit. Channelers could store extra energy in the batteries for use in both locomotion and pulse weapons. He made quick jumps and placed four explosive charges before returning to the far end of the street, well behind the action.

He was breathing heavily when he finally came to a stop. When the explosion hit the battery, it created an even larger explosion. The first mini-walker went up like a Roman candle, creating a pillar of fire where the operator had once been. Before the shrapnel could fall, the second one exploded, then the third, and finally the fourth. Hundreds of infantrymen had been knocked off their feet by the blasts, many of them never to get up again.

That level of destruction so far behind their lines could only be one thing: a wielder. The Rus with the Chronoburst brand was now actively searching the mass of his troops, looking for the fly in the ointment.

Then he saw Colonel Sobieski.

He disappeared, and several heartbeats later, they were standing face to face. The man said something in Russian which Stefek couldn't understand. No words were needed. They would fight, and one of them would die.

What the Rus didn't understand was that when two wielders share the same brand and are in proximity, their powers become synced. He no doubt intended to be first to stop time and easily kill his counterpart, but it didn't work that way. They both entered the out-of-phase universe where time stood still, and they were free to move.

They both drew swords at the same time, and when the Rus realized he was far from his men and had no advantage, his face took on a look of terror. Stefen lunged in, stabbing at the man's heart, only to have his thrust deflected at the last moment. The point still connected, and Stefek's sword penetrated the Rus officer's shoulder, sinking in deep. The man let out a howl that would attract no help, as they were still outside of time.

They began to duel in earnest, their sword blades flashing in the bright, late afternoon sun. It became apparent to both of them that their skill levels were not equal. Stefek had trained with a sword since his pre-teen years and was a master swordsman, even without his brand's power. Stefek pressed his attack, and it was all the man could do to stay alive.

The Rus took minor cuts to the midsection, the thigh, the thigh again, and even a long slash down his left cheek. Stefek decided to press his attack and put this pretender out of his misery… when suddenly, the man's Abyrinth ran out. He became frozen in time like everyone else up and down the street. If it had been a more challenging contest, Stefek would have felt bad about winning this way, but it was war, and the man was not his equal. He slashed at his windpipe, opening his throat and neck all the way until the vertebrae showed.

Stefek knew that his own well of Abyrinth must be nearly dry, so he made his way back to his side of the battle. When behind his lines, he rejoined his men and made sure they were properly deployed.

"Those mini-mechs that exploded. Was that your doing, sir?" the lieutenant asked.

"It was. Four mounted units, and I terminated two powerful wielders on their side."

Stefek wrote his after-action report that night at a hotel they had commandeered. What was not included in the report was that this was the first decisive victory for the Polish army since the war began. Their wins were few and far between, and only a miracle would stop their homeland from being annexed into the Rus Empire.

# Chapter 32

The following two months were the hardest of my young life. My brothers and a few others managed to secure the occasional victory, but overall, things were not going well.

My beloved Polska had long been divided into sixteen voivodeships. Podlaskie bordered Lithuania and Biała Ruś, and despite its defenses, it fell within a matter of weeks. Lubelskie was next. As the occupying forces moved into captured territory, Lubelskie also bordered Biała Ruś and Galacia, which the Rus called Little Rus. My brother won a significant battle in that region, but a week later, the Rus rolled in with an entire brigade, along with armor, mechs, mini-walkers. The order for retreat came directly from General Poniatowski.

I couldn't help but wonder how Stanisław was doing. He had all the ingredients for becoming a great leader, but he was only a few years older than me. He was my brother's age! He didn't have the experience to conduct a proper war.

I had not seen much action since leaving the capital. My orders always took me to places with minimal incursion by the Rus. I was pretty confident that Stanisław's hands were involved. When we parted, he really did seem taken with me, and maybe he was trying to keep me out of harm's way without playing favorites or diminishing my authority. Part of me appreciated the effort and the caring he was indirectly showing me. Another part of me wanted to be in the thick of it, killing Rus by the score and defending my homeland.

Word was, the capital itself was in danger. The royal family had already relocated to a castle in Poznan. The people, especially the blanks, were all encouraged to flee west, but most of them would have nowhere to go. Refugee camps had been established in Poznan, Wrocław, and Bydgoszcz, and everyone who could leave was abandoning their homes and heading towards them.

I got a telegram from Mother, saying she was preparing to take my younger siblings to stay with some family in Gdańsk. From what she said, it sounded like the barbarians were at the door already, and that Warszawa itself was about to be besieged.

My commanding officer was Podpolkovnik Nowak. The lieutenant colonel was in charge of a regiment under a Generał Brygady, the general of the Brigade. Because I had no subordinates and, truthfully, no responsibilities, when I asked for leave to check on the evacuation, my request was quickly granted. I was given a lieutenant, a non-commissioned officer, and ten enlisted soldiers to accompany me. We requisitioned a small troop transport, and in hours, we were heading east, towards the capital and my family's estates.

When we reached the suburbs, I was struck by the change in my hometown. There was nobody on the streets. Streets that had once been teeming with people going about their business, buying, selling, delivering goods, and making wares. There was garbage everywhere, building up in huge piles where people had to sacrifice belongings because they couldn't take them in their haste to leave the capital. It was known that the Rus forces were at Warszawa's doorstep, and they were well known for their mistreatment of noncombatants.

A scout ran up to me from the road ahead. She was out of breath and took a second to report. "Kapitan Sobieski, the bridge ahead has collapsed. We can't cross the Vistula here."

"Collapsed? Were explosives used, or maybe it was a natural disaster?" I doubted that very much.

"I don't know, Kapitan." She had her hair held back in a tight bun, and her utilities had the two stripes on the sleeve, signifying that she held the rank of kapral. She had a plain face and a thin, athletic body. I could tell that she was a blank like most of my crew. Over ninety percent of the population were blanks, but I still had very little exposure to them before the war broke out.

"Let's go check it out." She nodded and led the way.

When we got to the bridge, it was indeed crumpled, and the majority of it had crashed down into the river. I looked for signs of explosives. There were none. I tried to see if there were scorch marks from pulse weapons. Again, no luck. I was starting to give up hope that I could pin down the cause of the bridge's collapse when my second in command spoke up.

"It looks like a wielder did this," he said. Lieutenant Budny was at least two years older than I, and by the way he spoke, he was a graduate of some university. His manner was precise, and his words were always well thought out. He was a channeler, the only one with a brand, aside from me. He was tall, a bit over six feet, with broad shoulders and a narrow waist. His black hair was greased to a shine and was combed back in a very fashionable style. He had an anchor-type beard, just a small patch on the chin, and a thin mustache that didn't extend beyond the length of his mouth. It made him look older, and actually, quite handsome.

"How can you tell?" I asked. I was in charge, but I wasn't afraid to ask for help when I was over my head. "I don't see any signs of foul play, explosives, that sort of thing."

We were standing at the very edge of the break where the steel beams seemed to have rusted and crumbled, no longer able to bear their burden. He pointed at the rusted area, how it seemed to form a fairly straight line across the width of each steel girder.

"Definitely not natural. See the way the rust is in a straight line?" I nodded. "I've seen this before. I think it's the brand Unmaking Ember. The wielder can cause metal to rust, concrete to fall apart, wood to dry out and crack. It looks like normal wear and aging, but it lives up to its name. It unmakes things."

"That's very astute of you. Did you learn about the various brands at university?"

"It's a required course for those on the military track. We need to know how to deal with enemies that are wielders, and how to help our officers to maximize the use of their abilities."

"Did you come across my brand, Lieutenant Budny?"

"I've memorized most of the three hundred and fourteen known brands, but no. Your Abyrinth Embermark is either new or so rare that it hasn't been recorded yet. Because of that, not much is known about how strong your power is, or what its limits are."

"I've had it for a few months now, and I'm not entirely sure either." I looked around and found that aside from our small group, there was no activity anywhere near us. "Let's go to the next bridge heading into town. I have a bad feeling."

We mounted our troop transport and headed upriver until we reached the next main crossing. The Vistula cut Warszawa in half, and without the bridges, half the population, including my family, would be cut off from being able to flee westward. As I feared, the next bridge had suffered the same fate. We didn't even give it a cursory examination before heading upriver again.

"We need to stop whoever is doing this. Tens of thousands will need to cross these bridges in the next few days." I turned to a skinny kid under my command. "Radio leadership. Let them know which bridges have been sabotaged."

We picked up speed until we reached the next bridge. It was still standing, but I could see the Rus wielder attacking it. To me, his power looked like a fiery beacon in a dark winter night.

"Halt! Stop what you're doing!" Lieutenant Budny commanded. He held his pulse rifle in both hands, the butt in the crook of his shoulder, the iron sights lined up on the Rus soldier.

The man was late thirties, wearing a Rus officer's uniform. He looked up to see weapons aimed at him. Smiling, he waved his hands, and the lieutenant's pulse rifle rusted to dust in a second. The lieutenant pulled out his sword and started to run towards the man, but he only closed half the distance before his sword was turned to metal flakes in his hand, blowing away in the brisk midday breeze.

My crew was taking cover behind an abandoned car, trading fire with the Rus officer's squad. The car we were behind began crumbling, and two of my privates were struck by gunfire. I opened up with my pulse rifle, taking careful aim, and I fired through a newly-made hole in the car. I hit one of them, knocking the soldier back. Both sides wore the protective infantry armor, but a direct hit would still put someone on their backside.

We weren't losing the firefight, but we weren't exactly winning either. Their wielder would soon completely disintegrate our protection, and we would be sitting ducks.

I saw another car a half block away. Lifting that much mass wasn't easy, but it was nothing compared to holding up the cruise ship. I levitated the vehicle to a good twenty feet in the air, then threw it at the massed enemy.

Bullets and even pulse rounds might not be able to penetrate their armor, but a two-thousand-pound hunk of metal did the trick. They didn't even have time to scream as they were squashed.

The Rus officer looked horrified. Our brands gave us incredible abilities, the power to do superhuman things. What he just saw was a step beyond. The Rus had intelligence just like we did, and he probably knew who he was facing now.

I stepped out from my place of cover and concealment and began walking slowly towards him. He pulled his pulse pistol, but I could see the lines of energy around him and drew them to me. When I stole the Abyrinth from another wielder, they were only temporarily inconvenienced, but that was usually long enough for bad things to happen.

He aimed at me and tried to fire, but nothing came from his weapon. He tried a couple more times before giving up and throwing the pistol at me. With a wave of my fingers, I knocked the projectile aside, giving him a wicked smile as I got closer. Fear lit his face, and he drew his sword, ready to fight me without powers. I, too, drew my blade, and the duel commenced.

I took the classic first pose, the en garde. Belatedly, he too assumed the position. I took the initiative, lunging forward and attacking. My little brother had taught me the basics, and Krystian had worked tirelessly to give me a passable skill at fencing. I wouldn't stand a chance against my brothers, even my younger brother, but I inspected this balding, pudgy, unshaven excuse for an officer and felt confident that he wouldn't be skilled with a sword.

Indeed, he was not. We traded slashes, thrusts, and I parried everything that came my way with relative ease. I had seen what he had to offer and found him lacking. He was sweating profusely, his remaining dirty-blond hair plastered to his shiny head, and his moves were slow and lacked any particle of precision. He overextended on a thrust. I ducked, then made my own thrust. My thin blade sank deep into his side, going between his ribs and through both his lung and heart. The man stiffened in pain, expelling his last breath, then fell dead onto the paved street.

I wiped my blade on his uniform, then returned it to its scabbard. My crew gathered around me, all smiles and congratulations.

"I heard that Sobieskis led from the front. It's true for both the men and the women," a young woman said. She was one of my privates, in charge of the radio.

"I would never send one of you to do something that I wouldn't do myself," I said, soaking in their love. I was becoming numb to death, and the fact that I'd killed a man with my sword of all things no longer shocked me or made me want to break down in tears. "Radio headquarters to let them know what happened. Tell them that we are lending aid to refugees heading out of town."

Before we moved on, something caught my eye. Tucked into his leather pistol belt was a dagger. It was all too familiar to me, and I retrieved it from the corpse. It was identical to the one that I had been stabbed with at the Autumn Ball, down to the insignia on the pommel. The copper-colored owl seemed to stare at me with its hollow, soulless eyes. I saw the emblem and felt a cold shiver pass through me. This was something more insidious than the Rus. Someone or some group was at war with us, and we didn't even know anything about them.

# Chapter 33

Our investigation, and the hundreds of individual interviews we conducted, led us to Kraków. If there was a secret group trying to undermine the Polish people, trying to make us defenseless against the Rus, then we needed to at least know who they were. If we could understand why they were against us, all the better. My small crew agreed.

Julia Nowak was the plain girl, the private who worked as our scout and runner. Apparently, Lieutenant Budny's first name was Filip. Our new radioman was Private Jacek Demko, a thin boy, older than me by less than a year, but he looked like he was fourteen with his perpetually messy hair and greasy skin. Borys Wójcik was also a private, about twenty years old, with short brown hair, about my height, and, overall, very unremarkable.

Kapral Marcin Broz oversaw our logistics, ensuring we had food, ammunition, and whatever else we might need. He was shorter than me by a couple of inches, and his light brown hair was a mass of unruly curls, but the man was a genius. He was a scrounger of unmatched ability, and that made up for his complete lack of military discipline.

Sierżant Karol Antol was our weapons expert. He was well over six feet tall, taller still than my brother Stefek. He wore his hair cut to the scalp, and he had tattoos that spoke of some shady past before joining the military. His face was weatherbeaten and worn, like a mile of country road. His dirty little secret was that he was a delightful person. Once you got beyond the alpha-male vibe he put out, he was a good listener and had a quick wit. The reason he was on my team was that he knew every type of weapon, from a club to a mech. He knew how to maintain and repair them, and of course, how to use them.

Rounding out my crew was Starszy Szeregowy Izabella Bosak, a private who outranked a szeregowy and ranked below a kapral. Unlike Szeregowy Julia, Izabelalla was attractive, with more than a little sex appeal.

I hated to admit it, but she was a blank, came from a poor family, and was every bit as hot as I was. Her honey-colored hair fell to the middle of her back, and her figure was long and lean, but with curves. She was fast and stealthy, and better with a knife than anyone I had ever met. As a result, her place was cemented on our mission.

We left our military transport far outside town, thinking it would be better to travel incognito. Even loyal Poles were reluctant to speak to military officers, and the people we intended to question would reject us outright. It was Julia's idea to go undercover, and I immediately thought it was a great one. My aide was not as sure.

It took some time and a lot of my allowance, but we managed to get fashionable clothing for our night on the town. One very scrawny fellow, who didn't like having Karol sit on his chest, gave up the name of the Dom Szeptów, the House of Whispers.

"Tell me about the security at the door!" Izabelalla demanded, holding a razor-sharp knife to the man's throat. "Tell me now, or I'll gut you like day-old fish!" Her beauty would turn heads at any ball or state affair, but her mouth was not suitable for polite society.

"It's a very exclusive establishment. They won't let any common soldiers in," he spat the words, contempt thick in his voice.

"Kapitan! Can I kill this one? No one will notice. No one will care." She looked to me for permission.

"Not quite yet," I replied coolly.

"She extends your life, but for how long?" She barely grazed the skin of his neck, the blade drawing a thin line of blood. "Is there a password?"

I think we could all see the wheels turning in his head. He was deciding whether he could lie and get away from us without being discovered. He stuttered as he spoke. "Tatra. The password is Tatra," he said with manufactured confidence. "Like the mountain."

"Now, that wasn't too difficult, was it?" I asked. "Kapral, make sure he is delivered to the local constables. They are to hold him incommunicado until we return." I turned to the man. "If your password doesn't work, I will let this private first-class carve you into little, tiny pieces." My expression made it clear that I was not joking.

Sweat exploded from his forehead, and tremors began shaking him from the inside out.

"Take him away," I ordered.

"Hold on! Wait!" He thought nervously as we all stood, staring down at him. "That might be the old password. So sorry. The new password is bubonis."

"The Latin word for an owl," I said thoughtfully. We were definitely on the right track.

"Ah!" he exclaimed. "An educated soldier." He looked closer. "You're an officer? A daughter of noble birth? You'll fit right in, madam." He gave a slight bow of his head. "They should like you well enough."

"Get him out of here. Drop him off at the constable's and meet at the hotel in one hour."

I took the ladies shopping, and we guessed the men's sizes. We picked clothing suitable for an upscale nightclub. I was ready to go by seven and turned to my crew.

"Are you all ready to go?" I asked. They literally laughed at me. "Why are you all laughing?"

"Kapitan, no one goes to a club before eleven. Not a good club, at any rate," Borys said, taking a seat.

"We need to get our story straight," Marcin said. "If one of us calls you Kapitan, it's over."

The west and central parts of Polska were in turmoil. The wolf we feared for years was already inside our fence. But in the coastal region of Gdańsk, life went on without much disturbance. The trendy, seaside neighborhood had expensive restaurants that were full, with lines around the block. There were a variety of dance clubs, bars, playhouses, and other places where the rich could squander their wealth.

Amongst the hustle and bustle of the entertainment district, the House of Whispers was considerably low-key. There was no sign identifying the club, and the only indication of a nightclub was the presence of two large doormen. The guards were every bit as large as Karol and wore tight-fitting, expertly tailored suits. They had severe looks at rest, and their expressions soured as we approached. The brute on our right put up a large hand with fingers like sausages.

"This is a private club," he said dismissively.

"I know," I replied. I reached into my purse and pulled out one of the daggers, specifically the one that had cut my flesh. I held it, the owl insignia showing. The man took it, turned it over in his hands, then handed it back to me. He looked over his shoulder at his partner, who had a clipboard.

"Name?"

"This is Lady Jafra Sobieski, and I am Krystian Sobieski," my lieutenant said confidently.

The other guard was taking notes and checking his list. He nodded to the man with his hand still holding us at bay.

"It looks like you're on the list." He gave the others a dismissive look. "What about these?" he asked.

"This is my cousin, Milka Ostrogski," I said, indicating Izabelalla. When I told her she'd be passing herself off as my dear, deceased Milka, she was concerned they would check her identity by looking at her brand. I reassured her that in noble society, it is the height of rudeness to even speak of someone's brand, much less ask to see it.

I pointed at Karol. "My bodyguard." I pointed at Julie, Borys, and Marcin in succession. "Personal assistant, secretary, and he's both groom and social secretary."

It started to drizzle, and he stepped back under a small awning.

"Lord, ladies, you can enter, and you can bring your security man. The others can't come in."

The rain was slowly picking up strength. Filip leaned in. "The weather is only going to worsen. Is there some side room they can wait in?" It was not uncommon for finer establishments to have sitting rooms for servants and staff. He nodded to his partner with the clipboard, then, with a most unpleasant smile, he opened the door and ushered us in. The interior was a typical foyer, with chairs around the large oval room. A central hall went forward, but he led the excluded members of my squad to a room off to the left.

"You, wait in here." His voice was low, tinged with threat. "Lord Sobieski, a hostess will be along in a second to take you into the club proper."

I had never been to a nightclub before, but I was still surprised by the furnishings. The walls were dark, draped in velvet curtains in either dark purple or black. I couldn't tell because the lighting was dim; candles were in pewter lantern boxes hanging every few feet around the room. The right side of the room had large, circular windows that were completely opaque, looking like giant, inhuman eyes. I was sure that someone was watching us, deciding how to greet us once we got deeper inside.

"Lord, ladies, right this way, please." The young woman was dressed like a man, wearing tuxedo pants, a white shirt, a black tie, and a jacket. Her hair was pulled back almost painfully tight, which did nothing to soften her very serious expression.

I wondered if we'd miscalculated, dressing as we did. Izabel and I were the nobles, the wielders, so we wore the nicest clothes, along with my brother, Filip. The greasy little man we questioned told us that patrons wore the highest fashion, generally sticking to dark or muted colors. I wore a sleek black blouse that fit tightly and rode high enough to show a few inches of skin above the tight silk skirt, which was cut several inches above my knees. I can't remember ever going out in public so exposed. Izabel's dark blue, A-Line dress covered her midriff, but showed enough cleavage that any man with a heartbeat would do a double-take. Filip was in a black silk business suit that fit like a surgical glove. The rest wore nice clothing, not too expensive, but far better than what they could have afforded on their own.

What concerned me as we were led down a narrow, dark hallway was that our names were on the list. What the hell did that mean? Nothing good, considering their repeated attempts to kill me and people in my class. The walls were dark wood, stained and oiled to a light sheen. The floor was dark grey tile set in a very plain, almost hypnotizing pattern. The hallway seemed longer than the building looked from the outside, and it took a while to reach a heavy wooden door at the far end. A steel plate in the door slid aside, and two beady eyes looked out. They saw the hostess, looked us over briefly, then the door closed again. Several locks were audibly moved aside, and the door swung in, allowing us to pass.

The hostess ignored the doorman and continued walking at a brisk pace, assuming that we were hot on her heels. It was immediately clear that this was no dance club. It appeared to be more of a social club with dozens of people gathered into small groups. The room was as dimly lit as the foyer and hallway, with flickering lanterns everywhere. It wasn't a nightclub, but there was music. A small band played in the far corner; the music was muted, so it didn't overpower conversations.

Waitresses drifted around, trays full of whiskey tumblers, each with a couple of fingers of a dark brown liquid. I don't know why, but I grabbed one and put it to my nose. The alcohol burned my nose when I smelled it, and pushing good sense to the side, I downed the drink in a gulp. It burned the back of my throat and caused a burning sensation all the way to my stomach, where it mixed with the roiling acid and threatened to come back up. They called it liquid courage, and I was inclined to agree. Whoever these people were, they knew my name, and that got us through the door. I left the others and walked over to a small group that was engaged in an animated conversation.

"….heard that they will take the capital. A few weeks at the most," said a woman who was gently fanning herself. She was probably forty, with jet black hair that was sure to be colored. She wore a dark green dress, showing off a body that was not yet faded. I felt better that I was attired appropriately for this place.

"It may be too late to intervene." The man replied to her, then he noticed me. He was definitely in his forties, with a liberal sprinkling of grey in his dark brown hair. I could tell that he was older, but his face had the look of someone who had not led a life of labor. I thought that Filip was well dressed, but he couldn't hold a candle to this gentleman. "Miss? I don't believe that we've been introduced." He took my hand, kissing my fingers with a light touch of his lips. "Andrei Stoica, at your service." He indicated the woman. "This lovely creature is Freja Madsen."

"I'm pleased to meet you. Jafra Sobieski." I gave the slightest of curtseys. I could see energy clinging to both of them. I scanned the room and saw that nearly half of those in the room were either wielders or channelers.

"Sobieski?" he asked. "I believe that I met your father a few years ago. How is he in these troubled times?"

"Troubled times? This country is in a state of war, and I fear for our sovereignty." I took a drink from a passing tray. "He is well, but the front lines have moved perilously close to the capital." I sipped my whiskey this time, not letting the unpleasant burning sensation show on my face.

"Whiskey?" he asked. "You're barely old enough to be out by yourself. Should I have them bring champagne?"

"Yes, you must be careful, dear. Especially in a place like this. You could wind up pregnant, or worse!"

"I have my man, who will ensure I leave in the same condition that I arrived." I pointed at my personal giant, Karol.

"Oh! He's a big one," she said, sipping a pink-colored drink in a tall, thin glass.

"I didn't mean to intrude, but this is my first time here, and I was hoping to meet… like-minded people," I said, trying to sound confident. I opened my handbag and took the dagger halfway out, just enough to show the owl design on the pommel.

"Well," the man said. He looked surprised. "Where did you find that?"

"In my back." I smiled. They were both taken aback. "I have two of these, actually. I may be just a girl, but I'm hard to kill."

"Hard to kill or not, I would leave that in your bag. That symbol is well known here, and those who are most familiar with it are very serious people," the man said.

I wasn't surprised. I had no idea what the lore was behind the evil owl symbol, but I'd only seen it when people were trying to kill me, so yeah, I knew that it led to trouble.

"I detect accents. I hope you don't find me to be gauche, but I've not traveled…"

"Jeg er dansk. I am Danish," the woman said, raising her glass. "Andrei here is from… well, it used to be Transylvania."

"It is Moldavia now. Vlad Dracul gave us a bit of a reputation."

The older woman touched me on the arm. "You're too polite to ask us why we're here in your country." I tried not to give away that she was exactly correct. "I just arrived by ship, and I'll be heading to the capital tomorrow. Andrei is here for the same reason. Your king is trying to forge alliances, to form a coalition against Rus aggression."

"I had no idea, but that makes perfect sense. If they are able to annex Polska, the rest of Europa will be next in their sights. We have a common enemy."

"Do we?" the Moldavian asked. "Rus has not declared war on us, and we don't know for certain that they ever will. Out of courtesy, we are meeting with your king."

"Do you know who else is discussing possible alliances?"

"Unofficially? The Poniatowski family has been reaching out to every empire in Europa. Rumor is that your military is running out of mechs, armor, and the conscripts are poorly trained for combat." I knew that my face showed my displeasure. "No offense, dear. No country in Europa is prepared to defend against the Rus war machine."

"All the more reason to unite. It will be easier to swallow us a bite at a time. United? Rus would choke on us."

"You make a compelling case, Lady Sobieski. I am meeting with Prince Poniatowski the day after tomorrow. Let's see if he is as persuasive as you."

Prince Poniatowski. My Stanisław. Since smothering him with kisses when we last met, I hadn't had the chance to speak with him. He was the architect of our war effort, and I was a loose cannon, trying to uncover who was sending assassins to kill our king, and to kill me.

# Chapter 34

Interlude III:

The staff waiting room had a distinctly different vibe from the foyer or the hallway. The room was dimly lit, with sparkling white walls and a plain tiled floor. They had obtained a floor plan of the place from the local land registrar's office. It seemed to be an easy, in-and-out mission.

Julia was lifted to the air vent in the corner of the room. She pried out the slotted cover plate and handed it to Borys, who had pockets full of tools. She was thin and lighter than the rest, making her the natural choice to slip into the air ducts and navigate to a room marked on the plans as 'management office.'

Her instinct was to complain how dirty it was in the aluminum shaft, but she sneezed, and the sound echoed wildly through the ventilation system.

I definitely need to wash my hair tonight, she grumbled to herself. Good thing I'm not claustrophobic. She inched through on her elbows, pushing with her rubber slippers on the metal surface. Straight, straight, left, right, then left again. She passed out of the waiting room, over a supply closet, and then she moved over to another room that was unlabeled. She heard a slapping noise, grunting, then a sound she'd made herself when she was with her boyfriend. The room was dark, and she didn't know for certain what was going on, but she had a pretty good idea.

They allowed her five minutes to crawl from the waiting room to the manager's office. Their estimates were overly optimistic, and it took ten full minutes to reach the room.

When she reached the grate over the office, the room was well lit, and there were two men and a woman inside. One man sat at a small desk, piled high with papers, while the other two stood across the room, conversing with him.

The standing man seemed very animated. "She's out there, talking to the Dane and the Romanian."

"What are they talking about?" the seated man asked.

"It's too loud to pick up anything on the microphones. I've sent a server over there to try and eavesdrop. I'll let you know when she reports back to the bar."

The woman finally spoke. "We should take her. We'll never get a chance like this again."

"She's very dangerous," the standing man said. "We don't know the full extent of her powers, but what she did at the ball on the cruise ship was enough. Without a doubt, she bears a prime brand."

"This is one of our main goals. The time to strike is now!" she replied. Julia could see her face redden through the gap in the vent. "We immobilize her, don't allow her to fight back."

The other man sat forward, placing his hands flat on the desk. "She's right. This may be our best chance. It's time for the Court of Whispers to emerge from the shadows. Send out the signal. Put plan Gamma into effect." He got up, his chair scraping, and they continued to talk.

That was Julia's cue to start backtracking. She had to inform the others before this plot against her kapitan was put into action.

Sliding backward through the confined space was even tougher than going forward. What had taken a long time before was taking forever now, and she knew that time was of the essence.

Every inch was a chore; she was sweating profusely through the lovely dress that her commanding officer had bought for her. I'm not going to make it in time, she thought, feeling desperation creep in.

The next twenty feet felt like an hour, though it was probably just minutes. She heard a familiar sound, the sound of lovers who had slipped away from the crowd. The room below her was dark, and she couldn't see anything, and had no idea what was directly below.

I don't have time for this!

She kicked the vent and heard it clatter a second afterward, accompanied by a cry of pain. She shimmied backward and went through the opening with a speed and grace that surprised even her. She landed on the warm body of a man who gave out another scream as, like the vent, she rolled over his back and onto the floor.

"So sorry. Please continue!"

Julia ran to the door and rushed out into the hallway, making sure not to look back. The dark hallway was empty, and she ran to where the rest of the squad was held up waiting. She opened the door that had a deadbolt on the outside. She rushed in and pulled the door shut behind her.

"You weren't supposed to be seen!" Marcin whispered.

"I wasn't," Julia replied. "We have to move. They are going to try and kidnap the Kapitan!"

"Who is?" Borys asked.

"The Court of Whispers. Whoever that is. Doesn't matter. We have to make our play."


Lieutenant Filip Budny tried to keep his head on a swivel while at the same time appearing nonchalant. Unlike his boss, he couldn't look at someone and know if they were a channeler wielder. He had no royal blood, and he knew that he wouldn't go far in his military career without it, but he felt a duty to Polska, to her people, and his family. Going undercover was about as far from what he was commissioned to do as possible, but this was the mission, and he would perform to the best of his abilities.

The Kapitan was across the room, chatting up a couple of foreigners. Sierżant Antol was several feet away, not part of her conversation, but close enough to step in and protect her.

"You should put your arm around me," Izabelalla said in his ear. "I think it would help our cover."

"I am Krystian Sobieski. You are Milka Ostrogski." She looked at him dumbly. "We are first cousins. That may be ok where you came from, but the rest of society frowns on such things."

She gave him a dirty look, then smiled again as a tray of shrimp puffs passed. She crunched the pastry and looked around the room for anything out of place. She had a checkered past before joining the army, and her situational awareness was better than the rest of their little squad.

The dank, dark room was already creepy, and it was filled with equally creepy people. When they had come in, she saw that a man behind the bar wasn't mixing drinks, but was watching the Kapitan pretty closely. He spared a few glances for her and the lieutenant, but focused on Jafra.

A woman loaded drinks onto a large round tray before walking over to serve whiskey to the Kapitan and the man and woman she was talking to. After they took their drinks, she hovered nearby, close enough to hear over the soft playing of the band. The server set her tray on a tall table and pretended to wipe the table with a cloth from her belt for a long time.

"Krystian," she nudged the lieutenant. He didn't respond. She hit him harder, too hard to ignore. "Over there." She nodded towards Jafra, pointing with her eyes. "That waitress is spying on your sister." He followed her gaze. "She's reporting to that stiff behind the bar." He looked at the man over her shoulder. "Don't look too often. Use your peripheral vision."

She felt something, a feeling born from being in sticky situations in the past. Nothing happened for the next ten minutes, then she saw them. Two men and a woman were closing in on Jafra. They were dressed like the other patrons in fine clothing, very upper-crust types, but she could tell they were on the hunt.

"It's happening." She didn't wait; instead, she started moving through the room, jostling people aside if they got in her way.

One of the men had come up behind Karol and placed a hand on him. The large man wasn't happy about being touched, and when he went after the person who had laid hands on him, he found himself stuck fast. He had incredible strength, but try as he might, he was stuck to the ground like an insect on fly paper. He growled and thrashed around, but couldn't move an inch in any direction.

Jafra was staring at a young man across the room when a woman came up from behind and put both hands on her, causing her excruciating pain. She jolted, then spasmed as if electricity was passing through her.

Everyone in the club turned to see the disturbance and watched as a man put a cloth over her nose and mouth for several seconds until she was unconscious. He caught her and started to drag her away before a knife was stuck in his back. Izabelalla could kill with a single stab, but she stuck her knife in him a dozen more times before someone knocked her over the head with a bottle.

Filip put himself between his Kapitan and a wielder bearing the Torment Kiss brand. He reached inside his coat, but before he could pull his hand out, she had her hands on him. Intense pain shot through his system, like he was on fire and being electrocuted at the same time. He'd never experienced pain anywhere near as intense.

He was a military man to his core, and through sheer force of will, he reached into his pocket and pulled out a small pistol. It was a child's toy compared to his service weapon, but it could kill.

Every muscle in his body was contracting in pain, and he could feel his tendons trying their best to rip away from his bones. His breath caught in his chest, throat dry, eyes wanting to explode out of his head. He lifted the barrel and put a pulse round through the woman's face, creating a small hole on her left cheek, next to her nose. That stopped the pain immediately. His second shot made a small, circular hole in the middle of her forehead. She dropped, and he looked around for someone else to shoot.

Two men were dragging Jafra's unconscious body out a back door, while others were trying to attack him and the other two soldiers. Karol was hopelessly stuck to the ground, and whoever had done it was wisely hiding somewhere. Izabelalla lay on the floor, still unconscious. Three men rushed to block the kapitan's path; they stood defiant and proud. He was sure they were wielders, but he had no proof. It would come.

The music had stopped long ago, and the room was a chaotic cacophony of screams and curses. The man in front was yelling at the soldiers and the room in general, some threat, but in a language that none of them spoke. A crashing sound came from the back of the room as the rest of the squad poured into the room. They were all blanks, so they charged in brandishing gunpowder-based pistols. Julia was pissed and held her gun pointed at the wielders.

"Let the woman go, or I start blasting!" she screamed. The mousy, young private looked fierce in her bright red dress covered in dust, her brown eyes ablaze.

The man was a black silhouette in the poorly-lit lounge. He was tall and imposing, despite only being a formless, dark figure. He raised his arms, and thousands of three-inch-long thorn-like needles appeared. Everyone in a cone of space before him was struck. The screams of a few were replaced by the cries of pain from dozens in the room.

Julia ducked, covering her face and neck, but took a handful of needles to her forearm, side, chest, and right thigh. Jacek was directly behind her and took only a single needle to the knee. Marcin was hit several times and was groaning like he was in childbirth. Borys was struck in the chest and collar and took a needle to the eye. His screams overwhelmed all the noise in the room.

Julia began shooting, the crack of her shots ringing in the confined space. She hit the dark shape in the leg, and one of the men behind him in the stomach. She was reloading when a green gas filled the room. The smell was horrific, like rotten egg mixed with baby shit and a hint of skunk. The vile cloud rolled from the third wielder like a fog moving in from the shore in a vast, fluffy wave.

People were retching, and every eye in the house was watering with the foul stench. Julia couldn't concentrate on putting the new magazine in the grip of her pistol and dropped it as she lost her lunch.

A woman approached Julia with a knife in her hand. She grabbed the soldier by her long hair and was ready to slit her throat when a feral roar split the sound of crying and whimpering. She was pulled backward and down in a flash.

Julia and the boys watched as a creature, more wolf than man, ripped out her windpipe with a vicious bite. Blood coated its muzzle, and the yellow eyes were wide, hinting at human intelligence.

The first wielder peppered the wolf creature with needles. It sheltered its face, then, when the barrage stopped, pounced. The wolf-man landed on the man's chest, driving him hard to the floor. His head hitting the floor that hard may or may not have been fatal, but the slashes to his face, neck, and chest most certainly were.

Blood splashed everywhere, and everyone stood by in horrified silence as the kill was made. Two men at the back of the room had Jafra tied up, blindfolded, and gagged, and were trying to hustle her through a side door when the wolf caught them. The monster dug its claws into the back of one man and tossed him like a rag doll across the room.

The other kidnapper lifted a pistol, and a shot rang out. The wolf jerked back as hot lead pierced its upper shoulder. Blood exploded from the wound, but it seemed only to enrage the beast. Leaping over tables and a score of partygoers, the wolf-man seized the hand holding the gun and put a sharp, clawed thumb through the man's eye. It yanked his head to the side, giving easy access to the exposed throat. The sound of flesh tearing and spine crunching gave everyone in the room a queasy feeling.

With unexpected delicacy, the wolf slipped a claw under Jafra's blindfold, cutting it easily. Her eyes were huge, showing the horror she must have felt at that moment. It then cut the cord holding her gag in place, and finally, it cut the rope holding her arms tight behind her back. She fixed her dress as she stood, now recovered from the chloroform that had been used to knock her out. The wolf-man stood staring at her, looking at her in a way that didn't seem like he considered her an enemy or a potential meal. It seemed more like a protector than anything.

"I'm sorry, milady," Karol said, still stuck where he'd been since before she was attacked.

"I've had enough of this," she said with a finality that no one understood until a moment later. She waved her hand, and half the room didn't notice anything different. The other half were shocked to their core. Karol was able to move again, relief lighting his face. Several faces around the room, including both guests and those participating in the kidnapping, were in stunned silence. The most shocking revelation came when the wolf-creature began to change. The hairy body shrank, hair receding as if by magic. His muzzle receded, revealing a familiar face.

"Jaroslav?"

# Chapter 35

I was talking with the Dane and the Moldavian when my world erupted into unbelievable pain. It felt like a combination of acid running through my veins and electricity coursing through me at the same time. I could feel the touch of Abyrinth and was about to fight against it when a cloth was put over my nose and mouth, and then my world went black.

When I woke up, I was on the far side of the lounge area, tied up and lying on my side. I wanted to scream, but something was in my mouth, and I could feel a strap around my head, holding it in place. I couldn't see; there was cloth across my eyes, completely blocking out any light.

I had seen some crazy things in the last few months, done some things, but this feeling of helplessness had me panicking. I could hear screaming; people around me were getting hurt, possibly my squad, and there was nothing that I could do about it. It went on for what felt like an eternity, but I was sure it was only a few minutes.

It fell quiet, and I wondered whether the good guys had won or if I was about to be taken captive.

I felt something hard rub against the side of my head, and then the pressure holding my gag in place was gone. I spit the wad of cloth out as the same process happened to my blindfold. It was dark in the club, just as it was when we entered. Still, I had a difficult time seeing who my savior was. He rolled me over so that he could saw through the ropes holding my arm tied behind my back. When I was free, I rolled back to see who, or what, had saved me.

It was a man, but with the head of a wolf. He wasn't as tall as Stefek, but he was good-sized, with bulging muscles in the shoulders, arms, and chest. Every inch of him was covered in thick, dark fur. He maintained a low growl, and saliva dripped from his blood-stained muzzle.

I know that I should have been terrified, but I wasn't. I had never seen or even heard of such a monster existing. If he had wanted me dead, he would have killed me when I was helpless. He wouldn't have been the one to release me.

I maintained my composure and stood to face him and the rest of the mayhem that had ensued during my period of unconsciousness. I could see hundreds of people, including my squad, standing around, looking at the wolf, waiting for him to kill me. He had the aura of Abyrinth on him, as did many more in the crowd. I knew that it was a wielder that caused me that horrific pain. I saw people who looked like pincushions, with three-inch thorns stuck in their flesh. There was pain and blood everywhere. I wasn't a healer; that was my mother. What little I could do was to stop the madness caused by powerful criminals.

I pulled at the strings, gathering the strands and wisps of Abyrinth to me. Every particle of energy obeyed me. If it was serving another, it abandoned them and at my command, entered me, filling me with heroic levels of energy. It wasn't about energizing myself; it was about denying the bad actors in the room of their superpowers.

My plan worked perfectly, making the wielders temporarily the equal of blanks. And my blanks were anything but helpless.

I hadn't expected it, and I should have, but the wolf slowly morphed into a man. I watched the process with morbid curiosity. The muscles were still there, though smaller, and his height had been reduced by an inch or two. The fur gave way to a light dusting of arm and chest hair. The biggest change was the wolf's head, which transformed. The blood-soaked muzzle shrank to become the gentle, handsome face of the Bohemian. Prince Jaroslav Záhoř. Technically, the first man to kiss me.

"Jaroslav?" I couldn't help myself. He was the last person I expected to see.

"Jafra." He took a clean cloth from his man nearby and tried to clean his face. He was the self from the airship races, not the version from my Ascension Ball. He had dark hair, and there was no trace of the wolf or the cad. "We should have a doctor look you over. You might have been harmed by these terrorists."

"Jaroslav!" I said dumbly. I was still in shock.

"Jafra. I told you a bit about my brand, Trojvlk—the three wolves. I told you before that I have three states. This is the true me, the one before I faced my trials. You've also met me in my middle state."

"I remember. You're very bold in your middle state." I remembered the touching and the almost violent kiss he gave me.

"And now, you've seen my third state. The wolf."

"You're terrifying. You still have blood on your face." I pointed to a patch of fresh blood along his jawline on his left side. He wiped at it while I looked around. At our feet was a woman with her throat torn out. Others were lying around near us, who had suffered wounds attributable to some fearsome beast.

"Terrifying? I suppose so. Like you and the rest of the nobles, I didn't choose this particular gift. But I use it against my enemies, my country's enemies. I become the wolf to protect those I care about." He gave me a look that frightened me even more than seeing him in wolf form.

"I need to tend to my soldiers, but stick around. You have much explaining to do!" I wanted answers immediately. I needed to know what he was feeling in that moment. I knew his middle state had sex on the brain, but in his natural form, did he also have feelings for me? The welfare of my troops had to come first, so I rushed over to check on them.

By now, Karol was at my side, and while he looked to Filip and Izabel, I crossed the room to check on the others. No one died, but they were in bad shape. All of them, except for the kid, Jacek, had multiple thorns stuck in their bodies.

Borys was the worst. His left eye had been punctured, ruined. I didn't know that even my mother could have healed such damage. Mother wasn't around, but maybe there would be a healer in the room.

"There are many wielders here. Are any of you healers?" I shouted.

I was approached by the nice Danish lady whom I had been speaking to.

"I have the Embermark Restore," she said. "Of course, you took away everyone's power. That brand of yours is… incredible."

"My mother has a similar brand. I hate to ask, but could I see yours?" It was insulting to ask about a person's brand, and even worse to ask to see it, but if she had some power to immobilize or kill me, well, let's say I could learn from my mistakes.

I could see that she wasn't thrilled to expose herself, but she turned and lifted her hair. There, at the base of her neck, was the brand that I was so familiar with. I thanked her and filled her to overflowing with Abyrinth.

She began healing the worst first, and I helped to pull the needles from my squad members. It took time, but I personally pulled over twenty of the needles from my squad member's bodies.

"If we were wearing regular armor, we would have been ok," Jacek griped.

"You got one needle in a non-vital spot, you lousy shit!" Borys said, holding a bloody cloth to his ruptured eyeball. "I'll be wearing an eye patch for the rest of my life."

"You seemed to get your needles and all of Jacek's as well," I said, pulling a tenth from Julia. "I heard that you took out a wielder before he could even use his power."

"With a lousy, unpowered pistol. Put a ball of lead through his black heart." She smiled, then grimaced as I pulled out another needle.

Lieutenant Budny walked over with Izabel and Karol in tow. They all looked more ashamed than hurt.

"Kapitan... I want to apologize," he began.

"For what, Lieutenant? I understand that both of you killed an enemy before getting incapacitated. You stopped the one who shocked me, and the man who drugged me? Izabelalla put more holes in him than a golf course." All of my troops were older than me, and yet I was in charge, and I had to keep up their spirits. "You all saved me, and saved each other. I can see that we make a great team."

"Thank you, that is kind of you. With Karol's help, we collected all of the wielders and regular people who were involved in the kidnapping attempt. Once you turn on the power again, they will be hard to contain. I've called for a sealed hover bus to come pick them up." He was ready to turn and go. "We didn't include that shape changer that released you. He's still waiting to speak with you."

Jaroslav mentioned three phases to his change, but he didn't elaborate. I crossed the room to where he was talking with a couple of other men. When he saw me, he shooed them away. He wore what had probably been a very nice blouse, but it was now a mess of shredded silk hanging off his muscular frame. I had only seen him in suits and formal wear, but I had to admit, he looked very appealing without a shirt. His hair was a mess, and as I approached, he ran his long fingers through the tangled mess and smiled.

"Jafra. I'm so relieved that you're safe and relatively unharmed." One of his men handed him a jacket that he shrugged on, much to my disappointment.

"I thought I recognized you from across the room, just before I was attacked. What on earth are you doing here?"

"I was on my way to Warszawa to meet with your king. He has feelers out all around Eastern Europa. It sounds like things are getting desperate, and he is searching for allies."

"I understand that. I met other representatives from Moldavia and Denmark; they, too, were heading towards the capital. But why are you here?" I asked. I got frustrated, having to ask a question more than once.

"I received an invitation." He reached into his jacket pocket, pulled out a card, and handed it to me. The card was three by five inches and had writing in a supremely talented hand. The ink was gold and shone brightly, even in the dim light of the club.

"Your Highness, Prince Jaroslav Záhoř of Bohemia, you are cordially invited to a soiree to be held at Dom Szeptów, the House of Whispers, on (today's date). There will be representatives from all of the major houses in Eastern Europa, and vital information on Rus intentions will be discussed after the evening's festivities. Do not share this invitation with anyone, as the meeting will be top secret, and discretion is vital to the success of the resistance movement." I flipped it over, and in coppery foil was stamped the seal with the evil-looking owl. Just the sight of it sent shivers down my spine.

"You've seen that symbol?" he asked.

I pulled the dagger from my handbag. I handed the blade to him, trusting him as if we had known each other for much longer. He turned it over in his hand, studying it like a weaponsmith might.

"I'm afraid to ask where you obtained this," he said, handing it back to me.

"I was attacked the same evening that assassins tried to kill King Poniatowski. One of the assassins stuck this in my back."

"Are you sure it was just the king they were after? It is common knowledge in some circles what you are capable of. The Rus and other groups might see you as a threat." He pointed at the owl design on his card. "This group most certainly is out to get you. They are known as the Court of

Whispers, and I'm guessing this is their club. I should have put two and two together."

"And I stumbled in here, putting myself right in their hands!" I was mortified. My carelessness had caused death. Not to my troops, thank God, but to many. Borys was half-blinded, and everyone was harmed to some degree.

"How did you even find this place? I'm told it's very exclusive, and they jealously guard its very existence."

"We shook the trees, and a lowlife fell out. We questioned him, threatened him, and he coughed up the name and location of this place. We even got a password from him. As it turns out, we didn't need the password. At the entrance, I gave my real name, and we were told that I was on the list."

He looked concerned, he stared down, deep in thought, before meeting my gaze again. "It seems clear that you are a target of this subversive society. They don't want to kill you, but they want to kidnap you, and they'll kill whoever gets in their way." I could tell that he was racking his brain, looking for answers. "I don't understand why you would be a target. Your brand is powerful. Very powerful. But why go to the lengths that they've gone to?"

I took his elbow and guided him even further from the others. I could tell that he had a hundred questions, but he was patient and let me lead him.

"I was confronted by this woman who told me things that are still unproven, but have the ring of truth. She said that my brand is unique, the only one of its kind. Further, she said that it is called a prime brand, one of three. The theory is, if all three brands work together, their combined power would be impossible to stop."

"Who is this woman? Did you know her?"

"She gave me the name Hedwig, but later, I heard her referred to as Lady Rozalia Tarnowski. I'm not sure that either is her real name."

"If some secret cabal is trying to assassinate you, I swear that I'll track them down."

"And?" I asked.

"They'll meet my werewolf." Even though he was a mild person by nature, I could see he was seething with anger.

"I missed seeing the wolf attack, but I heard him, and the aftermath is… proof of his resolve."

"You speak of the wolf as a separate identity, but that's not the case. He is me."

"And the middle state? The wild, white-haired libertine?"

"Also me," he replied, and I could see that the confession was difficult for him.

"And the things he said… you said? Wanting me, lusting for me?"

He turned scarlet. "He voices things that I feel, but am too cowardly to say aloud."

I appreciated the honesty, and I saw that he was out of his comfort zone. I wasn't sure what to think about it. Every woman wanted to be admired, to be desired by men, but the way he kissed me…

"I've said too much," he stammered. He must have read my introspection as a rejection.

"No, Jaroslav. I bear you no ill will. In fact, I'm quite fond of you."

"And the libertine?" he asked, looking hopeful.

"He surprised me. He… you were very direct. I was caught off guard."

"That's not a rejection; I'll stop while I'm ahead. My instincts were on point. You are everything that a man could want and more." He paused, looking up to meet my gaze. "I've not heard any announcements that you've become engaged."

"The war has put a wrinkle in my plans to be wed and with child by now. No, I am not engaged. But, my mother is very much in favor of me marrying Stanisław."

"Prince Poniatowski?" He said the name with a distasteful sneer.

"You know of whom I speak." I wasn't going to let him off easily.

"The Commanding General of the Polska Army, who has never spoken a harsh word, much less led men into battle and spilled the blood of the Rus invaders."

"Isn't it common for tacticians, high-ranking generals, to lead from a position of safety?"

"I'm also an heir to a throne, and I fight the enemy with claw and jowl. I don't believe you can put the lives of others at risk until you've risked your own."

I looked at this noble son, a man born to privilege, in a different light. He could have easily led a life of leisure, spending his family's money until it was time for him to ascend to the Bohemian throne. Instead, he went against his naturally timid nature and hunted down the enemy, executing them without malice.

There was a world of difference between Stanisław and Jaroslav. Stan was taller, fairer, and… beautiful. In his military uniform, he was noble and imposing. The crisp lines, the medals, the gold braid and embroidery, the brass buckles and buttons shone to a sparkling finish. Since the king was so gravely injured, much of the country already looked at him as the de facto king.

Jaroslav was of similar social stature but different in appearance, manner, and outlook. He was two men in a single package. The prince was shy and thoughtful, funny in his own subtle way. I enjoyed talking with him more than anyone, even more than talking to Krystian or Milka. The cad was wild, fearless, and supremely confident. If they were a single entity, I would say I liked him as more than just a friend.

"You're traveling to the capital?" I asked.

"Yes. We need to meet with your suitor and his father, the king."

"How many are you?"

"Myself and two others. We are a very tight crew."

"You can travel with us. I have to report back to my brothers about this Court of Whispers."

"Agreed, and thank you. The trip is long enough, so I'll have the opportunity to present my case."

"Your case?"

"At your Ascension Ball, I told you that I would make you mine. I feel even more convinced that you are the woman I would make Queen of Bohemia."

# Chapter 36

Normally, it would have been a four-hour drive to Warszawa, but with refugees heading west and thousands of soldiers with their machines of war heading east, the roads were a mess. My squad, along with the Bohemians, piled into our troop transport, and we spent an inordinate amount of time idling on the highway.

While we were waiting, Jacek helped our guests sign on to the radio so they could communicate with their leadership. Even if I understood their language, I'm sure they were speaking in code to prevent outsiders from knowing their business. After several calls, each lasting five to ten minutes, a man named Radomír came to the back of the passenger cabin to whisper to Jaroslav. I could tell that he, too, was a wielder. When they were done, Jaro pulled me aside.

"It looks like this Court of Whispers is not a group exclusive to Polska. My family's agents in Praha have had their own dealings with terrorists, and in the aftermath, they've found the same owl symbology."

"We assumed that all of these attacks and assassination attempts were instigated by the Rus, but maybe they were really the work of this secret organization."

"Rus has dreams of empire. There's no doubt about that," he whispered to me. "They want to swallow Europa a bite at a time, and Polska, unfortunately, is the next in line to be conquered." He took my hand and locked eyes with me. "This court is something different altogether. We have evidence that they are behind the attack at your Ascension Ball and the assassination attempt  at the Autumn Ball."

"Regardless of our war with Rus, these cowards must be crushed!" I said, squeezing his hand tightly.

"There's more. My intelligence squad has been investigating a series of missing persons, and it appears the Court of Whispers may be behind them. Random people have been taken, with no trace of where they've gone. They are all over eighteen, and all are blanks."

With all of the horror of war, I was surprised that I wasn't jaded to human suffering. The idea that a person who was going shopping or commuting to work could be kidnapped and probably killed was making me feel their pain. There was so much ugliness in the world, it was hard to find any sunshine through the rain.

"Why do you think the murders are related to this evil owl group?"

"I feel like it's too coincidental. Dozens of people have disappeared, vanished without a trace. Then we become aware of this nefarious cabal. A group whose true intentions are still a mystery, but they are not afraid to send wielders on suicide missions."

It wasn't a direct line from the missing people to the Court of Whispers, but after what they tried to do to me, I agreed that it seemed likely. Our kind committed little, if any, crime, and in both recent instances, wielders were involved in the attacks. This Court of Whispers was more than a small, shadow group. They meant to upend the structure of life in Europa, and no doubt, there was some even worse master plan underway.

"I will reach out to my brothers. Find out if they can find out if anything is going on in the capital." He was still holding my hand, though neither of us had noticed how firmly we held onto each other. "Come to my house tomorrow. I am putting my team on forty-eight-hour leave. We can follow any leads that Stef and Krys might come up with."

I don't know why I was nervous about bringing Jaroslav home. We were going to compare notes and try to show proof that this secret organization really existed, and prove that it was responsible for the attempts on the king's life. It wasn't a date! Besides, his family held a higher standing than ours, even though they were foreign. A lot of the friends that I brought home were awed and intimidated by our mansion and grounds, but the only two boys that I invited to our house were both princes, and neither one was particularly impressed by our wealth or status.

"Welcome," Father said by way of greeting. I hadn't seen him for the last couple of months, and it felt like he had grown older. He bowed, Jaroslav bowed, then they shook hands.

"Thank you for welcoming me into your home," Jaroslav said.

Father regarded me with a critical eye. "Every time I see you, Jafra dear, you appear different. As if you're aging a year each month."

"I'm not sure how to take that, Father."

"This damned war is taking its toll on all of us. You are forgoing courtship for service to your country. Very noble, but it saddens me that your youth is squandered on such dangerous and violent pursuits." He turned to Jaroslav. "How is it in your country, milord?"

"There are subversive forces in Bohemia, trying their best to overturn our family and the government. We hunt them down and gather as much information as we can. We aren't on the front lines like Polska, but it's clear that Rus plans to add us to their real estate portfolio after they've taken your country."

"True. Their lust for land and power knows no limit."

"Jaroslav is going to meet with the king and the Commanding General. They are looking all over Europa for allies."

"Have you already made your decision, young man?"

"The decision is not mine to make. I'm here representing the crown. I will take any offers or requests to my father. In my humble opinion, we need to join this fight now. Have the war in Polska instead of Bohemia or Moldavia." He looked apologetic. "War is already here; best not to let it spread. That's my opinion, but I do not yet speak for my country."

"Father, it is getting bad out there. I know that you hate the idea of running, but the Rus are at the eastern edge of the city. They could be attacking as we speak. Please, take mother and head west. Today!"

He was a proud man, and our family had lived on the same plot of land for hundreds of years. The regular people, the blanks, might be alright, might be treated kindly by the invaders, but most of the nobles would be publicly executed. It was the last thing he wanted, but he knew it was time to leave.

As if on cue, all hell broke loose. There were shouts and the distant sound of cannons. A minute later, one of the grooms came rushing in, sweating and out of breath.

"Milord, armed men have breached the south gate and are advancing on the house."

For the first time in my life, I saw hesitation on my father's face. He was flustered and unable to make the correct decision. I didn't want to be disrespectful, but there was no time.

I spoke. "Mikel, fetch Lady Sobieski and the children. Take them to the garage." He nodded and rushed off. I turned to my father. "Sorry, Father, there is no time to collect any valuables or even clothing."

"You still don't know how the world works, dear daughter. Without something in your pocket, you'll not last a week." He jogged through the house to his study. Pulling back a large painting of his great-grandfather, he went for a wall safe. He fumbled a couple of times before getting the correct combination. The one-foot-square door opened smoothly, revealing a king's ransom in gold and jewels. There was a leather bag inside, which he stuffed with as much wealth as he could. The bag was completely filled, and there was still much more left on the small shelves. He looked at us with what I thought might be fear in his eyes. "Both of you, fill your pockets!"

To humor him, we each took a stack of gold bars. What I didn't want to tell him was that I had a gun, a uniform, and one of the most powerful brands. I wouldn't go hungry. I took him by the arm and hustled him to the garage, where Mother, Jurek, and Dominika were waiting. Mother looked terrified, and the children were a wreck.

"Everyone in the sedan," I ordered. "Father, you drive." My siblings jumped in, eager to escape the noise that was growing louder by the second.

Father got in, but Mother stood there looking at me. "Get in, dear, both of you. There's room!"

"I'm staying. I'm a kapitan in the Wojsko Królewskie. It's my duty to protect civilians and kill Rus. Go now! If I know that you've gotten away safely, I can fight without having to shield you, Father, and the children."

She wanted to stay and argue, but Father practically shoved her into the car. They all waved as he pulled out and headed for the north gate.

I turned to Mikel and pressed a couple of gold bars into his sweaty palm. "Leave Krystian's sports car, and take one of the other cars. Take whoever you can find and head east. If we have a home after this is over, we hope you will come back to us."

The man was, of course, frightened, but he was able to hide it well, and he looked grateful that we had not abandoned him and the others.

"Of course, miss. We'll clear out." A single tear rolled down his cheek. "Kill them, miss. Kill as many of the devils as you can!" Without waiting for an answer, he turned and ran.

After giving out all the orders, I turned to Jaroslav. He had changed. He had the same face, height, muscles… but his hair had gone white, and he carried himself with a confident swagger. He pulled off his jacket to reveal not one, but two pistols on his hips.

"The other guy is pretty good, but I'm ambidextrous." He patted the sidearms. This was the Jaroslav I met first. Like me, he wore a cocky smile and almost looked forward to the fight. I couldn't personally take out every Rus soldier by myself, but I planned to kill every invader that crossed onto my family's land.

"Ready to have some fun?" I asked as I pulled my pulse pistol.

He smiled. "Always!"

I took off at a jog, heading towards a pillar of smoke that had no doubt been our workshop. The air was filled with clanking and yelling as the enemy trudged through my property, breaking what they could in search of loot. We reached an outbuilding, where a soldier was banging around inside.

Jaroslav whispered in my ear, "If you see one with a pulse weapon like the one you're carrying, kill them first." It made sense. To carry one of these, you had to be a channeler or possibly even a wielder. Pulse weapons were silent, as they channeled power, and there was no combustion like regular guns.

The building had two entrances, and since they entered on the other side, I was sure they would exit through the door right where we were standing.

A female soldier burst through the door, rifle held at the ready. Jaroslav might have some hesitation when killing a woman. I had no problem with it. I put a round through her temple, and she dropped into his arms, now a lifeless corpse. A man on her heels didn't even notice until he, too, had his head ventilated. No more came, so we entered the building and shut the door behind us.

I looked out a window, trying to see how many there were. I turned to my partner. "Ten at least. That's just what I can see from here."

"Any officers? Anyone carrying pulse weapons?"

I looked again. There was a man about Stefek's age, with a lieutenant's bars on his collar. He carried a sword and a pistol similar to mine. I looked for traces of Abyrinth and saw the telltale aura around the officer.

"Just one. The rest are blanks."

"I don't know if you are aware, but they don't really like being called blanks."

In truth, I had never thought about it. I guessed it could have been taken as demeaning if you were a sensitive soul. I didn't believe that I meant it as a pejorative. I mean, they were lower than us. Everybody knew it, and they were fine with their lot in life. At least, I thought so.

"Hmph," I growled. "I'll block the channeler, and we both start blasting!"

"No," he said firmly. "You shoot from in here, where you have some cover. Your powers won't stop metal slugs from tearing you apart, and your mother isn't here to patch you up." He was commanding, and it riled me that he would order me around in my own home. "I'll circle the building and shoot them from the back." His plan was better, and that, too, got under my skin.

We agreed that I would give him a twenty count before starting. When I had counted off in my head and reached zero, I pulled the aura of energy from the officer, then shot at him from my position of concealment.

I was a good shot, but it took three shots to bring him down. The infantrymen were alerted by the first shot and were looking for the source. I took better aim, and my fourth shot took out a man carrying an enormous rifle. It looked like it could have shot me through the walls, and that meant he had to go first. I shot another man who was diving for cover behind a water barrel. I heard his cry of pain, and I saw the small fountain of blood as he fell behind the barrel.

I heard screaming, and then the sound of men crashing into the training stands to the left in our practice yard. There was no one to shoot at, so I slowly opened the door. I saw four soldiers who had been mowed down by Jaro's pistol barrage. I peeked out, and a shot nearly took my head off, striking the door just an inch above my fashionable beret. Well, damn.

I went out the back door, and like Jaro, I went around the building, but in the other direction. I came up behind two soldiers who had taken cover and were trying to gun down my friend. I made short work of them, and when I took their vantage point, I got to see Jaro in action.

He looked and moved like a gunslinger from the American West. He really was ambidextrous, firing his pistols from both hands, picking off enemies whenever they were foolish enough to show themselves.

Perhaps it was an effect of his transformation, but his reflexes seemed inhumanly fast. I saw him dodging bullets and returning fire with fluid strength and grace. I hadn't seen his wolf phase, but this middle ground was deadly and beautiful. He must have evaded a hundred rounds before taking a shot to the buttocks, of all places. I had to help.

I gathered strands of ambient Abyrinth and wrapped them around the troop transport that they were hiding behind. I lifted the vehicle ten feet in the air, then dropped it on them. Five Rus were smashed and killed instantly. The bumpers clipped a couple of soldiers, and they lay wounded. I made a dozen tentacles of pure energy and had each one grasp a practice sword from the rack near the gym. It was difficult to control so many separate items, but Jaro lay on the ground, tending to his wound, and was a sitting duck.

The enemy soldiers couldn't fathom that wooden swords were floating off a rack and were flying at them with great speed. Practice swords are typically not sharp or strong enough to puncture skin, but I was still very angry, and I stabbed at the remaining few men with such force that they were skewered. I caught one through the heart, and the other two got a wooden sword through the gut.

"I've seen you do feats of great strength, but now you are using your power with amazing skill and dexterity. You truly are a unique treasure." He gave me a sly smile, not acknowledging the wound he'd received. I was worried because he was bleeding quite a bit.

"That wound might be serious. We need to take care of it." I bent down to get a better look. There was a hole in his trousers, and the area was soaked. I needed to get to the wound, but I wasn't sure how to proceed. "Come in the house. We bought ourselves a little time."

We went into the kitchen, where Mother did a lot of her healing. I got a bottle of Father's best whiskey from the cabinet and handed the bottle to Jaroslav.

"Umm," I said hesitantly.

"Yeah, that's right. I have to take my pants off." He took a belt from the bottle and gave a deep growl as the liquid burned its way down his pipes. "Help me out of my boots?"

He sat on a wooden chair next to the breakfast table and stuck his leg straight out. I'd helped my brothers and father before, so pulling a man's boots off wasn't new to me. He watched me with amusement, evaluating my technique. When both boots were off, he stood and opened his belt. Never losing eye contact, he pushed the dark blue pants as far as he could.

"A little help?"

I squatted down, and he put his hand on my shoulder for support and lifted each leg in turn while I pulled his pants the rest of the way off.

I had admired his upper body before when he was in his natural state. The change added bulk to his muscles, and I couldn't help but notice that his legs were thick and sinuous. Each long limb was like a marble column, holding up the Parthenon. He wore light green undershorts that looked like they were military issue. He stood and hooked his thumbs in the waistband and was about to be nude from the waist down.

"Just in the back! Turn around and only pull down the back of your shorts!" Kind, gentle Jaroslav would have been too shy, but I guessed that this version was confident enough to get naked in front of anyone.

He chuckled and did as I asked. I should have directed my attention straight to the bullet hole, but almost subconsciously, I noted his nearly smooth buttocks and that his legs had very light hair like his chest.

"You like what you see back there?" he asked, laughter in his voice. "The front is even better, Jafra, my dear. I can make an introduction."

"Shut up while I clean your injury!" He sounded like he was joking, but my inexperience got my temper up. I had no desire to be introduced to what he had between his legs. I had no frame of reference, but it seemed substantial, and that sounded perfectly horrible.

I wet a towel and wiped the blood away, finding the tear in what was, otherwise, an attractive posterior. "It's hardly bleeding."

"When I use my brand, my healing is increased, and the wolf heals even faster." He craned his neck to look at the damage. "Still, I think I'll need a couple of stitches."

That's what I was afraid of. Mother never needed stitches. Minor surface injuries were nothing to her, and deeper wounds only took a little longer and a bit more of her power. I had tons of power, but none of it could be used to heal. I stood there for a long time, staring at the open wound.

"Wishing your mother were here?

"Yes," I admitted.

"So do I. Just do it. Please."

I got a medical kit from the pantry. It was nearly new because we always had a better option. I laid out the needle, thread, and bandages.

"Lie face down on the table. Maybe take another swig of the whiskey."

"Thought you would never ask." He took a heroic gulp, then assumed the position. I had changed Jurek's diapers, but until now, I'd never touched a man's ass. I couldn't appreciate it with blood still seeping from the hole. I sewed as quickly as I could, partially because I knew that more Rus troops would be coming any minute, but also because I felt uncomfortable with a nearly half-naked man in front of me.

"I'm sure that you're enjoying the view, but we don't have all day." He was having too much fun.

"Ok, I'm done. Now, get dressed. We'll take my brother's car."

He got up slowly, and it almost fell out when he was pulling his undergarment up. I didn't want to, but my eyes were drawn to the thick bulge. I was glad he kept it covered. But part of me wanted a peek.

"My eyes are up here, Jafra," he said, pointing at himself. He dressed quickly, had another shot of whiskey, then handed me the bottle. What the hell. I took a long drink because my nerves were shot. "Mind if I drive?"

"No problem, milord. I don't know how to drive, so go ahead."

He looked surprised. "You'll need to learn to drive. But not today." He took the keys from the peg, and we hit the road.

# Chapter 37

As we drove, I allowed myself to feel some of the loss. More of the Rus would be invading my family's property, and no doubt, when they found all of their dead comrades, they'd burn the place to the ground. Win or lose, my family would be devastated after the war. I knew that things could be rebuilt, but for the moment, I was saddened beyond measure.

"I'm taking us to the palace, dear. I'm still on a mission to meet with your king." He placed a steady hand on my knee. He did it so casually, like it was our hundredth drive together, and my knee was where he would always lay his hand. I wasn't sure what to do, but it took my mind off the loss of my home. What could it hurt? He wasn't touching my skin, just the leg of my camouflage pants.

He looked all around while we drove, constantly surveying the cross streets and keeping an eye on the rearview mirror. He gave my knee a gentle squeeze, then rubbed back and forth a little. He stayed on the lower half of my thigh, not too far up. I was trying so hard to pretend like nothing was happening as we reached the palace in what seemed like minutes.

"I'm sure that your parents and siblings got away safely. The streets west of your home are still free of the invaders."

He pulled the car up to the gate, where armed guards checked his credentials, then let us through. The gate guard must have called ahead, as Stanisław was on the front steps to greet us. He was more than a little surprised to see me, and it took a full two seconds for him to recover.

Greeting the Bohemian prince warmly, we made our way inside. The Zamek Królewski, or Royal Castle, was the royal family's residence since the sixteenth century, and was now the headquarters for the resistance. As castles go, it was not the most beautiful building from the outside. The main building was a reddish color, and it boasted three stories with a central tower. The inside was a different story. I was marveling at the Rembrandt collection when Stanisław pulled me aside.

"I'm surprised to see you here. With him." His annoyed expression matched his tone.

"Good to see you again, General," I replied. He may have been our next king, but I wasn't going to let him take that tone with me. I chose not to answer, and instead gave him my most withering stare.

"I've been expecting the prince. How is it that you're here, Kapitan?" He looked as handsome as ever. He didn't have his full uniform on; his tight dress shirt was even more appealing than his formal uniform jacket.

"My squad and I were heading back here anyway, so we gave Jaroslav and his men a ride. On our way here, we stopped at my parents' home. That's when the Rus struck. We got them and the children away in time, but as we speak, my house is burning." He was shocked. "We left plenty of bodies for the next wave to find."

"That close," he whispered to himself.

"If they reached my house, they can't be more than an hour or two from here."

Stanisław thanked me and ran off to join his father, who was speaking to Jaroslav. The palace was already at an alert status, but minutes later, things exploded. The royal guard was hustling people outside to board waiting armored transports. Seconds later, the king came out of the meeting room with Jaro a few paces behind. When he saw me, he rushed over.

"Jafra, dear! I hear so many great things about your military career so far. Please tell me your mother is alright! The two of you are the only reason I'm alive right now." He hugged me with his remaining arm, and I could feel his heartfelt appreciation.

"I haven't heard from my family, but we got them to leave before the Rus came. Prince Záhoř and I killed two squads of men before coming here. You should leave as soon as possible, your highness." I looked to Stanisław. "Have you heard from my brothers? I've not gotten a call from either of them in a while. They need to know about our home and that the family is fleeing west."

"My son will make sure word gets to your brothers." He turned to his son. "Take care of this. Your mother, sister, and I are leaving now. Meet us as soon as you can at the lake property." With that, he walked out, followed by the queen and Princess Jadwiga.

When the royal family was safely away, Stanisław came back to me. He had so many emotions playing across his face, I didn't know where the spinning wheel would land. Finally, after just standing in front of me for up to a minute, he met my gaze and spoke. "I should send you to the rear. Somewhere safe."

"General, there is no safe place in all of Polska. They'll take Warszawa, then within weeks, maybe a month, they'll own the country. I need to reunite with my unit. I can drop

Jaroslav back with his men. I gave my squad leave because I had no idea how close the Rus were. I'll get them, and we'll continue to follow up on this Court of Whispers. They're behind the attempts on your father's life, and God only knows what else."

"It sounds like you're choosing your own assignments now," he said bitterly.

"You're my prince and my commanding general. If you want me elsewhere, I'll go." I was not accustomed to any man other than my father giving me orders, but I was determined to be a good officer in the Royal Army. My only thought was revenge. Push out the invaders. Kill as many of them as possible.

Jaro was waiting near the door, talking to one of the Royal Guard who was in the trail group. Stanisław still leaned in to whisper to me. "You shouldn't be alone with that guy. I saw the way he took advantage of you at your ball."

"And after seeing that, you thought you could be next. You thought I was an easy fuck."

My course language caught him off guard. I wasn't too surprised by his reaction. No one speaks that way around the commanding general. But I had been in the midst of real soldiers. Men and women who shoot people and get shot at have little regard for the niceties of polite society.

"I admit, after what I saw, I thought you would be open to kissing on the first date, and you're hot, so I really wanted that to happen. After the way we ended our second date, I was given some hope. Kissing you was everything I had ever dreamed of. And more."

"I'm not a tramp like those party girls you had at the air races." The very thought made me throw up in my mouth just a little. "I imagine they did a lot more than kissing."

"I've kissed other girls in the past. I am older than you. I'm looking for a pure girl for marriage, and I'm glad you had the maturity to stop me." He looked over at Jaro, who was waiting patiently. "We're running out of time. You should go." He looked into my eyes; his were full of longing. I stepped up to him and hugged him tightly.

I whispered to him, "I can't kiss you in front of all these people, but I want to." I felt him tighten, crushing me against his strong chest. When we broke, I turned and walked away. It was not the time or place for a tearful goodbye.

"What are you going to recommend to your father?" I asked Jaroslav as we ran out to the car.

"Normally, I wouldn't want to get involved in foreign conflicts… but I can sense the future. They will annex Polska, rebuild for a year, then they will invade Bohemia. Together, we stand a better chance of curbing their hunger for other people's land."

"Did you radio your people?" We piled into the sleek sports car.

"Yes. I sent a coded message while you were chatting with your boyfriend."

"We've gone out, but he's not my boyfriend." I didn't know why I felt compelled to clarify. Whether Stanisław was my boyfriend or not, it wasn't Jaro's business. I wanted to kick myself, but Jaroslav made me nervous when he was in his intermediate phase.

He kept his eyes on the road, but had an evil smile. "Good to know."

We hadn't even reached the highway before the emergency claxon started sounding. By now, most of the citizens were aware that we'd been invaded. The sirens let them know that they were out of time, that the Rus were only minutes away. Shortly after the sirens began blaring, explosions could be heard throughout the city. Artillery was pounding the city, taking out bridges, power plants, and other vital infrastructure.

I can't explain the change that had come over me, but when I heard the sound of war, my instinct was to turn and drive into the teeth of the enemy. I had always been a girly girl, very feminine and well-mannered. I had never in my life harmed any person or creature, great or small, before turning eighteen. Since then, I'd stopped wearing dresses and makeup, and worse yet—much worse—I'd killed enough people that I'd lost count.

"People are rushing around, but I'm not sure they know where they're going," Jaro said.

I snapped out of my daydreaming and checked out the traffic around us. Most of the cars on the road were steam-powered, large and clunky compared to our futuristic hover car. The highway had gone from evenly spaced flows of vehicles to a free-for-all. They were trying to speed up, and when they did, many lost control. Accidents were happening all around us.

"We'll never get to the base like this." I was sure that my squad was there, waiting and getting their gear ready, but their leader wasn't present. "Let's go off-road."

He gave a grin, like a little boy who was given permission to misbehave. Hover vehicles usually stay within a foot or two off the ground, but on occasion, they can be taken to greater heights. We lifted out of the traffic jam and literally went off the road. We couldn't achieve the same speed on grassland and fields, but we were passing the evacuating civilians and were finally making headway. I can only imagine their anger at being stuck, either because they couldn't afford a hover car or, more likely, because they were blanks and couldn't harness Abyrinth.

We drove parallel to the highway and soon arrived at the main bridge across the Vistula. The riverfront featured high-end cafes and eateries, but the trendy area was deserted days ago by those who heeded the warning to escape. We needed to cross the river from west to east to collect our troops at the military base, but we were heading towards the enemy, not away from them.

When we arrived at Most Kierbedzia, one of the oldest bridges in Warszawa, I was crushed to see that it had already been bombed. The cast-iron bridge had been around since before the Night of the Comet and was a landmark of our capital city.

"I will radio ahead, see if any other bridges are still operational," Jaroslav said.

I got out and walked to the edge. The bridge was nothing more than a bird's nest of twisted metal beams now, broken at both ends. The whole center section had been ripped out and dropped into the river. I could see dozens of cars, and I assumed, still containing passengers, floating in the river. Some were right side up, some upside down. So many innocent lives lost.

"They are on the way. They'll be here as soon as they can push through traffic."

"They'll still be on the far side of the river," I said.

Above the din, I could hear a scream. A young woman, maybe a child, calling for help. I craned my head over the edge, looking in the direction from where the sound originated. Far down the lattice of wreckage, I saw a teenage girl, clinging to a deformed bridge strut. I tried reaching out with tendrils of energy, but she was too far away. I wasn't exactly sure what the range of my power was, but it seemed to be about a hundred feet, give or take.

I didn't think; I just started climbing down the wreckage. Massive pilings, with cores of steel and sheathed in cement, were driven into the ground near the western bank of the river. Beams wider than my body held a spiderweb of smaller beams, with vast chunks of wood and stone hanging like clusters of grapes. The section closest to the break was a ten-by-twenty-foot section of road, with thick wooden beams bolted to the metal skeleton. It was canted at a forty-five-degree angle, and I turned to scale my way downward, hand over hand.

"Help me!" came the girl's cry. "I'm losing my grip!"

I wanted to move faster, but just then, I realized how dangerous this was. I didn't have an irrational fear of heights, but I did have a healthy respect for them.

I safely reached the bottom, where another section of the bridge dangled from a pair of steel beams. Below was another section of road, a cement-covered steel surface with wooden slats sticking out like quills on a porcupine. I grasped the side of the twisted metal and swung my leg around to hug the beam.

I started shimmying down when I heard Jaroslav shout at me. "What the hell are you doing? Are you trying to kill yourself?" He was not happy.

"There's a girl down here. I'm going to save her." It sounded sane to me, in my head. Saying it out loud, I heard it and wondered if maybe I was crazy.

There was a loud explosion. I looked up to see a trio of mechs standing on the far side of the river. The opposite riverbank was nearly half a mile away, but the mechanical titans were silhouetted against the smoke-filled, sunlit sky. The mechs were firing rockets and shooting at anything that moved, including a handful of people trapped on both sides of the collapsed bridge. I felt the next impact, the whole chain of rubble that I was crawling on shook, and stone rubble fell on me like rain.

"They're shooting at me!" I screamed.

"They're shooting at all of us! Get your ass back up here!" he yelled back.

I wasn't halfway down yet, and I hadn't heard from the girl in a minute or two. I couldn't see below me as I reached the next clump of debris and was able to plant my feet.

"Are you still there?" I called out.

"Help me! I'm slipping!" I was much closer to her now, but her voice seemed even further away than before I started my descent. I thought that if I could see her, I might be close enough to wrap her in an energy tentacle, and then I would be able to pull her up.

"Hold on! I'm coming!" I said I was on the way, but the next section proved to be the most difficult to navigate.

The wind was blowing, making me cold on a warm day. I got down on my knees and tried to peer over the side of the cement block. I couldn't quite see, so I got flat on my stomach and inched out until my head was hanging over the edge. Another artillery shell hit somewhere above me, and the broken bridge section I was on lurched violently. I felt myself sliding; my head and then my upper body were over the edge, unsupported. The flat surface I was on tilted, and I rotated as I fell. At the last second, I flung my hand out and grabbed a metal cable, and instead of falling, I swung in a wide circle.

I saw her fall, and before I could react, she struck a large hunk of twisted, ripped metal and was skewered. A sharp, broken steel strut burst through her chest, like a volcano on an otherwise flat, featureless plain. I could see the blood fountaining around the wound. I was seconds too late to rescue her.

My hands were sweating, and I was coughing on dirt and smoke in the air. I felt my hand slipping, just as the girl's hands had given way.

I felt myself falling for the longest second in my life before I felt something grab me by the ankle. I jerked to a stop, then I felt myself being dragged back up onto the broken bridge section. When I turned around, I almost jumped out of my skin. Crouching over me was the werewolf. I had briefly seen Jaroslav's wolf form, but his standing over me with such intensity in his beast's eyes caused my natural fear of predators to kick in. I tried to cower, but he scooped me up and threw me over his shoulder like I was a sack of potatoes. With animal grace, he bounded up the twisted structure and got us safely to the roadside above.

I was placed carefully on the ground. I stared into the yellow orbs, looking for a trace of the prince. It was not an ignorant creature in front of me; there was a cool intelligence to the eyes. The muzzle wasn't frothy, the lips not pulled back, baring inch-long fangs. The coiled muscles along his long arms and legs hinted at his potential for speed and strength. He was a killer, but not in that moment. I knew I was not only safe with him but also protected.

It was my second time witnessing his transformation, but no less amazing. I had heard of certain brands that caused changes in their bearers' bodies, but this was taken to an extreme. The hair rapidly receded as the wolf's muzzle shrank, becoming the familiar face of Jaro's middle phase. His white hair was rustled by a breeze that rolled in off the water. His height lessened by two inches, and his physique softened, though in that state, he was still well muscled through the chest, arms, and abdomen. Thankfully, he'd retained his pants.

"Don't you ever do that again!" he admonished me. "That was foolish and dangerous!"

I watched as he retrieved his shirt and shoes and put them on. He was fluid in his movements, confident. I watched him and, for a second, got lost in my own thoughts. He snapped at me. "Do you hear me, Jafra? You might be strong, but you're far from being invulnerable." Fully dressed, he took my hands in his. "I couldn't bear it if anything happened to you."

"I appreciate you saving me." I felt guilty, like a child who had disappointed her parent. "You have feelings for me?"

"Yes. I told you the night we met. Wolves choose a mate and mate for life. I knew from how you look, from how you smell, that I wanted you." He took a step closer, and we were now only inches from each other. "You said that you're not engaged."

"I did."

He pulled me into his strong arms, crushing my body against his. Our first kiss was spontaneous, quick, and almost violent. He kissed me deeply, without haste, taking the time to sink into it. I hadn't given him permission to kiss me, but I didn't resist either. I saw it coming, and yet I still allowed myself the self-delusion that it was a surprise. My eyes closed, and I melted.

# Chapter 38

Things were exploding all around us, and everyone else had fled the scene. Jaroslav and I were the only targets left, and the Rus mechs were trying desperately to pick us off. A high-explosive shell landed not far from us, but that couldn't dampen his fire.

The first time he kissed me, I was the unwilling focus of his passion. This time, through inaction, I was a willing participant. There was no world around us, no imminent danger, no one to point out how wrong it was.

He devoured me, his lips ravaging mine, his tongue exploring my mouth. It was a cool afternoon, but his body was on fire, radiating heat as he pressed himself against me.

I should have fought back, but his smell, his energy… I became lost in his embrace. The fact that I found him extremely physically attractive didn't hurt. Even my sense of self-preservation deserted me. We should have run, gotten out of range of the mechs, but my whole world was consumed by the strong arms around me, the lips on mine.

He held me tightly with his left arm, and his right arm slid down my back until his hand cupped my left buttocks. It wasn't a soft caress, but an almost painful squeeze. He actually lifted me off the ground an inch or two.

A near miss rocked us and almost knocked us to the ground. It was time to go.

He released me, but took my hand, and we ran together to where we'd left my brother's car. We almost got there when I heard a whistling sound above us. I was rushing ahead when Jaro tackled me. We hit the ground hard, and he spun me so that he would land on top of me. He covered my head with his forearms and buried his face in my mop of hair. There was an explosion, then a second blast. I heard the shower of shrapnel, though I couldn't feel it with him on top of me.

I rolled him off me because he was heavy and his hand was holding my right breast. Not caressing or squeezing, but just kind of there. I was ready to be pissed except for two things. The car had been reduced to small, burning pieces. He had saved my life twice in the last five minutes. Secondly, he was peppered with sharp fragments of our vehicle.

I decided not to scold him for touching my boob and rolled him on his stomach to see how bad the damage was. Jagged shards of metal were sticking out of his arms, legs, and back. He was struck and bleeding in at least ten places, but the worst was a metal rod that went all the way through his left calf and a bit of sheet metal stuck in his back that was roughly triangular, and five inches on a side. I took off my camouflage jacket and tore it into strips. I went for one of the smaller pieces that was penetrating his posterior.

"If you keep touching my ass, I'm going to think you have a thing for me." He chuckled. I thought it might have been to mask the pain.

"If you weren't so careless, you wouldn't keep getting your ass shot off. Then I wouldn't have to play nursemaid. Again!" I pulled out the sliver and applied pressure with a bit of cloth. "This one isn't that bad. Might not even need stitches."

The bleeding wasn't out of control. I looped a band of Abyrinth around his waist to hold the bandage in place until the bleeding stopped. I did the same for six or seven other wounds to his legs, arm, and back. I saved the worst for last because, when I pulled out the metal shards, he would start bleeding in earnest, and I needed a plan.

"Ok, now for the fun part," I said. I cut his pant leg off and looked at the metal dowel that had passed through his calf and was protruding from both sides. I cut sections of my jacket and folded them until they were square and nearly an inch thick. "This is going to hurt."

He had been looking over at the enemy on the far side of the river. They were gone now.

"It already hurts. Hurts like hell. We need to move, so do it now. I think they are going down to the next bridge and will come back to finish us off."

As he said the last bit, I pulled the shaft out with a quick motion. He growled, but didn't cry out, and his only other reaction was to grind his teeth to the point of shattering them. I placed the bandages, wrapped a cloth around them, then wrapped them tightly with a band of energy. I tied off the band and hoped that it would hold. I was improving at creating structures that would last without my active supervision.

There was a far-off crashing sound that we both could guess the origin of.

"Do it. Do it now!" he grunted.

I pulled out the knife-like metal sheet, trying to pull straight to minimize additional damage. Blood shot out of the wound several feet from the gash in his back. I applied my last strips of cloth, almost my whole sleeve. I put on another band of Abyrinth and cinched it very tight.

"Hard to breathe," he gasped.

"Better than bleeding out." I helped him to his feet. "Thanks for protecting me." I could tell that he was in a lot of pain, but we didn't have time for pain. "Doesn't your wolf form heal even faster than this one?"

"It does." He looked me in the face. "I think it freaks you out." It did.

"Nonsense. Change. We might even make better time."

I had seen him change from the wolf to his other two forms on two separate occasions. This was the first time I had seen him transform from human to werewolf. It was the same thing, but in reverse, and it was much more unsettling. I had to loosen some of the tourniquets that I made to accommodate the wolf's larger body. I no longer feared him in this manifestation, but knowing that we had been kissing just minutes ago sent a chill down my spine.

"Let's go!" I said and led the way. He nodded and followed.

I could tell that he was still hurting. He walked bent over, his clawed hands almost dragging on the ground. His spine seemed to be trying to escape his body, the fur on his head stood straight up, and he was breathing in rapid pants. Even so, he was able to match my pace. As fast as we could, we headed away from the river and the constant bombardment. I saw his ears perk up and rotate even before I heard the sound myself. Military vehicles were heading our way.

"We'll never get away on foot!" I said. I saw a steam-powered delivery truck near a market alongside the riverbank, and I motioned for him to get in. I had seen my brother operate vehicles before, but this would be my driving debut.

I fired up the engine without any mishap. The wolf looked at me, but I had a difficult time deciphering his expressions on that canine face. He pointed at the gearshift and growled lowly. I put the truck into drive, and we shot forward. It almost stalled, but in seconds, we were rushing down the main avenue, perpendicular to the river. It took nearly a minute to get a feel for the steering wheel and how much to turn it to go left or right. There was debris and destroyed cars everywhere. I even saw a few bodies, those that had been unlucky enough to be where artillery rounds landed. I got the hang of it eventually and was swerving sharply to avoid obstacles in the road. I was proud of myself; I only hit two cars and one trash receptacle.

We got almost five miles away before we ran into a mass of Rus soldiers. I saw the mech ahead, towering over the one and two-story buildings in the small town. Jaro grunted and waved his long, skeletal fingers to the left. I turned down an alley, and we parked under an awning behind a deserted bar. Exiting the truck, we went through the open rear entrance.

There was no one inside, and we could see through the place and out the front windows. I was getting hungry, so I took him by his furry forearm and led him to the small kitchen. I raided a large refrigerator, filling a mixing bowl with fruit, cheese, tomatoes, and half a salami. I found a loaf of bread in the pantry, and we sat on the floor behind the bar. Jaro turned back to his natural state, not the white-haired devil.

I looked at his wounds, and they already seemed better. "Looks like you might live."

"Due to your ministrations, dear Jafra," he said, looking down and smiling. "We keep saving each other, just like our countries need to save each other."

I gave him his shirt and shoes that I had picked up when he changed. His three physical states were distinctly different from one another. I found it to be fascinating. The wolf could barely communicate; he was driven by animal instinct and rage. The intermediate state was characterized by wild confidence, capability, and danger. Now, in his natural state, the one he was born to and lived in until he got his brand, he was calm and introspective.

We ate in peace as the Rus soldiers could be heard a few blocks away, destroying property in their search for us.

"Can I ask you a personal question?"

He looked at me warily. "Yes."

"This is the version of you that was born, raised by your parents, and attended prep school?" He didn't seem too surprised by my question. Like the other version of him, he was tanned, tall, and well-built. His face had the same features, but this Jaroslav was calmer and more reserved. He brushed aside his rich brown hair and looked at me with eyes the color of a chestnut mare, but with a hint of red.

"Yes. This is the real me." He finished a hunk of bread and dusted his hands together.

"I understand the werewolf; he is there to be strong and violent when violence is needed. What about the other guy? Where did he come from?"

"There are a few brands that cause transformation, and there are a couple like mine that have a second transformation. I usually go by my full, given name, Jaroslav.

I refer to… the other guy, simply as Jaro. It makes it a little easier to differentiate the two of us.”

“It certainly makes the language easier, but in person, you two are very easy to tell apart.” I stood up and took a bottle of Cognac from a shelf above us. No one was passing the bar, but I joined Jaroslav on the ground.

“I just started drinking after my birthday, and now I seem to be imbibing more and more often these days. Pardon my poor manners.” I pulled out the cork and took a healthy draught of the potent liquor.

I thought Krystian would have approved of this bottle. It had notes of apricot, candied lemon, and possibly cocoa. It warmed me and soothed my senses with the heady aroma and the velvety texture that left a silky sensation on my tongue. I held the bottle out for him.

“No, thank you. I’ve tried drinking, and to be honest, I don’t much care for it.” Yes, they were different. I was drawn to this man, this thoughtful and intelligent man, but even though they shared the same body, I was much more physically attracted to Jaro.

“I just wanted a bit of a jolt. If you’re feeling better, we should see if the way is clear.”

I stood and offered him my hand. He stood with visible discomfort, but he didn’t complain in the least. Both versions were proud men.

We decided to abandon the truck and go out the front. They might have been looking for that vehicle, and we could do with something faster and with better handling. It was just starting to get dark, and we hoped that we could sneak out of town without further confrontation.

We never found anything as spectacular as Krystian's sports car, rest in pieces, but we did find a Mercedes hover car. The car was long and low to the ground, with a glossy, black body that looked out of place in the sleepy little town.

Jaroslav climbed into the driver's seat and started adjusting mirrors and seat settings.

"Are you any good at driving?" I asked.

"I'm very good. Buckle up." He didn't take off with a jerk, but very soon, we were going faster than I've ever driven in my life. He navigated around broken cars, damaged storefronts, and anything else that got in our way with a finesse that made my brothers look like novices by comparison. We got out of the city and found ourselves alone on a highway heading west. All the streetlights were out. It was darker than the inside of a tomb.

"Looks like the Rus took out the powerplant," I noted. "I don't understand why they are destroying the utilities and so many buildings. If their goal is to acquire our land for themselves, they'll have to rebuild everything. Very costly. Very wasteful."

"What you say is true, but I think they want to win first and worry about reconstruction later. Besides, they will make any surviving civilians pay for and perform the rebuilding."

"So, the loser of the war not only loses their land and their freedom, but they are essentially enslaved? Made to pay the aggressor for damage done to them?"

"That's not the worst of it by far," he said. He kept his eyes on the road, the headlights revealing a small section of the road ahead. I could see his handsome features by the dim light of the dashboard controls. With everything we'd been through and the pain that I know he was still feeling, he had a completely calm demeanor. He gave the impression of someone you would want with you in a time of crisis or in a negotiation.

"What they'll do to the citizenry will be much worse than what they are doing to your systems." He took a breath. "Any man who is high up in the Polish military will be executed, or at least taken prisoner. I'm told they don't treat their prisoners kindly. Most nobles will be killed, regardless of how benign their brands may be. They'll be looking to eliminate most, if not all, of the Polish bloodlines. Anyone who speaks against them or calls for revolution will be publicly executed. Dissenters, intellectuals, businesspeople, religious leaders… none will be spared. Of course, there will be sexual assaults; some men, but primarily women… and children. They won't just rape women, they'll gang rape them in front of their husbands, in front of their children. And the children? They'll be passed around like cigarettes. Toys to play with while waiting for orders to move on to the next doomed city."

I was silent for a good long time. I had gotten an inkling about the horrors he described, but I'd just become an adult, and it was all too much. I was still a virgin. The thought of a hundred Rus soldiers lined up to pump their foul seed into my untouched womb made me sick to my stomach. "That's why we need Bohemia, Germania, Moldavia, Serbia, and all the rest to come to our aid. If not for our sakes, for their own self-interests. Our war will become everyone's war, sooner or later."

We drove for an hour, and I was sure that we were in the middle of nowhere. There hadn't been any lights or signs of life for quite a while, until we saw what looked like a row of vehicles coming at us from behind. A long row of headlights that could only be an army, and I feared that it wouldn't be ours.

When he saw them, Jaroslav immediately pulled off the road. We came to a cross street, not even paved, and headed right, through the low-hanging branches of fruit trees and through open fields of wheat and corn. We drove by first-quarter moonlight, barely able to avoid hitting fence posts and trees that were encroaching on the ancient path. I turned, and I could see the string of lights heading down the road behind us.

"Turn off the light and stop the car!" I said.

He complied, and we were paused in near complete darkness. Trucks and armored vehicles passed on the road we had left only a few minutes ago. We sat motionless, waiting for the convoy to end, but there was no end in sight. It was cool in the front seat of the luxury vehicle, but not uncomfortably so. The heated leather seats were premium, and the fan was set to low, so the temperature was ideal.

"We may be stuck here for some time," he said.

# Chapter 39

"How are your wounds?" I asked him. He had bloodstains on his suit in several places, but they had dried.

"Mostly healed."

"Do you heal faster as Jaro?" I asked.

"I do." He looked at me, his big brown eyes boring into mine. "We may need to get out of here in a hurry. Better if I'm... at my best." He changed before my eyes. Especially in the dark, it was difficult to see anything, but by the faint light of the moon filtering in, I could see his hair change to silvery white.

Still, that's not how I knew he'd changed to Jaro. He must have given off different pheromones for each of his forms. I knew it was through a sense of smell, but I could feel a change in me. My body reacted to him differently. It was chemical, animal.

"Things aren't going well. We're pushing back against the Rus, but there are so damned many of them. Jaroslav's little speech earlier... it scared me."

"He was just trying to be straight with you, love. The main trait we share is honesty. He's a bit more subtle."

"If this is my last day on earth, if they capture me... I prefer to die before being taken prisoner."

I felt heat coming from him, warming the small cabin. The heat, his scent, the anxiety I was feeling? I wanted to escape, if only for a second.

I leaned towards him, kissing him on his full, luscious lips. It was like an electric shock passing through me. The excitement of such a bold act made me flush. I rested my hand on his chest and felt the rapid heartbeat, his body like a steam engine running near to overload.

Our mouths stayed fixed on each other as he pulled me across the seat towards him. He effortlessly encircled my waist and moved me until our legs were touching. Did I like being manhandled? Yes, it was exhilarating being dominated like that. I ran my fingers through his thick, silky hair, trying to pull him somehow closer, get his tongue even deeper in my mouth. His arm around me was made of steel, and I felt both bound by him and protected from all harm.

Everything faded into the background. There was no war going on with my countrymen dying, no column of enemy soldiers a quarter mile away, looking to kill or capture me. No family, no other man.

I had gulped whiskey a time or two, but the intoxication was nothing like this. We were starving, and only by consuming the other could we survive.

When our lips finally parted, his found the side of my neck. He licked lightly, bit firmly, and sucked until I was squirming with passion. There was an electric circuit that ran from my ear to the nape of my neck to my vagina. I had never masturbated, but I had washed myself daily, and I knew how sensitive that area was. I shivered with excitement.

As he tasted my neck, his right hand grabbed my left breast. Not a glancing touch, not an accidental graze. He squeezed firmly, mauling it through my uniform shirt.

I was a good girl, and I should have stopped this long before, but damn it felt good. His tongue traced lines on my earlobe as he hefted my firm tit. I don't know how long it all went on, and when he stopped for a breath, I was ready for more. With both hands, he untucked my t-shirt and pulled it out of my uniform trousers. He lifted it over my arms and completely off. I let it happen.

Was I a helpless participant? No. When my shirt was tossed up on the dash, I reached behind to unclasp my bra. He was marveling at my large breasts, but I was still eighteen, and when I pulled the bra off, they sagged only an inch. Their size and weight might haunt me someday, but for now, they were large and impossibly firm.

"Since the moment I saw you, I dreamed of this moment." His smile reminded me more of the wolf than of his other two manifestations. He held one in each hand, lifting them, feeling the gravity of them. He couldn't meet my eyes, as his were transfixed on my naked chest. He squeezed and rolled them, letting his thumbs brush across my sensitive nipples. My areolae are light pink circles, about an inch in diameter, and in the center, my nipples are a quarter inch long. As he touched them, they became firm and rubbery. He pulled me even closer and leaned down to take the first nipple, then the second into his mouth. He sucked and let his tongue roll them around.

I was losing my mind with the amount of pleasure he was giving me. I felt a wetness growing in my panties, and a smell of fertility and sexual arousal was becoming evident. His heightened senses and animal instincts made him even more susceptible to the chemical signals my body was giving off. With his face buried in my tits, I'm sure he could hear and feel how fast my heart was beating.

"I've never felt so aroused. I want you to experience a fraction of how stimulated I am."

This was going too far, too fast. I wanted to pull his manly face from my boobs, put my shirt back on, but I was paralyzed. I couldn't move, couldn't object. I was transfixed by my own lust.

He turned me and pulled me over until I was sitting between his legs with my back against his chest. He cupped my left breast from behind and undid the button on my trousers with his right hand. I started to squirm, but he held me tight to his firm chest, and with uncannily nimble fingers, he unbuttoned three more buttons in the fly of my pants. My lacy pink panties were exposed to the warming air in the car, and now, the scent of my growing passion was unmistakable.

"We should slow down. I've never..." It was really going too far. No matter how horny I was, I wasn't ready to get fucked.

Ignoring me, he slipped his hand down the front of my panties, sliding through the short, bristly hair that lay above my sex. His left hand pinched and pulled at the nipple, while his right hand went where no man had gone before.

The wetness allowed his fingers to slide up and down my opening, brushing against my clitoris. His hand went slowly, letting both of us become accustomed to his touch. His fingers traveled all the way down to the lower extremity, then back again. Torturously slow, his middle finger brushed my most sensitive skin. With each downward motion, then each upward pull, his fingers glided across my hardened clit.

"No," I said weakly. It was more of a reflex than anything. "Ugh, ugh," I grunted as waves of pleasure rolled through my body. I felt his finger dip inside, not too deep, but enough to add another layer to my rapture. I could feel his hardness against my tailbone as he worked. He was as excited as I was. He was squeezing my breast hard and pinching the nipple mercilessly. All the while, he got into a rhythm, pumping his finger, and now two fingers in my vagina, and because of the angle, every thrust in and out massaged my clit.

I felt his breath on my neck, his body supporting mine, his arms like coiled steel. My muscles tightened; my whole body arched and grew rigid. Then it hit me. A wave pulsed through me from head to toes. My heart was beating a mile a minute, my breath coming in ragged gulps. The wave became a series of waves, and heat flowed through me; my scalp tingled. I didn't black out, but my mind went blank for almost a full minute. Eventually, my rapid breathing subsided, and my senses returned. I leaned into him, more relaxed than I had ever been in my life.

His left hand still cupped my breast, though gently now. Reverently. He brought his other hand to his face, and I heard him sniff. When he took in my scent, I could feel his member trying to jump out of his pants. It was hard as iron, and I could only imagine how uncomfortable it was to have me lying on it.

I leaned forward and turned to face him again. I felt at peace, if only for a few minutes, in the midst of war. I kissed him softly. A thank you for such an unexpected gift.

As I kissed him, I rested my palm on the painfully hard bulge in his trousers. Not an accident.

"Mmmmm," he purred. I could barely make out his face in the near-complete dark. He had an expression that was lustful and yet disciplined. He wasn't going to ask.

I slid my hand up and down the length of the bulge, feeling his energy through the material. "I've never done this. Open your pants. I want to see it," I said breathily.

"You'll do more than see it, Jafra." He kept his eyes on me as he undid his belt. The sound of the jingling buckle filled me with both dread and anticipation. When the belt was opened, he popped open the button with practiced ease, using two fingers. Four more buttons, and his fly was open. I couldn't see anything inside; his underwear must have been some dark color. I know my brothers mostly wore tight white underwear, and his style choice caught me by surprise. He lifted his butt an inch or two and, with his thumbs, pulled his pants and underwear simultaneously, then pushed them down to his ankles.

There it was. His penis was a lighter shade than he was, and it almost glowed in the pale moonlight. He was leaning back on his elbows, letting me get a good look. It seemed to be lying on his tight stomach, but I could see that it was actually suspended a quarter inch or so above his abs.

He watched me, looking at the hesitation in my face. He wasn't pressuring me, and I was surprised by how patient he was. This was my choice; I wanted to do this. So, after long seconds of staring, I lowered my hand and placed it on the shaft. It was warm and soft on the outside. Beneath the skin, I felt the steel core.

"Grip it like you would a dagger handle," he said. We were both soldiers, and I knew what he meant. I wrapped my long fingers around it and lifted until it was standing straight out from his body. I put my other hand above my first hand, and almost covered it. More than just warmth, I felt masculine energy radiating through my hands.

I had a rough idea of what boys did with their things. I let go with my left hand and allowed my right hand to slide up and down its length. The skin near the top was loose and moved with the pumping motion, revealing the mushroom-shaped top part. The inside was stationary, rooted to his flat abdomen. I stared in awe at the thing, watching his large testicles rise and fall with each stroke. As I worked it up and down, he issued a guttural, rumbling sound. It was a happy sound, but I had to make sure.

"Am I doing it right?" I asked.

"It feels great, my dear, but at that pace, this could take quite a long time."

"I'm not going to fuck you," I said, not believing that the words came from out so easily.

"I expected as much. Let's try something."

He leaned forward and kissed me passionately as I continued to masturbate him. He leaned into my ear after lavishing me with deep, tongue kisses.

"I want you to suck my cock," he said. I looked at his eyes, and he was serious.

"Ugh, that's gross!" I exclaimed, but still I had my hands on his rod.

"It's a very natural thing to do. All woman do it for their man," he said as he caressed my breasts.

"Are you my man?" I could feel the juices flowing in my vagina as I stroked him faster.

"I'm a prince, and not too unattractive. I can get women. I told you at your Ascension Ball that I wanted you. I want all of you: your body, your mind, your undying love. I'll wait for that pussy, but my balls literally hurt, and we need to go soon."

"But… you want to put this in my mouth?" I sounded outraged, but I wasn't so naïve that I'd never heard of a blowjob. I had thought about it when Stanisław had rubbed his against me while we kissed. Now, I was holding another man's erection, and he looked like he might not take no for an answer.

"Your married brother probably gets it every night. Your mother might be shy to talk about such things, but I would bet my crown that she's done it for your father a thousand times." He could see the doubt in my eyes. "Start slowly. Give it a loving kiss."

I looked at my hand sliding up and down the thick, veiny shaft. Even if I wanted this monster in my mouth, it looked far too big. There was a drop of liquid in the slit on the top that seemed to taunt me. A couple of months ago, I had never kissed a boy or been kissed by one. Now I was contemplating putting my lips on Jaro's engorged cock. My pussy, as he called it, was tingling in anticipation. I had no intention of losing my virginity any time soon, but if it were up to her, I would have my legs in the air, getting deflowered already. What could a quick kiss hurt?

I leaned forward and to the side so I could place a kiss on the side of it. It was the kind of kiss that you give your grandmother. Quick, dry, without passion. I looked in his eyes and his impatient expression, and I knew he was not satisfied. I gave the side a few more pecks before he pointed at the bulging vein on the bottom of his penis. I tried to give it more of the same type of kisses, but when my lips touched the soft, warm skin, he put his hand to the back of my head and held me there.

"Kiss it like you kiss my mouth. It's still me."

I didn't have his animal instincts, but I was as susceptible to chemistry as the next person. There was a musky smell that fueled the fire in my loins. I was losing my natural reluctance, and I could feel desire taking over. I kissed the underside of his member with an open mouth, letting my tongue caress the velvety soft skin. There was no discernible taste, except for a slight saltiness. I started in the middle, kissing and licking, before working my way down. When I reached the spot where the scrotum began, I dove right in. I kissed his balls; the odd texture of the skin was surprising, though not off-putting. With some difficulty, I took one into my mouth, massaging it with my tongue.

"Careful with those!" he whispered.

"Let me sample the other one." I nuzzled his lightly-haired testicles, left then right, while slowly pumping his cock. He was as hard as rock, so I began kissing my way back up. I kissed and licked like it was an ice cream cone. I gripped the bottom firmly, giving the head extra attention. We both knew how it was going to go, and I didn't need his coaching.

It seemed so natural to put the mushroom cap in my mouth. I had to open wide to accommodate his girth, and the best I could manage was to get the head and one or two inches in my mouth. Even so, I felt like I was choking, and I had to back off to collect myself.

He leaned down to kiss me, only helping to stir my overheated blood. With gentle pressure to the back of my head, I was guided back to my task. I moved my head up and down, taking a little more each time, but never getting more than half his cock in my mouth. I felt full, and I could barely breathe, but I was starting to enjoy it.

I sucked him for what seemed like hours, though I'm sure it was not even ten minutes. My jaw was getting tired, and as exciting as this was, I was ready for it to be over. I think he sensed my lack of commitment and decided to take over. He put his hands on either side of my head and held me firmly. Lifting his pelvis, he began thrusting into my mouth. I was about to panic, but he didn't push too hard, and he gave me ample time to breathe. After a couple of minutes, his pumping became more erratic, and I looked up to see him lost in his own pleasure. He was grunting and moaning, and I felt his penis swell. A second later, my mouth was flooded with a foul, salty substance. It exploded out of him in high-powered jets, six or seven streams, until my whole mouth was full. I wanted to throw up, or at least spit it out, but he held on to my skull for dear life, his cock still pulsing and twitching. Finally, I had to swallow to save myself from drowning. He started to soften, and with a huge sigh, he let go of me. I coughed, and when I had recovered, I felt a few drops of the sticky liquid were on my chin, and a little more had spilled onto my heaving breasts.

Through glassy eyes, he looked at me. "That was incredible. I can't believe it was your first time."

"Asshole!" I said, punching him in the thigh as hard as I could. "You made me swallow that vile stuff!"

"I would apologize, but that would imply that I was sorry, and I'm not. I have many faults, but I never lie." His smile made me want to punch him again. In the face.

"Get cleaned up. Let's get out of here." He pulled his pants back on and was ready in seconds. He looked out the steamy windows. "Looks like the convoy has passed. It should be safe for us to drive out of here."

I wasn't sure if I'd been violated or not. I was totally into the kissing and having someone, especially a sexy man, touching my breasts… that was intoxicating. I hadn't signed on to have fingers put inside of me, but I loved it, and I want to do that again as soon as possible. Never in my life did I think I would have an erect penis exploding in my mouth, and that I would consume the product.

Would I do it again? Maybe after a few drinks.

Yeah, it wasn't that bad.

# Chapter 40

We drove to the next major intersection and turned onto a road parallel to the river. When daylight came, Jaro left, and Jaroslav reemerged. He tried the radio several times before we could reach my squad.

"Kapitan, where are you?" Jacek asked.

"I was on the other side of the river when the Rus pushed forward. My family home was attacked, and I assume it's burned to the ground by now."

"Terrible news, ma'am. We heard the sirens and got out just before their whole battalion descended on us. We crossed at a small cargo bridge up north."

"Where are you now? I'll come to you."

He gave me their location, and Jaroslav agreed to take me there.

"I can drop you, but I need to return to Praha and report to my father." The world was going to hell, and yet he had the brightest smile as we cruised down the highway at a good speed. He had bright white teeth that were utterly perfect. His hair was brown again, and as it caught the light from the morning sun, it looked like dark, clover honey. He had the same features, the same incredible body, but it felt as if I were traveling with a completely different person. Maybe he could sense the tension in me, the apprehension. After long minutes of driving quietly, he broke the silence.

"I hope you had a good time last night?" He smiled, then turned his attention back to the road.

"Um, yes." I was confused, though in retrospect, I shouldn't have been. "You remember…"

"Your naked breasts? The image is burned into my memory forever."

"And... what about..." I stammered. I wasn't used to being nervous in any situation.

"Putting my fingers inside you?" It seemed challenging for him to speak so openly. "Or you using your mouth on me? Jaro and I are the same person. Every liberty he takes creates a memory for both of us." He kept his eyes on the road, but continued. "I felt like a prisoner, trapped inside our head. I could see and feel everything, but when he's in control, I have no voice. If he pushed you too far, too fast, I apologize. Not for what we did, but how you were pressured into it. I don't regret what we did. Not at all. I can still smell you, your collection of scents that subconsciously excite me, get me so aroused that I itch under my skin. I'm trying to drive, but it's hard to shake the image of you, dim moonlight shining on your... oh my God, perfect chest. Hair down, flat stomach, and the most beautiful face I think I've ever seen. Jaro is bold, aggressive, and dangerous, but he saw you and knew immediately that we liked you. No, like is not the correct word."

He took a deep breath, his hands turned white from gripping the wheel so tightly. "That we need you, like the flower needs sunshine, like the earth needs the sky. I'll be king someday, if the Rus don't take my country too. And you are the only choice to be my queen."

I appreciated the honesty, the effort it took him to speak so boldly, when I knew it wasn't normally in his nature. "Are you proposing to me, Jaroslav Záhoř?"

"You know I cannot. And though you have the power to reject me, we both know that you don't have the authority to accept such a proposal, were it your inclination to do so."

"I understand that many blanks can marry whomever they want. They can consult their parents, but many elope and marry whom they want, without regard to station."

"We look down on them, see them as lower than us, but in many ways, they have more freedom than we do." He pulled up to a service station at the intersection of two major highways. "We're here."

"This talk is far from over," I said, ignoring the members of my squad who were watching us from inside the shop.

"I agree. I still haven't heard your thoughts on choosing me. Us. Jaro and I. And the wolf too, I suppose. A combination package, if you will."

"I haven't had time to process everything. I'm not so innocent anymore, and my mother was always very set on wedding me to Stanisław." He didn't look hurt. I think he had more people feeding him information than he would ever admit. "It goes without saying, but I'll say it anyway. If anyone learns what we did in this car last night, Bohemia will be searching for a new heir to the throne."

"Far from an idle threat. No one will hear it from me, and you and I were the only ones there. I know that the timing is shitty, but please think about us. You and I."

"I can't help but think about it. I did enjoy last night, every bit of it. I want to kiss you goodbye, but I won't." I cracked open the door and stuck one boot out.

"I understand, completely. Stay safe, dear Jafra."

"I'll try, but convince your father that it's in his best interest to join this defense of eastern Europa. We'll fall without help from our neighbors."

He nodded, and I got out. I walked towards my team, hoping they wouldn't see the change in me. I felt both dirty and exhilarated at the same time.

"Kapitan Sobieski, you've been incommunicado for nearly twenty-four hours. I have some urgent messages for you," Lieutenant Budny said, handing me a stack of dispatches.

I opened one from the general's headquarters first. It was directly from Stanisław, telling me to evacuate my squad east. It said that the Rus were only miles away. I read this one to my team.

"Um, yeah! We know, we were there!" Julia said, looking bored.

The next message was also from Stanisław. He stated that he was conducting an emergency evacuation of the palace and relocating the royal family to a secure location on the border with Germania. He said he missed me and thought of me often, and was sorry that his duties prevented him from seeing me. I read the first part of the message aloud, keeping the personal stuff to myself.

There was also a message from my parents. They were worried about me and were praying that I was safe. They said that they had arrived safely at the summer house in the far west of Polska, and were going to be sitting by the radio, waiting for word on how the war was going in Warszawa.

I got a message from both of my older brothers. They were on the front line every day, leading our brave soldiers against the Rus invaders. Krystian had gotten a minor injury. He neglected to go into detail, but insisted that it was indeed minor and that he would be fine.

The last message was from Lady Rozalia Tarnowski, also known as Hedwig.

*Jafra—*

*I hope this finds you well. My group is constantly on the lookout for the other two prime brands, and we think we are getting close to finding one of them. Meet my agent in Berlin. She will update you with everything you'll need to track down one of these special brand bearers. I'm not sure which one it is, but there are signs of an extremely potent wielder there. Find him or her, and recruit them to our cause. With three of you, we'll have a weapon to use defeat the Rus invaders.*

*Hedwig*

I didn't have any specific orders from Stanisław. He was up to his neck in responsibilities. The fact that he was administering our country's defense and was responsible for evacuating his family and staff must have been incredibly stressful. I was happy he still thought of me and was concerned for my welfare, but disappointed he didn't have a mission for my team. I was starting to guess he considered me a trophy to put on a shelf after we married, but not an asset to help win the war. After seeing what I could do, he still didn't consider me an equal.

"We have no official orders, but I do have a mission that I think will be very important to the war effort. Pack everything, all the food and weapons we can get into your transport. We're going to Berlin to locate a person of interest."

I could see the relief on their faces. We would be heading in the direct opposite direction of the fighting. Not being near the front meant safety to them, and they eagerly got us ready to roll.

"Kapitan. I saw that Prince Záhoř dropped you off," Filip said. "Is Bohemia thinking of allying with us? We're really taking a beating so far."

"He will recommend it to his father, the king. The way that Rus is taking over land, I don't know if any of our neighbors would be in time to help."

"So, you think it's hopeless?"

I was feeling grim, and it showed in the way I spoke to him. "I've no idea. I know that I'm your commanding officer, but I'm only eighteen. A few months ago, my biggest concern was finding a good match and starting a family. That all seems like a lifetime ago and is probably unrealistic at this point. I think the capital will fall, if it hasn't already. We are going to see if we can find a person in Germania who has a powerful enough brand that we can start fighting back in earnest."

"What if that wielder doesn't want to risk their life to help us?"

"I don't know. Beg? Threaten? We have to do whatever it takes to locate and acquire this person. You get us there safely. I'll be the one to try to recruit this person. We're meeting an operative in the city, and we'll know more after that."

He nodded thoughtfully and, with a tip of his cap, went back to supervise the rest.

We headed out within minutes and were cruising down country highways as swiftly as was safe to do so. I sat by myself for most of the trip; my mind was a million miles away. Less than a day ago, I was having the hottest, most romantic time of my life. The dream was over, and now I was back to reality, avoiding enemy patrols and driving to the border on a secret mission.

I should have been focusing on the mission, but I couldn't get boys out of my head. It was a unique problem to be courted by two princes, both destined to become kings someday. That is, if the Rus didn't kill us all.

My mother was enamored with the idea of me marrying Stanisław. I would move across town, and she could see me whenever she wanted, and of course, I would someday become our queen. Among all available Polish men, Stanisław was easily the most desired match. Thousands of girls my age across Polska were dreaming of him. Many would, and probably some had, thrown themselves at his feet. He was rich, influential, an actual prince for heaven's sake, and very, very handsome. On a scale of one to ten, he was an eleven. Maybe a twelve. He was the first man that I intentionally kissed, and I had feelings for him. Not love. Not yet.

If he knew what I'd done with Jaro, it would be over.

Jaro. Jaroslav. Two men, different personalities sharing a single body. A very nice body. Prince Záhoř was a quiet, sensitive soul. Intelligent, caring, competent. He was a joy to talk with, and in his own way, he was very handsome. His alter ego, Jaro, was Jaroslav on steroids. He had the same face, the same firm arms and legs, and rock-hard… abs. He was unapologetically lecherous, virile, and insatiable. Jaro was the perfect compromise between cultured Jaroslav and the wild beast that was his third manifestation.

The wolf. What to do about him? Jaroslav was still clearly in charge when he transformed into the wolf. I was saved by the wolf. Twice. But I still had to take into consideration that a man I was very interested in, one who was clear about wanting me in every way a man wants a woman, would turn into a hairy, violent beast.

# Chapter 41

"We're at the border," Borys said. He looked strange with the eyepatch. I felt guilty every time I saw it. "They're asking for papers."

I straightened my uniform, stepped out of the main hatch of the personnel transport, and approached the border guards. There were many border crossings between Polska and Germania; this one was in the countryside, and few people were trying to cross here. There was nothing around except a small shack for the border guards and a weighted metal boom gate that blocked the single-lane road but did nothing to stop vehicles from driving around.

A uniformed guard walked up, rifle slung over his shoulder. "I'm sorry, Kapitan. Please to turn around," he said in broken Polish. He was shorter than I was, with wispy golden-brown hair. He wore a green-grey uniform with a matching wool cap pulled over his head. His words were respectful, but his tone was dismissive. He didn't really look at me, instead looking at the massive personnel carrier we rode in.

"We have urgent business in Berlin. We need to pass." It was at this point that I realized my planning skills required substantial improvement. The toad of a man was completely unmoved, and I didn't blame him.

"Your country is at war…" he said mechanically.

"I am aware," I replied dryly.

"Naturally, tens of thousands of Poles are fleeing to neighboring countries, including Germania. We have been given strict guidance to only let a set number of refugees through each day. We already met the quota for today. Please to come back tomorrow and join the queue."

"We're not refugees," I said, pointing at the large military vehicle.

"Regardless, I have my orders." He was not convinced in the least.

"Of course you do!" said a woman's voice, coming from behind me. I knew it was Izabel, but when I turned, I was surprised. She was in uniform, but the top four buttons of her blouse were open, revealing her bright white T-shirt. It was tight, and her nipples were showing through the thin material. Her lipstick was not regulation; it was bright red and glistening. Her hair was lighter than the guard's, brown, but drifting into blonde, and hung in curly waves down one shoulder. She was taller than either of us, and even through her camouflage uniform trousers, her long, sinewy legs showed. She had rosy cheeks and brilliant, blue eyes. She oozed sex, and even I was temporarily caught in her spell.

"Miss…"

"What is your name, Sergeant?" She sauntered closer, coming within a foot of the flustered man.

"Ernst Weber. I'm a Gefreiter, a private like yourself," he stammered, then he looked at her from head to toe and back. "Well, not exactly like you."

"That's surprising. I'm not too familiar with German ranks, but you exude… authority. I was sure that you were a noncom." She achieved a perfect balance of seduction and subtlety. I saw it for what it was, but the private seemed too much under her power. "Call me Izabel."

"You are too kind, liebchen."

She smiled warmly at the affectionate address. "You flatter me!" Her long, delicate fingers lightly brushed the front of his chest armor. "You are the man with decision-making power here." She gracefully tilted her head towards his partner, who was lounging against the shack a few dozen feet away. "You decide who can pass, who must wait. We are meeting someone in Berlin, and it's very important to my kapitan." She rolled her eyes towards me. "I have no right to ask a favor of you, lieber, but we are not refugees, and we shouldn't count towards your daily quota. If you would be so kind as to let us pass, I would consider it a personal favor." His smile seemed genuine, pleading without being desperate, promising without being crude.

He stared at her for a long moment. Then let his eyes travel up and down her long, lean figure. "Your logic is without flaw, liebchen. Your party can pass." He tried not to smile and stayed hard and professional. "When will you return?"

"We are not sure. Not more than a couple of days, I would think," she replied. "You will be here when we return?"

"More than likely. I am here every day from early morning to late afternoon."

"I look forward to seeing you again, lieber." She leaned forward and placed a light kiss on his cheek, then smiled and turned on her heel. We got back on the transport and waited. With military efficiency, he marched over to the shack and barked orders at his partner. The gate was lifted, and we were on our way.

My respect was sincere. "That was amazing!"

"That… was nothing. You have all the tools, Kapitan." She surveyed me the same way the soldier surveyed her. "You could wrap any man around your finger with what you have under that uniform. You need more experience in the fine arts of flirting and seduction."

The men in the transport were noticeably silent, trying not to look in our direction.

"I get looks, but I've never been able to do what you just did."

"Using my sexuality as a tool?" she asked. "That's second nature to all women, but really harnessing the power? That takes a lot of thought and a bit of instinct. Be sexy, but not too available. There's a fine line between being a tease and being a whore. Crossing the line puts you at a disadvantage. You lose the upper hand, you lose your objective altogether." She pointed at her chest. "Suggestive, not slutty. I'm not showing any skin. Their eyes see that my blouse is open, and their minds fill in the blanks."

"You were a little familiar, but you made no promises to the man."

"I complimented him. Everyone likes to be noticed, recognized. I gave him attention. Men get so little attention that when you smile at them, they bend over backwards to get more." As we spoke, she buttoned up her blouse and put her hair back into a ponytail. "Remember. Be honest, be respectful, be kind. A desperate man will fall for anything, but in general, people can sense bullshit when it's piled too high."

"You're very resourceful, Izabel."

"Can I speak openly, ma'am?"

"Of course. Always."

"I have to be resourceful, use my brains, and whatever assets I may have. I'm one of those blanks that you nobles talk about behind our backs, and sometimes even in front of us. We tend to fade into the background."

"That's not true!" I exclaimed. How could she think such things? "My maid—"

"Stop right there. Your maid? I don't have a maid." She waved her hand to include everyone else. "None of them have maids. If your only exposure to the unconnected, unpowered class is through your servants, then you don't know what we go through. You don't know what we do to survive in our powerless world without any magic or superpowers."

"I'm sure I can learn something from you."

"You can probably pick up tips and tactics from each of us. They assigned us to you for a reason. This is war, and we need to do whatever it takes to win."

"That sounds good. For this mission, we're going to be in my world. Listen up, everyone! Let me give you some information." They huddled around me, listening attentively. "I've been consulting with someone back in Warszawa. She thinks my brand is one of three very unique brands that, when combined, will give us a very potent weapon to use against the Rus."

Julia cut in. "We don't know much about your brand, Kapitan. I know that you were able to shut off everyone's brand at the club."

"I didn't shut off their brand, I drained their Abyrinth. They still had their brand, but no energy to make it work. That's why I was also able to drain Filip at the same time."

"So, your power is being able to drain power from other wielders?" Jacek asked.

"My abilities include being able to see Abyrinth. It's everywhere, outside, in this cabin with us." They all looked around, trying to see for themselves. "I can harness it, make it obey my will."

"Yeah, I don't understand," Jacek replied.

"As I said, Abyrinth is the energy that powers the abilities of both channelers and wielders, and it's invisible to everyone but me, as far as I can tell. It's everywhere, floating in the air; it hovers over the lieutenant like a protective blanket." They looked at me like I was insane. Izabel and Marcin were very skeptical. Borys was busy driving, and Julia, Jacek, and Karol were neutral, listening and trying to understand. "I can manipulate this energy, including pulling it into myself. I can give it solidity, make it hold or lift things." I collected long bands of energy and wrapped them around Jacek, holding him tightly.

"Hey!" he said, looking down at his arms that were pinned to his sides. "I'm trapped!"

I used the bands like an arm, lifting him a foot in the confined space of the transport's cabin. He started whining, so I turned up his anxiety by slowly rotating him head over heels, then placed him back gently in his seat. The whole squad was goggling their eyes in disbelief.

"I can see where that would come in handy," Karol said, his voice low and gravely. "How strong is that ability?"

I thought about it for a moment. "I'm not completely sure. I picked up a mech once and smashed a tank with it."

That made them go silent. For almost a minute, the only sound was the steam engine and wind as we rumbled along down the autobahn. I think they were a little afraid, even though we were on the same team.

"So what are we looking for?" Filip asked.

"My brand doesn't show up in the registry. It's unique, a one of a kind. My contact refers to it as a prime brand. There are supposed to be two others, and when used together, they should be nearly unstoppable. Our country is in trouble, and like you said, Izabel, we need to do whatever it takes to win."

"You know the location of one of these other prime brand wielders?" he asked.

"No. They could appear anywhere, and like me, they might not know how special they are. I was given the name and address of a contact in Berlin. She thinks she knows who we're looking for."

"Please give Borys the address. We're getting close to the eastern side of the city." Filip said. He looked around. "Does anyone speak German?"

# Chapter 42

I checked us into the Hotel Adlon Kempinski using family credit. A suite for the girls and me, another for the boys.

Across from the Brandenburg Gate, the five-star hotel had been in operation for hundreds of years and was a landmark of the Prussian-Germanic capital city. The seven-story building was not an architectural wonder, with its square, boxy shape and teal-colored roof, but the inside was spectacular. It boasted grand ballrooms and two gourmet restaurants, one being a French-German café where I was to meet with Lady Margarete Krüger.

When I entered the room, I was able to pick her out immediately. In a room full of elegantly dressed people, she stood out from the rest. It was early afternoon, but she wore a blue satin ballgown in the style of a Baroque Rococo evening dress. Her décolletage was framed in high ruffles of gold-trimmed off-white lace. The satin bodice was tight, narrowing to a thin waist before the long panels of intricately embroidered blue satin blossomed out, forming a bell shape around her. When she saw me, she raised a perfectly manicured hand and offered a warm smile.

I had clothing delivered that morning, something in the Victorian style that was popular here. Finding a dress that would accommodate my figure was difficult. I settled for a more modern dress, and I felt like I stuck out like a sore thumb. Yellow was not really my color, but I wore a simple dress that reminded me of sunshine with short sleeves and puffy shoulders. My neckline was high, and my hemline was low. A respectable dress, if not fashionable. I wore no jewelry, which set me apart from the other ladies present. The poorest woman in the room was adorned with thousands of marks' worth of gems.

A maître d'hôtel showed me to her table and introduced me. "Madam Krüger, Lady Jafra Sobieski," he said formally, before bowing and getting my chair.

After I sat, she spoke. "Hot tea, please," she said. He smiled and evaporated into the back.

"Thank you for meeting with me," I said simply.

"Of course. I have been expecting you for a week. Hedwig let me know you would be seeking the other… well, you know." She sounded conspiratorial, whispering to avoid being overheard. That was strange, as our table was not at all close to the rest of the diners. The room was vaulted with gold-embossed coffered ceilings. The tall windows around the room had long cream linen drapes. The table had a spotless white tablecloth, a bouquet of seasonal wildflowers, two settings of spotless silverware, and peach-colored silk napkins.

"Hedwig is an interesting person. Not always what she seems to be."

"Well, my dear, to be honest, I don't know her that well. My brother is a member of this Brotherhood of Virtue."

"Hedwig mentioned it. They are trying to free up the stones for use by channelers and blanks."

"So I understand. Ridiculous. Everyone knows that only the proper bloodlines can acquire a brand."

"Agreed, but why are you helping her?" I asked. We were quiet while the tea was delivered.

"First off, I don't think anything will come of it. My brother is very dedicated to this group and thinks society would benefit if everyone had our abilities. Rubbish. Anyhow, he knows that I have contacts in Polska, and I knew someone who knew this Hedwig person. It took longer than I expected, but thankfully, you received my message."

"The Rus have invaded our capital, and things got a bit dicey." I looked down at my simple dress. "Please pardon my appearance. I wasn't able to leave with any of my things, and I've been trying to avoid the Rus at all costs. I hear they are not too kind to the better families."

"That sounds perfectly awful, dear. Things are quiet here. I hope you stay so you can avoid all of your people's troubles." She took a light sip of her steaming tea before plucking a schnitzel from the plate.

"Please let me know how I can get in touch with your brother. I was really hoping I could see him today, if at all possible."

"Today? My, that is a bit rushed." She thought for a minute. "This time of day, he is usually at his factory downtown. They are making munitions for the army, and they may be selling them to your military as well."

I got the address, then sat for the next hour as we sipped tea and nibbled light snacks. Every second, I was itching to get away and look for her brother. If he had as much information as Hedwig did, we would be able to locate this prime brand bearer in no time. When it was finally acceptable for me to do so, I thanked her and bid her auf wiedersehen.

The whole squad insisted on coming with me to see Herr Krüger. I was sure I could handle it myself, and I was the leader, but somehow I got outvoted. The personnel carrier was way too conspicuous inside a major city, so we parked in front of an abandoned building and covered it with a humongous tarp. We switched to civilian gear, though everyone, including myself, was packing heat.

"We're here to speak with Herr Krüger," I said to the guard at the front gate. He looked at me in my casual dress and comfortable shoes. I gave him some credit; he didn't stare at my tits. He looked at Filip, who was just behind my right shoulder.

"Sir, do you have an appointment?"

"I asked the question. Please address only me," I said, trying not to let my frustration take over.

"Please, fräulein, let your betters speak." He had a condescending look that made me want to smash his face with a metal pipe.

"She is in charge here," Filip said. "You must speak with her." His broken German did the trick.

He turned back to me, unhappy at the thought of dealing with a woman. "May I ask who is calling?"

"Tell the gentleman that it is Lady Sobieski. I am a friend of Hedwig."

He harumphed, then went inside to pass the message. Two minutes later, a man who could only be Karl Krüger came out from the main entrance of the building. The surly guard walked several steps behind.

I could tell Krüger was who I was looking for; I could see the aura of energy enveloping him. He took my hand in both of his and graciously kissed my fingers.

"Lady Sobieski. It's good to meet you. Hedwig has raved about you and has gone on at length about your… well, let's take this inside. Shall we?" He offered his arm, which I took. We started walking towards his factory when he looked over his shoulder at the members of my squad. Borys and Izabel were left in the car; the rest followed me.

"I've had trouble in the past. I never travel alone."

"Hmm, understandable. With the Rus swallowing sovereign nations like appetizers, I'm not sure there is anywhere that is safe these days."

We climbed some stairs just inside the large garage-style door. The factory floor was filled with men manning all sorts of milling and grinding machines. They wore protective gear because of the loud stamping, sparks, and other hazardous conditions. The second floor had a hall with offices for the accountants and clerks. At the end of the hall, there was a large office behind a heavy wooden door with the owner's name on a brass placard.

"Filip, you come with me. The rest of you, please wait out here," I ordered.

There was a coffee table with four chairs at the far end of his office. The desk was a large monstrosity made of highly polished cherry wood. A couple of curio cabinets lined the other end of the office, near the table. We sat in plush leather chairs and sank in pleasantly. The table held a small humidor of cigars, and the cabinets held strange artifacts, not only from Europa but also from Africa and the Orient.

"Drink?" he asked as he plucked a crystal decanter from a rolling tray.

"Yes, please." Filip gave me a look I couldn't quite understand. "For each of us."

He poured three glasses of the dark, mahogany alcohol. Filip stood, took his, and handed me mine. Our host sat across from us, holding his drink.

"Prost!" he said, holding up his glass. We returned the cheer, and we drank. The whiskey was not as good as my father's, but it was smooth and warmed its way down my throat.

"I don't mean to steal your thunder, as they say, but I know why you are here." He was as tall as Filip, but thicker in the limbs, torso, and face. The gentleman was balding, with neck-length hair in the back and sides. What very little there was on top was wiry and uncontrolled.

The day was cool, but the exertion of going down to fetch us and returning up the stairs had him sweating on his face and neck, causing damp spots everywhere on his smart business suit. He wore a light grey wool coat with a dark grey satin vest that seemed ready to pop all its buttons. A pocket watch chain emerged from the center button on his chest and dropped into a small pocket on his right side. He had a matching suit jacket hung on a wooden coat rack near the door, and next to it rested a walking cane with an owl's head, the shaft made of polished ebony.

"You know the name and location of a prime brand holder?" I asked.

"For certain, I know the name. He is my wife's nephew, August. August Vogel. I can't say that I know the man well, but we are family, and ever since he went through his trials, we've yet to see anyone with a brand like his. Hedwig has been part of the Brotherhood much longer than I have, and she told me his brand is unique. One of a kind."

"A prime brand?"

"Yes, I think that's what he called it."

"Where can I find him?"

"Tonight is Friday. More than likely, he'll be at Das Uhrwerkhaus."

"The Clockwork House?" Filip asked

"It's very trendy. He meets a lot of women there, and drinks more than a little on weekends."

"Would you say he's dangerous?" I asked.

He smiled. "He's very dangerous." He had a sly look. "Normally, I wouldn't be so free with information, but she told me what you can do. No need to hang me upside down for information. He has the only instance of the Chronovore Emberrift."

I turned to Filip. "He can travel through time."

"And some other neat tricks as well," the old man said, pouring another few fingers of the whiskey. "I don't know what all he can do, so don't bother. You can ask him tonight, if you have the intestinal fortitude to face him." His family pride was showing through.

"I have yet to meet the man, or woman, that I fear. You can let him know we'll be there at eleven tonight."


This was starting to become a thing, and it bothered me. We dressed up appropriately for the club, and when we showed up, we were let in because we were on the list.

"Well, Kapitan, you did tell them that we were coming. This time, we're not trying to sneak in."

The building was three stories tall and roughly a cube. It was called Clockwork House, so the décor made it seem as if the inside of a clock were attached to the outside of the building. Steam issued from exhaust tubes that protruded from the metal walls in seemingly random locations. A huge gear, eight feet in diameter, turned lazily next to the front entrance. There were a couple of gears of similar size where the second floor would be, and more on the third floor. Smaller gears filled many of the spaces, made of solid burnished steel, each gear and cog moving at different speeds. A shaft protruded from the center of the building, holding up brass clock hands, a short one for the hour, a longer one for the minutes. The hands were crafted in the Maltese style, with an iron cross midway between the post and the point.

We were escorted inside and taken to a private room on the top floor. I had my whole squad with me, and they didn't check us for weapons. That alone made me suspicious.

The room was comfortable enough for our small party. A table was laid out with meats, cheeses, and fresh fruit. A small pyramid had been erected with full glasses of champagne. There were plates of chocolates and Bavarian candies. A barman stood behind a solid wood bar, ready to pour any liquors we might desire, and a maid in black and white stood ready to attend to our every need.

We were encouraged to partake, and we did so with enthusiasm. I was accustomed to parties with similar extravagance, but to my soldiers, this was like heaven.

I wore a simple white evening dress, sleeveless, fitted tightly around the bust, waist, and hips. I didn't exactly scream army Kapitan with my moderate cleavage and skirt that nearly touched the ground, with a slit that started high on my thigh. The girls had to dress a bit more conservatively as they were carrying small pistols and a few knives. I already felt like a weapon, so I decided not to carry any on my person.

When he came in, I was a bit surprised. I don't know why I expected him to be my age, but he was older than Stefek, possibly in his late twenties or early thirties. I wasn't sure, I just knew that he was old. He had dark brown hair, cut very short, and his beard and mustache were closer to overgrown five o'clock shadow. His features were plain, but his eyes had a sparkle that hinted at some secret he had yet to share. He wore a very fashionable, shiny black velvet coat with metallic, indigo patterns throughout. His lustrous trousers broke evenly over violet leather Oxford shoes. He looked put together and rich, but he was far from what I found attractive.

"Welcome to my club," he said. "August Vogel at your service."

"Thank you for receiving us," I said as I watched him lounge on an overstuffed love seat. He looked confident, untouchable.

We made small talk for a while, which was required at our level of society. He and I spoke while Filip sat quietly in our circle, sipping a beer and not joining the conversation. The rest mostly ignored us. I could tell that they were trying to listen without being too conspicuous as they ate to bursting and drank, though not to excess.

"You met with my aunt?" he asked. Finally getting to business.

"Yes. She directed me to your uncle, who told us how to find you." I was drinking whiskey, and I realized that I was starting to like it. "He's part of this Brotherhood of Virtue. A woman in Polska named Hedwig has been trying to recruit me to the group. Are you a member?"

"Let's take this talk private," he said, looking at Filip.

"How do you mean?" I asked, not sure if he wanted to lure me to some dark back room.

He held out his hand, and I stared at it for a moment. His cheeky grin didn't inspire confidence, but I wanted to show that I wasn't afraid of anything. We were still sitting, but I took his hand in mine, and everything changed. It felt like a flash, but it was just a change in illumination. We had been in a dimly-lit private room, and now, we were still in the same room, the same chairs, but there was light outside the windows.

"I hope my time shift didn't cause you any distress," he said, letting go of my hand. "We didn't move an inch, as you can see, but we are almost twelve hours in the past."

"Chronovore Emberrift."

"I don't even know how far in the past or future I can travel. Like your brand, there's no instruction manual."

I looked down, and there was a pulse pistol on the coffee table between us. He had anticipated this meeting and set the stage in advance. How little did he know about my brand?

"Are you a part of this radical group?"

"The Brotherhood? No, I'm not much of a joiner. They want to give brands and power to the masses. I'm not a big believer in sharing." He picked up the pistol and held it loosely in his hand. "I am in favor of others sharing with me, though. Let's go for a ride." He waved the pistol at the door, and he followed me out. There was a car waiting, no driver. Whatever he had planned, he didn't want one of his thugs to witness.

"You're kidnapping me? The last guy who tried that got his lungs pulled out through his chest."

"I have something to show you. You'll find it to be the most interesting thing you've seen in your life, and that includes your trials." He gestured to the car. "You drive. I need to keep an eye on you."

"I have minimal driving experience. I hope we're not going far." I climbed into the driver's seat of his new Benz and stared at the controls. He pointed out the starter with the barrel of his pistol, and after a couple of tries, I got the engine going. He gave directions out of town, and after an hour and a half, we arrived. We parked and walked down a steep incline until we found ourselves at the mouth of a cave that looked very familiar.

"Yes, this is our Star of Abyrinth." At the trials, I entered the cave alone. Now, we were entering together. The trip took as long as I remembered, and when we finally reached the star chamber with the glowing stone, I felt a sense of déjà vu.

"This is exactly like ours. Not similar to, but exactly like our cave."

"I've seen your cave, and about ten other caves. They are all exactly alike. They can't be natural, but I've no idea how they were made, or by whom."

"How many caves are there?" Despite his holding a gun on me, I was genuinely interested now.

"As far as anyone knows, there are eighty-one." He strolled over to a placard bolted to the cave wall. I had seen similar; it showed hundreds of brand designs worked into a thick copper plate. They were arranged in a grid, organized by school or, for lack of a better word, magic.

I saw Stefek's Chronoburst; so powerful, it sat at the far left of the row of temporal powers. I easily picked out Mother's Hand of Mending brand. At the top of the list, not applied to the grid format, were three brands set aside from the rest. There was my Abyrinth Embermark; one of the other two would have to be August's Chronovore Emberrift.

That one. The brand had a clock with gears. A little too on the nose for my sensibilities, but not everyone appreciated subtlety. His club was modeled after a giant clock, turned inside out. August didn't seem to worry that anyone knew about his special abilities.

The third brand would be the Omniport Gatefold. It was exactly like the rubbing given to me by the British gentleman, Edmund Fletcher. The design was of a doorway, surrounded by energy tendrils.

August had me stand off to the side before he touched the copy of his brand on the steel plate. I could see Abyrinth flowing from his brand, through his body, then his arm, and into the seal. I thought it interesting that for the first time, I actually saw the flow originate with the wielder's brand.

There was hardly any sound as a section of the cave wall swung inward, exposing another chamber behind the main chamber where the trials were given. He waved me in with his pistol, feeling very at ease. I could have taken his gun away at any time, but I wanted to play along and see where this went.

There was another gem, mounted on a stone pedestal, but it glowed with a light that cycled between orange, gold, magenta, and ultramarine. The flashing lights were beautiful, but in just a few moments, I felt dizzy and worried my stomach was about to empty.

I saw him flinch; it was a strange movement. He did it again, and then cursed and looked very frustrated.

"What's wrong?" I asked.

"Nothing," he said through gritted teeth.

He went from calm to furious in seconds, and I had a hunch. I could see him trying to use his power, and I tried to pull the Abyrinth from him. I failed. I tried again, but apparently, he was immune to my shenanigans. More than anything, it confirmed my suspicions.

"You can't stop time around me?"

"Damn it!" he cursed.

"As prime brand holders, we have great power, but it seems that we can't use those powers against each other. Or maybe it's just in these star chambers. I'm not sure."

He aimed his pulse pistol at me and tried to fire, but it, too, was useless here.

"You brought me all this way to kill me? You could have done that in the car, or tried. Why are we here, and what exactly is your devious plan?"

His anger was irrationally virulent. We had only met a couple of hours ago; our countries were not at war… why was he seething with such anger?

"Gah!" he shouted, then turned and raced out of the chamber and through the tunnel towards the car. I followed as best I could, but my heels prevented me from running. When I got out in the open, the car was gone, along with my hope of working with one of the three holders of a prime brand.

"Fuck!" I cursed. I wasn't one to use profane language, but I was far from civilization with no way back. I decided to go back to the chamber and see what I could figure out. When I reached the outer cave, I saw that the door had automatically closed. It wasn't hard to figure out. I touched the symbol for my brand, the all-seeing eye, and the energy began to flow. Just as before, the hidden door opened, and I entered the secret room. I looked around the room for another plaque and was disappointed.

It was probably the single most careless thing I'd done to that point, but I approached the large gem with the rotating colors and placed my hand on it.

I felt a jolt through my system, not like an electric shock, more like a reflex that had been triggered. My hand cramped, grasping the glowing stone with painful intensity. I knew that until it was done with me, I wouldn't be able to disengage. My eyes were open, but that didn't stop the flow of images and information from dominating my vision. It was like either a dream or a premonition.

I saw a glowing figure, so bright that I couldn't tell the sex. It was like the sun in the shape of a person. The being was able to weave and control Abyrinth, with enormous webs extending from every inch of it. Energy flowed both ways, feeding the blinding light, while at the same time, shooting out to seize enemies. The glowing person passed through time, and I knew this more instinctually than from the changing background. Then I saw the wielder move through a hole in space and was instantly transported to the pyramids of Egypt, then to the Grand Canyon. Three distinct powers were at the person's beck and call, and they could bend reality with powers that defined time and space.

I didn't know the complete meaning of the vision, but it was clear that a wielder, a prime brand wielder, could somehow gain the powers of all three prime brands and become nearly God-like in ability.

I wasn't sure… ok, I was pretty sure that August had intended to steal the power of my brand. No doubt, he would have killed me right after. Something in this chamber would make it possible to transfer the power, or perhaps even the whole brand, to another person.

I wanted to see if there was a similar secret room behind the gem cave in Warszawa. First, I had to get back to Berlin. My crew would not be safe with this time-stopping asshole venting his frustration.

I called Filip on my hand-held radio.

"Why are you calling? You're in the next room over," he said.

"No. I'm not. Ok, I am, but I'm also a couple of hours from where you are." I couldn't stop the frustration from coming through. "Later tonight, Vogel is going to take me twelve hours in the past. We drove to the middle of nowhere, then he left me."

"I'll come and get you. Give me your location."

"No, he's already on the way there. He'll arrive long before I will. Act as if nothing is wrong, follow the plan as we laid it out. I have an idea, and I want you to get everyone on board." For the next several minutes, as I walked toward the main road, I told my lieutenant my new plan. I couldn't help thinking that it would be a suitable revenge.

August checked his watch, then smiled as he held out his hand. I took it, and we disappeared. A second later, he was back in his seat with a pulse pistol in his hand.

"Alright! Everybody against the wall!" he shouted. My squad gave him a quizzical look before gathering around him. "I told you to get over there." He waved with his pistol. "Get against the wall!"

No one reacted; instead, they stood there eating his food and drinking his liquor. Filip looked at him like he was crazy. He instantly became furious.

"Against the wall!" he shouted. His face was turning red with anger. "Don't think that I won't shoot you all!"

I was dressed as a server, standing right behind him. Just being in close proximity should have been enough, but I placed my hand on his shoulder to be sure.

"It's a very rude host that pulls a gun on his guests," Filip said.

August tried firing his pistol, but when in contact with me, his energy flow was neutralized.

"Lieutenant Budny, at least he didn't have a real gun. Just one of those magic guns that doesn't work when another prime brand holder is touching you," Izabela said, laughter just under the surface.

He jerked around, then looked up at my face. He was shocked, knowing that ten hours ago, he'd left me in the countryside.

"You left me too much time to get back," I told him, baring my widest, warmest smile.

"You were planning to steal my Kapitan's birthright?" Filip asked. "You were planning to leave her in an unmarked grave?" He punched the German noble crisply on the corner of the chin. The dandy's lights went out, and he crumpled to the floor. "That was very rude!"

"Tie him up," I told the boys. He was hogtied, and with guns drawn, we dragged him down the stairs and outside. The staff watched as we carried their boss through the bustling club like a game deer heading to slaughter. On the way out, Jacek pulled the fire alarm. Alarms sounded throughout the building, drowning out the live band. Clubgoers started running out of the club, fearing a fire that wasn't real.

I turned to my squad. "Take him over there." I pointed at a spot towards the edge of the parking lot. I could feel the dampening of my power until he was a good fifty feet away. It was subtle, but when he was far enough away, I could feel the release of the restriction on my ability. I assume that due to the nature of my brand, I was especially sensitive to the flow of Abyrinth.

Now that I was unrestricted, I wrapped giant tentacles of energy around the largest gear on the side of the building. With little effort, I ripped it from its axle. Like a child with an unwanted toy, I flung it off in the parking lot. What I could do still surprised my crew. I started plucking gears from the clockwerks, fueled by my need to vent my frustration. Each metal structure that I ripped from the walls would cause a tremor. Anyone who thought the fire wasn't real and it was safe to stay inside soon found out the truth. I began disassembling the nightclub, piece by piece.

August regained consciousness at some point, and I could hear him actually weeping. It took more effort, but I managed to completely wrap the building in a vise-like band and squeeze. The structure crumbled and fell in on itself. A cloud of dust tried to wash over us, but I formed a barrier around myself and my team.

"Ok. I think I'm done here," I said, feeling a little better. I turned to where Karol had been holding our prisoner, but he'd escaped.

"I'm sorry, Kapitan," the big man said. "He disappeared."

"Not to worry. It's hard to stop someone who can project himself forward or backward through time. We'll catch him next time."

# Chapter 43

Interlude IV:

*Journal entry, 5-20-2020*

*Generał Brygady, Stefek Sobieski, Commander, 3rd Battalion*

*The war started shy of three months ago, and it was essentially over. My home, the estate that I shared with my parents and siblings, which had been in our family for hundreds of years, was lost over two months ago. I heard from Jafra that she was there when the first wave of Rus attacked, and that she and some boy, also a wielder, were able to get the rest of the family off safely, and killed a whole platoon. I may have to move her up to second-favorite sibling.*

*Instead of reporting to me, she now reports directly to the prince, General Poniatowski. He's a good man, and I know that he likes my sister, but I fear that putting him in charge of our limited military resources has been a mistake. More than anything, he is defending his legacy, his right to someday wear a crown. He has a passion for the job and conviction, but he lacks the experience. We are close in age, but while he was living the high life in Oxford, I was here in Polska, fighting foreign incursions.*

*In all honesty, I think this war is lost. The royal family was evacuated over a month ago, and the only people remaining in the capital are soldiers. So many have fallen. I was promoted to Generał Brygady, the lowest rank in the general officer corps, but still in charge of a whole brigade. I have almost five thousand men and machines under my direct command. We've been ordered to make a last defense of Warszawa, and if possible, to protect the royal estate. I fear for the lives of my men and the*

Stefek had taken over a local police station for his field headquarters and was poring over dispatches with his command staff when the runner entered. The woman was holding her left arm with her right hand, blood seeping from a wound. She was out of breath, and her uniform was in disarray.

"General, they are on the move!"

"Thank you, private. Get yourself to a healer." He turned to his men. "Gear up. The time for strategizing is over. You all have your assignments; go out and lead!"

It was almost painful for him to send others out to do the fighting. He'd been given a lengthy lecture about not putting himself in immediate danger as a senior officer. His role had evolved to the point where he was to employ his mechs, tanks, and troops to maximum effectiveness. His gliders were coasting high above the riverfront and would be constantly reporting the locations of both his forces and the enemy's. Looking at his maps, he was concerned.

He could hear the explosions now, and it was all too much for him. Stepping outside, he looked to the east, towards the river, and he could see pillars of black smoke rising near the docks. Rounds were landing all around, and it was no longer safe, even this far from where the fighting was taking place. Making sure that he had his pulse pistol and saber, he went in search of one of his commanders. He found a young major a few blocks away, shouting orders to her platoon leaders.

"Major, how are you deployed?" he asked.

"They've already crossed at one of the bridges and are on this side of the river. Their mechs are out front, and they're moving north towards the castle. I have men with shoulder-fired rockets on top of all the buildings, waiting to catch them at choke points. If we can drop a couple of mechs in a tight street, we can block the tanks, and they'll have to go around."

"Very good. Put snipers in all the windows along the street. When their troops catch up, spring the trap."

"Yes, General!" she said, popping a proper salute.

Stefek checked the rest of his platoons and was satisfied that they were ready as they could be. The enemy force was reported to be a complete corps of soldiers, somewhere north of thirty thousand souls. The defenders still had twenty functional mechs and two dozen tanks, but the Rus probably had twice that. When he reached the end of the line along the southern edge of his defense zone, he saw what he feared most. The Rus were sweeping around his position to flank his troops.

Stefek was in a long street between rows of warehouses when he heard a shot ring out. There were enemy riflemen down that street who saw him first. He'd honed his reflexes to a degree unmatched by any human. The second he heard the gunshot, his power kicked in, stopping time. Even from a distance, he could see the muzzle flash. He ran forward at an angle. When five seconds had passed, his power was released, and time resumed. The bullets went past him to his left. The soldiers were taken by surprise, seeing that they'd missed and their target was now much closer. They re-aimed, but time had stopped again. He got closer and moved to his left. When time resumed, their shots were completely off the mark to his right. Stefek pulled his sword as he stopped time once again. Each of the three men received a quick cut to their throats before time resumed. They dropped their weapons and clutched at their fatal wounds.

Grabbing one of their rifles, Stefek crouched behind a corner and started firing into the crowd of invading soldiers. These were low-end troops, with no armor plating and only simple, non-pulse weapons. Head shot, head shot, neck, head shot. He took out five of them before they could pinpoint his location. They raised their weapons to take aim, but he was already gone.

I need to find their officers, he thought to himself. Killing their leadership is the only thing that will at least delay the inevitable. Planning out his route, he stopped time, moved to a covered location, then searched for the next stopping point. He was able to pass through the enemy ranks and into their rear without being detected. Men were marching in the warm summer sun, sweating under packs of gear, carrying weapons, ammunition, and other items required for an assault. He could see their faces, young men and women, pulled from their farms and factories, and sent a thousand miles west to attack people they didn't know, and had no problems with. There were true killers in the mix, men who loved to fight and slaughter, men who loved to claim the spoils, be they monetary or something more personal. The rest were youngsters, younger than him and his brother. Mostly boys, sent to fight in a foreign land for plunder that only their masters would enjoy.

That wouldn't stop him from killing them. Their officers would most likely be either channelers or wielders. If he could eliminate some of them, their side would lose both direction and powerful weapons.

He saw a young lieutenant with a pulse pistol on his hip. Almost certainly a channeler. He checked his magazine; only seven rounds were left. Taking careful aim, he squeezed off a shot. The young man moved at the last instant, and instead of a killing shot through the temple, he had lead pass through his jawbone, tearing off the lower jaw. Good enough. He was gone before anyone knew what had happened to their platoon leader.

He bounced around, looking for more targets. They were behind the lines, but the sounds of stamping feet and the hiss of steam-powered tanks echoed off the tight walls of businesses on both sides of the road. Finally, he found someone worth killing.

Sitting on top of a troop transport, there was an older man in his mid-thirties with a spotless uniform. His light-colored hair was tucked under a uniform cap, not a combat helmet, the insignia on the front proclaiming him a colonel. Stefek's intuition was that anyone able to reach such a high rank must be a noble, and therefore, a wielder.

Stefek got the man in his sights and fired. Like himself, the man's control of his brand was an integral part of him; he heard the sound of a gunshot where there shouldn't have been one, and his ability kicked in. The bullet passed through him, flying off and getting lost somewhere behind him. The Rus officer was ethereal, passing through the metal side of the transport and alighting on the ground, facing Stefek. The two men stood in the side street a hundred yards apart, sizing each other up, preparing to duel.

The Rus fired his pulse pistol, but Stefek seemingly disappeared into thin air. Stefek had sprinted the distance between them and was standing a few feet to the side, with his rifle aimed at the man's head. He fired, but again, the round passed through the phantom soldier.

Damn, this could go on forever, Stefek thought to himself. Then he had a thought.

"Quit hiding, General! You can't shoot me or stab me with that sword. I can become intangible, like a ghost!"

Stefek shot at him anyway, just to give him a false location, then stopped time and ran into a nearby building.

"Come out, General! Were you scared by a ghost? Are you afraid to face me?"

That went on for some time; the Rus was trying his best to goad Stefek into making a mistake. He waited nearly five minutes, spying on the wielder through a second-story window. When enough time had passed, it was clear that the colonel was substantial again. He stopped time, hustled down to the first-floor door, reset the time freeze, and then sprinted over to the caravan of troops. He pulled two hand grenades from a soldier's belt, pulled the pin, and stuck them on the colonel's belt. He was only fifty feet away when time resumed, and he dropped to the ground for his own safety.

The explosion was loud, and the sound reverberated in the narrow side street. Bits of Rus Colonel rained down on everyone around, as his soldiers searched for the enemy, but the enemy had stopped time again and run away. I enjoyed that more than I should have, Stefek thought to himself.

Over the next hour, he assassinated another colonel, two majors, five captains, and a score of lieutenants who were probably just channelers, but they became victims of opportunity. He had given the men their orders and placed his assets as strategically as possible, and now killing Rus leadership was the most effective way he could even the odds. Running by, he saw a tank with its turret hatch open. Dropping a few hand grenades in, he didn't even stay to see the resulting chaos.

Stefek returned to his side of the fighting and found his command squad. They updated him on how the fighting was going. Despite his efforts, not so well. The enemy was advancing more slowly than expected, but they were still advancing. He found out that they had been shelling the castle for an hour, and the company left to guard it was most likely dead by now. He received a report on troop strength, and more than half of his own battalion had been destroyed. A lot of good men and women lost their lives. The best of the Polish youth. The enemy had taken even larger losses, but they had started with so many more men that they were still outnumbering the Poles by more than three to one.

"Get Generał Dywizji Dabrowski on the radio."

"I'm sorry, General. The Major General is dead."

"How about General Kowalczyk, or General Dubicki?"

The radioman showed real fear, but performed his duty. "They are all dead, sir. You are the only general that we have left."

"What is the troop strength across the line? How many souls are left in our army?"

"I just finished collecting reports from the other command centers. We are down to around fifteen thousand men," the kapral stuttered, tears flowing down his dirty cheeks.

Stefek thought long and hard, weighing the pros and cons of continuing. In the end, it was a simple decision. He turned to the kapral.

"Have someone make a white flag, and walk out to the enemy line. Have them request a meeting with their leader to discuss terms."

"We're surrendering?" the young man asked.

"This war has been over for a while. It's time our people stopped dying."

# Chapter 44

Jacek ran into the hotel lobby where they were all staying. He was a naturally high-strung kid, but now he was even more worked up than usual.

"Kapitan! Kapitan!" he whispered, very loudly.

"Yes?"

"The war is over. General Sobieski has surrendered, and the king has agreed."

"From his summer home in Bavaria," I groused. "My brother is the last man standing, and will be known as the general who surrendered to the Rus. Great."

"At least he's alive," Filip said. "Most of the other generals were killed."

"Have you heard from your other brother?" Izabela asked.

"Krystian? No, not in weeks." It made me wonder why I'd not heard from him. "He was leading patrols in northern Polska along the border, last I knew."

"So, there's no Polish army any longer. Looks like we're all out of a job," Marcin said.

"What are you going to do, Kapitan?" Julia asked.

"I guess I'm not a kapitan any longer. Not your superior." I thought for a moment, but I knew what I had to do. "I'm not done fighting. I need to find out the secret of the prime brands and figure out how to use them against the Rus. I'll not sit quietly and accept occupation. When I see a Rus soldier, he dies!"

They all nodded in agreement.

"I'll stay with you… Jafra," Filip said. He was tall and strong, a true patriot.

"Me too," said Julia. "If you'll have me."

"Of course," I replied. "You're an essential member of this team." She smiled at the compliment.

"I'm in," Jacek said.

"Me too," Marcin added.

"You need me to have your back. None of these others can crack heads properly," Karol said.

"I have nothing better to do," Borys said. He readjusted his eyepatch.

It was quiet for a minute, and they all looked at Izabelalla expectantly. She looked grouchy, and I was sure she was going to decline. "Well, I'm used to being the hottest chick wherever I go, so I'm not too pleased to always be in the company of a stunner like you… Jafra."

"If you stay with us, you can be the sassy, streetwise one. I could use some tips on using what I have without giving away the farm, so to speak."

"You definitely don't want to give away the farm. Someone will be plowing your field without your permission." They all laughed, and it took me a second, but when I got the joke, I joined in.

"What do we do now?" Julia asked.

"First, we have to take off these uniforms. We travel without all the heavy armor and without military vehicles."

"Boss," Filip said. "Maybe we can investigate these missing persons. Many people who might otherwise fall through society's cracks have been going missing. I don't have anything solid, but my gut tells me that it's related to this Court of Whispers."

I thought for a minute. Losing the war was a shock, though we all thought it would be the eventual outcome. I wanted to track down that bastard, August Vogel, but he would be well guarded, and it would be a pain in the ass trying to figure out how to get around his power. He was a prime for a reason. I figured that if there was some conspiracy to kidnap and disappear people, we could help.

I looked directly at him. "Where do we start?"


It took a couple of days, but we snuck back into Warszawa. I had first heard from Jaroslav about the missing people, and it seemed to be a much more widespread problem than I thought. Every week, someone would join the ranks of the disappeared.

We found ourselves in a typical middle-class neighborhood on the outskirts of the city. We had to keep our heads on a swivel to avoid Rus patrols. It hurt my very soul to know that this was now their city.

We had stopped by my family's estate, and precisely as I had feared, it was burned down to the foundation. My house, the garage, the barn, and other outbuildings. They wanted revenge for the platoon that Jaro and I had killed, so they took it out on my property.

"This is the house?" I asked as I turned the map up and down. "I've never been to this neighborhood."

"I imagine not, princess," Izabela said. She was the first to lose the respectful tone that had been required when we were in the army. "Your estate was far away from where us little people live."

"Come with me to talk to the family," I said, ignoring her pettiness.

She went with me to the door, followed by Marcin. We tried to go out in small groups; more than three people together would attract too much attention. Before, I always wore dresses, usually very frilly, expensive ones. Only silk and satin could touch my skin. Women who wore such things were hunted these days. It wasn't safe to be singled out as wealthy, or worse, from a noble family.

Now I wear denim trousers with cotton shirts and a small leather jacket. I just couldn't cut my hair, but I did braid it, and now I usually wear it coiled at the back of my head, often under a hat. I didn't give up jewelry; instead of spending thousands of złoty on a necklace, I wore cheap, second-hand earrings, rings, and bracelets. They cost nothing compared to what I wore at the Ascension Ball so long ago, but they were shiny, and I liked them.

Izabellala just dipped into her closet. She was a blank from a lower-middle-class household, and what I wore now was what she wore every day when she was off duty. The only difference was that she showed more skin than I was comfortable with. She wore blue jeans so tight I think she had to lie down to pull them on. Her light-pink top had no sleeves, and I wasn't sure what was more distracting, her nipples, which were very easily seen through the soft cotton material, or the wide, deep neckline that showed a generous amount of cleavage. It would have been a convenient shirt if she were breastfeeding a baby, because her tits were at risk of falling out at any second.

"Quit staring! Yours are just as nice," she said.

"Lately, I've seen your breasts more than I've seen my own."

"Ladies," Marcin cut in. "It's not a competition. But if it were…" We both glared daggers at him. "I would be the winner!" He had let his curly hair grow out, and he wore a blue-and-white striped shirt that wouldn't look good on anyone, especially not on him.

We walked up to the address we were given and knocked on the door. It was a typical house for this area, one story, made of red brick, and barely over a thousand square feet. An old steam sedan was parked in the driveway, with a couple of minor dents and a little rust around the wheel wells. The door opened, and we were greeted by an older woman, a few years my mother's senior.

"Yes? Can I help you?" She wasn't too old, but I could see that stress had added years to her otherwise smooth features. Her hair was light brown with grey streaks and looked in need of a cut. Her housedress had a floral pattern and fit her chunky frame like a tent.

"Pani Wozniak?" I asked. She nodded. "My name is Emilia Filipowski, this is my colleague, Basia Janda," I said, pointing at Izabel, "and he is Bazyli Kijek. We are investigating the disappearance of several local people, and we were told that your daughter, Iza, went missing a few weeks ago."

The woman had looked defeated when she opened the door, but at the mention of her daughter, she went even more pale, and I could see tremors shaking her frail body.

"Could we please come in and talk?" I asked, using my best and friendliest smile.

"Yes, please come in." She opened the screen door and let us follow her into her small parlor. There was a couch and two chairs that surrounded a long, oval coffee table, stacked with old magazines and a cold cup of tea. Marcin stood until she pointed at a chair across the room at a small dining table. He pulled it over and joined us.

"Thank you for speaking with us, madam. I understand how difficult this subject must be for you, and we hope to learn your daughter's whereabouts, along with the many others who have gone missing in the last year."

"Where did you say you were from again?" she asked, not able to meet my eyes.

"We are private investigators hired by one of the other parents," Marcin said. He leaned into her, getting her to look at him. He had so much sincerity in his lie that I almost believed it myself. "As my partner said, there have been a string of disappearances over the last year. It happened before the war started, so we don't think it was the Rus. We believe that they are all somehow connected, so we're speaking with those closest to the missing persons, trying to get a better idea of what happened."

"Do you think that she was kidnapped?"

"A single person can fall into the lake and drown. A hundred people missing can't be attributed to accident or chance. There is evil out there, even more insidious than the Rus."

"Please tell us about the day she went missing. Tell us everything; any small thing might prove to be the key that we are looking for," Izabel said, taking the woman's shaking hands in her own.

She closed her eyes tightly, as a stream of tears ran down her tired cheeks. She sniffled, and we waited patiently for over a minute until she could compose herself.

"There is not much to tell. She worked as a server at a nobleman's house downtown. Not the royal palace, but some other minor lord's manor. She was often expected to stay late, or if there was some event, she might be asked to spend the night to watch over their children. But two days passed, and she never came home. I checked with her boyfriend, and he'd not seen her in days. I asked her employer, but they had let her leave two days earlier at her normal time. I asked her girlfriends, none of whom had seen her in a week. The police took a report and looked around a bit, but after I called them a dozen times, they said they had put the case on temporary closed status because of the time that had passed, and admitted they had no clues. None."

"That's terrible. Do you think it would be all right if we looked in her room?"

"I guess it would be alright."

"Please give Bazyli the name and address of her employer. We will see them next."

"I'll give the address, but I think they fled west, one step ahead of the Rus."

I got up and walked down the hall. There were three bedrooms; one was the master bedroom for the mistress of the house, another was full of junk and a sewing machine. The third room was obviously for a young, single woman. It was filled with lots of pink, with stuffed animals and a closet full of girly clothing. I wasn't sure what I was looking for; I only hoped that I would know when I found it.

Her things had been picked over, probably a couple of times, then put back meticulously by her mother.

I didn't want to tell this woman that her daughter was dead. Deep down, I think she already knew it.

I looked over the belongings of a simple person, a girl who could have been me, had I been born under different circumstances. War was the great equalizer; my being born to a rich, influential house was less important than the amount of food and supplies I had been able to accumulate and hide from the invaders.

I looked through a small chest of knick-knacks, awards for races almost won, tokens from male admirers, charms, and good luck objects.

Then it caught my eye. A small, round, coin-shaped token, the size of a five złoty coin. It had 'Potentia Ante Patriam' written across the top in an arch that followed the coin's edge. Along the bottom, 'Regno Pernicies' was written. My Latin was very poor, and I could only pick up on themes of death and destruction.

I turned the coin over in my palm to look at the obverse side and was greeted with a familiar emblem. An owl was set in relief, and it looked like it could fly away from the field behind it to peck at my eyes. There were many breeds of owl, but without a doubt, this was the sign of the Court of Whispers.

I pocketed the coin and joined the others. We observed the pleasantries, but were back in our car as soon as was polite. We piled into the steam sedan; it was clunky and slow, but able to withstand a lot more than Krystian's sports car. As we drove away, I showed them the coin.

"Not a coincidence," Marcin stated.

"No, not a coincidence. Did we miss these at the other houses?" I asked.

Izabel was driving. She looked over her shoulder at us. "Now that we know what to look for, let's specifically look for signs of the Court of Whispers. If we find even one more, we'll know."

"I noticed something else. It seemed that all of the missing people were over eighteen, but under thirty." I said.

Izabel spoke while navigating the city streets. "Something else. They were all blanks. People like me."

We went to three more houses that afternoon. Consoled three more sets of despondent parents. We scoured the next house and found nothing. One house had a father who refused to let us look at his son's things. I tied him up with bands of Abyrinth, including a gag, and left him in an easy chair in the living room.

"Don't you think that's a little much, Kapitan?" Julia asked. I shot her a look. "Jafra, wait, what?"

"No. What we're doing is important, and I won't let being polite…"

"Or respectful," Izabel offered.

"Or respectful, stop us from accomplishing our mission. Marcin, help me upstairs."

We went to the young man's room to see if we could find anything. We entered, and it was a lot messier than the girls' rooms. "Do all guys live like this?" I asked. "My brother's rooms aren't like this."

"Didn't you have a full staff of maids and other servants?" he asked. "Both of my parents work, and when left to my own devices, yes, the room I shared with my brothers was at least this messy, maybe more."

I couldn't imagine having to share a room with anyone. He was right about the maids, though. I guess my brothers threw clothes on the floor, and someone else picked them up. We dug through his closet and a small desk in the corner, where he painted small figurines. We spent ten minutes, and in that time, I think we touched every item in the room.

"Where exactly do boys hide their illicit goods?"

Marcin thought for a moment. "I've heard that sometimes people will wipe their boogers on the underside of a table or desk. Not me. It's something I've heard about." He was a terrible actor.

I was standing closest to the desk, and I got down on one knee and peered under it. There was a coin stuck in the middle of the underside of the desk. I tried to pluck it, but it was stuck firmly to the cheap composite wood. I eventually pried it off and took a look. There was a coin with a massive glob of chewing gum that the young man had used to hide it from his parents' sight.

"Ooh, gross!" I said before picking the gum off the coin. It was identical to the previous coin that we found.

Marcin looked at it, turned it around a few times, then handed it back to me.

"Exact match. We know who the perpetrators are. Now, how do we find them?"

There was a knock on my hotel room door. We were no longer staying at fancy hotels with endless amenities. We now had three rooms, one for the guys, one for the girls, and one for me. I was still the leader, even if we were no longer in an army where I was their commanding officer. I answered the door to find Jacek holding a radio.

"Call from Prince Záhoř," he said, handing me the radio.

"Thank you." I shut the door, took the radio, and lay on the bed. I hadn't heard from Jaroslav in weeks, not since he left to return to Bohemia. Funny, I haven't thought much about Stanisław recently.

In those rare instances where I had a moment of free time, I had thoughts of the scoundrel. When he was Jaro, he didn't treat me like a china doll, but instead, like an object of desire. When he held me, it was with strong hands that would have left bruises on my pre-war, softer self. I remember the scrape of his facial hair when we kissed, and how, even though it felt painful at first, I craved the raw maleness of it. Against my will, I longed for the feel of his hands on my body, touching me anywhere he wanted. It was consensual, but at times, I felt like I was along for the ride, allowing him to have his way with me.

"Jafra, are you there?" He was breathy, rushed.

"Jaroslav, how have you been?"

"I survived. I guess that's something."

Survived? What the hell? "Back up, mister. What do you mean by 'survived?'"

"Long story. Let's just say that my team and I have encountered some resistance while trying to uncover this mysterious people-stealing cabal. I'll give you all the details when I see you next. I called to check on you. I know that having your brother surrender the army was difficult for the country, but probably even more for you and Krystian. Polska is now a captured territory of the Rus Empire."

"We never stood a chance. I know that now." And I did. It was a hard pill to swallow, knowing that your country fought for its independence from foreign domination… and lost.

"My father was assembling our forces to join your Poles, but the Rus moved much faster than anyone anticipated. I'm trying to convince him that we should mount a campaign of liberation, but he probably won't move without the agreement of the Baltic States and maybe even Galicia. Little Rus and Biała Ruś are lost; they are now nothing more than vassals of the empire."

We were both quiet for a minute. He wasn't going to be charging to our rescue. Even if the decision were in his hands, Polska was a bad bet right now. He was still a prince of an autonomous country; I was a fugitive, a former noble.

"It seems like a long time since we parted," I said, breaking the silence.

"An eternity. Luckily, we've both had adventures to distract us. My boys and I were near the Slovakia border tracking down some Rus insurgents, and we got in a bit of a pickle. I heard a bit about your adventures in Germania. You disassembled an entire three-story building using your brand?"

"The owner pissed me off. He turned out to be one of the three prime brand wielders. He can travel forward and backward through time. It makes him really difficult to pin down. I need to track him down again, but I got distracted."

"Killing Rus?" he asked.

"No. The last thing I want to do is leave a trail of dead Rus. They would form an arrow, pointed at my squad and me. We're also looking into the series of people who have gone missing. You were the one who first told me about it."

"I remember."

"The disappearances are increasing in number, or so I fear. All of them are between eighteen and thirty, and they're blanks. What is most damning is that there is a connection with the Court of Whispers."

He whistled at the revelation. "How do you know?"

I told him about the coins and how we had searched the victim's residences. I was at a loss as to how to proceed. He had some ideas, none of which seemed particularly promising.

"How about if I come down and visit? I could bring my boys; we are a tight unit, and if things get dangerous, you could use some extra muscle."

I thought long and hard, wanting to agree, more than anything, to see him again. "Would it be you coming, or Jaro?"

"How do you know that I'm not Jaro right now?

I laughed. "I know."

"We're the same person. If finesse is needed, I will provide it. If violence is called for, I will provide that as well." There was a pregnant pause. "I want to see you again. You may have lost your home and title, but I'm every bit as taken with you as the moment we first met."

"I miss you too," I admitted. "If it's safe, join us here. Maybe together we can peel a layer from the onion that is this Court of Whispers."

I gave him my location, and he said that he would be at my side in twenty-four hours. I felt butterflies in my stomach. I wanted his help, but I needed his strong arms, his soft lips, his commanding presence.

This time, I swore an oath to myself. I wasn't going to get lost in the moment.

Deep down, I didn't even believe it myself.

# Chapter 45



They had followed the insurgents across the border with Slovakia and almost as far as Trencin. The Vlci Temna, the Wolves of the Dark, were not officially part of the army, so they traveled in jet-black, military-style clothing.

The three men stalked through the woods wearing black trousers tucked into their tactical boots, dark, long-sleeve sweaters, and fleece balaclava. They all had blackened daggers in their hands and pulse pistols in the small of their backs. They had been together for a couple of years and could communicate with hand signals as easily as speaking.

Jaro signaled to Radomír to approach the target from the left, and he signaled for Oldřich to move in on the right.

Oldřich moved first. He had the Stínový Vlk brand, also known as the Shadow Wolf. He could move silently and fade completely into shadow. He was the perfect spy or assassin.

A man who was clearly a soldier standing guard died without raising the alarm. With a hand over his mouth and a blackened blade drawn against his throat, he fell where he stood. Oldřich dragged his body ten yards until he could bury it in shadow. His partner saw the guard fall, but he received the same treatment, and still, no warning was transmitted. They had been guarding a warehouse that had only a single street light and was far from the city limits. Without being told, the shadow wolf found the door open and slid inside while being absolutely soundless. He returned in a few minutes with his report.

Whispering, he reported, "There are about twenty inside. Most are sleeping, but three are awake playing cards."

"Can we enter the area where the men are sleeping without passing the men who are awake?" Jaro asked. Oldřich shook his head no.

Jaro pulled his pistol, as did the others, and they crept in as quietly as they could. The inside of the warehouse was mostly empty, with a few crates near the door and stacks of wooden boxes lining the far wall. Men lay on the floor, on thin mattresses and worn, dirty pillows. All were dressed in their fatigues, though only a few had left their boots or jackets on. Twenty feet away, the trio of gamblers was hovering over a table, playing cards and betting rubles.

Jaro drew his pistol as they approached the circle of light; his two companions followed suit. They got within twenty feet before they were spotted. Jaro fired, his energy pulse punching a hole through the man in the center of the trio. Radomír shot the man on their left, and Oldřich shot the one on their right. The weapons were nearly silent, but the sound of falling bodies was not. The last to be shot was able to yell something in Russian before getting gunned down.

The men sleeping on the ground woke at the sound and reached for rifles that they always kept near at hand. Most of them were still in a confused sleep state, but their training had them locating an enemy target and shooting within seconds.

Jaro and Radomír pulled off their hats and shirts as they dived for cover. Jaro transformed into his third state, the werewolf. Radomír became a dire wolf, undergoing a transformation very similar to that of his prince and commander. He was nearly two hundred pounds as a man, and he was the same mass when he became a wolf. Where Jaro was half man, half wolf, Radomír's Železný Vlk brand, the Iron Wolf, made him into a canine that was much larger than the largest wolf, with dark grey fur streaked with white and skin that was as hard as iron. He leaped at the nearest soldier, a skinny kid who was outweighed by fifty pounds. The young soldier landed hard on his back with a two-hundred-pound beast on top of him. He cried out for only a moment before incredibly powerful jaws ripped out his throat.

Jaro was equally brutal in his attack. He leapt at a pair of disoriented soldiers, raking each of them from clavicle to belt with long, razor-sharp claws. The men screamed as they were rent limb from limb while still alive.

Oldřich took cover behind the overturned card table and shot pulses at anyone holding a weapon. The savagery of the wolves made quick work of the band of terrorist insurgents.

Jaro turned back into himself. "Anyone hurt?" he asked. Oldřich shook his head no. Radomír, still in wolf form, gave a low howl. He turned to show them a bullet in his hind quarter and another in his side.

Oldřich tended to the wound. Radomír would heal faster in wolf form, and using his limited Abyrinth on changing back was too stressful when he was injured.

"Jaro, we're not at war with Rus, and yet these bastards keep raiding into Bohemia. When is your father going to go ahead and declare war?" Oldřich asked. Radomír barked in agreement.

"I don't know. I've asked him a million times, but he doesn't want to commit. He buys mechs and tanks with all of his riches, and we are conscripting men and women at an alarming rate, but still, he waits. Perhaps he thinks he should be the equal of the Rus before declaring war, but we don't have their resources and never will be a match for them."

"True," Oldřich said. "Soon, we'll have Polish troops in Rus blue knocking at our gates. We'll be fighting against an army that we could have been fighting with. A missed opportunity. I'm worried that Rus will roll through Europa without any significant resistance."

"These guys came a long way through a couple of countries to cause problems in Bohemia," Jaro said. "I find it hard to believe Rus is so subtle. Let's check their bodies, see what we can find."

Radomír returned to his human form, his injury greatly healed. They rummaged through the pockets and gear of the dead terrorists and met back at the poker table. They laid out small devices, coins, daggers, pistols, and a few other small items. Jaro dug through until he pulled up a dagger that bore a familiar symbol. He showed it to the others, and they nodded in agreement. It had the glaring image of an owl.

"These men are Rus, but I don't think that Rus sent them," Jaro said, pocketing the knife.

"They are agitators sent by the Court of Whispers to turn up the heat on starting a world war?" Radomír asked.

"That would be my guess. I believe this group is behind much of the hostilities and may have hastened a war that would have happened eventually. They were the cause of the cruise airship almost crashing."

"The one where your Polish girl came of age?" Oldřich asked, sneering.

"The very one," Jaro replied. He puffed out his chest, not liking the vibe from his brother.

"I'm not certain your father would approve of your obsession with a foreigner. Especially since she is no longer at our level."

Fire lit his eyes as he stepped only inches from his brother wolf. "You have a problem with that?" Oldřich backed up a little, but didn't break eye contact. "Don't step away from your words! Do you question the lady, or do you question my choices? Neither one is going to make me happy."

"I'm not here to make you happy, Your Highness. I'm here to defeat enemies of Bohemia and to keep your ass alive."

Jaro looked him up and down, deciding whether to end his life or not. They had found out early that his wolf made him the strongest and deadliest of the three. He knew he could kill the man, but the fact that he was so upset made him put reins on his fury.

"Those are your duties. Who I pursue is not in your purview. For the record," he snapped, turning to include Radomír, "no one, not even my father, will tell me who I will court."

"Court?" Oldřich asked, astonished. "I thought you were just fucking her. Don't let anyone know you have more on your mind. You can never marry her!"

His reflexes in his intermediate phase were higher than most humans, and he had his friend and partner by the neck before the other two could react. With his heightened strength, he lifted him until only his toes touched the ground.

They had seen that same look in his eyes many times before, and they knew that he was on the knife's edge of violence.

With measured tones, Jaro spoke. "I love you both like brothers, but do not presume too much. I am your prince, and I will be your king, but we are not equals." Only the rapid beating of their hearts could be heard. "I will forgive this because of the bond we share, but if you speak against Jafra again, I will not stay my anger."

He let his friend down, and Oldřich wouldn't meet his gaze. Radomír was silent.

"I'm going back to Polska. You two find the link between these raids and the Court of Whispers. When we know about their infrastructure, we'll seek them out and crush them."

# Chapter 46

"Jafra, dear. This is your mother." The voice over the radio was very familiar.

"I know who you are, Mother," I replied. "How is Father?"

"Your father is fine. So are Jurek and Dominica. How are you, dear? Are you still in Warszawa?" Her voice sounded strained, and I worried that she couldn't handle all of the terrible things that had happened to us recently.

"No, Mother, the capital has fallen into the hands of the enemy. I am somewhere in Polska, and we are trying to track down some bad actors."

"If our army is defeated, disbanded, you should come here and join us. We still have money and a good reputation. We can try to rebuild here."

What was she talking about? Leave our country forever? "No, I have important work to do here. Stefak surrendered the army, but I'll never give up. I will see these invaders killed or driven from our lands!"

"Darling, please don't talk like that. You're a girl, a young woman. Fighting is best left to the men." She paused, and I was too angry to say anything. "There is some good news. I have spoken with the queen recently. She is still amenable to discussing a match with her boy Stanisław."

To be honest, I hadn't thought about him in a while. The fact that he was heir to a throne that might never be reclaimed didn't factor into my deliberations. He was perfect in so many ways—a perfect face, a perfect body, great hair, and despite evidence to the contrary, I knew he was highly intelligent. As the commanding general of the Polish forces, though, he was a failure. I didn't really know enough about tactics to pin the defeat on him or to know it was inevitable all along. What I did know was that he didn't stir feelings in me, not the kind I would need to bear him children and wake up next to him every day for the rest of my life.

"I am much too busy, Mother. I lead a small group, and we are doing what we can to advance the resistance." I paused for several moments. "If I die, know that I died to free Polska."

There was much crying, but in the end, I made no commitment to rejoin them and made it very clear that I was not ready to enter into an engagement with Stanisław. She was crushed, but it was my life, and I couldn't marry to help my family. Besides, as a girl, I would be leaving our home to live in my husband's home. How would that help House Sobieski?

Thinking about men brought Jaroslav to mind. He would be arriving in a day or so, and I wasn't sure how I would act. I may have still been eighteen, but I was legally an adult and a military officer. Of an army that was disbanded.

I missed his smell. I wanted to be swept up in his arms and held tightly against his chest. I would bury my face in his shirt and take in his manly scent.

I closed my eyes and was transported back to the few hours we spent alone together. The heat of his skin as he crushed against me, his arms holding me, made me feel more secure than at any time since the war began. The way he kissed me was passionate and forceful. When we kissed, I felt like he needed it as much as I did, like war was poison and my lips held the cure. I recall my mind going blank, and only the feel of our tongues intertwining was real to me. Gasping for breath as we tried our best to devour each other. The scrape of his stubble on my porcelain skin was opposed by the softness of his lips on mine. Too few kisses.

I remember his hands on me, the first set of hands to touch me intimately. As I remembered, I could feel his hands on my breasts. Starting with caresses, then moving to rough squeezes. I thought of what he did with his fingers, how he touched me between my legs and played me like a cello. He knew the cords that sent me over the edge, giving me pleasure that I never knew was possible. I felt myself getting excited at the memory, tingling in my nether region.

Lastly, I thought of how, after giving me pleasure, he dominated me to get his payment. Was I forced, or was I a willing participant? Not forced, but I knew that I wouldn't have gone that far without being coaxed. It was a combination of curiosity and desire, made reality by a dominant male.

I wondered for a second if I could be talked into doing more. One minute, I thought that I would never submit before marriage. The next minute, I was picturing it happening.

I wasn't sure if I was ready, but I'm not sure anyone is prepared until after the fact, when they realize that the moment was written in their book of life. Just like death, it happens when fate, or God, dictates it to be the right time.

At some point, I had fallen asleep. The transport jarring to a stop woke me, and I looked around, a bit dazed.

"We're here, Kapitan," Julia said.

I had stopped trying to get them to call me Jafra. Stanisław might think he removed me from the army, but I no longer recognized his authority. I gave the others the right to walk away, and not a one even considered leaving. When we met, I had a lot more to lose than they did, but now that I had lost the mansion, the wealth, and social status, we were equally fucked.

She could see the confusion on my face. "We've arrived at Lodz."

The prince may have lost faith in me, but I'd fought and bled, and he had not, so I had some cachet with my fellow soldiers. They had let me know that my brother Krystian had been taken prisoner and was being held in Lodz. I had no idea where Stefek was. I assumed he was making sure his wife was safe and far from Warszawa.

I was told that Krystian had come across a lovely Rus girl named Irina. What he didn't know was that she was one of the infamous Nikolaeva sisters. They had a reputation for being rotten to the core. Most of the Rus sent to invade Polska were conscripts. Men and women who were forced to travel a thousand miles to attack people they had no genuine ill will towards. It's easy to hate invaders, but much harder to hate the people you are terrorizing. With that in mind, when my brother saw a beautiful, young Rus maid, he let the wrong head do the thinking.

"What do we know about these women?" I asked.

"Bitches," Izabel corrected. "They are the enemy, and these two, especially, are bitches. I'm told they are quite attractive. No doubt they used their feminine wiles to snare your brother in a honey pot."

I looked at Filip, who nodded. "We are simple creatures."

Marcin sat across from me in the back of the vehicle. "Despite the coarse language, Izabel is right. We men are taught not to harm women, but these two are killers and our enemies. They are very dangerous, and if you get the chance, kill. Don't search your soul for a more peaceful option. Stabbing the bitches in the back is the safest and best thing you can do to save your own life and the lives of the rest of us."

Filip looked at his notes and read them aloud. "Irina and Sofiya Nikolaeva. Sofiya is the elder by a year. Sofiya is, wow, she's six feet tall, about one hundred and sixty pounds. She has light brown hair, cut short, well above the shoulder. Thin body, no chest, but a healthy behind."

"How is her ass relevant?" Izabellala asked. Both Julia and I nodded in agreement.

"Ask your brother," he replied with a smile aimed at me. "She has a mental ability to cause mass confusion; her brand is called the Mindshard. Basically, if you are in her line of sight, she can turn you into a lost simpleton." Flipping the page. "The younger is Irina. She has blonde hair, almost white, and it's cut to mid-back length. They are both beautiful, but Irina is considered the true stunner. She stands at about five feet seven, about a hundred thirty pounds. Athletic figure, curvy, and she has very classic Rus features. She has the Arcstorm brand."

"What is that?" Jacek asked. "I don't like the sound of that."

"It gives the bearer the ability to launch electric shocks."

"Holy crap," Jacek remarked.

"Not lightning bolts, but still, serious shocks. Possibly lethal." I had to study the brands in school, and though I hadn't memorized them all, that one popped into my head because I'd thought it was cool. "Where is he being held?"

"County jail, of course," Filip answered. "Already built, serves the purpose."

"My brother can melt and reform metal at will. No regular jail cell can hold him."

"It must be so cool to have a brand," Jacek sighed.

"It has its positives and negatives. I'm sure he was captured for his name as much as his brand."

"You know that this is probably a trap," Filip said. The mood in the car became somber. "They've been killing a lot of wielders. They might be holding him because he's a good kisser, but more likely, they're trying to lure you into their clutches."

I hadn't thought about it, but it made perfect sense. I was a rarity. I had also caused Rus a lot of resources. If they thought they could control me, they would do what they could to take me alive. We talked about strategy until my head hurt. We stopped at an abandoned farm and parked behind the house, out of sight of the road.


Julia was the mousy type and didn't even look like the teenager that she still was. She'd gotten harder since the war started, but for today, she fell back on her humble appearance, wearing a dirty, white cotton dress with scuffed, brown canvas shoes. She carried a loaded handgun, but no one could see it inside her basket of baguettes.

I was happy to see her return unharmed. "Are you ok?" She nodded. "Have a seat. Here's a glass of wine," I said, handing her a glass. "How close were you able to get?"

She sipped the heady drink, then sat back in the rusty metal chair and smiled.

"Very close. I saw the morning changing of the guard and the evening shift change. My brother did a little time…"

"Reeeally?" Borys exclaimed. Do tell!"

"Shut up," Filip said. "Continue, please."

"It's a county jail, not a federal facility, so they usually house not more than a hundred prisoners. They have three eight-hour shifts, with a kapitan, a sierżant, and six or seven guards. They might also have extra staff to process paperwork or maintain the facilities. There are at least three times the required number of guards going in and out. A lot of what I would call hard men. The guards in jail can be assholes, but these 'guards' are killers, for sure."

"I wish I could say that I was surprised, but this is what I expected. What I'm not sure about is how many of them are channelers or wielders." I thought for a minute. "Did you see the sisters?"

"No, didn't see any women at all."

"I know they're close. I can almost sense them. Did anyone stop you? Give you a hard time?" She shook her head.

This troubled me. We could hold our own against a couple of dozen soldiers, especially with my abilities, but a couple of high-powered wielders could turn the tables and get us all killed. I explained that I should get close to see if I could sense anyone with special abilities.

"I know you're the boss, but that's a really bad idea," Jacek said. I could see from their faces that he had spoken for all of them.

"If this is a trap like I'm almost certain that it is, they'll have your description. They weren't looking for someone like Julia." Filip thought about it. "Or, they knew she was casing the place, and let her come back to us with information that is incomplete and gives us a false sense of security. The place might be crawling with wielders, or they might have a way to neutralize your brand."

I wanted to argue, to tell them that I was the only person for the job because I was the only person alive who could tell if someone was powered without looking at their back. I was ready to pull rank, flaunt my power, but I was beaten to the punch.

"I'll go inside," the large man said from somewhere far above me.

"Karol, I should go."

"No, Kapitan, it must be me. They know you, and they're waiting for you to try and break in."

I looked at the giant of a man, a protector who was easily the most gentle person on the team. "How are you going to get in?"

"Well, if you're a criminal, they send you to jail." He put a gun in his waistband and took off his dog tags. He already had a week's growth on his chin; he didn't look like a prim and proper soldier. The others took it well, but he could see the consternation on my face. "Don't worry. I'll take a few shots at a cop, miss of course, and allow myself to be apprehended. Easy."

I protested, but was outvoted. The big man gave us a sheepish grin, then went out into the night. I had a difficult time getting to sleep, worrying about a man older than me and almost three times my weight. In the morning, we got an early report from Julia.

"He was at a late-night bar and grill, and after a couple of drinks, started shooting at a moose head on the wall."

I was confused. "A moose head?"

She looked at me like I was stupid. "Yeah, a moose head. A hunting trophy. Anyway, believe it or not, two security men held him down until the constable arrived. He was carted off to jail for holding and will be processed later today."

"Is it normal for a person to be taken to jail before seeing the magistrate?" Filip asked.

Marcin answered, "No, not normally. They would usually be taken to a smaller facility, but it was Friday last night, so he can't be arraigned until Monday. Because it will be almost three days, they took him to jail for holding. I imagine his immense size made the local authorities think twice about trying to hold him on their own."

"Au contraire, mon frère." Julia was whispering, even though we were in a secure location. "I spoke to some people who are still loyal... frankly, almost everyone is loyal to Polska. They say that, true, he did shoot the moose, but when the constable arrived, he took Karol to prison and gave some of the boys a wink. He could have housed him at the city jail, but Karol whispered to him for a good minute or two, and it was off to the county lockup."

"I'm so glad to hear that we're not alone out here." I felt a sense of pride in my countrymen.

"So, they will find out on Monday that there are no witnesses," she pulled out Karol's gun and put it on the table, "and no weapons were found on the suspect. He will be set free and will return to us with a report before lunch."

Filip stood up and spread out the plans of the jail that he'd obtained from the city records office. "That gives us two days to come up with a plan to break out Colonel Sobieski."

"And not get ourselves killed," Izabel said.

"And defeat the Nikolaeva sisters, who are no doubt in or around the prison," Jacek added.

"And take on not only five times our number, but fight against an unknown number of channelers and wielders," Borys groused. "I was worried that this would be hard."


"Jafra, you have a visitor," Izabel said, a devilish grin on her face.

A visitor? What are they talking about? I turned around to see Jaroslav enter the room. He had two men behind him, the other members of his team. His milk-chocolate hair was cut short, not as short as a soldier's, but much shorter than the last time we were together. His team had similar cuts, like they had cut each other's hair in the middle of a forest somewhere.

"Vlci Temna?" I asked.

"What?" Marcin asked.

Jaroslav smiled as he ushered his men in. "Some call us the Tri-Wolves; in our country, we are known as Wolves of the Dark."

Radomír leaned against a wall, reaching for his pack of cigarettes. "We heard that one of your team was captured last night." He went to light a smoke, but the women all stared daggers at him, and he put them away.

"We're offering to help you break him out," Jaroslav said cheerily.

"He's getting out on Monday," Julia said before biting into an apple. Jaro and the others looked confused. I explained the plan to them, and they still weren't sure.

"My brother Krystian was captured. We are going to break him out."

Oldřich spoke first. "We have gone on missions with Krystian before. He is a good man."

"If you'll have us, we will help you."

"That's a relief," Filip said. "Now we're only eleven versus forty-something."

"When Karol gets back, we'll have a better idea of what we're up against," Borys said.

"Have you heard of the Nikolaeva sisters?" I asked.

"Radomír, you've met them before," Jaroslav said with a chuckle.

"I certainly have. The older one is… meh. The younger? Quite lovely. I can see Krystian falling into her web." Radomír sat on a bench between Jacek and Marcin.

"Okay, Jafra, do you have any kind of a plan?" Jaroslav looked exasperated with his own men.

"We're... working on it."


Monday came and went, and there was no sign of Karol. Julia was working all of the sources she'd developed in the few days that we had been in town, and they were either missing or had become useless. I was really starting to worry, but Jaroslav kept a cooler head.

"No doubt some local has turned on us for an extra ration of bread, or to get out of being beaten to death. It would seem that your teammate won't be coming out without our assistance."

Julia entered, and the look on her face was one of defeat. "The local magistrate will not be helping us." She sat down, tears staining her cheeks. "He's hanging from a light pole downtown."

"The whole plan is busted. I suggest we break in and take our chances."

I looked at Jaroslav, wondering if he was really the more contemplative of his manifestations. He was supposed to be the calm one, the thinker, but he was ready to go. I had ideas and pieces of a plan, but not a complete one. I've been accused of overthinking things sometimes, so, with the lives of my soldiers, the Czechs, poor Karol, and of course, my brother in my hands, I said, "Fuck it. Gear up. Let's go!"

They all looked at me like I was crazy, but they geared up, and in minutes, we were on the road. The Rus might have been expecting us to make our eventual jailbreak at night, but it was nine in the morning, and shit was about to hit the fan.

We pulled up in our armored personnel carrier a few blocks from the prison and parked in an alley out of direct sight. We piled out, all of us with armor, guns, and knives, as well as swords for Filip and me.

I was about to give out assignments when I felt something. They all hovered, waiting for me to speak.

"There's a channeler." I followed the trail of Abyrinth that seemed to be flowing to a spot in a second-story window, a block down and a block over. "Probably a sniper, second floor, over there." I pointed. Oldřich took off some of his gear and handed it to Jaroslav and Borys.

"Let me take care of this." He almost ran down the street, but didn't make the slightest sound. Most of my crew looked at Jaroslav and Radomír.

"He is the Stínový Vlk," Jaroslav answered their obvious question. "The Shadow Wolf. His brand allows him to move absolutely silently and to disappear in shadow. He is the fastest and deadliest knife fighter I know. That sniper is as good as dead."

True to his reputation, Oldřich returned five minutes later and signaled 'mission accomplished' to his teammates.

"Time for me to gear up." Jaroslav concentrated, and I saw the hair on his head go from luscious brown to snowy white in only a second. He stood a fraction taller and looked noticeably stronger. "Alright, let's fuck some stuff up."

Izabelalla approached the main entrance of the prison, her hips swaying like a pendulum. She wore a tight pink cashmere sweater that seemed demure yet showcased her attributes to best effect. Her black leather skirt was just as tight and shockingly short. I watched her walk and was amazed at how confident she looked while balancing on black four-inch heels. Even from a hundred feet away, I could see the guards' mouths hanging open.

The prison had a fifteen-foot-tall chain-link fence with coils of razor wire lining the top. Fifty feet from the gate was the building itself, a massive three-story building with tiny, barred windows every ten feet or so. The red brick was seamless and featureless, giving it a bland and oppressive feel. Probably what they were going for.

The men were all smiles as she approached and started making conversation. She talked to them for several minutes, occasionally pointing at us where we were standing around a street vendor, before they laid down their weapons and ran off down the street. We jogged over to join her.

"That went well."

"What did you say to them?" I asked.

"First, I made sure they were Polish and gave them the opportunity to get the hell out of here. I want to spare as much blood of our countrymen as possible." She pointed at a nice sedan, parked in the warden's parking spot. "That car is owned by the Nikolaeva sisters. They are on-site today; they come every other day or so."

"Did they know about any other channelers or wielders inside?" Filip asked.

"They said that there are nearly a hundred soldiers in there, maybe a half dozen are channelers. There are some high-ranking Rus soldiers whom they don't know much about."

"A hundred?" Julia asked. "I guess I didn't get an accurate count of how many went in and how many came out."

"Ya think?" Jacek asked.

I couldn't read Jaro and his boys, but my crew started to look pessimistic. In my opinion, we had passed the point of no return. I started shooing them back.

"Everyone back. Get back." I kept waving at them. "Get ready to run inside, armed and ready!"

"What's the signal?" Jacek asked from across the street.

I saw vast clouds of Abyrinth in the air, surrounding us and floating around like cottony clouds that skimmed the ground. I controlled the power, causing it to coalesce and wind into long, thick tentacles. I reached with the tentacle and wrapped it under and around the sedan. Such a beautiful car, long and aerodynamic, with a white metallic skin, chrome trim, moldings, and bumpers.

What the rest saw was a large car flying up about a dozen feet, then flying backward past their position and down the street to about one hundred feet distant. I may have thrown like a girl normally, but with my power, I threw like an Olympic javelin thrower. The car easily tore through the fence and crashed into the prison's front entrance. I had thought about caving in a side wall, but there were prisoners there, and I didn't want to hurt anyone who might be held there as a prisoner of war. The building shook from the impact, and the whole front was caved in.

Everyone followed my orders and rushed the building before the car had settled. I moved it out of the way, and they surged forward.

In the lead were the Bohemian wolves. They held pulse pistols and fired as they crossed the threshold. My unpowered crew, aside from Filip, were using Sokół semi-automatic service rifle, Szabla revolvers, and enough grenades and ammunition to fight a war, which is what we planned to do.

Jaro was first through the breach, a pistol in each hand and a wide, manic smile on his handsome face. He shot at anything that moved, taking out guards left and right. The same for his brethren, killing wholesale and moving through the halls as fast as they could run. Filip kept pace a step behind, and he was followed by Julia, who was out for blood.

I tried to keep up, but I didn't like the idea of anyone sneaking up on us, so I followed close on the heels of Marcin and Borys. They were ready to fight, but the boys in the front didn't leave them many targets to shoot at.

The inside of the prison was as dull and nondescript as the outside. There was a long hall with many offices and administrative rooms, and at the far end, there was a steel door with a window. I was worried that we would have difficulty getting through the locked door, but guards rushed through it from the inside. What happened next shocked everyone, including me, though I had expected it.

Jaro changed into his werewolf, and Radomír transformed into a large dire wolf with iron-hard skin. With animal grace, they leapt into the mass of Rus soldiers trying to storm out the door. Rado took a man down and went for his throat, ripping it out with a yank of his massive, fang-filled jaw. Blood sprayed like a lawn sprinkler, coating his steel gray fur as he moved on to the next victim.

Oldřich slid through the cramped opening like a thread through the eye of a needle. He had inhuman speed and dexterity, his foot-long daggers slashing wrists and throats with graceful ease.

I had watched Jaro in action, but not in his third state. He was no longer the man who held me in his arms and kissed away my better judgment. He was a feral demon from one of the lower pits of hell. His wiry legs propelled him like a spring releasing its tension. With his arms outspread, he raked an enemy on each side with his long, knife-like claws.

Men were screaming, and curses in Russian echoed in the narrow hallway beyond. A soldier shot him in the arm, and he flinched with the force of the impact, then ignored the pain as he sank his long fangs into the face of the man. As he crunched down on the narrow skull, skin tearing and pulling away, he punched his fist through the man's chest to grip his beating heart before extracting it from its cage of ribs.

The three wolves were more beast than men, using their heightened speed and strength to overpower their opponents.

My soldiers were even more dedicated to the cause because this was their country, and these men had taken it. Unlike the wolves, they relied on their training to systematically lay down fire without hitting our allies or each other. I was pretty sure that Marcin missed everything he shot at, but I really appreciated him stepping out of his comfort zone and risking his life to join the rescue mission.

Julia wasn't accurate either, but she made up for it by firing constantly. I don't know if it was nerves or anger;

probably some of both. Izabelalla was there, but she hid behind the boys as much as possible. When opportunity arose, she would peek out and fire off a shot. Filip was firing his pulse pistol on rapid fire; he was accurate and deadly. Borys held a shield and gave protection to the others; he wasn't as accurate since losing an eye.

The big surprise was Jacek. Though older than me, he seemed like a greasy kid, but he was perhaps even a better shot than I was. He controlled his fire, picking and hitting what he aimed at without fail.

It sounded foolish, but I wasn't worried about my own safety. I felt like everyone was my responsibility, including the wolves. My troops followed me in a desperate bid to rescue my brother. They were dedicated to the resistance and to freeing Polska from Rus domination. Still, their willingness to risk themselves for one man, a man they didn't know, was touching, and it placed a ton of responsibility on my shoulders. Jaroslav and his partners were friends with my brother, but I couldn't help thinking their decision to join us was based on how Jaroslav felt about me.

I finally got past the door and into the hall to see the chaos that had erupted in the jail. The Bohemians went down the center, leaving body parts and a bloody smudge on the painted cement floor. My crew left cleaner bodies, just a few holes here and there.

I saw Julia fall, and I ran over to check on her. She had taken a bullet to the thigh and a second to her forearm. She had been tough as nails a few seconds ago, but now she was wailing in pain and holding on to her arm wound. Neither looked life-threatening at the moment, but I applied some field dressings and, with a whisk of my hand, slid her down the hall, then behind a door.

Ok, I am angry now. There were still about eight Rus soldiers who were hunkered down behind overturned metal tables. I wove the Abyrinth in the air, creating long, thin ropes that I controlled like a snake charmer controls his snakes. There were eight cords of hardened energy, one for each of our enemies. I sent them out until they looped around their necks, then I tightened the nooses. Lifting them, I allowed them to kick and struggle as their air was cut off, and they slowly choked to death. I heard a couple of gasps of surprise, but I was too engrossed to give them any attention. One or two of them had stopped moving when I suddenly felt like the world had been turned upside down.

A wave of confusion flowed through the room, causing everyone to drop their weapons and forget what they were doing only seconds prior. I forgot where I was, why I was there. I literally couldn't string two thoughts together.

I saw out of the corner of my eye a tall woman with short hair hitting a giant wolf with a steel pipe. The wolf howled but seemed too confused to run from her. A shorter woman ran in, and lightning arced from her fingertips. She went from person to person, making them dance with the electricity flowing through their bodies. I felt like this was bad, like I should stop this somehow, but… I lost my train of thought.

A loud noise came from behind me. It hurt my ears, and two more loud bangs followed. The fog that hung over my mind cleared, and I was brought back to reality as if I'd been slapped in the face.

Borys, Jacek, Marcin, and Izabelalla were all lying on the ground, steam rising from their bodies from the electric shocks. The woman who had been shocking everyone, Irina Nikolaeva, stood still, in a state of disbelief. She looked at a woman I assumed was Sofiya Nikolaeva, lying on the ground, bleeding from three bullet holes.

I turned to see Julia lying on the ground, a smoking gun in her hand, and her head resting on the ground. I rushed to her and was relieved that she wasn't dead.

"You killed her?"

"Somebody had to. You all started drooling and walking around looking at the ceiling." With effort and a little help from me, she got into a sitting position. "I guess her ability to make you all simpletons has a range, and I was down the hall. I crawled here and saw the other one shocking the guys." She smiled. "I can hit what I aim at if I have a second to concentrate. Three rounds, tight pattern through her black heart."

"Somebody help me!" I heard a woman's voice say. I saw Irina on her knees, trying to revive her sister. She held the woman in her arms as tears flowed down her beautiful face.

I walked over to stand over her. She was an invader; she had harmed my troops, my friends. Her sister had beaten the wolves unconscious with a steel bar. I was out of sympathy. My lieutenant was the only other person left standing. I gave him a knowing look.

"Filip," was all I needed to say. He pulled his pulse pistol and, without ceremony, put a pulse round through the back of her head. Her perfect features exploded, coating her sister with brain and gore.

"What the hell happened?" Izabelalla was pulling herself off the floor. Her hair was frazzled, and she looked like she had been through a war.

In the next couple of minutes, the rest recovered from their electrocution, and Marcin attended to Julia's wounds. Jaro had returned to his human form, but Radomír stayed as a wolf.

"Rado, find Krystian."

The wolf nodded once and started sniffing around for my brother. I followed, with Filip and Jaro behind me. The wolf sniffed here and there, checking out each cell. We passed one with a large man inside who looked very familiar. He'd been beaten and was slumped in a corner. I summoned tendrils of Abyrinth, and with an anger barely under control, I ripped the bars from their mounts on the concrete floor. Filip rushed to help the big man up.

When he saw me, he mumbled, "I'm sorry, Kapitan."

"It was not your fault, Karol. Some person in town betrayed us. Filip will take you back to the rest of the team."

I continued the search with Jaro and Radomír. We found ourselves in the back of the kitchen, and the wolf sniffed and pawed at a door set into the floor. When Jaro opened it and lifted the door back, I could see that a steep ladder dropped down to a dark basement below. I tried to go down, but Jaro cut me off.

"I know that you're a strong, capable woman, but please, dear Jafra, let me go first." His smile was reassuring, and I regretted that we had to jump straight into action without having time to catch up. I could see that his bullet wound had partially healed, but was still oozing blood. He spun around and went down the steep steps like they were a ladder. Radomír tossed him a light before following him down. I brought up the rear as shots rang out.

It was dark, and I couldn't get my bearings until I heard a familiar snarl. I listened to the sound of flesh being sliced and torn from a person. The fact that I knew what that sound was horrified me.

With my new sense, I could see a blanket of energy wrapped around what I knew was Jaro in his werewolf form and, lower to the ground, Radomír in his wolf form. I saw a very faint source behind a concrete wall, and in the corner of the room, a third powerful source of Abyrinth. I was still by the door and found a light switch. I turned it on to find no one there. I pulled at the strings of energy, leaving whoever it was without Abyrinth. A tall, pale man popped into view, with greasy, short, black hair and greasy skin. He wore the uniform of a Rus major and looked surprised to be discovered.

"Well, hello there," he said in broken Polish.

"What is your name?" I demanded as I pulled my gun. I didn't need the gun, but it helped to convey the seriousness of the situation. He stepped over the flayed corpse of one of the guards and saluted.

"I am Barón Major Sokolov of His Majesty's Royal Army."

"Is my brother behind this wall?"

"Um, if your brother is the Sobieski, then yes. His ability to melt and mold steel makes him especially difficult to contain. Here, let me show you how the lever works." He tripped a secret lever, and a foot-thick section of concrete rotated out into the room. I saw Krystian inside, sitting in a corner and holding his hands up to shade his eyes from the light. He had evidently been kept with little food and water based on his weight loss, and in the dark, as there was no light fixture in his eight-by-eight cell.

I stepped in and helped him to his feet.

"We're out here fighting, and you're in here resting?" I joked.

"You're doing so well. Didn't think you needed my help." He stumbled out, looking weak. Like Karol, he was bruised, but his bruises were yellowing with age. He was probably beaten, then thrown into the cement box, and only fed and given water a couple of times in the last week.

"Do you know this man?" Jaro asked, pointing at the Rus.

"Jaro! Good to see you!" He looked at me, then back at Jaro. "You'd better be treating my sister respectfully. If not, when I recover, I'll kick your ass." He looked at the major. "He never touched me."

"He says his name is Barón Major Sokolov," Radomír said, pulling the man along by the sleeve.

"Sokolov? As in Colonel Dmitri Sokolov?" Krystian looked energized, despite his haggard state.

"You know this colonel?" Jaro asked.

"His soldiers committed the massacre at Lublin. The colonel became a giant, with the strength to match. He executed my squad by squeezing their heads in his massive hand."

"That sounds like the same thing that happened at Braniszów," I said. I looked at the group around me. "We may not be able to defeat the Rus, but this colonel needs to die in the most painful way possible."

# Chapter 47

I sent for all the healers I could find. Nobles were extremely difficult to locate, and I feared I would have to bring in a healer from a neighboring country. Julia was hurt badly, and a few of the others were in danger of long-term internal injury from electrocution.

With Jaro's permission, I sent Oldřich and Izabelalla to run down a lead. The Rus major had heard about the Court of Whispers, but he didn't know much more than we did. He'd found out that they were behind a string of terrorist attacks in Moscva and around the country. His opinion was that they were trying to push Rus into war with the West and the rest of Europa. He did have intelligence that there was a high-level member of the Court in Warszawa.

After everyone was healed and we had replenished our supplies, we would be heading back to the capital. I got Jacek's radio and decided to call in with our current status.

"Kapitan Sobieski calling to check in with General Poniatowski," I said into the radio. There was some static, then silence, and after a full two minutes, Stanisław came on the line.

"Jafra? How have you been?"

"A lot has gone on since I saw you last. I'm sorry that I haven't checked in for a while, but I've been chasing down wielders who carry prime brands."

"Catch me up. I'm not sure what that even means."

"Every brand has been given to dozens of wielders across the world. There could be ten others who carry the exact brand you bear. The exceptions are the prime brands.

There are only three, and each is totally unique. I carry one, I found a Brit who has one, and a couple of weeks ago, we left Germania, where the third one is.”

“That’s very interesting, but how is this helping our resistance? I am living in seclusion in a foreign land while my country has been stolen from me.” He sounded tense. I guessed that he was starting to regret his decision to declare war on a much larger country.

“You mean our country. We all lost our homes and fortunes. Many tens of thousands have lost their lives.” He replied with a grunt. “I’ve been told that if the three prime brands work together, their power can become a great weapon that we could use to free us from the Rus.” I could hear him grumbling to himself. He was under a lot of stress, and I felt bad for him. He was first in line to become king, but now it looked like that would never happen.

“I’m skeptical, but at this point, it may not matter. How are you, dear? I felt better when you were serving under your brother, but after having you report directly to me, I think you are less safe.”

“I’ll admit, a lot has happened. My team and I snuck back into the capital. I went home to help evacuate my family just as the Rus invaded our property. I got them out in the nick of time. I stayed to fight with Jaroslav—”

“Jaroslav? Are you talking about that Bohemian?”

“Yes, Prince Jaroslav Záhoř. We met him in Gdańsk. He was on his way to meet with your father when we were all attacked at a club. We found out that the club was run by a secret society that is trying to gain access to Abyrinth’s Fire.”

“He traveled with you from Gdańsk to Warszawa?”

"It was safer to travel in numbers. He had his team, and I had mine. Anyhow, I got my family out, but they were already attacking our outbuildings, and so we had to stay and fight."

"Both teams?"

"I had released my team for some leave. It was only a dozen soldiers. The two of us were able to kill them. My body count has grown since I last saw you."

"I bet it has," he replied. I didn't like his tone in the least. "How long were the two of you alone together?" Restrained anger simmered in his voice now.

"Are you asking as my commander, or as a suitor?"

"You don't ask the questions here. I do."

"So, neither." I was not in the mood for his temper or his childish behavior. "I'm still here, in our country. I'm risking my life and the lives that have been entrusted to me to fight the invaders, the army that conquered our country. You and your father rule in absentia."

"You can't speak to me that way! I'm the Commanding General!"

"You rule over an army that has surrendered. Your family was chased from your ancestral home and from the country they ruled over. Take off that fancy uniform made for parades, with a chest full of medals that you never earned, and put on what I'm wearing. Camouflage utilities, made for fighting. No medals, no ceremonial swords, no niceties that we can no longer afford. You have a strong brand, one made for fighting. Come home and fight with us! Get blood on your hands!"

There was a long silence. I wanted to go further, but I stopped myself.

"I should have known better than to give a girl any responsibility. You're away from your parents for a minute, and you become a whore."

I felt like I had been slapped in the face across our radio line. A whore? I wasn't exactly innocent, but I was technically still a virgin. My anger was about to boil over. I wanted to vent on him, tell him how wrong he was. But I was maturing ahead of schedule, and I decided to be the bigger man. Sort of.

"You would know about whores. Apparently, you spend a lot of time with them." When I spoke, I was remarkably calm. "I'm not sure which is worse, flaunting your whoremongering at the airship races, where those in the public can see your shame, or having your sex parties in the royal palace. Humiliating your family's name and our country's reputation. Very sad."

I could feel the hatred on the other end of the line. He was seething, at a loss for words. I had scored my point and was content to wait for my prince to regain himself.

"I'll not stand for your insubordination or your lack of discretion. There's no room in our forces for a whore who doesn't know her place. I strip you of all rank and discharge you from the Wojsko Królewskie. I'm going to have your team reassigned. Now you can fuck whomever you please."

"I always could, Stan. I just chose not to. The Wojsko Królewskie went away when our country was taken over. I don't need your permission to fuck anyone, and I don't need your permission to keep fighting for our country's sovereignty. If I die fighting for Polska, that's a fate I can live with. Marrying a coward and a cad like you? That's something I couldn't."

I disconnected and sat back. I had burned a bridge, not just for myself, but for all of House Sobieski. My only regret was that I had no regrets.

# Chapter 48

I sat on a log down by the river. I told the teams about my exchange with Stanisław. I told them everything. The ladies were shocked, enraged. The guys were ready to kick his ass for me. Jaroslav looked like he was about to turn into the beast that was part of him. I could feel the anger and bloodlust radiating from him.

In the end, they all agreed to continue our side quest. We were going to investigate the terror cell in the heart of Warszawa and confront the Court of Whispers once and for all.

I wanted to be alone, so I walked for half an hour and found a quiet location to rest and contemplate my next move. Everything seemed so turbulent. Of course, there was the war, which had displaced my family, my people, and turned me into a violent person. My oldest brother was still out there somewhere, possibly running with his family, or perhaps mounting his own resistance to the invaders. My personal life was up in the air. I was still young, but when people were dying all around me, I felt like I needed to put aside my doubts and fears and embrace every day like it was my last. At the moment, Jaroslav walked up to me, then stood there waiting.

"You followed me?"

"Obviously. I saw that you had slipped away from camp, and I wanted to make sure that you were alright. I have heightened senses, and it was pretty easy to follow your trail." He inclined his head towards the log I was sitting on. "May I?"

"Yes. Please sit. I should have invited you to come. I've been meaning to be alone with you since… well, for a long time now."

He sat close, but not touching me. I could smell him; it was a slightly different scent than Jaro's, but both gave me a warm feeling inside. His smile was shy, and I could tell that these types of interactions were not easy for him. He held out his hand, and it was like a reflex when I took it in mine. He looked at me with his deep brown eyes, the rich color matching his short, spiky hair.

"I know you think that things might have gotten out of control, but that's not the case. From the moment I met you as Jaro, then again as Jaroslav, I've known that you are destined to be mine. War has gotten in the way of my pursuing you, and it's still not the best time to open my heart. I know that I may die any day, and I accepted that long ago. If I die protecting Bohemia, or protecting you? I would die a happy man."

"I was just thinking the same thing. No one is promised tomorrow. I could live to a hundred, or I could be killed the next time I take a stupid chance, and things don't go my way. I've given up on having titles like lady or princess…" My heart was racing as I let myself sink into those eyes.

"I don't plan to leave you again. I'll be by your side as we crush the Court of Whispers and until both our countries are made safe from Rus. We'll hunt them down, destroy their weapons, and kill their soldiers. When both are safe, you'll join me in Praha as my bride and future queen."

I thought about the two men in my life. Two handsome men who wanted me, not just physically, but found me worthy to stand beside them and rule their respective countries for the rest of our lives. They each had their positives, and to be honest, both had their negatives. Marrying Stanisław would have eventually made me queen in my own country. He was inhumanly handsome, strong, and had a great body. That arrangement would have pleased my mother to no end. Choosing anyone else would be a slight to her greater life experience.

Marrying Jaroslav would see me whisked away to a foreign land. Bohemia was our neighbor to the south, and it would be a day's airship ride or a couple of days by train, but it would still not be Polska. He was handsome the way he was, and his alter ego was even more attractive, with his defined muscles and supremely confident swagger.

Tabulating each man's qualities should have wound up in a virtual tie, but to me, it wasn't close. Jaroslav loves me, and… I love him. There, I've said it. Ok, I've thought it.

Stanisław wanted me because it was a sound political move, and hey, I was not bad to look at. Does he love me? Would any real man call the love of his life a whore?

He'd lost me long before then, but that glimpse into his character solidified the poor impression that I'd gotten of him. My decision was made, and I felt like the weight of the world had been lifted from my shoulders.

Almost like I was attacking him, I leaned over and kissed his lips. Not a hot, romantic exchange, but a hurried, desperate need for me to show my affection. I lasted only a second and caught him completely by surprise. We parted, and I looked deeply into his eyes.

"I love you." Simple and to the point.

He took a moment to let his emotions equalize. "I love you too, Jafra. I always have."

I didn't consider it poetry or some oratory that would move men to go to war, but when he spoke to me, I felt him touching my very soul. Deep in the brown forest of his stare, I could see a man laying his heart open and telling me the absolute truth, with no boundaries and no qualifications. He didn't need to fight for me, though he had on multiple occasions. He'd risked his life for me, killed for me, and recently, taken a bullet for me.

I went in again for a kiss; again, I was the aggressor. We kissed, and it was sweet, pure, but that was not what I wanted at that moment. Not what I needed.

With his arms around me, his mouth on mine, I think he felt my indecision. Easing me away from him, he began to change. I saw the color in his hair seep away into the void. He grew even bulkier, his arms firmer, and his whole body tightened with taut muscles. The most remarkable part of his transformation was his demeanor. He still radiated an undying love for me, but he had a confidence that I found intoxicating.

"Jaroslav loves you as much as a man can love a woman, but he relies on me to express it." He put a hand behind my back and another on the back of my head. Forcefully, though not aggressively, he pulled us together and kissed me. My eyes instantly closed as I let his tongue invade my mouth. It swirled around, the firm tip dancing on the roof of my mouth, the thick shaft wrapping around my yielding tongue. I wrapped my arms around him, not quite able to reach all the way around his broad, muscular back. He pulled me onto his lap, and my legs naturally wrapped around his waist. I felt his chest against mine, his manhood straining to escape its denim cage.

We kissed and touched for a long time; it was enough to get my motor running. I pushed on his chest, separating our bodies. He looked confused for a second, then looked pleased as I reached down and pulled my sweater up, pulling it off and throwing it on the ground behind the log we were sitting on.

He openly ogled my chest, then brought me in to nibble on my ear. His tongue traced the inner ridge of my ear before sucking on the lobe, then he gnawed on it playfully.

The breath exhaling from his nostrils while my earlobe was in his mouth drove me absolutely crazy. I gripped his back, my fingers digging into his shoulder blades as he moved to my neck and traced a line from my ear to my collarbone with his mouth. He licked and sucked, and I knew he could feel how fast my heart was beating through his soft lips.

"Remove your brassiere," he said breathily. He pulled off his shirt, then stared as I nervously unhooked the garment. I sat on his lap, and we looked at each other's bare chests.

His was large and flat, with areolas a little smaller than half złoty silver coins. I could tell that he wasn't flexing, but still, a shallow valley was formed by his highly toned pectorals. A little black hair ran from his collarbone down past his navel and disappeared into the top of his jeans. Even at rest, the valley continued to separate two columns of roughly square abdominal muscles. My brothers had the same, but they looked more defined and, well, sexy on Jaro.

He squeezed my right breast and corralled me with his right arm. He took my aroused nipple into his mouth and suckled like a baby before flicking it with his tongue and chewing lightly on the now erect flesh. He gave each breast his attention, spurred on by the low moan building somewhere inside me.

I stood up and climbed off his lap, staying directly in front of him. I lifted my boot, and he took the signal to help undo the laces before pulling it off. After both boots were set neatly behind him, I undid my belt, then slowly opened the buttons on the front of my uniform pants. I never lost contact with his eyes as I slid out one long leg, then the other. I threw them on my jacket and t-shirt.

He was a wise man, and he said nothing, letting me make my own decisions in my own time. With my blue eyes locked on his brown, I hooked my thumbs in the waistband of my black, lacy, bikini pants, and pulled them down to the point where they would fall on their own.

Since becoming a woman, this was the first time that I had been completely nude in front of a man. I could see the heat rising in him, but he looked at me, taking in my pert but large breasts, my stomach that had only gotten flatter since joining the army, the wide hips, and long, athletic legs. His gaze passed over my groin, where a trimmed patch of hair lay between my torso and vagina. He stared for a long time, and I could tell that he was saving the memory, seeing me at my most vulnerable for the first time. His smile grew, and it was one of pure bliss and satisfaction.

He stepped over by the pile of my clothes and laid them out flat on a pile of orange, yellow, and red leaves that had fallen. He added his shirt, then, like me, began to take off his shoes.

"Wait!" I said, almost pleading. I stepped up to him and squatted before him. I undid his laces and helped him out of his boots, with as much care as he had done mine. I lovingly removed his socks and placed them inside his boots. I stood and worked the buckle on his pants. For better or worse, being in the army meant that both sexes wore essentially the same clothes. I deftly opened the belt, then worked the buttons with ease. He looked down at me, his expression calm, but as full of life as I had ever seen a person's face. Not breaking the connection between our spirits, he pulled down his trousers and boxers at the same time, stepping out one leg, then the other. He added them to the nest he was making.

I stared at his ass as he bent to smooth the clothes. Nearly hairless, it displayed glutes that looked carved from stone. His thighs were thick like Christmas hams, with cordlike tendons attaching to the back of his knees. His calves were high on the leg and looked as firm as tempered steel. As he bent over, I saw his egg-sized testicles hanging down between his thighs. They looked like large stones swaying in a tight leather purse. When he was finished, he turned back to me, and my eyes fell to his penis. His cock. It was only semi-erect, yet still intimidating.

"Come sit," he offered. I was scared, excited, maybe a little light-headed. I joined him on the mattress made from our clothes. He kissed me softly, tenderly. I had thought that he wanted nothing more than to penetrate me, take my virginity. I was sure that was his end goal, but he was in no hurry, and that put me at ease.

We went slowly, his mouth on mine, his hand cupping my breast before running it down my side to knead my hip and buttocks. I let my hands travel all over his body, missing nothing and lingering on his balls, tickling his shaft. It was time.

"Jaro, I want you to be my first," I said, though even I could hear the wavering in my voice.

"Are you sure? We can wait until after marriage, if you're truly in love with me." He sounded sincere, but he was hard as steel, and I knew it pained him to be so noble. Would he be able to wait to consummate our union until after a priest blessed it? I actually thought he would.

"We both said it. We're going to take on the Court of Whispers and hopefully put an end to their instigation of this war. And I, at least, will pledge myself to pushing the Rus out of Polska. Tomorrow could be my last. You're the man for me, and if it makes me a whore to make love to you, then so be it!"

I lay down on my back, letting my legs fall apart. I had never felt so vulnerable in my life. I wanted this, I was ready, but I was terrified. I expected him to leap on me and slam his hard member in me. Instead, he looked down at my naked body, but focused on my face. He had a warm smile that would have been more at home on Jaroslav than on his Mr. Hyde.

Instead of lying on me, he lay down next to me. I went to talk, but he shushed me gently while stroking my hair. He kissed my eyes, my cheeks, then lightly kissed my lips while his hand squeezed my breasts and pinched my nipples between his strong fingers. He kissed me passionately, tasting my lips, sucking my lower lip, and chewing lightly on it. His hand glided down the plane of my stomach, making it flutter with anticipation. I knew where he was going, and his taking so long to get there was driving me crazy! After what seemed like an eternity, his fingers reached between my legs to softly cup my sex. He held it there, feeling the heat radiate from my loins. I lost myself in his kiss, so when his finger parted my lower lips, I was momentarily shocked.

Using my own wetness, he glided two fingers across my clitoris, making me quake with lust. It was only the opening salvo of a war to bring me to climax. Keeping his mouth on mine, he worked my button as a master pianist does the keys of a Steinway. I felt a sensation building in my lower abdomen, a rush of blood to my hypersensitive genitals, then the explosion. My body jerked involuntarily as waves of pleasure cascaded throughout my body. I clutched at him, my nails digging into the solid flesh of his arm. I bit his lip, much harder than I would, even when playing at love. He slightly grunted at the pain as he moved his hand back to the curve of my thigh.

"Oh my God!" I got out between gasps of air. "That was even better than before!" I looked at him, remarking how incredibly sexy he was. "I still want to… I want you inside of me." I should have been mortified, saying what I just said. I should have turned beet red, but it was the truth, and it felt natural for me to tell him.

I looked at his cock. Though impressive, it had lost half its tumescence. "Do you want me to…"

"No, there's more work to be done," he said while taking a position between my legs. He pushed my thighs apart and lowered his head until his mouth met my vagina. "You're not yet ready for me." His smile had a touch of the old rascal that I had fallen in love with. "Lay back and close your eyes." I did as I was told. There was a light breeze wafting over my naked body, chilling me, making the fine hair on my arms and neck stand on end. My nipples were erect, but became rock hard as I felt kisses around my area.

He kissed the outer lips, then licked in long strokes. I wanted him to rush to my clit, but he tortured me by devouring every other spot, including the soft skin on the inside of my thighs. When I thought that I couldn't take it any longer, he finally began to flick my most sensitive spot with the tip of his tongue. He swirled around it in endless circles, then toggled it back and forth like a light switch.

I felt the familiar feeling, the one that I'd had two times in my life, counting today. My orgasm was building slowly, like a bonfire that was getting more fuel every few seconds. I knew it was coming soon.

I felt the crescendo so close, then he took my pearl in his mouth, applying suction. His timing was perfect, and I lost all control of myself. I clawed at the clothes beneath me, my back arching as if I'd been struck by an electrical current. Pleasure that I'd never thought possible coursed through me, catching my breath, making my heart skip a beat. I eventually had to push on his blonde hair to get relief. He smiled at me as I lay there trying to catch my breath.

"We can stop here," he said, and I believed he meant it, though he would suffer and maybe regret being a gentleman later. I looked at him through hazy eyes. He was so beautiful. His body was perfect, his face warmed my heart. And whether he meant it or not, I loved him for giving me another chance to back out.

"Does it get even better than that? I don't think my heart can take it." I knew that I must have had a stupid smile on my face, but I didn't care.

"Probably not, but it's something that we can enjoy simultaneously, and it brings a man and woman closer, if they truly care for each other." I looked at his staff, now nearly full mast.

"It looks like we both enjoyed what you just did."

"I enjoy giving and receiving."

He crawled up until his knees were under my bent legs. He grasped his shaft and gave it a few slow tugs, bringing it up to full inflation. He guided it up and down my dewy slit, getting my natural lubrication on the head. It felt nothing like his mouth and was very different than his fingers. Maybe it was because I knew what it was, but it was different and breathtaking.

He pushed against my opening, and though it felt like I was being split apart, I don't think even the crown was inside me. I was very wet, and it helped a lot. I was more relaxed than I had ever been, until I felt the intruder storming my gate.

"I'm sorry, dearest, but this next part will be… uncomfortable."

With a violent thrust, he tore through my maidenhead. Uncomfortable was not the correct term. It hurt! He applied steady pressure, letting me acclimatize to each fraction of an inch. With a bit of pain, I felt the head pass. He slowly pushed, like a train easing into the station. It took a long time for him to get even half of himself in me, and that was enough time for the pain to subside. Mostly.

I didn't realize that I had been hyperventilating. I felt him pulling out, and I was afraid that he would stop because of my reaction, but he pushed back in, deeper this time. He gripped the underside of my thighs, pushing them apart and up towards my body. My muscles were not used to bending that way. He got closer, his body hovering over me as he thrust deeper and deeper. He looked at me for signs that he was hurting me, and finding that I was ok, he picked up his pace. In less time than I would have imagined, I was hurting a lot less, my tight leg muscles relaxed, and I began to enjoy it more.

I watched his face as he worked. His expression was a mix of pleasure and concentration. I knew he loved it, but he was so worried about hurting me that he wasn't letting himself go wild. It was my first time, and even in this, he made it about me.

I stroked his chest as he thrust into me, picking up the pace a little more. I could feel him inside me, firm like an oak, reaching further than should be possible. I felt full. It was a strange, but intensely satisfying feeling. He was in a position where his thrusts hit my sweet spot, but I was worn out and not sure I would achieve a third orgasm.

His face got red, and his grip on my thighs was vice-like. I knew that his climax was seconds away. I wanted to see his face as it happened, to see how much pleasure my body gave him. He gave a titanic grunt before pulling himself out of me. A torrent of white lava exploded from his cock, spraying my stomach and breasts with globules of his pearlescent seed.

He took a second to calm himself, his breathing rapid but evening out. I saw love in his face and contentment. He had accomplished what we both wanted, and in the least painful way.

I've heard that men wanted to finish inside the woman, but he knew that as a virgin, I was not taking any precautions. He had not anticipated this happening, so he, likewise, wasn't prepared. Getting pregnant in the middle of a war was poor timing.

We cleaned ourselves with river water and put our clothing back on. As I was buttoning my blouse, I watched him. Even putting on his clothes, he moved with grace and precision. I thought it a shame to cover that statuesque body, but we had things to do.

We walked back to camp hand in hand. I relived every detail, focusing on the emotions he stirred in me. If we both survived the next few weeks, I would be his… and he would be mine.

# Chapter 49

There seemed to be no rhyme or reason to the abductions. They happened mostly in the lower to middle-class areas of Warszawa. I suspected that was because they were less likely to be missed. Missed by their families, yes, there was a string of broken hearts among the families of the taken. But the upper-class, the nobility? They didn't even know that it was going on. The one thing that I knew for sure was that there was some connection to the Court of Whispers. They were the architects behind the abductions, and I still had no idea what they had to gain.

It may have been a gigantic waste of time, but I decided that we should stake out the Polska Abyrinth's Fire. The stones played a large part in our world's trajectory, both going forward and reaching back to the Night of the Comet. The stones might have been buried for millennia, but we'd had a couple of hundred years of their influence on our lives and our society. It had been almost two weeks since we had put eyes on the ravine where the cave was located, and I was beginning to think that my instincts were wrong.

Jacek came rushing into my tent. "Kapitan! There's movement down by the cave."

We had twenty-four-hour eyes on the trail that led down to the cave; everyone got a turn to lie in a bush with a pair of binoculars. I grabbed my gun belt and went out to fetch Jaroslav and his guys. They were accustomed to covert missions, and I didn't want to scare off whoever was sneaking down into the sacred area. Each of the men was twice my size, but they were almost soundless as they moved through the brush and leaves. I was a lumbering ox by comparison.

Borys was lying there, monitoring the comings and goings. He handed the glasses to Oldřich and reported to me.

"Kapitan. I saw two women and four men enter the cave. They are all still inside."

"Any idea who they are?"

"No. I know they aren't military. One of the women and two of the men were older, but otherwise, nothing." He thought for a minute. "The older ones were dressed fancy, like you, Panisko. Um, sorry, ma'am."

"Yeah, watch it, cyclops!"

Jaroslav suggested, "If we go to the entrance, do you think you can tell how many are wielders?"

"Doubtful. The cave is far too deep even to sense them." I accepted the binoculars from Oldřich and took a look. "I see an outcropping near the entrance. I can go by myself and hide behind it. When they come out, I'll be able to scan them for Abyrinth usage."

"I don't like it," Jaroslav said plainly. He'd become even more protective of me since our romantic interlude in the woods. Things in the bedroom were getting better every time we tried it. I almost felt like I was cheating on someone after being with both Jaroslav and Jaro a couple of times over the last two weeks. He claimed that they were the same person, but I had enough first-hand experience to the contrary.

Oldřich looked at him with barely concealed disdain. "She is a kapitan in their army, and a very powerful wielder. She can handle it."

"I could prowl around in wolf form," Radomír offered, trying to break the tension.

"Thank you, but no, Radomír. I'm not sure about Bohemia, but in Polska, they shoot wolves for the crime of being wolves. I'll go alone." I turned to Jaroslav. "I'll be very sneaky, so don't worry. When they come out, follow them. I want to see where they go from here."

I didn't wait for any further argument, but started down the hill towards the cave mouth. I moved quickly because I had no idea how long they would be inside. I was in the open, and this was the most vulnerable part of the plan. I couldn't safely dress in my uniform, so I wore heavy boots, loose denim, a white undershirt, and a heavy grey wool sweater. With no makeup and my hair pulled back in a ponytail, I slid down the dry, rocky grade on my ass. I prayed that they didn't have their own spotters because I was not stealthy by any stretch of the imagination.

The first time I was here, I was scared, but I had family members present, fully supporting me. On my third trip there, I was scared, but my comrades were far up the hill, too far to help me if things went sideways.

I reached the bottom, covered in dirt, with the worst road rash ever on my backside. There was the trail that led off to the road above, the clearing where the warden would give his instructions and the family would gather, and, of course, the rocky entrance to the cave.

I had just crossed the open stretch when my senses lit up like fireworks. I could feel the approaching energy, the kind only radiated by other wielders. It was like I had X-ray vision. I could see their clouds of energy and knew they were less than a dozen steps from the entrance and from catching me.

I tried not to kick too many rocks as I ran full out towards the rocky crag of stone that separated the cave entrance from the rest of the hillside.

Five feet. Three feet.

I hit it hard, bruising my hands and one knee. I pressed myself as flat as I could against the stone surface, trying to blend in somehow.

"Take them, and get them inserted as quickly as possible. The Rus may try to camp on this location, and we'll lose access to it," a male voice said. I closed my eyes and concentrated. I could make out six distinct energy signatures. Two were wielders, the other four were channelers. Why would channelers be allowed in the gem chamber? I hadn't learned much, and it bothered me.

I felt all of the signatures moving further from me, so I risked a peek. The older woman in a heavy wool coat walked gingerly up the trail towards a waiting hover limousine. Beside her, the older gentleman was steering a hovering platform with four bodies piled upon it. I could see his power attached to the platform, making it levitate, and I could see that the inert bodies were the channelers. Six entered under their own power, but only two were able to walk out. Even from a couple of dozen yards, I could see that the channelers were dressed in very inexpensive clothing.

Channelers typically made much more money than blanks; they could have afforded much better. Nothing was adding up… then it struck me! Were these the people who had gone missing all over the capital for the last year? I knew there was a connection to the Court of Whispers, though it wouldn't hold up in court; I thought I had a pretty strong case.

What I couldn't figure out was: what were they doing with the people they kidnapped?


I never would have expected Karol to be good at tailing people. He was so big that he drew attention just walking down the street.

Somehow, he followed the car carrying the unconscious channelers to a power station southwest of downtown Warszawa. I thought the facility was closed, but when I arrived, it seemed fully functional.

From the outside, it resembled a cathedral, its façade two stories high, wrapped in brick and stone, with blue-stained-glass windows. There was a large dome section on top of a two-story glassed-in chamber. Behind the main facility was a factory floor, with three smoking, cylindrical chimneys that reached high up into the air, belching dark coal smoke. Hundreds of workers could be seen maintaining the many boilers, their miles of piping, and copper kettles. Gears and pistons could be seen at the rear of the building, creating and distributing energy to thousands of electrical supply lines.

"Here?" I asked. It seemed like an unlikely place to be taking their prisoners.

"Yes, Kapitan. It was night by the time they got here, and the night shift had a fraction of the personnel of the day shift. The hover car was backed up to that small door over there." He pointed at a rather nondescript freight entrance with a rolling garage door that was several hundred feet away from the loading dock. "Workers stay in the rear, either performing maintenance on the steamworks or unloading supplies at the docks."

Jaro looked closely at the situation. "A large distraction," he said as he pointed, "right over there, would be quite fortuitous."

He was trying to be funny, but as I considered him in the bright light of the short November day, I saw his strength and commitment, traits that he possessed in all three of his states. Jaroslav was the more thoughtful, the considerate intellectual. Conversation with him was more compelling, and at times, I preferred his calm. When it was time for action, whether in battle or in bed, Jaro was my first choice. I marveled at how close I felt to him after so few actual days spent together.

"I could find us a car," Marcin offered. "Borys can blow it up. He has spent a lot of time recently making pipe bombs and IEDs. I think being asked to make a car bomb would be the height of his week."

"You two coordinate that. Make it go off at one thirty in the morning. Don't get caught."

"Not to worry, Kapitan. We're actually getting good at this revolution stuff."

I laid out the rest of my plan to the others and told them to eat and get some rest. It would be a long night.

We were holed up in a local hotel, and since everyone here was aware that we were a couple, I shared a room with Jaroslav.

"Jaro, you need to do something for me." I held his stubbly cheek in my hand, forcing him to meet my stare. "Tonight is very important. Everyone's security is my… second-highest priority. Completing the mission, bringing the Court of Whispers to heel, should be everyone's highest priority. You've saved me before, and I've saved you, but tonight, don't sacrifice the success of the mission to come rescue me, if it comes to that." He nodded. "I mean it! Mission comes first."

"We have had some abductions in Praha, too. Not as many as here, but it's my responsibility to protect my people at all costs, even at the cost of my life." He pulled my hands from his face and held them in his. "As much as it may hurt me, I will not save you at the expense of crushing this evil cabal." He leaned in and kissed me. Not with the burning passion of a lover, but with the affection of someone who truly loved me.

I fell into his arms, embracing him, allowing him to envelop me. I had no plans to die today, and if things went well, we would all have a celebratory breakfast together, but I knew that facing this group was deadly serious, and the chance for someone to get harmed was high.

I loved my life, as turbulent as it was, and I was still eighteen. I longed for many years, filled with marriage, children, travel, and service to my countrymen. Though if I married Jaroslav, the Bohemians would become my citizens, and their welfare would be my responsibility.

He hadn't proposed to me. Even so, we both treated our relationship as if the proposal had been made and accepted, and at least for my part, I felt like I was engaged. I had to be sensible and protect myself. I was already giving him the benefits of a wife without the title.

Now that my title was forfeit to an invading army of Rus, I was common, and Oldřich openly hated that his prince was involved with me. Nobody said anything in the languages that I spoke, but I could tell that the King and Queen of

Bohemia may no longer see me as a viable choice for their son.

I wanted to surrender to him physically, right there and then, but all of us had to get our heads straight. Tonight will be the culmination of months of work.


As the hour approached and we assumed our positions, I recalled the reason I was so concerned about this mission, more than the others we had carried out: the Abyrinth. I could sense more of the energy localized in the power plant than at any time since taking my trials. A single channeler was a candle in my other sense, a small light in the dark. A wielder was a lantern, shining brightly, but not able to illuminate more than a small space.

What I witnessed was a forest fire. In a concentrated area, there were hundreds of separate embers, sparks, and torches. Together, they created a fiery conflagration of the mysterious energy that was now the basis of our societies.

Access to Abyrinth could make a man king, while the lack of it would doom him to obscurity and mediocracy. Something very wrong was going on there, and for the security of Polska, and possibly the whole world, we needed to know what it was and stop it.

The car exploded spectacularly. I would have to commend Borys' work later, assuming we all made it out. The electricity generation section of the plant was illuminated from sundown to sunup with hundreds of lights, affixed to almost every surface. The distribution area and administrative offices were shadowy by comparison. I knew Oldřich was out there somewhere, but the only way I could pick him out was that I knew where he was going. I caught a glimpse of him as he passed through a circle of light right next to a side door. Otherwise, he was invisible.

It was only seconds before there was a faint crackle on the radio, followed by two distinct clicks of the transmitter. That was the signal to move. A second round of explosions went off, and we all ran the hundred yards to the unlocked side door. I piled in with my team, filing in behind me.

"Jafra," Filip said. "Do you have an idea of where the wielders and channelers are?" He had a better understanding of how my power worked than the others, and he knew I could see them like fireflies on a dark night.

I closed my eyes and concentrated. "I see two wielders on this level, and a half dozen channelers." I turned to my crew. "No offense, but blanks are, well… blank. There could be a million or none. You guys don't show up on my radar." I thought again, letting the whisps of energy flow to me, telling me a story about the person from whom they emanated. "One wielder upstairs, and…" What I found next caused me to gasp audibly. How could it be? "There are channelers down below us."

"Below us? I wasn't aware of a basement level in this facility," Filip said. He'd studied the schematics and was in charge of guiding us when we reached the inside. "How many channelers?"

"Hundreds."

We were knee deep, no… neck deep in this raid. It was too late to go back. I had no idea how we would defeat hundreds, maybe a thousand channelers, in a secret underground chamber. I had no idea how large the room or rooms were; they had to be massive to accommodate that many people. They could all be carrying pulse pistols and waiting for us.

"A wielder and two channelers over there." I pointed to a suite of offices to our left. The area we were in had a high ceiling, which was almost three stories high, with offices on the left and workshops on our right. Along the wall above, a row of smaller offices with large windows looked down on the worker bees below. Stairs ran up the far wall to the supervisors' offices, and another flight led to the executive level above the factory floor. The place smelled of lubricants and mildew. I pitied the blanks that had to work in such conditions. "The other wielder is through those doors with four more channelers. I'll go left with Karol, Julia, and Jaro. The rest of you, flush them out of the meeting rooms to the right. Be careful, there may be significant non-powered guards."

We split up, and I let Jaro take the lead. He changed into his werewolf form for the increased strength and night vision. It was dark as pitch inside, and turning on the lights would make it easier for them to find us.

It was a good plan, but it didn't work. The large open office was the worst possible place to try to move unnoticed.

We were sneaking around a long row of desks when we came under fire. There was the flash of regular guns, along with their ear-splitting cracks. I saw rounds of hardened Abyrinth streaming from pulse pistols, invisible to everyone but me. I followed their path back to the source. I saw the channeler that was firing, not only their energy aura, but I saw where the energy left the muzzle of their pistol. I couldn't actually see him, but I could see enough to guess and shoot.

I fired in the direction of the shooter, loosing a dozen pulse rounds where I knew he or she had to be. The firing stopped, and a couple of seconds later, I saw the Abyrinth being surrendered to the atmosphere.

Please God, forgive me for taking life. I sin for the sake of my country and her people, I prayed silently. They were my enemies, yet I still hated to kill.

I heard a barrage of shots ring out, then a cry of pain from very near me. It was a male voice, so I knew it must be Karol. Jaro was in wolf form, and Julia was right next to me.

With a bestial growl, Jaro leapt into the air, far higher and further than a man could. In the dim light, I couldn't make out the details, but I heard the rending of flesh and the cracking of bone. Men screamed their last as my lover ripped the life from them.

I grabbed Julia's collar, and we moved together, trying to flank the enemy by circling the outer wall of the office. As we were creeping around, Julia put new clips in her pistols. She tugged at my sleeve and signaled that she was going to charge. I nodded and prepared to cover her.

We were to the side of where they were concealed. I don't know how many blanks there were, at least a dozen. With a pistol in each hand, she charged out, guns blazing. She took out three that I saw before they even knew that she was there.

I was a step behind, and when they turned to return fire, I fired. Julia was a decent marksman, but pistol shooting was one of the areas where I really excelled. They had their eyes on my diminutive partner and didn't notice me picking them off with well-aimed shots.

I hear a scream, female this time.

"Damn it! I fucking got shot again!"

"Julia, are you ok?" I called out. She was ten feet away, but I couldn't see anything.

"No, Kapitan! I got shot! Again!"

"Are you going to live?"

"I hope not. This fucking hurts! Ma'am."

You get weird thoughts at the oddest times. I thought of how quiet she was, and, well, uninteresting when I met her. She had changed a lot since the war started. She was an unmitigated badass now.

I had cleared out most of the soldiers near us, so I crawled low across the floor, trying to stay beneath the top of the desks. When I got to her, I started running my hands over her thin limbs. Her thigh had a wet spot where warm blood was seeping between her fingers.

"Is this the only one?" I asked

"Yeah, uh, yes, ma'am."

I hadn't thought of this before, but I knew it would work. I moved her hand away, then wove strands of Abyrinth together, making them flat like a wrap bandage. I created a strip about four inches wide and sealed it around her leg. The bleeding would slow, if not stop altogether.

I pulled out her first-aid kit and found a morphine syrette, which I stuck in her leg. I could barely see, but I saw her face relax immediately, and I felt much of the tension leave her body.

"I know you're starting to get loopy. Don't shoot any of us."

"Yes, ma'am."

I heard Jaro on the other side of the room. I almost pitied the soldiers he was fighting. I was rushing over to help when the world turned upside down. I was floating in the air, and in seconds, I was bumping against the high, thirty-foot ceiling. I saw that everyone was equally affected.

Looking down, I saw Julia hanging onto a desk, but Jaro, Karol, and I, along with a dozen guards, were all floating lazily through the air. I saw the wielder below; she was hiding behind some cabinets. I could shut off her power, but that would drop us all like a ton of bricks. Likewise, shooting her would send us all crashing down.

I reached out with the power, wrapping firm coils of energy around each of us, but not the guards, then I took aim and put a pulse round through her forehead. Not bad for floating upside down and slowly spinning.

I let us down easily, and the dozen guards fell as gravity reasserted itself. Several of them were ok, though not unharmed. Some fell very badly, and were not getting up any time soon. Jaro ripped into a guard, pulling out his throat with strong, clawed hands. Karol had another guard in a bear hug, and the sounds of his rib cage cracking and breaking were drowned out by his screams.

I don't know how things were going on the other side, but I saw a channeler, and I knew it was Filip. It seemed that every wielder and channeler had a unique energy signature. Cool! I saw two other wielders, and I somehow knew that they were Oldřich and Radomír. I wanted to clear this level before going upstairs. I thought that the mastermind of this branch of the Court must be upstairs. I started heading towards our teammates.

"Come on!"

Pistol in hand, I started running toward the wild action by the plant entrance. The lighting was better there, and I could see that my team had their hands full. I started firing into the crowd of guards when I felt like I was punched in the back. I had a searing pain between my shoulder blades, just a couple of inches from my spine. I dropped my gun and fell hard, only catching myself at the last second. Searing pain shot through me, even worse than when I was stabbed a few months ago.

I saw Jaro turn; his snout was dripping blood, and his eyes shone like burning coals. He stared at me, some sixth sense telling him that I'd been harmed. I waved him away from a distance. As much as he cared for me, he respected my wishes to put the mission first, before any one person's welfare. He turned and launched himself at a handful of the enemy, and instead of being aware of my surroundings, I watched him. I saw a handful of guards with rifles pointed right at me, and maybe it was the pain from my gunshot, but I froze.

A second later, I felt massive arms envelop me. Not a wielder or a channeler, but a normal person without powers, put his body between a hail of bullets and me.

It was Karol, and I felt him holding me suffocatingly tight.

With our bodies pressed together, I felt the bullets strike his body. He was so large, so dense, that they felt like weak punches, the type Jurek used to give me before Father had a talk with him. There were so many, at least twenty, and

I knew that he wouldn't survive such a barrage. Tears flooded my vision as Karol fell over, still on top of me.

From beneath his bulk, I saw my troops. My friends. They were in as bad condition as Julia and I were. I saw Izabelalla on the ground. I had no idea what her condition was, but she wasn't in a pool of her own blood, so I had hope.

All of these people, regular people like I was before taking the trials, and my incredible power couldn't even see them. If she were a channeler, I would know if she were alive or dead.

Filip was with the wolves, taking the fight to the enemy. He looked a little haggard, and I thought I saw him limping, but he was alive and fighting like hell.

Jacek looked unharmed, but he was stuck behind a workbench, and there were enemies all around him. Borys lay a few feet from him. He had his eyes open, staring off into the distance. The pool of blood he lay in made it pretty clear he was dead. Marcin was nowhere to be seen, and I feared the worst.

"Jacek!" I screamed above the cacophony. "Turn the lights on!" I pointed at a row of light switches by the main entrance. It was too far for my power, and too far to see clearly. "Turn them all on!"

He nodded nervously, then sprinted to the switches. The lights flicked on, one row at a time in rapid succession. The dark had hidden the blood and chaos that reigned in the vast space. The guards were still on one side, near the outer wall and the power plant door. A quick glance told me that Izabel was breathing, and that Marcin was on the far side, providing cover fire for the wolves and Filip.

Try as I might, I couldn't get Karol off of me without using my power. I hated having to dump him off like dead weight. I was saddened beyond measure, frustrated, and angry. My Abyrinth sense couldn't detect blanks, but my eyes could.

I had never controlled so many objects at one time. It was much more complex than what I was required to do in my trials. I wrapped energy around every one of the guards, picking them up a dozen feet in the air. Some dropped their guns, others screamed in panic. None of that mattered. I began spinning them, faster and faster, until there was a tornado of flesh. Men who worked for this Court of Whispers, men who'd shot me, hurt many of the others, and killed Borys and Karol—none were spared. I spun them around at a dizzying speed; they were hard to make out, just blurs of brown uniforms and their pale faces. When they were spinning as fast as I could make them, I released them towards the far wall. They struck the unforgiving surface and splattered like insects on a car's windscreen. They formed a heaving, bleeding mass that would produce no survivors.

I tried to stand, but my legs shook, and I could feel hot blood flowing down my back. Jacek came over, wanting to help me, but I weighed almost as much as he did. He got me on my feet, but I had to lean on him for support. Jaro loped over, followed by his boys. He and Radomír stayed in their lupine forms; they had numerous bullet wounds, and they had increased healing when engaging their abilities. He barked at me, a strange sound that I would have to try and forget when he was making love to me. I had no idea what he was trying to say, but I got the gist of it.

"Jacek, I need you to take charge down here. We're all pretty banged up, but we can't stop now. I have to go upstairs. Whoever is pulling the strings on these abductions and terror attacks before the war, possibly even instigating the war itself, is upstairs waiting for justice. Izabel and Julia are both hurt. Bring the car around and get them to a healer." He nodded and rushed off to bring around a regular steam transport.

Marcin came up and started tending to my gunshot wound. I refused pain relief; I needed my wits about me. He put some powder on the wound and placed a wad of cotton from a med kit.

"Kapitan, can you put one of those invisible bandages around this, like you did with Julia?"

I nodded. I put the wrap in an X across my shoulders, holding the cotton compress over the hole in my back. I turned to Filip, who, with a seeping wound in his calf, seemed to be the least injured of the crew I was planning to take upstairs.

"Kapitan Sobieski… That, whatever you call it… I've never seen anything like it. I've seen you do some incredible things, miraculous things, but if I live to a hundred, I'll never see anything like that again."

"Disgusting is what it was," Marcin piped in. He pointed at the bloody mound of pulp and the dripping red splotch on the wall near it. "They deserved it, one hundred percent, but it was really gross."

I ignored him and turned to the wolves. "Can you all continue, or are any of you too injured?"

Jaro shook his head no, Radomír howled, which I took as confirmation that he was going with us. Oldřich looked grim, but otherwise unharmed. His stealth made him difficult to see, much less harm. Marcin tended to Filip's wound, and again, I applied a band of Abyrinth before tying it off.

"Let me lead the way," Oldřich said. He pulled his cloak over his head, casting his sharp features in shadow. We all followed him up the stairs that led to the uppermost floor. I was supposed to be in charge, but I was in a lot of pain, and I didn't trust myself to be the point of the spear. Filip was second in line, with Radomír, Jaro, and then me. Jaro's shirt was missing, but he still wore torn and bloody uniform trousers. His wounds had stopped bleeding; it was remarkable how fast he healed in his Mr. Hyde and werewolf states. I held on to his belt to steady myself as we climbed a half dozen flights of stairs. Then something felt... off.

"I don't sense the wielders up here anymore!" I whispered loudly. I wasn't sure why I was whispering; the plant floor and offices below were a war zone, with dead and dying everywhere.

Aside from being inhumanly stealthy, Oldřich also had superhuman strength and speed. He motioned for us to wait, then he exploded up the last flight of stairs and into the offices above. He was gone for no more than two minutes before returning.

"It's all safe. Come on up."

When we reached the executive suites, there was a whole different feel to the place. The space was decked out with lush furnishings in the highest quality woods, brilliant silk tapestries, and area rugs that looked imported and very expensive.

We looked from office to office, and in the largest room, we found the missing wielder. She sat in a broad and tall office chair. A small pulse pistol lay in her dead hand, her brains fouling the exquisite leather.

"Who is it?" Filip asked. He stared at the body, dressed in a white-and-blue day dress, with diamonds in her ears and gold on her fingers.

"She told me her name was Hedwig. I've also heard her called Lady Rozalia Tarnowski," I replied. "It seems that every word she told me, all the help she was giving me… was all a lie."

"What did she say?" Jaro said, putting his human hands on my shoulders. His touch felt comforting, despite my sudden overwhelming feeling of disillusionment and loss.

"She said she was part of a secret group called the Brotherhood of Virtue, and she wanted me to help her find and control the other two prime brands. Instead, she was the head of the local chapter of the Court of Whispers all along."

He wrapped his arm around me as I stared at the corpse. I was tired of being in charge, but quitting was not an option.

"Let's go downstairs. I still sense hundreds of channelers down there."

"We should wait, find a healer." I felt weak and a bit dizzy, so Jaro helped me walk down the stairs. I was ready to fall down, and he was trying to stay strong, but I saw the weariness in his eyes and a slight shaking in his arms.

"I need to see what's down there," I insisted. Jacek had returned with the car, and he was loading the girls in with help from Marcin. "Jacek, there's a healer a few miles from here…"

"Magda? Yes, I know her. Don't worry, I'll drop them and come back for all of you."

I nodded; my strength was waning fast.

"I'll look for the entrance to the lower chamber," Radomír said before switching to his wolf form. He loped off at a trot, sniffing and looking for anything unusual. He passed through the large double doors into the power plant's generation room. A minute later, he ran back, changing to his human form and sliding to a stop before us.

"I found a hidden door at the back of the loading dock."

I righted myself, gently removing Jaro's steadying arm, and walked. The rest followed and were as enthusiastic as I was, which was not very much at this point. Hundreds of channelers? If they were armed, we might die instantly. I could absorb a tremendous amount of Abyrinth, but the full load from a hundred or two hundred channelers? Doubtful.

When we reached the doors, there was the type of lock on it that I had only heard about, but never seen myself. Filip stepped forward and channeled his energy into the device, pumping out streams of pure power until we all heard an audible click. He pushed open the door to a large freight elevator.

"Allow me, Kapitan." He entered, and we followed closely. He felt with his hands until he found a light switch. We were so far beyond having the element of surprise that none of us cared to try to be subtle. With his pulse rifle in the ready position, Filip slid open the door as soon as we settled on a level that must have been a hundred feet below the surface.

When he jumped out, there was no one there. A bit of a let-down if you ask me.

We followed him down a short hallway that dead-ended at a double door with another complex lock. He was about to exert more of his energy when I stopped him.

"I'll get this one." He stepped back, and to everyone's surprise, I started to blast the door with my pulse rifle. A few well-placed shots, and the locking mechanism was decimated.

"I could have done that," he groused as he opened the doors. He walked in, and I followed.

We were not prepared for what was inside. There were metal racks stacked ten feet high with shelves that held bodies, and there were five to a rack. There were dozens upon dozens of racks, supporting hundreds of channelers. Each one had rubber hoses feeding something directly into their stomachs. They appeared to be naked; their shoulders were bare, but they had blankets covering most of their bodies. I could see more than the others, and the sick truth became almost immediately apparent.

"They're all channelers."

"How do you know?" he asked. He knew my ability, but I guess he was shocked and wanted confirmation.

"I can see the Abyrinth on them." I watched the flows; I could see small rivers of energy flowing upward, rising. "There!" I said, pointing to a glowing gem that was suspended from the ceiling. There was a gem that looked eerily similar to Abyrinth's Fire. "Their energy is being siphoned off and is flowing into that gem!"

"To what end? And how did they get so many channelers?" Filip asked.

"It looks like they are trying to create their own Abyrinth's fire," Radomír said.

I nodded in agreement with him. "As far as getting all of these channelers? I think they made them." I turned to Jaro. "The missing young adults, blanks who are over eighteen. I think this is the one thing Hedwig said that may have been the truth. I think they are exposing blanks to the gem, which is turning them into channelers. They become batteries to create their own private gem." I pointed at the glowing stone over our heads.

"We have had a rash of kidnappings in Bohemia. They may have a facility like this in Praha."

"I'll call on the radio, get some doctors to come to help us safely remove them from these contraptions," Filip offered.

"I wonder how far-spread this Court of Whispers is?" I wondered aloud. "There may be cells in every major city that have an Abyrinth's Fire gem throughout Europa. Maybe even in the new world."

# Chapter 50

We had dismantled the Court of Whispers' schemes in Warszawa almost two weeks ago. At least I think we did.

We had changed locations three times already, and were getting ready to move out again in the morning. I didn't know for certain if the Rus were looking for us, but I figured that it was better to be safe than sorry. They were looking for anyone not toeing the line, not bowing down to the tsar. There were rumors—more than rumors—that there had been many public executions across the country in the last month.

We were in a seedy motel on the outskirts of Wrocław, taking up several rooms for Jaroslav's guys and my crew. Everyone was healed within a couple of days, and some of them were even relearning how to smile. Most of us had to recover from both our physical injuries and mental injuries.

Over the course of months spent closely together, we'd become tight-knit, like a family, but losing two of our own had hurt all of us deeply. I gave them the opportunity to leave the unit, to go off and see if their families were still alive. None of them cracked, and there was no chance they were going to stop until they themselves were dead or Rus was driven from our land.

I lay in Jaroslav's arms as we tried to get some good sleep before hitting the road again. There was no marriage, and maybe there never would be, but we were happy.

Wrocław was not too far from Bohemia, and even if he said nothing, I knew he longed to see his homeland and visit his family, but he kept his promise never to leave my side. I could have gone with him, spent a week or two in his castle, but I was dedicated to continuing the resistance. Part of the reason I was reticent to visit his family in Praha was the bile coming from Oldřich. I didn't believe that he hated me personally, but it was pretty clear that he didn't think the Bohemian royal family would accept me. I thought about how little I missed the title, the money, the influence.

Well, I missed the money.

There was a knock at the door. "It's me." I heard Filip's voice.

I walked to the door and opened it a crack. "What's up?"

"Someone is here to see you." His shit-eating grin had me both apprehensive and intrigued. He stepped aside to reveal my brother. "Krystian!"

I closed the door, looked down to make sure I was wearing clothes, then undid the lock and flung the door wide. I threw myself into his arms and hugged him fiercely. It hadn't been so long since we rescued him from the clutches of the Nikolaeva sisters, but a lot had happened since then. I invited him in, and he gave a knowing smirk when he saw Jaroslav pulling a shirt on.

"You've given up all pretense to propriety, little sister?" He turned to Jaroslav and bowed. "Prince Záhoř."

"We had to rescue you from falling for a honey-pot scheme, and you have the nerve to question my choices?"

"No, I just like to see you turn red," he said, laughing. He took a chair. "Hey, lieutenant, get in here!" Filip must have been just outside the door. He slid in, closing the door behind him.

"I would ask you what you kids have been up to, but there's no one in eastern Europa that hasn't heard about what happened back at that power station in Warszawa. So instead, I'll tell you what I've been up to." There was a knock at the door. "I sent that scrawny fellow to get some ale and whiskey." He went to the door, opened it, and accepted a couple of packages from Jacek.

"What did you wind up doing with the Rus Major?" Jaroslav asked.

"Baron Gavriil Sokolov? It's funny you should ask." He uncorked an ale for each of us and took a sip before resuming his narration. "I brought him with me."

"With you?" I asked. I was perplexed.

"Me and the soldiers that I've collected. It's taken weeks, but I've contacted some other officers, and we've been traveling ahead of the Rus. As you know, Stefek surrendered the army when they overran the capital and captured the royal residence, but half the country had not yet fallen under their control. There are still thousands of our brave soldiers who would prefer death to surrender."

"But how are you here?" I asked. "Our location is supposed to be secret. We were going to relocate after breakfast, and even we don't know where we're going."

"A very simple solution. I have the services of a bloodhound." He turned to Jaroslav. "No offense."

"I know what a bloodhound is," he replied.

"Wait, that's a wielder that can locate anyone. They hold some token of the person, and they can follow them anywhere in the world."

"Yes, Jafra. I found your emeralds where you hid them back home." He pulled the gems out of his breast pocket and handed them to me.

"How did you know about my toilet safe?" I asked, feeling violated.

"I found it three years ago. Good idea: the Rus never found them."

"Ok. What crazy scheme do you have cooked up?" I tried to sound cynical, but I was excited to see if my older brother could pull a rabbit out of his hat.

"We can't win the war with the men I've collected. We lost when we had ten times our current number. But, we can strike a blow that will shake their confidence and may bring allies to our cause." He looked pointedly at Jaroslav.

"How many soldiers do you have?"

"Seven thousand. Give or take. A handful of mechs, but no Goliaths or tanks." My brother tried to act casual, but I could tell that he was anxious. "The plan is to take out Colonel Dmitri Sokolov and as many of his men as we can. He's a truly evil bastard, but perhaps the only life other than his own that he values is that of his brother."

"Let me call my father. See if he can step up," Jaroslav said, darting out the door. He never said it, but I think he felt guilty that his father waffled until it was too late to save Polska.

"So, we're hanging the brother out as bait, and hopefully the good colonel will come running to the rescue."

"Running is the operative word. He has more than ten thousand soldiers, airships, tanks, mechs, and God help us, at least a few Goliaths. If he believes that his brother's life is in imminent danger, and it is, he will have to leave the machines and transport as many infantry as he can, as fast as he can."

"When do you expect his main body to arrive?"

"Three days."

The plan had too many moving parts, and we were putting it together much faster than I was comfortable with. The good thing was, I didn't have to be in charge this time.

I still had doubts, wondering whether, if I had been a better leader, Karol and Borys might still be alive. Julia only complained a little, but I had gotten the poor girl shot. Twice! Krystian was not only my superior in the army, but also older and infinitely more experienced than I was. Except for my brand, he outclassed me in every area.

We arranged our limited resources around Oława, not far from the Oder River. The area we chose had shallow, mirror-like pools, knee-deep grasses, and narrow causeways. The bog was in a perpetual mist, with great clouds of mosquitoes, snakes, and blood-sucking leeches.

We commandeered a small cannery on the river, forcing anyone wanting to approach to come from the other direction, passing through the bog. We set up a makeshift prison for the major and leaked his location.

The Rus were already close, so it was less than forty-eight hours before they closed in on our location. Fighting in a swamp was going to suck, but it was our country, and we knew the terrain better than they did. We had scouts everywhere, and we knew hours in advance when they would arrive and from which direction.

Jacek rushed into the command tent that we had set up almost a mile from the cannery. "They're here. As usual, mechs in the lead, but no airships or tanks. A battalion of infantry is trailing behind."

"Mechs in the swamp?" I asked.

"Yeah. This should be good." Krystian was smiling. "We dug all kinds of holes out there and let them fill with swamp water."

As predicted, the mechs lumbered into the swamp with their guns blazing. We had mortar units dropping high-explosive rounds on them, and two artillery batteries were trying to set them back, but they were heavily armored, and the best our crews could do was scratch their paint.

Jaro wasn't thrilled about it, but he let me move in closer, alongside my brother. We saw two mechs struggling through the muck and brush. These weapons of war were incredibly powerful, but with each step, the muck and mire sucked at the legs, trying to root them in place. They eventually fought their way through, but their progress was impeded far more than their Rus commanders expected.

I could hear my brother giggling as the lead mech passed through a zone marked by bent branches. The forward leg stretched forward and sank ten feet into the muddy, algae-covered ground. It lurched forward at forty-five degrees before I gave it an Abyrinthpush. The mech fell face forward into the muck, arms swinging around like a fat man who fell and couldn't get up. The mech that was following closely behind had to stop abruptly, spinning on its waist joint, looking for danger. Scores of soldiers were following fifty feet behind, and they, too, were sensing danger.

We had bodies in the trees and behind every fallen log and rock. The air was filled with lead as our soldiers mowed down the Rus soldiers, who were hopelessly stuck in the mud. On Krystian's command, the ships that we had on the river opened fire. Their large caliber shells were up to the challenge of piercing mech armor. The standing mech was battered by shrapnel near misses, but after a few test rounds were walked in, the mech took a direct hit in the center of the main cabin. When the smoke cleared, it stood standing, but the driver and the whole front of the war machine were missing.

I didn't have my brother's or Jaro's experience in battle, but I was starting to develop a danger sense. I looked at Krystian, who was still celebrating, but when I looked at my man, I saw a different picture. He was running towards me as fast as the soft, wet terrain would allow. As he ran, he pointed upward, and my eyes followed his direction.

The swamp was already dark and murky, but a shadow was falling over us, and I saw the noses of two airships peeking out from behind the canopy of trees overhead. I felt like I'd seen a lot at this point, but what I saw next blew my mind.

I had never seen a Goliath in person, but heading towards us at a glacially slow pace was one of the dark green behemoths, suspended by ten-inch diameter cables from four of the Black Ships. Its cab was actually larger than the cannery where we were holding our prisoner. It was set down straddling the downed mechs; they looked like newborn pups next to the mother wolf standing over them. The foot pads were so massive that the giant walker was in no danger of sinking into the mire.

Just by looking at the thing, I knew it had too much mass for me to lift or even push. It ran on advanced steam, so

I couldn't drain any Abyrinth because it didn't have any. I gawked at the metal monster and felt fear. How could such a monstrosity ever be defeated?

A booming voice echoed out the Goliath in passable Polish. "This is Colonel Dmitri Sokolov, and you are engaged in an illegal action. The Polish military has surrendered, and none of you will be afforded prisoner of war status. Release Barón Sokolov, unharmed, immediately! Your lives are already forfeit, but if the barón is returned, it will not be necessary to teach you a lesson, as we did in Braniszów."

"What do you know about this colonel?" I asked.

Krystian looked defeated. He had been hoping to lure the colonel out into the open, but he was as safe in his Goliath as a babe in its mother's arms.

"He's a liar. I saw him in action, and he takes pleasure in murder and massacre. I think we should kill this barón. He'll kill us all regardless, and probably destroy a few of the surrounding towns just for good measure, regardless of what we do."

To illustrate the colonel's lack of patience, he started to lob fire bombs into the surrounding woods. I doubted that they could see our men, as most were well hidden, but they probably had enough munitions to level the swamp and every living thing within.

Trees were exploding all around us, and Krystian didn't need to tell me that it was time to go. He was shouting orders to his men and women, staying behind to make sure they heard and obeyed his orders to retreat.

I heard a whistling sound and looked up in time to see bombs falling on our position. It was too late to get away, so

I instinctively wove an Abyrinth shell around us. The bomb landed a dozen feet away, where it exploded and pelted my shield with shrapnel. I felt the energy take the hit, and though it weakened, it lasted long enough to weather the first barrage. Krystian was shocked by the rough shards of metal seeming to bounce off of nothing, inches from our faces.

"Is that your doing, Jafra?"

"Yes."

"That's a new trick. When did you learn to do that?"

"About thirty seconds ago," I replied, pulling him along. "We need to evacuate! Sound the retreat!" A bomb went off nearby and tossed us both a dozen feet away. I landed face down in a slimy puddle. I pulled my head out of the stagnant water to see Krystian wrapped awkwardly around a tree. I saw him twitching.

"Krystian!" I screamed. No response.

All around me, the world was on fire. I crawled through the mud and grasses; I was scratched by bushes thick with briars, and I felt blood oozing from my scalp, dripping into my eyes. I reached for him, turning him onto his back to check his condition. His breathing was ragged, and his eyes were a roadmap of blood-red lines, the pupils mismatched and dilated. I tried to wake him, but he was unresponsive.

I was pretty sure we were both going to die. I thought it highly likely that we were all going to die in the next few minutes. The ground had the consistency of pudding, and still it shook with the force of the bombs dropped from above, and the bombardment the Goliath was directing at us.

As I wrapped my brother in bands of Abyrinth and levitated him inches above the ground, I prayed to God to deliver us from certain death.

My prayers were answered.

I heard explosions from above, far above. I had Krystian behind a large tree trunk on my way to the river. High up in the sky, even above the Dark Ships, I saw smaller airships that were soaring and diving at high speed. They were far away, but when I saw fire blossom on the surface of the ships, I understood what was going on. The Black Ships ceased their bombing run and tried to flee the smaller craft, but were hopelessly outmatched when it came to speed.

They were trying to make an about-face, and even I knew that was a terrible idea. One of the ships erupted into a massive fireball when its gases were ignited simultaneously. The gondola remained mostly intact as it fell from the sky in what seemed like slow motion. When it hit the ground, it cracked like an icicle falling from the roof and striking the hard ground. To add insult to injury, the burning envelope landed on the fractured structure, ensuring no one would survive.

The small fighters were maneuvering the airships until they were over the Goliath, then they really poured on their weapons fire. A pair of them passed over where I was taking refuge, and I got a good look at them. They were one- or two-person airships, not the titanic gas bags like the Black Ships, but essentially powered by channelers. They had long, swept-back wings attached to their sleek, aerodynamic frames. Even at a distance, I could see the flows of Abyrinth emitting from the rear engines, and not at all on the lift surfaces.

Jaro slogged his way through the muck until he was by my side. He had a satisfied smile on his face that would require more explanation.

"Why the grin?" I asked.

"My father sent a squadron of our new fighter airships. I told him how well the airship you bet on at the air races performed, so he commissioned a dozen to be made. They have regular guns alongside pulse cannons, in case they run out of conventional ammunition."

Another two explosions rocked us, shaking the air and blasting us with heat, even from a hundred feet below. It was bright daylight above the tree line, but the explosions were blinding. Again, in slow motion, the metal gondolas with crew members and at least a partial load of bombs fell from the sky. The fighters pushed them until they were over the Goliath, and the metal colossus couldn't move fast enough to escape tons of metal and fiery gas landing on it.

"Prince Záhoř, I do believe you've outdone yourself."

He didn't even attempt humility.

"This is not over yet. Let's get Krystian to the ship. There are a couple of healers aboard." I looked at where I had left my brother, and my heart tore in two.

Jaro went to his friend, my brother, and his mood turned instantly dark. "He's not doing well." Emotion caught in his voice. Not just for my brother, but most likely for me as well. He knew how close we had always been.

"He's dead," I said plainly. I was too tired and too heartbroken to mince words. "The essence that surrounds all wielders has left him."

Jaro took me in his arms and held me tight, not as a lover, but as two people trying to survive in the midst of an untenable situation. He crushed the air from my lungs, but I didn't care. There were still hundreds, if not thousands, of Rus soldiers walking around the woods and the swamp. I knew we should leave, but I needed another minute, one last minute to grieve for Krystian.

I couldn't cry. Not yet. There would be time for that later.

I buried my face in Jaro's chest, feeling the heat of his body against me. My nerves were calming, my blood was slowing its breakneck pace through my veins, and I was almost ready to leave when the sound of metal being bent and ripped apart brought me out of my darkness.

There was a pounding coming from the inside of a hatch that was on the side of the Goliath, still visible beneath the burning husk of one of the Black Ships. We saw the metal bending, tearing, and then the door burst outward. A fearsome creature climbed out of the wreck, its face a mask of vengeful anger.

The massive creature looked like the monster from Mary Shelley's novel. The disfigured features were even more horrible from being burned in the fiery wreck. I knew from Krystian's description that this was the demon, Colonel Dmitri Sokolov. He took such pleasure in killing captured soldiers. He ravaged whole towns, killing every man, woman, and child.

What affected me most directly… was that he was directly responsible for my brother's death.

"You're not running, girl?" he slurred, his mismatched features drooping. "I dreamed of a girl like you. Yes, she looked exactly like you. Take out your tits; let me see how deep the resemblance runs."

"Jafra! Let's run!" Jaro said, knowing how unbeatable this giant was.

Only the colonel's character matched the ugliness of his form. I thought back to my third trial, and the evil Rus colonel that I had been married to. Did he somehow share my experience while I was connected to Abyrinth's Fire?

I pulled my sword. I had equipped it knowing that I would be in battle, but it was usually my weapon of last resort.

"A sword?" he asked, coughing with laughter. "Look at me, girl! Do you think that puny blade can harm me? My skin is as tough as a rhinoceros'. My muscles are strong enough to break me out of that metal coffin." He waved his meaty hand at the grounded Goliath, flames still licking its sides.

I assumed the en garde, first position, legs bent slightly, sword arm extended towards the brute. He chuckled and lurched towards me. In the short space between us, he built up some momentum. His face was beaming with the thought of crushing my skull in his meaty palm.

At the last second, I pulled the Abyrinth from him.

As it did with Jaro in his wolf form, he reverted to a normal, unpowered human. His forward motion carried him onto my blade's point. His now very human face was twisted with shock and pain. My sword entered his lung and passed through, coming out his back. He made no scream; instead, he clutched at the steel that passed completely through his torso.

I withdrew my blade, letting his blood fountain from his body.

"Damn you, witch!" he screamed in Russian.

I advanced on him, my reserves filling with energy stolen from him. He held up his hand in defense, and I chopped down with my sword, the blade slipping between his ring finger and middle finger. It sliced through his hand, down to the wrist bones. He growled in pain, tinged with hatred.

"That's for our soldiers that you executed, without trial, without mercy." I stepped to the side and hacked at his other hand, taking it off cleanly at the wrist. Blood poured out, and he had no way of even applying pressure to the amputation.

He should have tried to run away, but his arrogance and pride prevented him from doing the only thing that could have conceivably saved him. I saw the slight bulge of his penis and stabbed just below it. "I cut off your balls, because I know that in your dream, you rape the woman who you say I resemble. That's what rapists deserve."

I sliced across his bare stomach, deep enough to free his intestines. "That is for the cities that you have destroyed. The thousands of innocent Poles you've killed."

He was a broken man, death imminent. I put the point of my blood-drenched sword to his sternum and looked in his anguished eyes. I pushed with all my might, plunging the blade through his black heart. "This is for Milka."

# Chapter 51

With the Black Ships set ablaze and the colonel's Goliath destroyed, cleaning up the leaderless Rus soldiers went smoothly. I lost a brother, but thankfully, I didn't lose any more of the soldiers that had been entrusted to me. We had won the day, and the detestable Colonel Sokolov was very, very dead.

"We need to leave here; sooner would be better than later," Jaroslav said.

I was able to feel again, and I threw myself into his arms. He held me for a long time, not attempting to break the embrace, not speaking. I sobbed into his shoulder until a feeling of calm washed over me. When Krystian died, for a moment, I was sure that I would never find happiness again. It would be hard, but Jaroslav's arms were exactly where I needed to be.

After some time, I said, "Thank you, dear. You saved the day by sending in those airships. Please give your father the heartfelt gratitude of the Polish people."

He kissed me deeply, then stared down into my eyes, his eyes gleaming like stars on a cool autumn evening. "Why don't you tell him yourself?" We were walking to a waiting hover sedan. "We are close to the border, and of all people, you need to lay low for a bit." He held the door for me. "Praha is a few hours east of here. We can be there before dark."

I sucked in a calming breath. I had to steel myself before continuing. "I cannot think of anything I would like more. Getting away from the death, the devastation… but I don't think your family would accept me. A year ago, I offered a connection to one of the leading families in all Polska. Now,

I'm nothing." I didn't say those words with a victim mentality. My family no longer had wealth or status, and they were refugees in a foreign land. Jaroslav could find any number of more suitable candidates.

"Remember when we first met?" I nodded. "I told you that you would be mine. Jaro wants your body, but I want all of you. From now until the end. My mother thinks highly of you, and Father will love you like a daughter. Let me show you Bohemia. I want it to become your new home."

"Oldřich clearly dislikes me, thinks that I'm not a worthy mate for his prince. Radomír is silent, but I think he also agrees that your parents will not see me as a good match for you." I surprised myself with how calm and rational I was being. The emotions that I feared would explode all over this good man were held at bay.

"They will accept you. Trust me."

I trusted him, but I didn't believe him. I had to bury my brother and check on the rest of the family. Stefek was in the wind somewhere, and I needed to find him. For better or worse.

"I can make no promises, but I'm open to meeting them."

He seemed happy about my decision, and that went a long way towards making me happy again.

My crew was given a week's leave, and we promised to meet in Praha. Arrangements were made for Krystian's service, and I would have to call my parents very soon. As we drove, my mind wandered to many unsolved mysteries.

I wanted to know more about the origins of Abyrith's Fire and the other stones around the world. Who put them there? They were obviously not natural. And when were they installed on the strange mechanical pedestals? I thought that the vision I had gave me more insight than anyone alive, and I might be the only one on earth who could unearth the mysteries of these seemingly infinite power sources. Were they tapping the very life essence of our world?

Bearing one of the prime brands gave me incredible powers, but I felt there was much more to it. We were supposed to pool our abilities and use them for a higher cause. Control over time, space, and energy would allow me to crush the Rus, but I would have to be as evil as Hedwig and steal the brands from the others. The German was an ass, so stealing his brand wouldn't be the end of the world, but the Brit, Edmund Fletcher, was a good guy, and no matter how much it would help me to liberate my country, I didn't know if I was capable of such treachery.

The colonel was dead, and so was the liar, Hedwig. I found the man of my dreams, but I lost my brother. My world had been turned upside down, and there was a mountain of things still to do, but it could all wait until tomorrow. Tonight, I would drink wine and sleep in Jaroslav's arms.

Author's Note:

Science Fiction is my first love, but Fantasy was right there. I love reading and worldbuilding, and I've been writing on and off since I was in junior high school. Now that I have the time and energy, I am really pursuing writing with everything I've got. I have a series of Hard Fantasy books out, and I'm working on other projects as well. I have so many ideas in my head that I'm dying to get them on paper.

This is my first foray into the Romantasy genre, and I hope that you enjoy it. I put a lot of research into the geography and language of the Polish people because I wanted the story to be as realistic as it could, within the framework of an alternate timeline. This is the first book in a planned trilogy, and I also plan to write other trilogies in the same universe.

Thank you very much!

M R Goodrum

Check out my website: Worldbuildingpress.com

Email: mrg@worldbuildingpress.com

Instagram: mrgintl

Facebook: Author page

https://www.facebook.com/profile.php?id=100095161151723

Facebook: Author page

https://www.facebook.com/profile.php?id=100094028413995

www.ingramcontent.com/pod-product-compliance
Lightning Source LLC
Chambersburg PA
CBHW070300310726
48976CB00005B/1503